Lynn

SWEET FANTASIES . . . SUDDEN FEARS

With her face pressed against the soft hair on his chest, Acadiana listened to Jonas's heartbeat for what seemed like hours before she was eventually lulled to sleep. . . . But sleep eluded him, and the darkness tortured him with visions of what marriage should be, of things he had never needed or thought he wanted—talking, sharing, and loving —until, in quiet desperation, he gripped Acadiana's shoulders and shook her until her eyes opened, wide and startled. His voice cut through the blackness like a steel-edged knife.

"Why do you hold yourself from me?"

Time hung suspended. The very air seemed to have been sucked from the room as Acadiana stared back at him with deep, fathomless eyes. Her whispered response, when it finally came, held the fierce and fatal sound of one doomed.

"You would have my soul!"

Jonas could not deny it.

D1444116

Bayou Dreams

LIBBY SYDES

A DELL BOOK

Published by
Dell Publishing
a division of
Bantam Doubleday Dell Publishing Group, Inc.
666 Fifth Avenue
New York, New York 10103

The trademark Dell® is registered in the U.S. Patent and Trademark
Office.

ISBN: 0-440-20574-3

Printed in the United States of America

Published simultaneously in Canada

June 1991

10 9 8 7 6 5 4 3 2 1

RAD

To my parents,
Joan and Eddie—
your unconditional love
has been the cornerstone of my life.

With deepest gratitude for your wisdom and support, I want to thank my agent, Sue Yuen, my proofreader, Lisa Brooks, the Murfreesboro Writers' Club, and the Heart of Dixie Chapter of RWA (especially the Huntsville Hussies). And to author Myra Rowe for helping a fledgling take flight.

Prologue

~❧ ❧~

The settlement of New Town,
Louisiana, 1814

Jonas Courtland gazed out the multipaned window, a triumphant look on his arrogant face as he stared out at the sleepy Bayou Teche. He was a striking man with sapphire eyes set in a rugged suntanned face. The near victory was an almost tangible thing, embracing the man like a rich cloak. He ran long, slender fingers through his sable-brown hair as he pondered the document he had just been handed. The simple, handwritten piece of old paper represented the passion that had consumed him for more than a year.

Jonas was obsessed with obtaining the Hamilton property. And that obsession was an unkind thing, wreaking havoc on his mind and heart until they no longer functioned in the capacity for which they were created.

He tapped the paper impatiently against his muscular thigh, then turned abruptly, towering over Henry Smith, the spineless man who served as lawyer for the Courtland estate.

"At last." Jonas beamed, showing straight white teeth that strongly contrasted with his skin.

Henry returned his employer's smile with a weaker version that looked suspiciously like a grimace. He was tired of the chase, and prayed that this old piece of parchment would finally satisfy his temperamental patron.

"I knew you would be pleased, Mr. Courtland. It took us long enough to locate the heir." Henry tried to make his high-pitched voice sound soothing. "The document was registered in St. Martinville. Hopefully we will be incorporated as a township soon and won't have to travel the nine miles to *le Petit Paris* to locate important records."

Jonas nodded absently, his eyes scanning the paper for details. "This is barely legible," he said, his enthusiasm dampening as he held the faded document up to the window. It was the time of day known as first dark, when the bullfrogs and katydids began their evening symphony and the chatter of starlings could be heard in the high bamboo hedges. The Courtlands' negress, Mattie, had not yet lighted the evening candles, but that was not the source of Jonas's mild aggravation. His deceptively calm tone sent a chill crawling up Henry's spine, warning him that the poor condition of the document was beginning to creep into Courtland's previously euphoric disposition.

"But quite legal," Henry quickly reassured him. How blasted long had he been working to obtain this information? For over a year, it seemed as if his sole purpose in life —at least according to Jonas Courtland—had been to find this paper. However tattered and worn it was, he had exhausted all means of finding anything more concrete. "Can I be of further assistance?"

"I have everything I need for now," Jonas said. He turned silently back to the window to study the bayou in the distance. Greenish-brown ripples splashed against the bank then retreated to roll lazily backward. A mourning dove cooed its loneliness from a giant live oak nearer the house. Henry knew by Mr. Courtland's stance that he had been dismissed. Unable to stifle a sigh of relief, he hurried through the French doors and almost collided with Minette Courtland as she entered the room wearing an angry scowl.

Whereas Henry felt dwarfed by Jonas, he stood eye to eye with this grande dame, but she was as formidable as her son. Not wishing another confrontation, he quickly stepped out of her way.

Minette suppressed the urge to bare her claws and shout "boo" at the timid little man as he scurried out of the room. However, intimidating Henry Smith was not her desire or her purpose this evening. She merely nodded a curt dismissal and pulled the door shut before speaking sharply to her son in a heavy French Creole accent.

"Monsieur Smith had encouraging news, yes?"

"Good evening, Mother," Jonas greeted her, undaunted by the dowager's displeasure. "You're in a lovely humor." His jubilant mood was not to be denied, not even by the one person who had tried in vain to turn him from what she deemed a ghost hunt.

"Pooh!" she huffed, pushing past him with an arrogant flip of her wrist. "You have the information you have been wasting time seeking, yes?"

"I have the document naming the heir to the Hamilton property. It appears that an Abe Hamilton owns it all. The address, by the way, is the same one you gave me for Armand Hamilton's brother near Providence Lake."

"I thought you had your friend Charles make inquiries when he became engaged to Grayson Hamilton's daughter," Minette said. Satisfaction gleamed on her aristocratic face. "That got you nowhere."

"That was a year ago," Jonas replied indifferently. "Charles will marry in three weeks. As his best man, I will be properly introduced to the family and can pursue purchasing the land on a more personal level. This fellow might even be living in Providence. If I can talk to him, it shouldn't be too difficult to buy back the property. I assume he can't have much interest in it —no one has been out to check on the place in the ten years since the Hamiltons left."

"You assume too much, Jonas," Minette snapped. "The grounds have been well tended."

Jonas shrugged and sent his mother a smug grin. "I didn't say the man let it go to ruin, but that fertile soil has remained undeveloped for a decade. What a waste. *Grand-père* would have apoplexy if he were alive."

"Your illustrious grandfather is the reason the property left Courtland hands to begin with."

"Granted, he sold it as a gross error in judgment."

"He was reeling drunk!" Minette exclaimed bitterly.

"Exactly! It was a mistake! A mistake he regretted the rest of his days," Jonas returned. "Have you forgotten that Father spent the last years of his life trying to retrieve the property? Out of respect for him, I am determined to get it back. Do you deny the fact that the land should rightfully belong to us?"

Minette would not debate this issue with her single-minded son. Of course the land should belong to them! Land is everything to a planter. But this parcel had been squandered by a foolish old man who had tried once too often to recapture his youth. Even her own dear Jon had become obsessed with retrieving the property before he died. There were times when Minette almost felt as if the land were cursed. She was by no means a superstitious woman, but over the years so many lives connected with those arpents along the bayou had been strangely and viciously lost. If the idea had not been ludicrous, Minette would have sworn that an evilness inhabited that place.

"You are as hard-headed as your *père* was, Jonas!" she spat out as she tossed the eerie thought aside and began pacing the elegant library. This obsession with the land had to stop, she thought. Her son had had time for little else over the past year. There were other responsibilities pertaining to Courtland Manor plantation that needed to be considered. He should be settled, married, and producing children to inherit his father's domain. She stopped abruptly and turned to face her oldest son with a quelling look. "Enough of this talk. I have other matters to discuss with you."

Jonas braced himself for the tirade he knew was forthcoming. The age-old discussion was wearing thin on his patience. With a frown he turned toward the soothing swish and placating roll of the bayou.

"When are you going to announce your engagement to Mary Elizabeth Clayton?" Minette insisted more than asked.

"I am not engaged to Beth," he answered coolly over his shoulder.

"But you are considering her, yes?"

"You know I am." Jonas sighed. As much as he hated his mother's interference, he knew at thirty years of age it was time to marry. Beth would make a perfect wife. Sweet and docile, she would make a lovely addition to any man's life. What the two of them lacked in romantic love was more than compensated for by the friendship they shared.

"I believe she is quite taken with you, and her father is making a name for himself in our little society, even though he is an *Américain.*"

"Enough, Mother! Do not go on so! We are all Americans now, are we not? Father even had a bit of English blood, I am told."

"Never admit such a thing," Minette said crossly. "There is trouble brewing with the British, I guarantee."

"We will discuss this and other things when I return from Providence," Jonas conceded, secretly pleased to have struck a tender spot in his mother's Creole armor. "I am sure Beth won't make other arrangements before I get back. Now if you will excuse me, I have packing to do."

Excuse him? *Non!* She would not excuse him. This was something that should be settled. "Marriage is not an arrangement," she began. "It is a partnership." Actually, Minette did not care what her son called it, as long as he didn't present the proposal to Miss Clayton in those terms. Beth was not the sort of girl men made "arrangements" with. Minette knew Jonas cared for the lovely young woman, and she approved the match. Beth would be easily manageable in the years ahead, and Jonas would surely come to love her. They already respected one another.

Jonas sighed and smiled at his mother in an endearing yet patronizing way. "Your marriage to Father was like that, a partnership based on love. I am not so cold that I wouldn't prefer that type of relationship, but I do not consider it necessary when there are perfectly suitable matches to be made for monetary gain." Here he stopped and raised his arm only to let it fall back by his side in mock resignation. His voice took on the quality of one beset by life-shattering troubles. "Besides, Mother, there are just no more women like you left in the world. I must be content with doing my duty as I see fit."

Minette scoffed at the ridiculous notion and the rakish quirk of her son's lips. "Do not trifle with me, you insolent . . ."

Jonas turned a deaf ear and waited for her to finish. Even his mother's constant badgering could not dampen his spirits as his mind returned to one Abe Hamilton. The faded document was just what he needed to continue his quest for the land that should be his. When her speech ended, Jonas turned back.

"I leave within the week for Charles's wedding. Upon my return, I will speak to Beth. Good evening, Mother."

1

P rovidence, Louisiana

"Oh, Acadiana," Katherine cooed, "isn't this just the most wonderful day! The sun is shining, the birds are—"

"Katherine, please spare me. I simply cannot take any more of your inane jubilation. *Mon Dieu,* you shall burst before your wedding if you do not calm down." Exasperated, Acadiana fell back on the bed and watched unenthused as her cousin danced gaily around the room in a primrose taffeta day gown the exact color of her pale yellow hair. Raising up on her elbows, she eyed Katherine speculatively. *"M'sieu* Charles must be coming this morning."

"Coming? No, dear cousin, he is already here. He brought Jonas Courtland with him, and they have been locked away with Father all morning, discussing heaven only knows what." Katherine stopped her spinning and pouted daintily, fluttering her blond lashes behind an ivory-handled fan. "Why, I haven't even been called down to see Charles yet."

"Called down?" Acadiana teased in a voice that was remarkably cool and clear when compared to Katherine's pet-

ulant tones. "Since when do you need to be formally requested? *Mais oui,* you have been sneaking off to meet with
Charles secretly for a week now."

Katherine paled. "Do hush! Someone will hear you! Besides, we didn't do anything improper—for an engaged couple. All I did was let Charles kiss me. You know"—she
lowered her voice to the tone she used when telling a juicy
secret or scandalous bit of gossip—"you know what I mean,
Cade. A *real* kiss! The kind one gets behind locked doors!"

Acadiana squeezed her eyes shut. "Behind locked doors"
was how Katherine referred to anything that happened between a man and a woman that one simply did not discuss.
And she had no intention of letting her cousin elaborate
now.

"It was wonderful," Katherine continued dreamily. "You
cannot possibly imagine how wonderful. It nearly made me
swoon with delight." She clutched her hands to her heart
and floated into a chair.

"Everything about Charles nearly makes you swoon,"
Acadiana taunted her merrily. "And no, I can't imagine. I
have never been hopelessly in love as you are now, and if it
makes me half as dim-witted, I hope never to succumb to
that blessed state of the heart."

"You are impossible, Acadiana. I do love you though,
and I shall miss you ever so much when I am gone." Katherine sighed. "But I cannot think of that now. My darling
Charles is downstairs, and I shall not wait a moment longer
to see him. Now, do get ready."

"Me?" Acadiana asked. A bothered expression knitted
her forehead and caused her dark eyebrows to almost
touch. "I see Charles every day, and I do not care to watch
the two of you moon over each other. Besides, I want to go
riding," she added.

If Acadiana had been honest with herself, she would have
admitted that she was just a mite envious of Katherine's
newfound exuberance. But to act so silly and ridiculous

over a man was something her mind simply could not understand.

"Not to see Charles, you goose. I have already told you that Jonas Courtland is here. Since you are both to stand in attendance, it is only proper that the two of you be introduced."

"Another time," Acadiana said coaxingly. "There is a full week before the ceremony."

"No!" Katherine's mouth pressed into a little moue. "Charles is expecting us. Please, Acadiana. He says Jonas is from an old aristocratic family and the ladies find him devastatingly handsome. You will need an escort for all the parties we have planned, and since Mr. Courtland doesn't know anyone here . . ." She made a half-circle with her hand and let it drift.

Acadiana scooted off the bed and leveled her cousin with a stern look as she spoke. "Stop matchmaking, Katherine. I've never met a man yet that devastated me."

Acadiana's frown darkened considerably. The last thing she needed right now was another man thrown carefully in her way. Her uncle had been parading what he considered worthy subjects in front of her for years. Everyone, except Acadiana, despaired of her ever choosing a husband. It wasn't that she did not want to marry, but she had dreams to fulfill before committing herself to someone else.

Both girls turned at the slight knock on the door and smiled as a very round black face with equally round bright eyes peeked in. Pearlene grinned, showing a wide mouth of teeth.

"Y'all ready, Miss Katherine? Some men be waiting down to the parlor for you. Ooo wee, miss, they sure do be handsome."

"Pearlene!" both girls exclaimed at once.

"Well . . ." Pearlene shrugged then grinned, her bright eyes on Acadiana. "I know what Miss Katherine's going to do with Mr. Charles, but what about you, Miss Cade? You going to take up with that man what's with Mr. Charles?"

"Oh, Pearlene, not you too." Acadiana sighed. Her violet eyes narrowed and an impish grin flitted across her lips. "I guess I'll take up with him as soon as you take up with old Jethro out at the stable."

"Ooo wee, chile! I ain't about to jump over the broom with that man. You'll die an old spinster woman if you wait on that. You sure will," Pearlene pealed as she headed for the door. "Y'all hurry up now, you hear? Don't want to keep those fine men waiting."

Jonas Courtland stood next to his longtime friend Charles Nolan in a small but elegantly furnished room. The simple planter's cottage was warm and cozy, but Jonas's thoughts were not on the pleasant surroundings. His face was furrowed in a perplexing frown as he stood listening to a stocky gray-haired man, his earlier excitement beginning to fade at the older man's discouraging words.

"I wish I could help you, Mr. Courtland, but for the life of me, I can't imagine why Abe Hamilton would be listed as heir to Armand and Elaine's land." Grayson Hamilton shook his head in confusion and turned to his wife. "Elizabeth?"

Demurring as always to her husband's judgment, Elizabeth shook her head and gave Jonas a soft smile. Her hair was a pale blond lightly touched with gray, and her unlined face had protested aging with genteel grace.

"To my knowledge there has never even been an Abe in our family," Grayson continued. "Do you have the document with you?"

"Yes, sir, and I assure you it is legitimate. See what you can make of it," Jonas said as he handed over the worn paper.

Grayson studied the document carefully for a minute until a smile began to form on his stern face. He gave Charles a knowing grin while showing him the paper, then proceeded to hand it to his wife. Elizabeth's eyes rounded perceptively before she shoved it back at him.

"Look here, Mr. Courtland, I see your problem," Grayson said. "This is not Abe but the initials A.B.H., an easy mistake given the sprawling signature. This would be *Cade* Hamilton." He glanced up and chuckled self-consciously. "Now you do have a problem, if you expect to purchase Cade's property."

"I am prepared to offer quite a reasonable sum, sir," Jonas said with a confidence that was as much a part of the man as the land he was trying to reclaim. "Is there any way I can get in touch with him while I am here?"

"I have never known Cade to be overly reasonable." Grayson laughed lightly before his pudgy face settled into a sober expression. "As to your question, Cade will be here any moment, Mr. Courtland, but you are well advised to use caution when mentioning the land." He sent Charles a shrewd look and both men began to chuckle, while Elizabeth stood by in vague discomfort and cast her husband a pained look every few seconds.

"Jonas, you certainly have your work cut out for you," Charles said with a gleam in his eyes. "But I will guarantee you one thing: It will be the most pleasant work you have ever engaged in." He clapped his friend on the back in a patronizing manner and continued to smile along with Grayson.

"Gentlemen, I fail to see the humor in this," Jonas stated, put out by their remarks. "I assure you, this is a very serious matter to me."

"Cade will think it a serious matter also," Charles stated, all teasing gone from his voice now. "If you only knew how serious."

Jonas's next response was cut short by the vision of a very lovely lady entering the room.

"Mr. Courtland, I have the pleasure of presenting my daughter, Katherine," Grayson said with obvious amusement. "Cade is coming shortly?" he asked more as a statement. "Mr. Courtland is interested in meeting and speaking with my ward about some land."

Katherine lifted her eyes to the handsome man standing before her. Charles was right, she thought. Tall and broad-shouldered, strong but pleasant features, any woman would find Jonas Courtland gorgeous. Except Cade. Not when she found out he wanted to discuss her land. "Uh-oh." Katherine groaned before she gained her composure. "I mean, oh! I am so very pleased to meet you, Mr. Courtland." She curtsied awkwardly then glanced hesitantly at her father. "Cade is a bit indisposed at the moment. I had better go check on the situation."

Without regard for proper deportment, but knowing she would have to answer for her rude behavior later, Katherine bid a hasty retreat and rushed out of the room, the flounces of her skirt bouncing up and down as she took the stairs two at a time.

"Cade . . . Cade!" she called breathlessly when she reached their bedroom. Twin beds of pine, covered with beruffled quilts to disguise their simplicity, sat against one wall. A small dressing table with mirror was against another, while a tall armoire provided the room's only other adornment save the hand-stitched pictures hung throughout.

"Are you getting ready?" Katherine continued unnecessarily, for she could see that her cousin was even now tying the waist strings of a disreputable pair of pants. "Father is expecting you!" she emphasized without success as Acadiana knotted the laces. Katherine clamped her mouth shut to avoid blurting out anything about the land. Cade would never *ever* come down if she knew someone was asking about her property.

"Katherine, I told you I am not coming. I have things I need to do today," Acadiana responded. She ignored her cousin as she pulled on a tall leather boot.

"But Father is expecting you. You know how testy he gets! If you make him cross, I swear I shall never forgive you," Katherine pouted.

"I shall attempt to go on living," Acadiana teased, "despite my fall from grace."

"What shall I tell them?" Katherine asked pleadingly. "Father will be so miffed. I don't think you are being very considerate, Acadiana Hamilton."

"Tell them anything you like. *Oui,* tell them that I will be down after a while," Acadiana replied flippantly.

"That's not funny! You have no intention of showing up, do you?"

"I'm sorry, Katherine, but you shall have to entertain the wonderful *M'sieu* Courtland on your own this morning. I am going riding."

Acadiana turned her back to her disgruntled cousin and pulled on the other boot that just reached the bottom of the worn-out knee breeches she was wearing. She methodically plaited her long, dark tresses and tucked the braid under her cap.

"Cade!" Katherine wailed. "You can't go down dressed like that! Father will pitch a fit!"

Katherine loved Acadiana like a sister even though her cousin had a mile-long stubborn streak and a complete disregard for proper behavior. She never knew quite what to do when Cade was in one of her moods.

"I'm not going down like this." Acadiana smiled. "I'm going riding." She gave Katherine a peck on the cheek, then stuffed her scraggly shirttail into the pants.

"But they will see you—" Katherine began.

Even at twenty years of age, Acadiana had the agility and slenderness of a much younger girl. It was evident in most of her mannerisms that she had not yet accepted the maturity imposed on her by adulthood.

"Non," Acadiana reassured her. "I will go out the window."

With that she scurried out and swung long, sleek legs over the window ledge. She hung on to the rough timber in such a precarious position that Katherine held her breath in anticipation of disaster. After finding a foothold on the trellis, Acadiana shimmied down the lattice, careful not to disturb the clinging vines that were weaving their way toward the sun.

"Oooh! You've done it now, Acadiana Hamilton," Katherine called down to her before flinging herself away from the window. "Father's going to be unbearable for the better part of the day, and it's all your fault!" Katherine tried to collect herself and began thinking of excuses she could make to her father before going back downstairs. As furious as she was with her cousin, as incapable as she was of understanding Acadiana's strange notions, Katherine would defend her to the death. There was a bond between them as strong as that of natural sisters. Although she wouldn't lie, Katherine would find some way to pacify her father.

Acadiana lost her footing on the last section of framework and fell to the ground with a thud. *Mon Dieu!* She hoped this was not an indication of how her day would go. Rubbing her abused posterior, she surveyed the grounds in all directions, then scampered across the yard to the barn, calling for Jethro. The wizened old black man met her at the gate with a warm expression on his face.

"I saw you coming, Miss Cade. You best not let Master Gray see you dressed like that. He's going to have my skin and yours too."

"He won't see me, Jethro." Acadiana smiled. "He's busy in the parlor with a guest. Is Shawnee ready?"

Jethro knew that rascally grin meant trouble. "Ain't nothing to get ready," he grumbled, "unless you's figuring on riding with a saddle this time." Jethro rolled his eyes heavenward and mumbled the words that had become a ritual over the past few years. "It ain't proper for a young lady to be riding the way you do and dressed the way you are. And you knows it!"

"It will be all right, Jethro," Acadiana said brightly. She stood on tiptoe and kissed his leathery cheek. For as long as she could remember, he had been her accomplice, and Acadiana remained undaunted by his scoldings.

A slave since birth, Jethro could well understand her need for a bit of freedom every now and then. Warm summer days just beckoned a man to laze away the hours on the lake bank, smelling the honeysuckle and waiting for a perch to snap at his line. But understanding this did not change his feelings of responsibility toward the ragtail young lady.

"Don't be turning your girlish charms on me. One of these days it won't work no more!" Jethro said with a sternness he knew was futile. This little girl had him wrapped so firmly around her finger he didn't know why he bothered to fuss with her. "And don't be kissing this black face of mine! You ain't no poor white trash. Now git on afore Master Gray come out here and has my poor old tired hide."

Purely for the sake of rebellion, she kissed him on the cheek again and hopped astride her horse. "I'll be back before he even knows I'm gone," Acadiana said sweetly. She gave Shawnee a lusty kick and headed down a path toward the lake.

"I's heard that too many times to believe it," Jethro called after her. He shook his graying head and muttered to himself, "That girl ain't took no saddle. She'll be gone all day. Master Gray'll have my hide."

Acadiana ignored the old man's rambling as she cantered away. Her Uncle Grayson didn't hold much with slavery and never abused the few who served him. She followed the trail for several minutes, enjoying the warm sunshine and the solitude of the woods. She let her mind wander as the smell of fresh cedar wafted over her, her body moving in rhythm to the horse's light-footed pace.

Preparations for Katherine's wedding had kept her confined to the house for the better part of a week. She would quite simply go mad if she had to stay there one more minute. It was truly better for everyone concerned, she reasoned, if she got away for a while. Besides, she couldn't stand the thought of having to meet another of Charles's stuffy old friends. *Mais oui,* Katherine was happy enough with her beau, Acadiana thought, but she wanted no such thing for herself. She had met enough of them to know she could do without a man in her life right now. She had dreams, goals to achieve, before making a commitment to another human being.

Coming to a gathering of vines that had intertwined themselves to form an awning, Acadiana dismounted and picked her way along the overgrown lake bank in search of the trotline she had previously set. She pushed her way past a surly willow, then braced against a huge cypress, grabbing hold of the rough bark that grew in ridges around the tree. She stepped cautiously onto a tree root, aptly named cypress knee for its bent-leg look, where it jutted from the shallow water. Balancing on one foot, she reached for the overhanging branch to steady herself as she searched the murky water for some sign of her line.

"Ooh!" She gasped suddenly. Losing her foothold, she dangled from the tree limb. "Shoo! Shoo, snake!" Acadiana kicked at the offending water moccasin with the toe of her boot. It raised a laggard head and slithered off the root into the water. Acadiana stretched a slender leg down, fumbling for a secure spot on which to stand. She succeeded by wedging her boot between the cypress knees and bracing her other foot against the tree.

"Well!" she huffed, disgusted with her carelessness and the awkward, straddled position she was in. "This is all I need. If I split the seams of these breeches, Pearlene will fuss for a week. I declare, you steely-eyed serpent, if I ever catch you back here, I am going to skin you!" Acadiana shook her fist heavily in the empty air, an act that threw her off balance and sent her floundering to the water below.

"*C'est magnifique!*" she fumed as she sat on the slimy, moss-covered lake bottom, hanging her head in hostility while the muddy water soaked her tight-fitting pants. She beat at the water with a clenched fist, venting her anger on the ripples that spread out around her. The brief tantrum complete, she eased herself up and sludged through the sucking mud to the bank. Once on dry land, she gave a sharp whistle, and Shawnee trotted over.

"We are doomed, *mon ami.*" She sighed as she pulled herself over his warm back and hung there, utterly dejected, while deciding what she must do.

"I'll never get back in the house unnoticed. I'll be dripping water everywhere. Stupid snake!"

Acadiana sat upright and urged the steed on, fussing and mumbling the whole way back. Accustomed to such outbursts, Shawnee disregarded her bad humor and loped back to the stable.

Eyes bugging, Jethro started toward her when she reached the fence. Acadiana threw her hands over her ears to block his scurrilous voice and stomped off toward the house. She had decided that the best line of defense was a frontal attack, and headed straight for the main entrance. She swung the heavy oak door open and tramped through the entrance hall toward the stairs, leaving a trail of muddy footprints behind.

Katherine, standing next to the parlor door, threw her hand over her mouth to silence a startled gasp as Acadiana hurried by. "Cade! What happened?" she whispered so her father wouldn't hear.

Acadiana ignored her and continued past, a squishing sound emanating from the seat of her pants. She was intent on getting to her room before an outburst of tempers could fly from her aunt or uncle—or both.

Jonas turned just in time to see a fresh-faced youth rush by in sopping clothes with a snarl on his face. He was startled to hear Katherine call out the name "Cade" and took a quick step closer to get a better look. His eyes flared in triumph as he took in the scene. A kid! This Cade was just a lad. Jonas chuckled inwardly. Things were looking better all the time despite Charles's warning. He could handle a youngster with little effort, and soon the land would be his again. With a grin that reeked of victory he accepted the brandy Charles offered him and turned back to the occupants in the room.

Acadiana doffed her wet clothes, rinsed off, and dressed hastily, trying to make herself presentable before someone could come to make inquiries. Now, she supposed, she would have to meet *M'sieu* Courtland just to make peace. Her uncle would never make a scene in front of a guest. *Mon Dieu,* but her day had been ruined.

She made one last brush through her softly curling hair before tying it back with a ribbon. A few stray curls refused to be tamed and framed her face in wispy abandon. Acadiana adjusted the low neck of her ivory taffeta dress, then pulled her chemise up to fill in the neckline with its stand-up ruffle. The ankle-length skirt was embroidered with delicate violets, so she quickly snatched a purple satin sash to tie at the waist. Taking a deep, fortifying breath, Acadiana smoothed the folds of the gown, squared her shoulders, and left the room to approach the parlor with a bright smile as if nothing were amiss.

Jonas stopped in midsentence, one eyebrow lifting in appreciation when a young lady entered the room and walked over to stand beside Grayson Hamilton. She was the most unusual female he had ever seen—not beautiful exactly, but pretty enough in an innocent sort of way. There was an earthy quality about her that seemed to radiate from within and flow vibrantly to the surface. How he could tell all this at first glance quite escaped him, but there was something familiar about the way she breezed into the room, and Jonas suspected there was more liveliness to this girl than her demure countenance suggested.

Jonas found himself entranced as he detailed her features. This was no classic beauty. Her hair was much too dark—almost ebony, with just enough sparkling highlights to keep it from being coal black. Her figure, although shapely, was too petite to be considered fashionable. Even her skin did not bear the ivory cast of a well-guarded female. It was a golden sun-kissed hue, as if she had gone outdoors without her bonnet too many times. Gauging her assets singularly, Jonas found there just wasn't much to recommend her, but collectively they formed a stirring combination.

His lazy perusal reached her eyes, and all previous thought paled. Those glorious eyes were the strangest, most intriguing shade of violet he had ever seen. They were complemented by long, dark lashes and had just enough of a tilt at the edges to lend an air of mystery. Staring at her piquant face, Jonas was suddenly quite sure a weaker man would drown in those eyes.

Propriety demanded that he drag himself away from his errant thoughts to be properly introduced. He looked to Charles for assistance, but Grayson suddenly pulled the girl forward, a hint of mischief in his voice as he spoke.

"Mr. Courtland, I would like for you to meet my niece, Cade," he said. " 'Cade' is short for Acadiana. Acadiana Belizaire Hamilton, I would like for you to meet Jonas Courtland. He is very interested in speaking with you, my dear."

"My pleasure," Acadiana said politely as she lifted a dainty hand to the most striking man she had ever seen. In a strong chiseled face, his dark blue eyes glittered boldly with a mingling of something like shock and amusement. His smile was polite, though she sensed it covered some hidden secret, just as his relaxed stance concealed an inner strength that his towering height couldn't deny. She felt even smaller than her five feet three inches while her eyes traveled the length of him. Buff breeches were molded to his muscular legs, and his broad shoulders bulged with overworked muscles beneath his cutaway tailcoat. He gave the appearance of being elegantly attired, although his shirt had no front frill, and he wore no cravat.

Devastating, Katherine had said. Acadiana quite agreed. Though she would have never admitted it, not in a lifetime, Acadiana found, much to her wonder, that one Jonas Courtland quite took her breath away. *Fie on you, Cousin,* her eyes seemed to say as she cast Katherine a sideways look. Katherine winked back a pompous *I told you so.*

"The pleasure is mine," Jonas said graciously, taking Acadiana's proffered hand. This couldn't be the kid he had seen stomping through the hall just moments before, yet the name was the same. . . . The slight grin on his face broadened as he turned to look at Grayson. "Is there more than one Cade in this household?"

"Ha! We can't handle the one we've got," Grayson joked. No one saw the satin slipper peek out from under Acadiana's gown, but Grayson felt it when it stepped lightly on his toe. "I mean no," he confessed awkwardly while casting her a disapproving frown. "There is only one Cade."

Jonas turned to look at Charles and could well understand his friend's amusement at his expense. "Charles, *mon ami,* you did not tell me that all of the Hamilton women were so beautiful. Did you perhaps think you could keep them for yourself?"

"Precisely," answered Charles. He knew his friend's game and was quite willing to play along, but if Jonas thought he could win Acadiana's land with flattery, he was in for a rude awakening.

Jonas smiled and secretly concluded that Charles's previous statement was correct. This would indeed be the most satisfying business venture he had ever had the pleasure of pursuing.

Everyone relaxed and wiled away the day in warm conversation, and it was some time before Jonas was able to corner Acadiana away from the others. She had captured his attention for most of the afternoon with her charm and easy conversation and, of course, those eyes. They compelled a man to take a closer look, yet there was also a guarded expression in their violet depths that held him at a distance.

Jonas had watched her covertly during the evening meal while trying to keep conversation with those around him. There was something about this girl, he decided, a restlessness eclipsed by restrained tension that seemed out of place in their informal setting. She held herself aloof, inviolate, without appearing to do so as she answered his inquiries politely and laughed often with her cousin Katherine. Her manner with Charles was teasing, but not at all flirtatious.

In all, she gave the illusion of being perfectly content with her surroundings. She was poised, Jonas had to give her that, but he couldn't shake the niggling feeling in the back of his mind that said something about her was different. A fleeting glance perhaps, a second's unguarded look— something told him that a part of her was completely detached and held aloft from everything around her.

This Acadiana Belizaire Hamilton, possessor of the land he had desperately been coveting, was like a wildflower growing among a well-tended garden. She was without the polish of her Aunt Elizabeth or Katherine, but reflected her own unique beauty. There was something intrinsically alive about her. It challenged him in a way he did not completely understand, goaded him to delve a bit deeper into the complexities of one Acadiana Hamilton. In essence, he found her most desirable.

"Miss Hamilton," Jonas said with a grin after carefully maneuvering her away from her family, "correct me if I am wrong, but did I see someone running through the house earlier in wet boy's clothing?"

"Now, *M'sieu* Courtland, what would *someone* be doing in boy's clothing—and wet, did you say?" she asked with a twinkle in her bright amethyst eyes. "Surely you were mistaken."

Intrigued by her mysteriously coy manner and the aplomb with which she stood her ground, Jonas's smile widened. "Shall I ask Katherine who was tracking mud all over the hall floor? She saw the little scamp."

"You may ask anyone you like," Acadiana replied with a terse grin that bordered on the sarcastic. "But I assure you, Katherine is very loyal." She raised her eyebrows and inclined her head toward her cousin.

"Loyalty is an admirable trait," Jonas conceded. "Shall it be our secret?"

"I have no secrets," Acadiana answered. "But if you insist on seeing phantom boys running through halls, by all means, *M'sieu* Courtland, humor yourself."

You have secrets, Jonas thought as his gaze swept the petite woman standing before him. "I would rather you humor me, Miss Hamilton," he said in a deep drawl that sent involuntary shivers chasing up Acadiana's spine. She took an unconscious step backward to distance herself from his direct stare.

Jonas had never met a more wary yet self-assured woman. There was no doubt she was the one he had seen in those form-hugging wet pants. He hadn't appreciated their tight fit then, but he was trying to conjure up the captivating vision now.

Baiting her did no good. She seemed to enjoy their volley of words, and nothing daunted that calm, serene exterior. "I wonder," he mused aloud. "Does nothing ruffle your feathers?"

"I've sprouted feathers now?" Acadiana sent him a deliciously innocent smile. "First a boy, now a bird. What an adventuresome day I am having."

"Touché." Jonas chuckled, nodding his head to concede the win. "Witty, and beautiful as well. Is there no end to your charm, Miss Hamilton?"

"Perhaps not," she said playfully. "At least *I've* yet to find one."

"Enchanting," he murmured, but decided to put an end to this meaningless play on words, enjoyable though it was. A part of him wanted to explore further the depth of this intriguing woman, but that desire did not take precedence over the real reason he was speaking with her. He wanted her land, and as she was amiable enough, beguiling even, he could foresee no problem in settling his business with her now, then pursuing more intimate avenues once that was done. "I was wondering if we might discuss more weighty matters."

"I am at your disposal, *M'sieu* Courtland," Acadiana said, confused by the subtle change in his tone. "But I cannot imagine what we would have to discuss of such a serious nature."

Jonas took the document from inside his breast pocket and handed it to Acadiana. "This property belongs to you, I believe?" he said, little knowing the devastating impact that simple utterance would have on her.

The corner of the room in which Jonas and Acadiana stood took on a palpable stillness. The murmur of voices from the others, the tinkle of crystal from refilled glasses, even the hum of nighttime insects was only a muted backdrop that couldn't penetrate the suddenly thick air surrounding them.

Acadiana swallowed and stared hard at the parchment until her eyes misted over and she could no longer make out her father's handwriting. *"Oui,"* she whispered as her fingers curled around the paper and she clutched it to her breast. She lifted her head slowly and everything about her, from the fierce spark in her violet eyes to the squaring of her shoulders, radiated tension. *"Oui,"* she repeated more forcefully. "Where did you get this, *M'sieu?"*

"My man finally located it in St. Martinville. I have been searching for the owner for over a year now."

"Why?" Acadiana's tone was wary, her entire body stiffening by degrees as if she expected disaster to come crashing down upon her.

"I wish to purchase this property," Jonas said, and added the outrageous price he was willing to pay.

"Non." It was little more than a whisper, yet it carried the ring of defiance and sounded almost threatening. "It is not for sale. Not at any price. *Pardonnez-moi."*

Acadiana turned quickly to leave, but Jonas reached out and caught her arm. She paused immediately and only the narrowing of her eyes warned of her ignited wrath. She glanced down at the strong fingers encircling her forearm, then lifted her eyes to Jonas. "Unhand me this moment, *M'sieu* Courtland, or suffer the consequences."

Jonas's smile flared briefly in amusement as he met the challenge sparkling from her violet eyes and his fingers flexed tighter. "Whatever it costs, whatever it takes, I'll have that property," he said quietly. Acadiana jerked on her arm but he refused to release her. "I only wish to detain you long enough to settle—"

"*Adieu, M'sieu,* we have nothing more to discuss," Acadiana said, and promptly sank her teeth into Jonas's fingers. She nearly had them jerked from her head when Jonas snatched his hand back.

A violent curse hissed past his grim lips and was met with Acadiana's satisfied smile. "I think we understand each other," she said demurely, but her eyes were cold as a winter wind when she turned her back on him and walked away.

"I think perhaps we do." Jonas smiled in kind. "I think perhaps we do."

2

The sleepless night had not been kind to Acadiana's physical or emotional disposition. Jonas Courtland's stunning face had taken on demonic proportions as he encroached upon her dreams, waving the document before her with a satanic smile and taunting her with lurid threats. Knowing that dreams were not fact but only distorted fragments of reality did little to ease Acadiana into the new day; she was plagued with enough true nightmares of a day long ago that she was fearful of the significance of these new night terrors. The morning had passed in a hazy blur of activity, and the afternoon had also offered little rest.

She had fussed and fretted half the day getting ready for the soiree, the evening party being hosted by Charles's parents. After the restless night she couldn't find anything about her looks that she liked, and was quite agitated. Never had she met a more stirring and unsettling man than Jonas Courtland. He was by far the most handsome man she had ever had the misfortune of encountering, and he did not even seem to notice her. He didn't pass many of the little pleasantries or indulge in idle chitchat with her. The very things that bored her to tears with other men might have been pleasant with him. *Mais non,* all he could talk about was her land. When he had taken a moment last night to speak to her alone, it was only to discuss her property. Well, it might just be property to him, but to Acadiana Belizaire Hamilton it was a legacy. Her dreamfields—hers! How dare he? How dare anyone!

Her land was all she had left of a life long past, parents long dead. How could anyone think she would let go of it for any price? And Jonas Courtland had offered an exorbitant amount of money! It had taken her breath away in the second before it had completely inflamed her. One could not possibly place monetary value on a legacy.

M'sieu Courtland could just go on back to the bayou with his arrogant, willful self. He would never get her land!

Acadiana should have known that he wasn't interested in her—*only* her. She knew, of course, that she wasn't beautiful—not like Katherine with her golden hair, sky-blue eyes, and buxom figure. But hadn't she had almost as many offers of marriage? Why, only last year a young cattleman from Natchitoches had come with his father to buy cotton. Richard Whittington, professing undying love and devotion, had even tried to kiss her. Although flattered, she had turned him down—turned them all down. She didn't want to get married yet. She wanted to go back home to *her* land!

Acadiana knew she was different from the other girls of the area, knew that she would never be like them. Too much had happened after her parents' death. If the men of polite society knew about her past, they probably would never have asked for her hand. Several, in fact, had withdrawn their attention once they discovered the truth. And that was just fine! Maybe it *had* hurt just a bit at the time. But that was long ago, and Acadiana told herself she didn't want to marry any of them anyway.

If she could just hold out for three more months without Uncle Grayson arranging a suitable marriage for her, Acadiana could go home. She would be of an acceptable age to live on her own then.

Uncle Grayson had tried to give her free rein to choose a

marriage partner, but she had stunned him by refusing or being rejected by them all. After Richard, he had given up. He had warned Acadiana that the next time he would arrange the marriage himself, and she would not be consulted. That is, if another suitor could be found in view of her most recent reputation. She had been dubbed the ice maiden.

What did they know? Acadiana thought indignantly. She wasn't cold at all, but rejection had caused her to build an emotional barrier around herself. If she appeared haughty or aloof at times, it was merely because she didn't want to involve herself too closely, or invite the ridicule that she knew hurt her aunt and uncle far more than it did her.

Three short months before she could return home. She might be dubbed the *spinster* maiden, but she could leave without bringing shame to Uncle Grayson's family.

Well, she thought wryly, she was certainly safe where Jonas Courtland was concerned. The only man who had ever been disconcerting to her peace of mind was only interested in her land. That was just fine. She certainly was *not* interested in him—not *that* handsome man with his dark blue eyes and winning smile. Not one single bit.

"Cade, are you ready?" Katherine asked as she came bouncing into the room they had shared for the last six years. "Well? What do you think?"

"You look lovely as always," Acadiana replied.

"Not me, silly, Jonas Courtland. What do you think of him? Isn't he the most dashing man you have ever seen—next to Charles, of course."

"I think *M'sieu* Courtland is an insufferable wretch," Acadiana said, throwing her head back with a haughtiness that she wasn't really feeling at the moment. Just being in the same room with Jonas had made her heart race and her skin tingle strangely. His persuasiveness alarmed her, overpowered her in ways she had never encountered, and she couldn't even discern the reasons he affected her so. Acadiana only knew she was in danger of losing her land, and with that loss came the danger of losing control of her life. That thought was intolerable.

"Acadiana Hamilton!" Katherine sniffed delicately. "How can you say such a thing about Mr. Courtland? He is so handsome and quite polite. And Charles says he has tons of money—not that it means anything to you after spending all those years you-know-where."

Mon Dieu, Katherine couldn't even say it. Acadiana's eyes rose to meet her cousin's, distress sketched along the planes of her face. Taking a deep breath, she confessed.

"Oh, Katherine! I swear, he makes my hands sweat!" Her cousin's mouth dropped open and Acadiana almost giggled, but her anxiety ran too high for her to indulge in such lightheartedness. "For some reason I feel very foolish and jittery around him. Ah, Katherine, it is the oddest thing imaginable. And that's not the worst of it. He wants my land! He wants to buy the only thing I have left of *Maman* and Papa. Last night when I thought he was being so nice to me, he was only interested in my property."

"Fiddle, Cade! What are you saying?" asked Katherine, eyeing her cousin somewhat skeptically. She had never seen Acadiana, normally so strong and self-assured, so utterly out of sorts.

"He is after my land," Acadiana returned heatedly. "If you could have seen his eyes, heard the tone of his voice—I tell you, *chère,* he is dangerous. He will not give up easily. But he shan't get it!"

"Pooh!" Lifting her fan from the tabletop, Katherine snapped it shut and pointed it straight at Acadiana's dainty nose. "I did see the way he looked at you. He couldn't take his eyes off you. It was as if he were looking into your very soul. Why, Charles only looked at me like that after I let him kiss me. Your land isn't all Jonas is interested in, I can tell you that," she continued with a passion that was lost on Acadiana. "It's silly for you to get so upset over it. Just tell him no. Why you want to keep it though is beyond me. Whoever heard of a woman farmer?

"Anyway, Jonas is your escort tonight, and this is so important to me. Please, Cade, be polite for my sake."

Katherine just didn't understand, Acadiana thought, not that it mattered. Their love for one another was unconditional. Each had her foibles, but overriding that was the love and companionship they shared.

"Have I ever done anything to embarrass you?"

"Nothing you got caught at," Katherine hedged.

"You know I would never do anything to hurt you," Acadiana said soothingly. "It will be a wonderful party, and I'm sure I will have a grand time."

Acadiana knew there was no sense in upsetting her cousin. Katherine had done nothing to deserve that. It was that man, Jonas, who was causing her to feel nervous and edgy. For Katherine's sake, she would play her part as gracefully as possible.

The evening was progressing nicely, Acadiana supposed. At least she knew that Katherine was in a state of bliss, since she appeared to be floating across the large octagonal tiles Charles had imported to decorate the home they would share. After becoming engaged, Charles had renovated his small cottage into a raised-basement plastered brick house. The squat feeling caused by the heavy hipped roof was softened by the elegant stairways mounting from the lower galleries both front and back. The most lavish renovations had been done on the inside. The rooms were ornamented by paneling, wainscoting, and cornices of wood. All were incorporated in the setting for the main fireplace with its pilasters, which rose to form a double cap on the molding.

Acadiana was as pleased as Katherine with the richness of what would soon be her cousin's new home. Her good humor, however, did not extend beyond that. Acadiana had lost all pleasurable feelings since Jonas had asked her for the first dance. Although she had refused, insisting she did not dance well, the arrogant man had offered to teach her. When she told him she wasn't in the mood for lessons, he dragged her out in the midst of the other couples before she could protest further. She did her very best to step on his toes, but the odious man picked her up under the arms until her feet dangled clear of the floor, and it was either give in or utterly humiliate her aunt and uncle.

Once defeated, Acadiana grudgingly allowed Jonas to glide her across the floor. She ignored the brush of her body against his dark green tailcoat and fawn-colored trousers, ignored the fact that her own gown of forest-green silk, beribboned at the border and ruched at the neck and wrists, made them look like a matched pair. And most assuredly, she ignored the way her flesh tingled like an unholy caress beneath her delicate lawn petticoat. If there was one thing she could attribute to salvaging an otherwise horrible evening, it was the fact that while Jonas was deliberately stealing her breath with each sway of his powerful body, he talked of trivial things and didn't once mention the land. For that, she was extremely grateful.

Jonas chose to ignore Acadiana's discomfort and the fact that she would have rather been anywhere than in his arms. He was too caught up in the violet eyes and her soft body pressed against his to dwell on his anger. The tempting morsel in his arms temporarily overshadowed his thoughts of the land, and he felt an immediate surge of discomfort in his loins. The arousal caused him to instinctively press closer. When Acadiana stiffened and sent him a glaring look of reprisal, Jonas recovered himself and remembered the real reason he was pursuing a dance with the little witch. He didn't care for amorous cat-and-mouse games, especially with unresponsive women. Yet he was inexplicably drawn to this one.

With great effort he refrained from mentioning the one subject that seemed to send her into a maelstrom of emotion so fierce it reminded him of a lioness protecting her den. The casual evening the night before had quickly become charged by his first mention of the land. What a change had come over the girl! What he had mistakenly thought was an appealing young woman, turned out to be a stubborn, hot-headed minx.

She would have to talk to him about it sooner or later. He would never give up trying to get the land back, but he didn't wish to see those intriguing eyes turn murderous again in a public place. No matter how much he longed to press the issue, Jonas restrained himself. Obviously any further dealings with Miss Hamilton and her land would have to be done in private.

Acadiana excused herself as soon as the dance was over. Jonas found himself on Katherine's arm, being introduced to every available young lady in the room. Jonas and Acadiana had barely spoken two words to each other since then. Each time she glanced his way he was engaged in conversation with another beauty. A new face, especially one as handsome as Mr. Courtland's, was a rare treat in this frontier region of Louisiana. Most of the guests were locals, the Hoods, Larches, Dempseys, and Browders, but many were from Charles's hometown of Natchitoches. Still, Acadiana was familiar with them, for she and Katherine had traveled there every summer to visit Aunt Elizabeth's relatives. There were a few young ladies hovering around Jonas that she didn't recognize, but the others were annual acquaintances. Everyone seemed to be quite taken with him.

Just look at that silly Sarah Cox, Acadiana thought as she leaned against the window frame in an effort to catch the night breeze. She is fluttering her lashes so hard one would think she has dust in her eyes. Acadiana sneaked a peek through her own half-lowered lashes as Jonas inclined his ear to the flirtatious debutante. *I'll bet he is not after* her *land!*

She was bored and irritable and hot and—"Oh! I've got to get some air," Acadiana huffed as she moved through the stuffy room. She would slip out for just a little while and pay a visit to old Jean Baptiste, a trapper from the marsh-lands and former acquaintance of her parents'. After years of trading with the Indians, he had finally married and come to this area with his new bride to try his hand at cotton farming, but his wife had died and the crops had failed. Still, the old man remained just on the outskirts of Charles's land, living off his trapper's experience and whittling statues for barter or sale. Acadiana started for the door when she saw a familiar couple slip quietly out into the garden. She suddenly changed her mind, and with a mischievous grin, she went in search of Katherine.

Finding her cousin engaged in conversation with a prudish old widow, Acadiana determined that Katherine needed rescuing. She made apologies to the dowager and pulled her cousin to the side.

Leaning close, she whispered in Katherine's ear, "I just saw Samantha Hutton leave the room with David Monroe."

"Cade, really! Samantha always sneaks out with stuffy old David," Katherine replied.

"I know," Acadiana said slyly. "Are you thinking what I am thinking?"

"Cade, no!" Katherine giggled. "We can't."

"But of course we can."

"No, I refuse! It has been years since we pulled one of those stunts. We just can't. If Charles found out—"

"He won't. *S'il vous plaît*, Katherine, this is our last chance to do something wicked before you are married. After that you won't be able to do a thing," Acadiana pleaded.

"Oh, I don't know," Katherine said peevishly, but her eyes were sly.

"Do you remember the time Samantha lured Charles into the garden with a fake message from you?"

Katherine's eyes narrowed and her lips pursed into a little moue. "Ooh! And then threw herself at him! Charles swears he was repulsed, of course, but that was a very underhanded thing for her to do. I also recall that she told Mr. Broussard about all those years you spent you-know-where. Then he quit calling on you. I always thought y'all made such a sweet couple before Samantha stuck her nose in it."

Acadiana reserved comment on the last statement. If anything she should thank Miss Hutton for getting rid of the weak-minded *M'sieu* Broussard. It was hard, however, to forget Samantha's interference in other matters. For some reason, the girl had made rabid attempts to damage Acadiana's reputation over the last few years. Acadiana didn't give a fig for what people thought of her, but she cared dearly for her uncle and his family. Every disparaging remark Samantha viciously tossed out reflected on them also.

Her smile might have been innocent-looking, but the light in Acadiana's eyes was anything but. Katherine didn't have the heart to refuse.

"It would be quite nasty, wouldn't it? And Samantha does deserve it . . . and I won't be able to do anything like it ever again. All right," she giggled. "Let's do it! Get the punch."

The girls headed for one of the serving tables before Acadiana suddenly stopped. *"Non!* Not punch *this* time, Katherine. For our very last prank we will use champagne."

"Excellent!" Katherine tittered. "But if we get caught, you will have to do all the explaining to Charles."

"Oui." Acadiana took Katherine's arm and walked toward the butler. "Slow down. We must look very refined."

"Of course," Katherine said with a giggle as she raised her chin in the air with an arrogant tilt.

They each took a glass of bubbling liquid and sipped it as they leisurely strolled around the room. They curtsied or nodded to the guests as they gracefully made their way to the other side. Once there, they each took a fresh glass and slipped outside.

"They will go down to the goldfish pond first," Acadiana whispered, "then they will come back by the old granddad oaks."

"I know, I know!" said Katherine. "Hurry before someone spots us."

They sneaked through the garden like two accomplices in

crime, carefully guarding their glasses of sparkling refreshment. When they reached their destination Katherine looked skeptically at the twin oak trees.

"I don't know, Cade," she said, shaking her head. "I don't know if I can get up there in these skirts. What do you think?"

"Shhh!" Acadiana whispered. "Come on, I'll help you."

"Who is going to help *you* up?" Katherine rasped.

"I'll manage," Acadiana said as she took the champagne and placed both glasses on the ground. "Up you go."

She took Katherine's foot in her cupped hands and began to hoist her up to the lowest branch. She teetered unsteadily as Katherine sought to gain control of the massive tree. Acadiana pushed, shoved, and lifted the wobbly foot. Exasperated, she finally put her hand under Katherine's bottom and hurled her up. Katherine squealed as she flew over the limb and almost fell off the other side.

"Shhh!" warned Acadiana.

"You almost threw me through the tree!" Katherine exclaimed in a gruff whispered voice.

"I'm sorry," Acadiana giggled. "I couldn't get you up."

Acadiana stood on tiptoe and handed the champagne to her cousin, then proceeded to climb the twin tree. She fought her way up past the clutching branches that were wont to tangle in her voluminous skirts, then pulled herself out onto a sturdy branch where she could see the ground below and Katherine at the same time.

"Do you see them yet?" Acadiana asked.

"Not yet. Can you reach this champagne?"

"I can try," Acadiana said as she scooted along the limb on her stomach.

"You are going to ruin your dress, Cade," Katherine whispered as she stretched out her hand with the glass.

"Shhh. Here they come." Acadiana grabbed the glass, then steadied herself on the limb. "You go first, they are almost under your tree. For heaven's sake, don't let them see you."

The couple stopped beneath the branches of the twin oaks and turned to face each other. David reached out his skinny arms and gathered Samantha to his spindly chest. From above monstrous mosquitoes attacked Katherine's face and arms. It was all she could do to keep from slapping them away as she waited. At a nod from Acadiana she tipped her glass ever so slightly and let a few drops of the liquid dribble over the edge to the top of Samantha's head. She waited a second, then repeated the act on David.

Samantha brushed back the drops with a gloved hand, then leaned her plump frame into her escort. "You don't think anyone will catch us here, do you, David?"

"I am always very careful, my dearest love," he said in a nasal voice as he shook his head free of the occasional drops.

"We really shouldn't be here," Samantha said coquettishly. "It would rightly ruin my reputation if we were caught."

Acadiana stifled a giggle as she thought of Samantha's dubious reputation. The girl had a list of beaux a mile long.

"My darling heart," David said, sucking in his stomach and throwing his shoulders back from his lanky frame, "I would defend your honor to the very death if someone dare say a word against you."

"David, you are so gallant!" Samantha crooned. She ran one long fingernail down the buttons of his vest, stopping just as she reached the band of his breeches. "I thought I saw you looking at that Hamilton girl tonight. Is that true, David?"

Monroe's Adam's apple bobbed up and down as he stared at Samantha's finger circling his navel. "W-which Hamilton?" he squeaked.

"The wild one." Samantha pouted, running her finger back up David's vest. "She is so . . . so common-looking. I can't believe someone as sophisticated as you would find her attractive."

Acadiana suppressed the urge to claw her way down Samantha's back and patiently waited for revenge.

"I would hardly call either of those girls ugly," David began, sweat breaking out on his brow as Samantha's fingers continued their seductive path. "You must admit they are both very beautiful." Samantha withdrew her hand suddenly and acted as if she might move away. "Uh, of course, whatever you think, my dear. Everyone pales next to you."

"*Were* you looking at her earlier?" Miss Hutton simpered while slipping her finger just inside David's waistband.

"Absolutely not!" David gasped. "Oh, Samantha, lower."

The branch on which Acadiana was perched began to bend and she made no effort to stop the champagne from spilling freely on Samantha's head. She wished with all her heart at this moment that she had a bucket of manure.

"Mercy me, is it beginning to rain?" Samantha said, squinting up.

"I certainly hope not," David whined. "Our time together is so very short."

Acadiana saw Katherine smile mischievously as she tilted her own glass to dribble a bit of the champagne down.

"I do believe it *is* raining," Samantha complained. "But there is not a cloud in the sky."

Acadiana tilted her glass again and let a few more drops fall down to the couple below. She waited just a moment, then released the rest of her champagne on the duo. Taking a deep breath, she whistled a shrill warble, then ducked her head in the crook of her elbow to smother her laughter.

"A bird?" Samantha gasped. The horror of it struck her swiftly, and she began sweeping wildly at her hair and shoulder. "Oh, David, it was a bird!" she screeched. "How could you bring me here?"

"I don't know, my fairest love," he apologized, and reached to take her arm.

"Don't touch me!" she shrieked, flailing her arms about to brush him away. "It got on you too!"

"Oh, Gawd!" he cried, then began wiping frantically at his coat.

"You clod! It's all your fault!" she wailed. Livid with rage and disgust, Samantha spun away from him and began running back toward the house.

"But, my dear, my sweet," David whined, trailing after her, looking like a stork with his long, awkward strides.

Acadiana was barely able to contain herself. When the couple was just out of sight, she burst into peals of laughter. Katherine joined in the revelry, clutching her branch for dear life as tears streamed down her face.

"Cade," she said between gasps of air. "Cade." Whatever she meant to say was lost as she continued to giggle uncontrollably and finally buried her face in her arm, unable to go on.

"Oh, oh, my." Acadiana gulped, wiping at her tears and trying without success to stifle her own mirth.

"That was our best one ever," Katherine declared.

"Better than the time we painted our faces black and ran through the quarters yelling 'slave uprising'? Or the time we went swimming in the raw and Uncle Grayson found our clothes and thought we had drowned?"

"Ooh." Katherine grimaced. "He was a tad bit cantankerous over that one, wasn't he? We had to listen to Mama preach for three days on the proper deportment of young ladies."

"Do you think it did any good?" Acadiana queried.

"Certainly," Katherine said in her haughtiest voice. "I am up in this tree in my best dress, aren't I?"

Another round of laughter overcame the girls, and it was a full two minutes before either could catch her breath enough to ease the ache in her ribs.

Katherine was finally able to choke off the last bit of laughter, though it threatened to erupt again at any moment.

"Cade?"

"*Oui?*"

"Why do you think David continues to sneak off with Samantha? Why doesn't he ask her to marry him?"

"It's like Uncle Grayson says. Why buy the cow when you've got free milk?"

Both girls broke out once again in a fresh torrent, giggling, tittering, and shaking the tree limbs until they almost toppled from their perches. The girls were hopeless in their efforts to compose themselves until Acadiana realized that someone was wandering down the lane.

"Shhh! Someone is coming," she whispered.

Katherine gasped. "Mercy! Who is it?"

"I don't know. Hush, before they hear us."

Acadiana crept farther out on the branch to see who was walking down the dark path. She couldn't make out their faces at first, but the deep drawl carried by the breeze was unmistakable and effectively crushed her good humor.

"I know I heard them out here somewhere," Jonas stated, "giggling like schoolgirls."

"Are you sure?" Charles asked. "I don't see or hear a thing."

"I passed near here a few minutes ago. That Hutton girl was running back to the house like a demon was after her. *She* certainly wasn't the one laughing."

The cousins stared at each other's broad, devious grin. Acadiana shrugged her shoulders and put a finger to her lips. Katherine slowly dropped her head to her arms and waited for them to pass.

The men continued to look around, then stopped beneath the tree. "I don't see them anywhere, Jonas."

"Well, they are not at the house, and I know I heard some sort of carrying-on out here."

Charles smiled. "I wouldn't put it past those two."

Jonas surveyed the garden, listening for more than the call of the mocking bird or the *tap tap tap* of the ivory-billed woodpecker. "Katherine seems so quiet. Not one to sneak off and leave her own party."

"She is until she gets around Cade." Charles laughed. "There is no telling what that girl has her doing right now."

Acadiana sent Charles a glare that would have split his skull if such a thing were possible. Katherine shook in her hiding place as she tried to squelch the laughter that threatened to bubble anew. She covered her mouth with her sleeve but could not stop her body from rippling with suppressed mirth.

Charles looked up at the sound, but, seeing nothing, leaned casually against the tree trunk. "I love this spot," he said wistfully. "Right under this tree is where Katherine first kissed me."

Katherine's head shot up and she stared at Acadiana in embarrassment. Acadiana could not see her cousin's face too clearly in the dark but knew it was flaming red.

"*First* kiss?" Jonas taunted. "You mean there have been more? I wouldn't have figured Katherine for the type."

"We *are* engaged," Charles said. "She hasn't let me go too far, though it's not been from lack of trying."

Jonas chuckled and slapped his friend on the back. "Why, Charles," he said drolly. "You never had a problem with the ladies before."

"Why, Jonas," Charles said just as blandly. "That's because they weren't ladies." Deep, masculine laughter consumed him until his chest heaved with guffaws. All of a sudden he was hit in the head with a champagne glass, which was followed by an outraged squeal. Katherine lost her perch in her quest for revenge and careened over the side, clutching the branch.

"Charles Nolan! You . . . you snake!" she yelled, dangling from the tree.

"Katherine!" He was stunned as he looked up to see her gripping the limb above him. "What are you doing up there?"

"Get me down!" she demanded, kicking her feet in midair.

Charles grabbed her waist and placed her firmly on the ground. "Katherine, what in heaven's name—"

Katherine shrugged his hands off and stood facing him with pronounced anger. "Charles! How could you?" she cried.

"How could I what?" he said, lowering his head to stare down at her in a condescending way. "What were you doing up there?"

"Climbing trees," she retorted before turning her back on him in a huff.

"Where is Acadiana? I know she's here somewhere."

"Well, maybe she was," Katherine said pertly, "but she is gone now. I must go back to the house and repair my dress."

Katherine lifted her chin and stomped off with as much poise as she could muster while experiencing total humiliation. Charles followed behind, glaring at her swinging backside and trying to smother a grin.

"I'll be along in a minute," Jonas called after them, casually leaning back against the tree. Folding his arms across his chest, he lifted his knee to rest a boot against the oak and ran his hand across his chin for a moment, then looked up into the darkness.

"You can come down now, Acadiana. They're gone."

A gasp was heard from above. The leaves rustled and a dainty slippered foot appeared in the darkness. Acadiana dangled from the limb a moment, shaking her skirts out, then dropped agilely to the ground in front of him.

"How did you know I was still here?" she asked, brushing the bark from her dress. Sticky sap gummed her fingers and made total repair impossible.

"Just a hunch," he said, offering her his handkerchief. "I remembered how *loyal* Katherine is."

"Very astute," Acadiana said. "Now, if you will excuse me, I'd better return to the house. I promised her I would explain things to Charles if we got caught."

"I think they need to be alone right now," Jonas said,

and reached out and took her wrist. There was just a hint of restraint in the hold, which caused Acadiana to stiffen. She looked down at his hand furled around her small wrist, felt the strength and purpose there along with the rhythmic heat of human contact where her pulse beat against his thumb. She was unused to being touched so by a stranger and tried to pull away, but his fingers tightened.

Her heart began to pound jerkily in her chest, and she was suddenly afraid that it would stop beating all together. *Le bon Dieu,* this Jonas Courtland was an impressive, handsome man, but too domineering. His presence did crazy things to her insides. If only circumstances had been different . . . Acadiana sent her ebony curls swinging as she shook her head to clear the wayward thoughts, then looked up to see Jonas staring down at her.

His brooding eyes appeared almost black in the moonlight. *Looking into your very soul,* Katherine had said. Acadiana thought he looked more like he was stripping her of her dignity.

He wasn't. Jonas was quite vividly stripping her of her clothing and lingering over the thought of what formed the swells and curves beneath her formal gown. Acadiana shifted nervously and began tugging more forcefully to escape his hold. His grip changed and the hand, which had been locked around her wrist, was now rubbing her flesh intimately. Her luminous eyes widened, and it was Jonas's turn to shake his head to clear the thoughts that were sending fire to his loins. He released her wrist but let his fingers drift down to linger beneath hers. Acadiana snatched her hand away but still felt strangely imprisoned.

"Escaping your cousin's party?" Jonas asked to deflect her thoughts. She looked ready to turn tail and run. "What would everyone think?"

"I don't give a hoot what the little socialites think," Acadiana returned before realizing he was baiting her. Her violet eyes narrowed and a playful grin crept across her mouth. "Why, *M'sieu* Courtland, whatever are *you* doing here? Surely you aren't bored with Charles's party also. What would all the young ladies think who are so desperately vying for your affection? I am sure you are sorely missed."

"No more than you, Miss Hamilton. Why, I haven't been able to speak more than two words to you all evening with so many gentlemen admiring your beauty." He grinned and leaned back against the huge old oak.

"My beauty! *M'sieu,* I fear you have had too much to drink—or your eyesight is extremely poor," she returned in feigned astonishment.

Jonas pushed off the tree to tower over her, and Acadiana found him suddenly very intimidating.

"I make it a habit to never drink too much, and my eyesight is perfect. You are by far the most beautiful woman here."

Acadiana was taken aback by his compliment and did not quite know what to say. Her heart was pounding at a rapid pace again, and she got the sudden impression that she should not be here. To top it all off, she was blushing. How very strange indeed.

"Cat got your tongue?" he teased.

"Pardon?"

"You seem at a loss for words. What were you doing in there anyway?"

"In the tree?"

"Back at the house," Jonas replied. "I mean, what were you *really* doing in there, Miss Hamilton? You look beautiful, say all the right things, make all the right moves. But you are just going through the motions, doing what is expected of you. Am I right?"

"Mon Dieu," Acadiana exclaimed beneath her breath. Her eyes lifted to meet the man's, and exasperation was written all over her delicate features. "I am that obvious, *oui?* Katherine will just die! I promised to behave myself in front of everyone."

"Katherine will not die." Jonas snorted. "She is too taken

with Charles to know what is going on around her. You play the part well, Miss Hamilton. The question is why?"

"It is best," Acadiana said softly. "I owe it to my uncle. It's not so hard really, just bothersome at times. I usually like the parties. I just have other things on my mind these days."

"The land?"

"Yes . . . *my* land," she said slowly, defensively. "You must understand, it is all I have left of my parents, and somewhere inside I feel that it is all I have left of me." A soft moan followed, and her next words came out as an almost desperate plea. "Why do you want it so badly? It can't possibly mean the same thing to you."

"That is where you are wrong," Jonas said in a cold, flat tone that was ominously clear in the dark night. "My grandfather sold it to your father one night when he was quite intoxicated and incapable of making wise decisions. He never meant for the land to leave our family and regretted it for the rest of his life."

Made anxious by his disclosure and the determination in Jonas's voice, she retaliated in defense. "I will never sell. I am truly sorry about your grandfather, but I will never *ever* let go of the land. It is mine!"

"We shall see," he taunted. "I'm a determined man."

"No more determined than I am," Acadiana countered, stepping back, then turning quickly to go back to the house.

She had taken only one step before Jonas halted her. Catching her by surprise, he grabbed her arm and spun her around to face him. He was standing so close, Acadiana could do nothing more than stare at him, wide-eyed. His arms encircled her, and with a quick jerk, Acadiana found her stunned and rigid body pressed against his.

Jonas's look was piercing as he delved deeply into her angry eyes to touch the woman hidden within. He had watched her reactions around other men earlier in the evening. Cool and aloof she had been, with a haughty grace that shouted she was untouchable. But with Katherine, she had shown a warmth of affection that could not be disguised. With him, her eyes had changed completely, yet not at all, as if the look she reserved for him was a mixture of the two.

It had been his intention to finish their conversation privately before she could retreat to the security of the house when he grabbed her arm, but his intentions were swept away by the closeness of their bodies, the whisper of warm, humid air surrounding them, and even warmer flesh. "Is it true what they say, Miss Hamilton?" Jonas drawled in mockery. "Are you really an ice maiden despite those fiery eyes?"

Acadiana gasped at the insult and sought to pull away. Her eyes darkened to a smoldering purple and her lips parted for an angry retort. She got no further, for at once his mouth was pressed to hers, and she was so shocked it took her a moment to respond. She jerked her head back and broke contact, but Jonas's hand immediately shot to the back of her head and held her immobile, while his lips once again pressed to hers. Acadiana had never been kissed before, and this powerful and insulting possession was certainly not what she had expected. His mouth moved over hers in a hungry, conquering way, overwhelming in its intensity, bleak and cold in its intent. Devoid of all tenderness, the kiss reeked of confidence and victory.

Acadiana had never been so insulted or at such a disadvantage. She felt rooted to the ground, unable to move, as if her strength were being sapped with each breath leaving her body. Her heart was racing uncontrollably again, and she didn't like the way her knees were weakening, turning to jelly beneath her. The instinct for survival rose within her, and with renewed vigor she groaned a protest and struggled against him, her hands folding into fists. She raised them to beat at his chest and shoulders, alternately pushing then pounding, while trying to dislodge his hand from her head.

Jonas's fingers tightened in her hair. He was past accepting denials of any kind from this woman, and his arm pulled harder against her waist. He lessened the pressure on her mouth just enough to play lightly upon her lips, nipping then tugging at them with the expertise of a master. Acadiana's angry groans turned into moans of pure distress. She could not break his hold, could not get away. In the space of a heartbeat, a new fear quickened within her, a woman's fear of the man who held her so effortlessly yet with steel strength. She was acutely aware of the power in the muscle-taut body that pressed against her, of the large hand splayed across her back. The night surrounded them in its darkness, and there was no one to come to her aid. And horribly, with earth-shattering clarity, she became aware of the lean hips that began to grind against hers until she was backed against the rough oak tree.

The bark cut into her back and Acadiana felt smothered by the force of emotions assailing her—anger, trepidation, disbelief. For the first time in almost a decade she was frightened, truly frightened, by the man and the vague but intense power glowing in those sapphire eyes. Summoning every ounce of strength she possessed—which seemed pitifully slight at this point—she raised her knee, then slammed her heel down atop his foot.

The blow connected on two vulnerable parts of his anatomy, and Jonas growled then shoved her at arm's length. He was shocked to find his breathing labored and irritated beyond endurance to realize that this tiny female could cause such an eruption of dark hunger within him. Common sense and good judgment were only shadows lurking in background, unable to gain solidity in a mind now cloudy with a desire both heady and unreasonable. The scent of her enveloped him, the feel of strained but supple muscles rippled beneath her silk gown to ensnare him. He was helpless to deny the fact that at this minute he wanted this woman with almost the same ruthless passion that he wanted her land—almost.

He stared hard at her and continued to grip her arms tightly as he watched the fury growing in her eyes.

"You . . . you dare accost me?" Acadiana grated out, her breathing harsh. "When my uncle finds out—"

"What?" Jonas mocked her. "You have never been kissed? Go tattle your little news, Acadiana. You are so near spinsterhood, your uncle will think I have done you a favor."

Acadiana jerked away and swung an open palm to strike him, but Jonas easily dodged the intended blow. He grabbed her wrists and pinned them to her sides as he leaned forward.

"Icy . . . yes, but even ice can be melted," he warned her. "We shall see. . . ."

He laughed coldly as he released her and walked confidently back to the house. Staring at the retreating male figure, Acadiana was left with a destroying sense of vulnerability. Breathless, shaken, she was utterly bewildered over the conflicting emotions tumbling throughout her.

3

Acadiana took deep breaths to still her trembling. What an odious man, she thought, and bold! For all his handsome exterior and gentleman's manners around others, Jonas Courtland was nothing short of despicable. How dare he take such liberties! Gingerly she put her fingers to her lips, then snatched them back. The kiss may have begun there, but it had quickly spread currents to the rest of her body, leaving her limbs quaking and her emotions mangled.

She couldn't go back to the house now. *He* was in there. Acadiana did not like the idea of retreating, but her pride had just suffered a severe blow when she had not been able to defend herself. She knew she could not face the beast without her cheeks turning to fire and would have to compose herself first.

Hiking her gown up to her knees, she ran through the garden until she reached the back gate. Without the light from the house, she was forced to pick her way slowly through the woods as she searched for Jean Baptiste's shanty. Since the Louisiana Purchase a tide of pioneers had been pushing toward the Mississippi southwest down the river network. Wood runners and trappers were being replaced with plantation owners, and Providence town was almost big enough now for a charter. Still, the land beyond the cultivated acres of cotton, rice, and small patches of sugarcane remained untamed, full of bear and wildcat, the bayous and lake full of alligator, garfish, and monstrous snapping turtles. Great hulking shapes loomed before her as Acadiana moved through the giant cypress trees rivaled in size only by the red gums and white oaks. Skeletal fingers reached out to snare her hair and dress as she crept past dripping moss. Eerie rustlings mingled with the evening fog and magnified to become wraithlike specters that sent her already frayed nerves humming. She stanched macabre thoughts of goblins and spirits and midnight lurkers. The only hellish host she knew was one Jonas Courtland, and she fervently wished he would go back where he belonged.

Catching sight of old pots strung on the trapper's drying racks, she raced in that direction. The fires burning there, to ward off mosquitoes, cast a feeble glow that created ghostly shadows that danced along the walls of the structure.

"M'sieu Jean?" she called tentatively as she approached the handhewn timber shack.

"Entrez, Cade!" a voice bellowed out before the door creaked open.

Giddy with relief, Acadiana entered the small dwelling and raised on tiptoe to kiss the huge man's cheeks. Gigantic arms wrapped her in a quick squeeze before the man motioned her toward a three-legged stool.

Jean Baptiste was an enormous man with meaty arms and bulging chest muscles. A shock of thick white hair crowned his head, lending him a robust but stately look. He stretched his massive legs out in front of him and settled back in an old wooden chair for a chat.

Oui. He chuckled inwardly. This *bébé* of Elaine Belizaire, she love to chat.

"What you come to this old man's house for, eh?" he blustered in a deep-echoing voice that had cowed many a brave man.

"I just need to visit, Jean." Acadiana sighed, used to the old Cajun's gruffness. "A man has come. He wants to buy my land."

Jean was instantly alert to the sadness in her voice and the look of tired desperation on her face.

"This is not too bad, no? You told him you would not sell?"

"*Oui.*" Acadiana smiled in an effort to ease her distress. "But he is so determined! I cannot explain it, Jean, but I think he will stop at nothing to get it."

"*Sacré!*" Jean stood up suddenly, sending his chair crashing back against the cypress wall. "If he has hurt you—"

"*Non!*" Acadiana hastened to reassure him. "I am afraid, that is all. I don't have the money to keep the land, but I cannot sell it. You know how it is; it is too awful to think about."

Jean relaxed somewhat and walked to the corner of the hut that served as his kitchen. "*Café noir?*" he asked, bringing out two exquisite demitasse cups that looked out of place in their humble surroundings.

Acadiana thanked Jean as she took the strong black coffee and waited for him to sit back down.

"Tell me about my people," she urged.

"How many times I got to tell you that old story, eh? For sho you get tired of it someday."

"Never." Acadiana giggled. Tough old Jean loved telling the tales as much as she loved hearing them. They gave her a secure feeling, a sense of belonging. A hope, perhaps, for the future through knowledge of her past.

Jean righted his chair then cleared his voice as if preparing for a grand oration. "It started at the time of *le Grand Dérangement—*"

"In 1755," Acadiana said expectantly.

"Who is telling this story, eh? Do not interrupt!"

Smothering a grin, Acadiana scooted onto the floor, pulled her knees up to her chest, and listened with rapt attention to the story she had heard too many times to number.

"Your *grand'mère* and *grand-père* were part of the exile, a sad t'ing, that." Jean shook his head as he always did when recounting the tale of how the British had taken over the French settlement of Acadia and forced the Acadians to flee their Canadian homeland with little more than the clothes on their backs.

An aggregate of sound—crickets, bullfrogs, owls—mingled in the damp night air to create a melodious background for the weaving of Jean's story.

"Adrian and Marie Labiche were not separated at the first like so many others," he began. "Long time they wander, combing the streams in pirogues, walking barefoot, all the time trying to get to French territory. But then it happen! Your *grand-père* took sick. Marie nurse him best she could, but he die. Poor Marie, she want to die too. She with child now and no family, nowhere to go."

"That is when she met Matthias Hamilton, *oui?*" Acadiana intoned. "He took pity on her and—"

"Who's telling this story, eh? Do not interrupt!" The sternness of Jean's voice did nothing to chastise Acadiana, but she tried to remain silent as he continued. *"Oui,* Marie was very beautiful; and *M'sieu* Hamilton, well, he fall in love with her. When he ask for her hand, she say no at the first, but he was so good and patient that finally she grow to love him back. That's when Marie marry him—right before your papa was born."

"But Marie was still lonesome for her friends," Acadiana began.

"You have heard this story, *petite?*"

Acadiana managed to look contrite as she hid a smile behind her coffee cup. Jean was not fooled as he stared at the bright amethyst eyes so like Elaine's. He had known this girl since she was a small child, before he had left on a trading expedition, before her parents were brutally killed. This child of Armand and Elaine had always been too inquisitive and full of fire for her own good. He sent her an indignant snort for good measure before resuming his tale.

"After your papa was born, *M'sieu* Hamilton agree to help Marie find her people. They go to New Orleans first, but guess what?"

"Louisiana had been transferred to Spain," Acadiana chimed in. "It was no longer French territory. No one in New Orleans wanted the immigrants, and they were sent to other areas. Marie and her new husband were sent to the Poste des Attakapas on the Bayou Teche."

"Oui," Jean agreed. "I t'ink you do know this story." At Acadiana's eager nod he continued. "It take them a month, traveling the water routes to reach their destination. By now they were poor refugees, cold and hungry, and 'bout eaten up with the swamp fever. Your papa was only a few years old, and Matthias Hamilton wanted to go back to his home in the eastern colonies."

"But he stayed," Acadiana said softly.

"Oui, he love that Marie and her son; he do anyt'ing for them. By now, Marie got herself another *bébé* on the way."

"Uncle Grayson," Acadiana said brightly.

"That rascal?" Jean bellowed. *"Non,* they found him in a gator nest for sho!"

Acadiana began to giggle at the disrespectful idea, then rose to pour more coffee. Jean sighed as she sashayed by with the natural allure of her mother. What would happen to Elaine Belizaire's daughter? he wondered. How long could an idle existence at her uncle's contain her? Not long, he reckoned. Born and reared the first ten years of her life in the swamps, Acadiana had a wildness about her that didn't take well to the quiet life.

A gentle breeze wafted through the open window, bringing with it the scent of summer that so reminded Jean of his own sweet Jolie, and Marie, and Elaine, and all women of great strength and beauty. He thanked Acadiana for the coffee, then waited for her to sit back down before finishing his tale of the hardships and struggles her grandparents had found in this new land. He ended with Armand Hamilton's marriage to Elaine Belizaire, then rose and gave a mighty yawn and stretch.

"So, Cade," he said jovially, "you have had enough?"

"It's never enough." Acadiana sighed. The story always soothed her, made her remember that her own trials were paltry when compared to the adversity her grandparents and all the Acadian people had suffered. "But now I must return to the party. I fear Uncle Grayson will already be looking for me." She didn't mention Jonas's name to Jean, tried mightily to push the domineering man's presence from her mind. She knew he was staying at Charles's house, so there was no way she could avoid him when she went back there. But she felt stronger now after talking to her dear friend. She was, after all, descended from those courageous Acadians. Something as insignificant as a kiss from an over-bearing, handsome Creole could not, *would not* bother her.

"Come then," Jean said softly, noting the introspection that weighed heavily on her piquant face. Elaine's *bébé* was up against something she had not had to deal with before. He wondered just how she would go about dealing with the man who wanted her land. She was resourceful, had courage and stamina. She had been through much over the past years and she had survived. He would not worry. But he would keep watch. He pushed the rickety old door open and bowed gallantly to allow her to pass. "I will see you back."

Acadiana paced back and forth across the hardwood floor of her bedroom. The carpet had been removed for the summer, and her heels clicked out a steady rhythm that ran contrary to the erratic pace of her heart. Things had not gone well at all in the week following Katherine's party. Acadiana felt as if she were living on the edge of a rocky bluff, tossed this way and that by a vertiginous wind, and about to be thrown to her doom at any moment. Never one to yield to topsy-turvy emotions, she berated herself constantly.

This is so witless, she thought as she fidgeted with the small puffed sleeves of her gown. Foolish to feel this way because of a single kiss.

But it wasn't just the kiss that had sent her body tumbling into a whirlpool of emotions so foreign they played havoc with her mind. It was the force behind the kiss, and the man behind the force. It was his daring and his strength, his absolute flouting of what was proper, as if he answered to no one, no inner conscience or sense of right. As if he cared nothing for her feelings but would do anything to gain his own end. Acadiana's dignity and sense of justice had been trampled. Jonas Courtland had caused her to feel more anger than she had ever before felt; he had also made her feel weak, defeated. And that was unforgivable. He was determined to get her land, and she sensed by his boldness that he was not above any means to get it. She would need her wits and strength to combat him. Weakness could be an enemy that would destroy her.

She tried to force the thoughts from her mind as she tugged on the bodice of the gown she had just donned for Katherine's wedding. But the thoughts lingered like pesky insects buzzing and stinging, offering no rest. The gathered bosom was so tight Acadiana feared she would pop out with each irritated breath she took. Her skirt was flared in front and pleated full in the back and sides. The pastel-pink fabric was sheer and worn over a lining of satin of the same color. In her dour mood she tried hard to appreciate the long hours Aunt Elizabeth had spent cutting scallops with a pinking tool for the ruffles that were used on the neck, sleeves, and skirt.

Her fingers fumbled as she jerked on the long formal gloves, and she cursed her nervousness over the fact that the dishonorable Jonas Courtland was downstairs this very minute waiting to escort her to the wedding.

With her usual flair for the dramatic, Katherine had arranged this little meeting without Acadiana's knowledge. Before she knew what was happening, her cousin had routed everyone from the house, leaving Acadiana no choice but to allow Jonas to drive her. She would get back at Katherine for this infernal matchmaking! Hadn't she seen him enough this past week—across the dinner table, riding along the lake bank, and at every social function she was required to attend.

She always steadied her nerves enough each time to make polite conversation with those around her. She never talked to *him* though. She couldn't. Every time he looked her way, made some seemingly innocent comment, Acadiana blushed outlandishly and remembered the kiss. She was tempted to tell her uncle what had happened and have him kick *M'sieu* Courtland out on his arrogant backside. But she was too ashamed to tell, too ashamed of her own chaotic feelings, and too caring of Katherine to spoil her cousin's happiness with the ugliness of what had happened.

So, she avoided him with every bit of cunning she possessed and every excuse ever invented. Still, there were those times over the past week when it had been impossible to escape his presence, when even her convoluted mind could not come up with a plausible reason to excuse herself, and she would be forced to suffer being in the same room with him. To add to her unease, he seemed to sense her failure to extricate herself, and every time she looked up he would be staring at her, staring with those brazen blue eyes that had the power to set her to shivering in the hottest part of the day, while he sat back relaxed and grinning like a satisfied wolf.

With more spirit than composure, Acadiana set her chin stubbornly and decided that this man would not ruin her day. She would inform him quite frankly that she expected him to behave like a gentleman. She would agree to be polite if he afforded her the same courtesy. She also decided that she wouldn't get within ten feet of him when she could help it.

Acadiana descended the stairs and approached the parlor cautiously. Jonas stood, almost like a ship's captain with his legs braced apart and his hands clasped casually behind his back, studying a painting on the wall beside the fireplace. Even in her anger, Acadiana had to admit that he was the most handsome man she had ever seen. He was attractively attired in dove-gray nankeen knee breeches that were tightly fitted and outlined his long, muscular thighs. His black velvet waistcoat contrasted sharply with his white shirt, stock, and cravat, along with the silk stockings that emphasized the strength of his calves. He was stunning, and much too stirring for the fragile composure Acadiana was trying to hang on to.

"Do you like it?" she asked curiously.

"It is as beautiful as the artist," he answered without turning around.

Acadiana was momentarily bedazzled by the compliment, and her determination sagged. She should thank him, she knew, but couldn't seem to force the words out. She took a step closer, and Jonas turned around.

"You did paint it, didn't you?" he asked with a slow grin because he already knew the answer. It was an excellent rendition of the land that had once belonged to his family. The only difference between the property now and in this painting was the magnificent house of Greek Revival design and quaint gazebo that the artist had added with unfailing detail. "There is no house," he said simply, and without malice. He could sense the dedication that must have gone into producing this work. "No house like this one, at least. There is just a cottage there now."

"My parents' cottage," Acadiana said in an almost dreamy whisper, caught up in the painting she had worked so hard on, her eyes caressing every detail of her legacy and her hopes. "But someday this house and the gazebo will stand, not in the place of the cottage but several arpents away, near a place my father had begun clearing. Children will play along the bayou again. My dreamfields will be planted, and the harvest rich."

The words were spoken softly, but they carried such weighty determination, such ultimate emotion that Jonas stepped closer and lifted Acadiana's chin.

"So much passion," he whispered, "locked up inside that icy façade."

Ever so slowly, he lowered his face to hers. Acadiana could see his lips getting closer, could feel his breath on her inflamed cheeks. She tried to take a quick step backward, but like the one other time she had been kissed, strong arms reached out to encircle her and she could not move, was forced to stare up at him in rising anger and trepidation as he drew nearer and nearer. She turned her face aside to avoid him and jerked violently in his embrace. This cannot be happening again, she thought hysterically, but knew it was when all her struggles proved pointless. His hands followed every twitch of her body, containing her without seeming to do so, then eased up her arms until his palms cradled each side of her head and turned her back to face him.

"Do not do this!" Acadiana whispered fiercely, her heart pounding as if rushing toward its final stroke. "I will not allow it. I—"

He was too close now. Her lashes fluttered down to shield her violet eyes, and to hide from him her vulnerability. Never would she be caught again like this, like some poor trapped animal in a hunter's snare awaiting the death blow. A tremor of apprehension shivered through her body as she braced herself for the insult. Jonas's lips brushed hers, feather light, almost not real. Acadiana groaned low and twisted again as heat flared across her skin, staining her cheeks a fetching rose. Her body grazed his in her struggles, back and forth, to and fro, and she felt as if she were sinking into some hot, dark abyss. Then as quickly as it began, the kiss ended.

Caught off guard by the impact of what should have been

a simple gesture, Jonas jerked back suddenly. The charge racing between them was a tangible thing, full of sparks and fire. He had meant the kiss as a truce, to show Acadiana that, unlike the other night, he could be gentle. But something had happened when he touched her. A flame, bright and consuming, had reared its brilliant head. Jonas knew such heat could not be extinguished here in her uncle's parlor. He had been a fool to step so close to the fire.

"I think we had better go, while we still can," he said in a husky voice, his eyes narrowed upon her in mingled portions of surprise and heat and deadly aggression. "But make no mistake, we will at some time finish what was started here."

Acadiana's eyes shot open, and her cheeks burned a dull red. *"M'sieu* Courtland," she said softly, dangerously. "We will *never* finish anything. We are done! You will never touch me again, I swear it." She couldn't think of anything more to say in her befuddled state, so she swung away from him and marched toward the door.

"Chérie," he drawled in amusement at the sight of her stiff shoulders and swinging backside. "If I had known it would upset you so, I would have stayed to finish the kiss."

Acadiana's maledictory reply was something Jonas had never heard come out of a lady's mouth. Like the ominous rumble of an approaching thunderstorm, his dark laughter crawled up Acadiana's spine and followed her all the way to the waiting carriage.

4

K atherine was beautiful in her mother's wedding gown of ecru silk as Charles proudly escorted her down the aisle of the small wooden church. Acadiana looked on, melancholy in her happiness for her cousin. She would miss Katherine's flighty, romantic visions, which had been a buffer for her own more solid and tactical approach to life. Although so different, they had complemented one another over the years and had learned to accept differences as a necessary part of growing.

Acadiana slipped into the shadows as the men moved the benches aside to make room for the reception. From there she could watch Katherine's blissful progress around the room without infusing her own sadness into the occasion. Katherine was the sister Acadiana had never had, and she would miss her terribly.

"Strange, I didn't figure you for one of those ladies who cry at weddings," Jonas said, startling Acadiana from her wanderings as he handed her his handkerchief for the third time since they had arrived at the church.

"Don't be ridiculous, *M'sieu* Courtland. I never cry at weddings—or anywhere else, for that matter. It is just that this is Katherine, and . . . well . . . it's just that this is Katherine."

"I understand," he said solicitously.

"Do you really?" She sniffed. "I wish I did." With that she turned on her heel and left.

With Katherine on his arm, Charles walked up after the odd exchange and smiled at his friend's beleaguered expression. "How much longer can you stay, Jonas? I had hoped we would have more time to visit."

"I'll have to be here for a while longer," Jonas said, covertly watching the swirl of satin and petticoats swish away. "I've made no progress with Acadiana on the land deal."

"Now, Jonas," Katherine gently scolded. "Cade will never let go of her land. It has been her dream forever and ever. She would positively let it go to rack and ruin before giving it up. The only man who will get her land is her husband."

"Her *what?*" It was a near shout.

"When she gets one, of course." Katherine laughed. Her voice dropped to a conspiring whisper. "Which will be soon if Papa's warning holds true. She has turned down so many offers of marriage, you see, that Papa says he is going to give his consent to the next suitable request with or without her permission."

"I pity the next man foolish enough to step forward," Charles broke in. Despite Katherine's indignant look, he continued, "It will take a tight rein to control her."

"Charles, how could you?" Katherine pouted. "Cade is a dear, sweet girl. She will make some man a wonderful wife someday . . . somehow . . . some . . . Oh!" Her eyes filled with tears, and she puckered her bottom lip out defensively. "I just know she will when she settles down. Tell him, Charles. Tell Jonas it's just an overflow from all those years she spent you-know-where. You can't expect her to be like everyone else. She has been through so much."

"Yes, dear," Charles said, sliding Jonas a knowing look.

A distraught bride was the last thing he wanted on his wedding night.

Jonas suppressed the snarl that threatened to curl his lips. He gave Katherine's strange words about Acadiana's behavior only brief consideration, relegating them to the back of his mind, as he did most of Katherine's unceasing prattle. However, he did have to agree with her earlier statement. Jonas had no doubt that Acadiana would let her land continue to idle away before giving it up. He needed that land and the revenue its crops would bring to support the mill he was converting over to steam power. He watched as the object of his aggravation strolled by. *I'm stubborn too, you hard-headed vixen,* he thought. *I'll find a way to make you change your mind.*

Jonas spent the better part of the week contemplating and agonizing over Katherine's words. With a regret that felt tantamount to a death sentence, he finally concluded that it was time he marry. With Acadiana would come the land, a beautiful wife to grace his home, children, and a hostess for social obligations. In essence, a pretty, ornate piece to acquire—something to own to complete his life.

Somehow, this Acadiana Belizaire Hamilton did not seem to fit the mold of the dutiful wife he was carving, but she *was* heir apparent to the land. That was enough for now. With the wedding would come the bedding, Jonas thought as he mounted his horse and headed in the direction of the Hamilton cottage. It would be very satisfying to break through that icy barrier and teach her the delights of a warm and willing woman.

He had to admit that he was troubled about her past. What had happened to shape that defiant nature? What if she had come from a sordid, ugly life? Raking his fingers through his hair in an impatient gesture, Jonas scoffed at his own misgivings. She certainly seemed immaculate enough, even immature at times. Having made it a point in his adult life to stay away from the innocents, he had no call to feel angry with the idea that Acadiana might have been intimate with other men. It was none of his business what she had done prior to her association with him, but damn it all, it did bother him. He tried to push the hypocritical thoughts aside, but they dogged him with relentless aggravation. He was finally forced to ask himself, if he knew what her past involved, would it matter? And Jonas knew without reserve that no, in the end nothing mattered but acquiring the land. Still, his curiosity lingered.

Her parents had died ten years earlier (brutally slain, it was whispered), and she had been with the Hamiltons for the last six. What had happened to the other four? Katherine had hinted at something the day of the wedding. Now he wished he'd paid closer attention to her. Whatever Acadiana's past was, no one was talking.

Even having spent quite a bit of time with the Hamiltons over the past three days, Jonas was no closer to finding out. Acadiana always treated him with polite but cool regard, in deference to her aunt and uncle, he was certain. She continued to dodge his inquiries about her past with a mysterious twinkle. Shrugging her shoulders, she would repeat that she had no secrets. She also refused to discuss the land, getting frigid if he pressed the issue, and she never allowed herself to be alone with him.

Against his better judgment, but seeing no other alternative, Jonas decided that marriage would be the likeliest choice. These thoughts continued to churn through his mind as he dismounted in front of the cottage and handed the reins to Jethro. Acadiana had forced him to take matters into his own hands. Even so, he wasn't sure that he was ready for marriage—especially to her. A mighty leap into the treacherous Mississippi River seemed a calmer path than what he was now contemplating.

But for all her rebellious nature, Jonas found Acadiana beautiful and subtly alluring. She could be witty, charming, and quite polite, he admitted, as long as he didn't bring up the subject of her property. But always, even in her quietest of times, he glimpsed a wild, free being lurking beneath the cool and gracious façade.

Once he had made up his mind, Jonas courted her with all the ardor of a smitten lad. Never one to falsely play the lovesick suitor, he found the game sickeningly prosaic, but gave it his best effort nonetheless. Acadiana seemed to sense his devious intentions and never gave him more than an innocent grin when he played the fool's advocate. But Jonas could see the fire in her eyes, knew by the rapid flushing of her cheeks when he was near that she was fighting emotions she tried hard to conceal.

What would it take to bring her around? Time was short; Jonas needed to return home. He would stop these wasted efforts, he thought as Pearlene opened the door to admit him. If what Katherine had said was true, he would not need Acadiana's consent for the marriage. But would Grayson really carry through with his threat? Jonas knew the man was attached to his niece, and he would have to be very convincing in order to succeed with his plans.

Acadiana gamboled down the stairs in a jovial mood, looking as animated as a playful kitten. The glow on her cheeks seemed to reflect the mauve gown she was wearing. Tightly fitted at her waist, it was low cut, exposing her creamy shoulders. The skirt rippled down in tiers to her pink slippered feet, and tiny rosettes were fastened at the waist.

Katherine was back from a wedding journey to Charles's hometown and ready to make her first visit as the new Mrs. Nolan. Acadiana had missed her beyond belief. With nothing to occupy her time except Jonas's constant visitations, she needed a nice long chat with someone other than that unpleasant creature. He hadn't tried to kiss her again, but she would be glad when he was gone. She was so nervous and trembly when he was around. She had felt the same churning stomach and breathless sensation each time he was present. Acadiana had concluded that she suffered some severe malady brought on by his mere presence. The way her body heated up and her breathing grew shallow, it was certain she was coming down with lung fever.

Thank goodness she would not have to suffer his presence today. This day would be spent with Katherine. In a lighter mood than she had felt for weeks, Acadiana skipped down the stairs. When she reached the bottom step she darted toward the garden door. As soon as she rounded the corner, she ran straight into Jonas's solid chest. He put his arms around her intimately and stared at her heaving bosom. The golden flesh straining against its silken bonds beckoned to him like the dangerous song of a Siren and threatened to cloud his mind and overshadow his purpose.

"Miss Hamilton, I didn't realize you were so eager to see me," he said in a low tone as his gaze rose to devour her flushed face.

Acadiana felt the heat rise to her cheeks with the sapphire eyes that were so boldly following a path of exposed skin. Resentment warred with embarrassment, neither gaining the upper hand but fusing to cause her whole body to stiffen.

"*M'sieu* Courtland," she replied coolly, trying to appear unaffected. "Excuse me, I didn't see you." When he did not seem inclined to release her, she began to squirm frantically beneath the hands that were sending strange flashes throughout her body and interfering with the regular beat of her heart. Even her breathing was affected. *Lung fever!*

"Please call me Jonas," he crooned, mocking her feeble attempt at escape. As her body wriggled against his, he felt an immediate and rigid response, and his voice reflected the physical reaction. "In this position we should certainly be on a first-name basis. Don't you agree?"

Acadiana wouldn't agree with anything he said. Disarmed by their close contact, the way his body seemed to be fitting itself to hers with scalding sureness, she fumbled with an apt and scathing retort. He had her flustered now, catching her so unaware, unprepared, and she couldn't seem to find adequate words. Her embarrassment was the only worthy emotion she could effectively name. Every other feeling was too wanton for her to dignify. Acadiana laughed in a ridiculously strained pitch to cover her inability to handle the situation gracefully.

"Unhand me, *m'sieu*," she managed to say lightly, unwilling for Jonas to see how he was dismantling her composure, and unable to gather the iciness she had used to repel other men. "My aunt warned me about men like you. What would she think if she walked in right now?"

"Your aunt?" he teased her. "I should think you would be more concerned about your uncle. He is meeting me here any minute. What do you suppose he would think?"

"Mon Dieu," Acadiana swore beneath her breath, casting a furtive glance around the room. "He would undoubtedly think the worst. Let me go before he finds his favorite niece in this compromising position."

Ah, sweet destiny, Jonas thought, and angled his body even closer to proceed better with his plans. The layers of clothing between them might as well have been nonexistent for all the protection they afforded him in the instant his body grazed hers. Jonas was startled by the surge of energy that hummed through him and caused his body parts to tighten further.

"I rather like this 'compromising position,'" he said, bringing his face down to within an inch of her pert nose. "And I rather like seeing you squirm."

"You are not acting the gentleman," Acadiana scolded, disturbed by the heat in his eyes, a heat that she feared was mirrored in her own. But an even bigger concern was the thought of her uncle walking in and finding them like this.

"You're right," Jonas agreed, "but I will consent to release you on one condition—a small kiss to show your affection for our . . . ah . . . friendship."

"There is no friendship," she spat out. "Uncle Grayson will be here any second; he is never late. You let me go!"

"One small kiss," Jonas pressed, stalling for time. Things

were falling into place much nicer than he had anticipated. "One kiss—just a small one."

"*Non,*" Acadiana said viciously. "You are insane if you think you can play your evil games in my home. Have you no care for what my uncle will think of me? Have you no shame for yourself?"

"None," Jonas replied flatly. "Give me a kiss, or I'll take it."

He would. Acadiana knew only too well that he would. She also knew she would have to get out of this man's arms before her body melted into a substanceless heap at his feet, so overwhelmed and defenseless did he make her feel. And she must get loose before Uncle Grayson walked in. She would never hear the end of it should he find her wrapped in this despicable man's arms. She glared at Jonas banefully, her voice suffused with wrath when she spoke.

"One small kiss? Then you will let me go?"

At a nod from Jonas, she raised on tiptoes and planted a sisterly peck on his cheek. He swiftly turned his head to catch her lips and watched with amusement as her amethyst eyes widened. His hand quickly rose to the back of her head to entrap her, while his lips captured her angry gasp and took advantage of her slack mouth. His tongue plunged inside, causing her to shriek with disgust, but his mouth caught the sound and she began to tremble and stiffen by degrees. Though she pushed against his chest furiously, her neck weakened with the strain and finally lolled back against his palm.

Jonas continued the calculated assault patiently, strategically, matching every jerk and twist of Acadiana's body with a countermove of his own until Grayson finally strolled around the corner. Jonas quickly loosened his hold and managed to look sheepish at being caught. Fury erupting in her eyes, Acadiana jerked out of his embrace, turned abruptly, and stepped right in front of her uncle.

"C-Cade . . . Jonas?" Grayson stuttered.

Acadiana took one startled look at her uncle and knew

she couldn't deal with him right now. "Hello, Uncle Grayson. Good-bye, Uncle Grayson. I am off to the garden." Without a backward glance she rushed out, leaving Jonas to explain their situation to her irate uncle. "Deceitful wretch!" she muttered to herself. "Serves him right." Feeling very smug that Jonas would finally get his comeuppance, she set out to find her cousin.

Reading her thoughts, Jonas sent a mocking grin and bow to Acadiana's retreating figure. Revenge would be his —as would the land—very, very soon.

Katherine was waiting for Acadiana in the garden. Her face was aglow with a happiness that seemed to envelop her like an aura as she wandered aimlessly around the honeysuckle vines. The barest whisper of a breeze stirred the yellow petals, dispelling the heat and filling the air with a sweet fragrance. As soon as Acadiana stepped into view, a smile burst forth from her cousin, and they rushed to greet one another.

After a quick hug, Katherine danced back and clutched her hands to her heart. Her eyes were twinkling with anticipation as she spoke.

"Oh, Cade, I know I promised to tell you all about the wedding night, but I'm just not sure I can now."

"Mon Dieu," Acadiana grumbled. "If it is that bad, I don't want to hear it." Jonas had soured her gay mood, and she wasn't sure she wanted to hear her cousin prattle on about things that happened *behind locked doors.*

Katherine grabbed Acadiana's arm and pulled her away from the house, well out of hearing range. "Oh, no, Cade, I did promise," she said, much more interested in telling the shocking news than Acadiana was in hearing it. "Of course, you must realize that Charles and I are married, and that's the way it is with all married couples. But I must admit, it quite shocked my sensibilities as a properly brought up young lady at first." She stopped to pick a camellia bloom and began plucking anxiously at the petals until a shower of dark pink drifted down to carpet the ground at her feet.

"Charles said it was necessary, and I would get used to it. He even said I would begin to enjoy it."

Katherine's face turned positively colorless, then flushed a vivid red. "Oh, Cade, I am so wicked! I'm already beginning to enjoy it. I just feel so . . . so wanton." She fanned her face furiously with the denuded bud to cool her cheeks. "It was so wonderful." She sighed, then proceeded to go into exact detail of their blissful time together.

Acadiana had a basic knowledge of coupling from having grown up around animals, but Katherine's talk of honeyed words, kisses, and carnal caresses quite embarrassed her. It also disgusted her, and she told her cousin so.

"It is not disgusting," Katherine said petulantly. "It is something that a wife must do to keep her husband happy." She tilted her chin up with a look of superiority, too pleased at having shocked Acadiana to let it rest. "Men have certain needs, and *that* is one of them."

Acadiana had done so much more in her short lifetime than Katherine ever hoped to do. Having been shocked time and again with tales of past adventures, Katherine was quite pleased to finally have the upper hand. She could not resist flowering their conversation a tad bit.

"Besides, Charles says that anytime a man kisses a woman—*really kisses her*—that is what he is thinking about."

The vision of Jonas's kiss came rushing back to Acadiana with clarity. All color drained from her face, then rushed back a fiery scarlet. Oh! He couldn't have been thinking that. *He just couldn't!* But the memory of his lips on hers, the way his body had fitted itself to hers, made her heartbeat pick up and her blood rush hotly through her veins. Acadiana was suddenly very much afraid that the arrogant *M'sieu* Courtland had been thinking just that. She squeezed her eyes shut as if that would block the vision and took a ragged gulp of air.

Katherine watched a number of emotions chase themselves across her beloved cousin's face. Saddened now by the somber mood, she spoke in a meek voice. "I'm sorry, Cade, I shouldn't have told you such personal things."

"*Non*, it is all right," Acadiana lied with false brightness. "I am sure that I just don't understand the ways of a mature married woman." She thought that it sounded like a most disagreeable situation married or not, and confirmed her determination to remain unattached.

"Of course, dear, you could not possibly understand such things until you are in love, as I am with Charles." Katherine said, pacified now.

The rest of the afternoon went very well despite their previous conversation. The girls laughed and teased as always, and Acadiana was quite pleased to find that marriage had not changed Katherine overmuch. Arm in arm they returned to the house where Grayson was fairly exploding with pent-up anticipation.

"Ah, Katherine, glad you're back," he said with an impersonal hug before turning his full attention to Acadiana. "Cade, that dress looks wonderful on you."

"Uncle Grayson." She smiled. "What's the matter with you? You look like you're about to burst." She kissed his cheek out of obligation, though she was exasperated by his flushed face and bright eyes. They told her quite clearly that Jonas must have given her uncle a plausible explanation for his earlier trickery. Damn his wretched hide! Grayson had apparently not felt it necessary to give Jonas the dressing down he deserved, or Acadiana would be hearing about it now.

"Don't be coy with me, child," Grayson replied with an audacious wink. "Your suitor has spoken to me."

"Suitor?" Acadiana asked, mildly perturbed. Now, who could have stopped by the house to cause her more problems? She was sure Richard Whittington had gotten the message—

"Sweet girl"—Grayson laughed—"Jonas has declared himself. I must say, after I witnessed what was going on between you two, he spoke none too soon. I should be quite angry, but given his intentions, I will admit that I am very pleased and happy for the both of you." He squared his shoulders and puffed his chest out like a pompous rooster at his own generosity. "I suppose I can forgive you that one indiscretion."

Acadiana could feel her heart sinking dreadfully to the pit of her stomach. She was becoming very nervous about what her uncle was saying and more so by the elated look on his face. "You are pleased?" she managed to ask as she forced a smile.

"Of course I am pleased." Grayson was almost blustering. "Jonas informed me that he was here to formally request your hand in marriage. By the way you two were carrying on, the request came none too soon. If I wasn't so overjoyed by the match, you would receive a stern lecture on proper behavior. As it stands, I was thrilled to give my consent to his proposal of marriage."

If Grayson had not looked quite so delighted, had not been rocking back and forth on his heels quite so gleefully, Acadiana might have been able to dismiss this conversation. As it was, that sinking feeling in the pit of her stomach changed to full-blown panic.

"Marriage? You gave your consent?" she asked shrilly. "Where is he!" *Why, that black-hearted, low-life scoundrel! Of all the underhanded, despicable . . . Why would he do such a thing? The land! Mon Dieu, he is trying to steal my land!*

"Jonas?" asked Grayson, misconstruing her panic for excitement. "Don't worry, child. He said he had business to attend to, but he will be back first thing in the morning to discuss the arrangements with you. As a proper gentleman he wanted to obtain my permission first."

"Oh, Cade, I am so happy for you!" Katherine squealed as she threw her arms around Acadiana's neck. "I just knew it! Charles said you two would be perfect together. Oh, he was right, so very very right. We must make plans

right away. I am sure Mr. Courtland will want to marry
you quickly so the two of you can return to his home."

Fearing her head was about to be snapped from her
shoulders, Acadiana gritted her teeth and managed to
smile. "I am sure he will, Katherine," she drawled sweetly.

Fear began to overpower the shock of Jonas's treachery.
To think that he would go to such lengths to have her property made Acadiana's heart flutter painfully in her breast
and her palms to grow clammy with the certainty of his
betrayal. She had underestimated him, underestimated his
ruthlessness and determination. But no longer. Now that
she realized the extent of cunning he was capable of to get
what he wanted, Acadiana would take action to protect
herself. If she thought it would do any good to protest, she
would raise a ruckus that would bring the roof caving in.
But Grayson's eyes were too bright with excitement, his
smile too satisfied. He would never back down on his word
to the sneaky *M'sieu* Courtland and lose his chance to see
his niece wed.

An elfin gleam crept into her eyes to disguise the scheme
brewing there. She knew she would have to make plans
quickly, go along with the family tonight so they wouldn't
suspect anything. But in the morning, she would flee.

Acadiana rose at dawn. The sleepless night had pressed
its mark on her, creating deep shadows beneath her eyes
and causing a weariness that was more heartfelt than physical. She went to the wardrobe and pulled out a soft, worn
hide tied with rough leather straps. She buried her face in
the pouch and inhaled the rugged scent. Memories of another time past came flooding back, coursing through her
veins like liquid fire. She didn't want to do this. One fat tear
plopped onto her hand as she stared down at the pouch.
Aunt Elizabeth had been like a mother to Acadiana for six
years, and she would worry. It was so unfair! But the decision had been forced upon her.

She stole quietly down the stairs, then tiptoed across the
brick walk to the kitchen. She added several staples to the

pouch, then ran to the stable. She could hear Jethro's muffled snores coming from the loft as she eased the gate open. With a sigh and what she hoped wasn't to be a last glance around the small plantation, she quickly mounted Shawnee bareback and set out for her imaginary mountaintop.

There were not actual mountains anywhere near, but she would go to a secret place that served as her hideaway. She would need a few days to think things over before facing her family and Jonas again. She knew in her heart that when she got there, she might not be able to return home after what Uncle Grayson had said. She knew also that if she could not settle this, she might have to keep on going north to the real mountains for a few more months until she came of age. She couldn't think clearly now. She would get away first, then make her decisions.

Jonas arrived at the Hamilton house by eight o'clock. He knew the hour was early for a social call, but Grayson had assured him that Acadiana was an early riser and that that time would be appropriate. He also knew that he was in for a confrontation with her. But, he reminded himself, Grayson had given his consent, and that was half the battle. He had already convinced himself that what he was doing would be good for both of them. Now, if he could just make Acadiana see that.

Confounded woman! he thought with ire as he rapped on the front door. He had never failed with anything he had pursued in his life—least of all a woman's affection. Maybe that was part of the allure he felt. She was a challenge and worthy of the conquest. Her light, easy manner spoke of grace and intelligence at times, but she could turn cold and calculating quicker than any woman he had ever known. It was as if there were two persons residing inside that beautiful body.

He fully expected to be greeted by those bright eyes flashing fury when he arrived, but what he got was a quiet household and a hearty handshake from Grayson, who promised that Pearlene had already gone to fetch Cade. Grayson was sure he didn't know why she wasn't already down; she always rose before everyone else.

Pearlene returned much later with a terror-stricken look on her face. The whites of her eyes bulged while her head bobbed up and down in a birdlike motion. "That chile ain't no where to be found, Master Gray. She sure ain't," she cried, ringing her hands in her white apron. "I looked everyplace I know to look, and old Jethro says that wild hoss of hers is gone, and the saddle and bridle still be here." Tears began to pool in the servant's dark eyes, and her full bottom lip began to tremble. "You know what that means, Master Gray, you sure do. That chile has gone and done it to y'all again. She sure has. What's got into her this time, Master Gray? Why'd she go and do that to y'all again?"

"Oh, Lord, Pearlene." Grayson groaned, rubbing his brow with shaking fingers. "Have you checked her wardrobe? We would know for sure then."

"Yes, sir. I checked it after I talked to Jethro. That sack of hers be gone. Miz Lizbeth seen me in there too, and she'll be down here any minute in a fit, 'cause she knows there's only one reason I'd be looking in there."

"What is going on here?" asked Jonas, becoming more bewildered with each confusing disclosure. He watched Pearlene wring a tattered handkerchief and Grayson's flushed face get ruddier by the minute. "What was Pearlene searching for, and where is Acadiana?"

"Grayson!" shouted Elizabeth Hamilton, flying down the stairs in a flurry of motion. She had managed only to tie a bonnet around her chin and throw a shawl over her shoulders before running down in her cotton nightdress. Grayson was so appalled by her outrageous display that he jumped in front of Jonas and threw his arms wide to hide his wife's near nakedness.

Jonas stood head and shoulders taller than the short man, and continued to stare at the disheveled woman's wild flight.

"Why was Pearlene searching Cade's wardrobe? Has she done it again? Tell me, Grayson! Has she—" Elizabeth reached the bottom step, and her shoulders slumped. "She has. I can tell by the look on your face. It's this business with Mr. Courtland, isn't it? We should have known, should have been prepared."

"Oh, Lordy, Miz Lizbeth, she's done it again," Pearlene wailed. "Come on now, you sure need to lie down."

Elizabeth Hamilton thought Pearlene was the one who looked as if she needed to lie down. Composing herself, she clutched her shawl tightly against her neck and turned to her husband. "Grayson? She's gone. What shall we do?" The words were spoken calmly enough, but her hands trembled and her face was ashen.

"What the hell is going on around here?" asked Jonas, fast becoming irate. Elizabeth Hamilton looked shaken, the servant hysterical, and Grayson as if he'd like to drop off the face of the earth. "Would someone please tell me whatever it is that is happening here? Where is Acadiana?"

Forgetting his wife's dishabille, Grayson turned around to face Jonas. "Uh, well, Mr. Courtland," he hedged, stalling until he could think of what to do, what answer to give. "It appears that Cade will be indisposed for several days."

As Jonas's anger mounted, so did his voice. He was close to shouting by the time he spoke. "I repeat, what is going on here?"

Elizabeth squared her shoulders at his tone of voice and crossed her arms over her waist with a look of defiance that vaguely reminded Jonas of Acadiana. "He has a right to know, Grayson. He *is* going to marry her."

"Now, Elizabeth, I don't know . . . it is up to Cade to discuss such things," Grayson muttered.

"I have a right to know *what?*" Jonas asked between clenched teeth, thoroughly exasperated. "Acadiana is obviously not here. Where has she gone? And *what* is missing that makes you so certain she will be 'indisposed for several days,' as you put it?"

"You might call it a travel bag, Mr. Courtland," Elizabeth began delicately before disregarding forty years of strict and proper upbringing and blurted out, *"Oh, tell him, Grayson!"*

Grayson sent his wife a pleading look, then threw his hands up in resignation. "My niece is gone, Jonas. She has flown. We don't know where, but she will be back in a few days . . . two weeks at the most."

Astonished by the girl's audacity in leaving without telling anyone, Jonas exploded. "Two weeks! Of all the idiotic . . . harebrained . . ." At Elizabeth's stricken look, he lowered his voice. "Is she with friends?"

"She is not with friends," Grayson began slowly, wondering how much he should tell this man whose annoyance was quickly turning into rage. "She is not with anyone. She is alone . . . and she can't be reached."

"This is insane!" roared Jonas, forgetting Elizabeth's sensibilities. He began pacing across the wooden floor, trying to assimilate the vague information, then turned to Grayson. "How can you be so sure that she hasn't just gone riding?"

Grayson sighed and looked up with a browbeaten expression. He'd had such hopes for this union. It appeared his niece was going to ruin it all—again. "She has done it before," he said frankly, "many times since coming to live with us. It has been over a year since the last disappearance. I suppose I thought she was through with that tomfoolery."

In deference to the older man's weary look, Jonas tried to rein in his anger and motioned for Grayson to continue.

"Look, Mr. Courtland, there are only two things we do know. One is that Cade can take care of herself. The other is that she will return when she gets ready. She always returns—usually in a few days. Only once did she stay gone for two weeks."

"And when, pray tell, was that?" Jonas asked with a mirthless laugh.

"Uh . . . well . . . actually, Mr. Courtland, it was

when I told her that I would accept the next suitable marriage proposal. That was about a year ago," Grayson said sheepishly, glancing to Elizabeth for help.

"I am going after her," Jonas said. His lips twisted in a satanic grin. "This is utterly ridiculous! I find it hard to believe that you don't have more control over your ward, Mr. Hamilton. I don't have time for her childish shenanigans, and I won't remain here until she takes a fancy to return."

"Don't, Mr. Courtland! I mean, you can't . . . What I mean is, it won't do you any good to go after her; you won't be able to find her." Making note of Jonas's seething countenance, Grayson sighed and threw his hands up. "It is impossible to track her. Please don't look at me as if I have lost my wits! We tried to find her many times at first. We finally gave up two years ago. She'll come back when she's ready."

Jonas was quite certain that the whole family had gone mad. There was a mere slip of a girl out alone at the mercy of God only knew what, and they couldn't track her down. He stared at the miserable faces around him and knew he would tolerate no resistance from this family.

He spoke calmly but firmly to Elizabeth. "I will bring her back, madam, rest assured. Can you tell me which direction she usually takes?"

"Toward Natchez, but she stays away from the populated areas. We have never really known where she goes, but I have heard her talk about crossing the river to get to a hillier region." Elizabeth sighed. "You will not be able to find her. No one has ever been able to. But I will feel better knowing that you are searching for her."

"Good heavens, woman!" Jonas railed anew. "That is dangerous country."

"Possibly not, if you find her before she reaches the river," Elizabeth said calmly.

Jonas's shock was complete. Before he could say anything further, Grayson drew himself up to his full five feet four inches, cleared his voice, and confronted him. "Sir, if you do find her—which I seriously doubt—I expect your intentions to remain honorable."

Jonas chuckled with only slightly amused humor. "I assure you, the only intention I have at present is turning her over my knee." He turned abruptly and stormed from the house, leaving Elizabeth aghast and Grayson snickering with ill-disguised mirth.

Cade has met her match this time, her uncle thought cheerfully despite the fact that his wife was glaring at him. "Yes, well," he mumbled. "Let us hope that Jonas can find her before she comes to harm." He didn't think to tell the man to guard himself. Cade could be quite unpredictable when threatened.

Jonas didn't bother to return to Charles's to change. He was dressed casually enough, and planned to catch up with Acadiana and return her before nightfall. She only had a few hours' head start, and he felt he could make up the time by setting a vigorous pace. An avid hunter in his youth, he didn't think he would have any trouble finding the rebellious little minx. He need not have been concerned in any case, for as Jonas started out he was certain the entire Hamilton family was indeed somewhat daft. Acadiana's trail was as clear as the nose on his irate face. If she had made any effort at all to cover her tracks, he could see no such evidence.

He traveled hard for most of the day, stopping only long enough to rest his horse and cool his temper, which alternated between simple ire and downright outrage. He had hoped to catch up with her along the way, give her a piece of his mind, then return her safely home by first dark. She had better not cause any more trouble, Jonas mused. With the mood he was in now, he would take great pleasure in planting the palm of his hand to her insolent derriere. Maybe *then* she would cool her unruly behavior.

The sun beat down with relentless fury, fueling the anger of the lone rider as he made his way through the fields.

Brief respite was offered by the intermittent wooded areas where pecan, hackberry, ash, and oak abounded along with cedar and cypress trees. But along with the cooling shade came the thickets of briars that waited to lash and stab any trespasser. Jonas mounted his sorrel after a short reprieve and scanned the area ahead of him, hoping to see some distant movement that would denote a horse and rider.

He had to give her credit, he thought. The mere slip of a girl, as he had referred to Acadiana, certainly had a lot more endurance than he had anticipated. Had Jonas not followed her trail so closely, he would have sworn that she was hiding out with friends. How else would she care for herself? She couldn't possibly carry enough food with her for one week, much less two.

The trail was becoming more treacherous now. The little rebel was leading him farther and farther from civilization. There would be nowhere to seek shelter here from either friend or foe.

The initial shock that a gently bred young lady would take off on her own had long since been burned from his mind by the suffocating heat and humidity. He was forced to allow a grudging respect for her tenacity to creep in, but suspected her untalked-about past had something to do with her resilience.

The warm evening sun was sinking too fast to continue the quest much longer. No matter how hard headed Jonas thought the little hellion was, she was out there alone, at the mercy of the elements and other more ferocious dangers. The river traffic of the last several decades had brought gangs of desperadoes and the pirate business flourished. Although a great earthquake in December of 1811 had drowned out the nest of the pirate Bunch, a locally famed Robin Hood, it wasn't known where the river bandits hid out now. No matter how much he denied it to appease his sense of guilt, Jonas felt responsible for Acadiana. The last light of day gave way to encroaching darkness, and he was forced to dismount and bed down for the night. And

pray that she was safe—wherever she was. His last thoughts
that evening as the crickets and bullfrogs began their evening chorus in the wooded copse were of stormy violet eyes
glaring at him above an impudent smile. He would catch
her on the morrow, he vowed. Then he would proceed to
tame that unruly nature of hers if it was the last thing he
did.

5

Acadiana banked her fire in the pale moon-
light, then stretched out on her bedroll. A pinpoint of stars
twinkled overhead in the black sky, illuminating the night
and glittering their welcome. Ah, sweet freedom, she
thought. It felt so good, so right. She hadn't needed this
feeling in a long time. Oh, but she needed it now! She didn't
want to think about what her uncle had said, but his words
kept reverberating through her mind. Sooner or later, she
knew she would have to make a decision.

She could easily hold out here in the wilderness for another three months, living off the land as she had been
taught to do ten years ago. But then what? There wasn't
enough money left in her trust to run a plantation, much
less start anew. Perhaps she *should* marry Jonas, be a dutiful wife, and give up her dreams. And perhaps she should
just hand over the title to him. It would be the same thing—
the loss of independence, the death of hope. A mournful
sigh caressed the darkness, laced with pain and fear but not
resignation. She would not give up. She could not.

Acadiana let her mind wander back to the fantasies she
had carried for years about the way life would be when she
returned home. She would recapture the land, taming it as

her father had done to produce a splendid living in the small settlement. Her parents' cottage would serve as her home until she could build the house of her dreams. She would raise a passel of children to play along the bayou as she had, and next to her would be the man, as yet a nameless face—the husband of her own choosing whom she would love and cherish for all times. Prosaic dreams, childish imaginings. They almost seemed foolish now, but they were hers. And she would hold on to what hope was left to her with every ounce of strength and determination within her.

Another sigh penetrated the ebony night and seemed to skip along the moonbeams, haunting in its sadness, taunting in its uselessness. *Le bon Dieu,* she couldn't dwell on those youthful fantasies now. Maybe in a few days when her mind settled and she could see things more clearly, then she would think about them, chart again her course for the future.

It had been a long, grueling day. Acadiana had become unused to hard riding over the last year, and it had taken hours of combing the backwaters of the Mississippi River to find a place safe enough to cross to get to the main river. Flooding from spring rains had trapped off marshes and bogs that would eventually dry up with the summer's heat. She'd expended much time and energy wading through the swampy areas. Once she had reached the winding Mississippi, Acadiana had followed it in a southward direction to reach the camp she had made for herself almost six years ago. She needed this place to get away when the pressures and inconsistencies of her life took their toll. Here she was free—free to be herself, and free from the expectations of others. After a few days of rest, she might catch a ferry and cross the river to Vicksburg or travel farther south and cross near Natchez, where she could hide among friends until her birthday. From there she could send word of her safety so her uncle wouldn't worry, and also warn him that she would not return home until Jonas Courtland was gone.

Utterly exhausted by the day's ride, the decisions churning through her head, and her guilt at running from her family, she dropped her head to the crook of her elbow and drifted off to sleep.

The constant buzzing and humming of insects invaded her consciousness and awoke Acadiana to a blazing dawn. Iridescent rays flashed across the horizon, welcoming the day with rosy golden fingers. She stretched languidly in the morning glow and rose from her pallet. The nippy air caressed her body, causing her to shiver and rub her arms briskly to ward off the damp chill of heavy dew. Teeth chattering, she rolled up her blanket and tossed it into an abandoned sod hut she had erected half a decade ago. Retrieving her saddlebag, she began to gather the things necessary for a delicious stew.

Acadiana crouched in the brush and waited impatiently for a rabbit. It took over an hour to bag the hare, and she was sure she must be going soft after a year of leisure. Her muscles ached; her reactions were slow. She should have returned to her haven long before now to keep her skills well honed. Nature was not kind to the weak. Her survival depended on the ability to stay quick and alert. After she got her fire burning again, she skinned and gutted the game, then left it to soak while she added other ingredients from her saddlebag into a charred pot. With the stew simmering over an open fire, she set out to repair her hut.

The year of absence had taken its toll on the small dwelling, and the sight of its crumbling walls irked her conscience. After going to live with her uncle six years ago, she had slipped away many times to come here and escape the stodgy plantation existence, to relive another time in her life.

Acadiana smoothed out the shallow floor in the interior of the hut with loving hands, then began packing clay and Spanish moss into the cracks along the rounded walls. With the sides of the structure finally secure, she climbed to the top and began layering palmetto leaves on the roof to prevent further leakage.

Her renovation complete, she strolled over to bathe in a sandy inlet created by the Mississippi, careful to stay well back from the main thrust of the dangerous river with its whirlpools, eddies, and undertows. The water was cold and the air crisp, but it helped to invigorate her, clearing her mind and body from the tiring journey and oppressing thoughts. She swam with easy, languid movements through the rivulet that flowed more than surged over sand and rocks shining in the morning sun.

She wandered to the deepest part and let the current swirl around her hips as she raised slender arms to the sky to bask in the warming rays of sunlight. Throwing her head back, she let her raven locks fall to tease the water bubbling about her hips. The midmorning sun warmed her face as she stared longingly at the brightening azure sky, and remembered peace—a peace so long past that she wondered if it had ever truly existed.

Jonas steered his horse up a grassy slope to avoid a dense thicket of briars, then stopped in sheer amazement. He might have expected anything by now. Anything, that is, except the beautiful Indian maiden stepping out of the water with only a short skirt of animal skin around her hips and a soft leather wrap that bound her breasts. Hair, black as a crow's wing, fell in riotous curls over her shoulders, then plummeted below to slender, rounded hips. The luscious mane was held out of her face by a leather strap that ran across her forehead and was tied on the side. Small wet feathers hung from the ends of the beaded strap to tease her bare shoulders. The beguiling maiden lifted her head and amethyst struck sapphire in a scorching exchange as their eyes met and locked.

"Acadiana?" Jonas called in stark disbelief. "What in the—"

"Damnation! Hellfire and damnation!" Acadiana stormed, on the run.

She leapt over the rocks, splashing along the sandy edge in an effort to gain solid ground. Jonas quickly swung his legs over the saddle and dropped to block her passage. Accurately gauging her need to reach her horse, he bolted in that direction and had her in two long strides. Never in all of his thirty years had he seen anything more beautiful, more wildly alive than what he was holding right now.

"What are you doing here?" Acadiana yelled, struggling to free herself from his iron grip. She twisted, turned, and wriggled spasmodically in an attempt to escape. "I knew better!" she fumed, outraged more by her own lack of caution than her capture. "I knew I should have covered my trail!"

"Hold still!" Jonas commanded. He had a firm grip on her upper arms, but her sleek body was wet, and he was having a hard time holding on to her jerking frame. "Why did you run away?"

"You know why," she spat out, eyes blazing furious violet sparks. "You tricked me. You went to my uncle behind my back!"

"What would you have done if I had come to you first?" he taunted.

Ignoring the gibe, Acadiana rammed her elbow into his ribs. "Loose me! Go back and leave me in peace!"

His grunt of pain was followed by a tightening of his hands, and the tone of his voice held a threat. "I am not going anywhere right now, but when I do, you are going with me."

Oh, the arrogance of the man! The utter and absolute conceit! If he thought he could bark orders and expect her to obey— "You wretch! Unhand me this minute or I'll . . . I'll . . ."

"You'll what?" He laughed lightly, sarcastically. "You're not in a position to do much of anything right now. But if you promise to be a good little girl, I'll let you go so that we can discuss this calmly."

"I don't have anything to discuss with you," she said. "Now go away!"

Her breasts heaved with her angry efforts to draw air. Jonas dropped his eyes to the straining golden mounds and wondered if the leather ties would hold.

His voice carried a sensual gruffness when he spoke. "Ah, love, we have much to discuss. Will you behave?"

"I'm not your love! And I'll not promise you anything!" she threw out, her black curls swinging wildly with the shaking of her head.

"Then I suppose we will be in this position for a very long time. Of course, I won't mind at all. You are most beautiful when you're angry, and I can think of any number of pleasant things that can be accomplished while holding you this close." A fire danced in his dark blue eyes, the heat of it reflected in his voice. "You, my ice maiden, are even more gorgeous than I imagined with your clothes *off.*"

A shriek rent the air, causing the horses to shuffle nervously and smaller animals to scurry for cover. "You insufferable fool, let me go!" Acadiana howled.

She strained back as far as his hold would allow and stared furiously up at him. But she didn't like what greeted her. There was something dangerous in his eyes and something predatory in the flash of white teeth against his bronzed skin, like a hungry wolf about to pounce on its hapless prey. His thick sable lashes veiled a burning intensity that was beginning to make her more anxious than angry. She renewed her struggles with vigor, fighting now for more than her freedom.

Jonas tightened his grip and pulled her to him. Her writhing body pressed the hard length of his and served to arouse his amusement and something more that Acadiana didn't comprehend. She felt his limbs go taut, his steel fingers cut more deeply into her arms. The strange light in his eyes dimmed, and his mouth was suddenly set in a controlled line.

"Hold still, Acadiana"—he growled the warning—"or I won't be responsible for my next action. You are too beautiful and much too indecently dressed for this to carry on much longer."

His words hit her like a dash of icy water. Acadiana froze immediately as his meaning, if not exactly clear, at least convinced her of its implied threat. Previously unthought-of visions ran rampant through her mind, Aunt Elizabeth's warnings of men and their unruly passions, Katherine's whispers about men and their ways with the type of women who incited those passions. She was alone here with no protection to rely on but her own strength, which seemed little match for this man's greater size. She shuddered with uncertainty and stared up at him, breathless, too afraid to move.

Jonas knew he should do something, say something to calm her fear, but he wanted her so badly right now that it was clouding his reasoning. Her half-dressed state and her sleek limbs rubbing and struggling against him were having a disastrous effect on his composure. He wasn't sure he could voice the words that would put her fears to rest.

Skittish as a cornered doe, she quivered. Her voice came low and raspy as she surrendered the plea. "Jonas, I will be good. I promise."

"You won't fight me or try to run away?" he asked.

"I will not fight you."

"Or try to run away," he added more firmly.

Acadiana knew that she would run if she got the chance, so she did the only thing she knew to do. Like a viper, she bit down on his hand, then kicked him hard on the shin.

"You she-devil!" he hollered as he released her to grab his throbbing leg.

Although her bare foot had to hurt more than his leg, Acadiana quickly took this opportunity to flee. She stumbled back out of his grasp and took off running. Certain that Jonas was in hot pursuit, she ducked behind the hut and let go a shrill whistle. As soon as Shawnee picked his way around the mound, Acadiana leapt onto his back and urged him onward with a kick of her heels. The horse startled and lunged forward, hurling tufts of grass and dirt in his wake.

Acadiana leaned low over his mane, gripping the coarse hair in her clenched fists, her heart beating wildly against her breast. Her ebony hair whipped around her face, and she had to brush at it with the back of her hand to free her vision. Shawnee galloped across the hollow at a thundering speed, in accord with Acadiana's wishes. They were harmony in its purest form, Jonas had to admit as he seized the reins of his horse. The imagery of a winged stallion and his goddess flashed across his mind, but he smashed the fanciful thought for more logical thinking.

He mounted his sorrel and swept a westward route, giving chase with a more tactical approach. He topped a hill and cut Acadiana off before she could reach the next ridge where the forest thickened and pursuit would be slower and more dangerous. Shawnee balked at the sudden appearance of another steed and reared up. Jonas cringed, a warning strangled in his throat as the horse's hoofs pawed the air, and he thought Acadiana would be unseated. But she remained steadfast, one with the animal as if born to that perch.

As the sorrel pulled alongside the fleeing girl, Jonas leaned over and snatched her around the waist, dragging Acadiana from her horse and across his saddle. A scream rent the air as Acadiana found herself heaped facedown across the hard leather in front of her captor. She squirmed frantically to free herself, grinding one hip against his solid thighs. Jonas sucked his breath in at the sudden friction and commanded her to be still. The sight of her slim thighs and small rump twisting and wriggling were enough to stir him, but to have those same, virtually unclad parts of her moving against his groin were enough to drive him insane. He set his jaw with an effort to attend to his purpose and commanded her again to desist.

Shawnee snorted and pranced, pawing the earth around him nervously as his mistress continued to twist and writhe in the man's grasp trying free herself. With the palm of his hand firmly on her back, Jonas forced Acadiana down, then careened his horse back toward camp. Tears of angry frustration burned behind her eyelids, but she refused to let them fall as she thought of every vile punishment she would inflict upon him if she ever got loose. She got no further than dismemberment when the breath whooshed from her as her chest hit the saddle. Acadiana felt as if her teeth would be knocked from her head as they galloped back to the hut.

Upon reaching their destination, Jonas dropped agilely from the sorrel and pulled Acadiana down with him. As soon as her feet touched the ground, she began pounding his chest with fury. Her original plan thwarted, she didn't try to escape again but stood defiantly to fight. As if she were nothing more than a pesky child, Jonas pushed her back at arm's length but discounted her ability to use her feet to gain freedom. She kicked wildly at him, coming dangerously close to a most private area that would have been his undoing. With a purpose, Acadiana swung her foot again at that sensitive region before Jonas picked her up roughly under the arms.

"I'm warning you," he growled, "if you continue to act like a spoiled brat, I'm going to treat you like one and turn you over my knee. We'll see how feisty you are when I peel back that skirt and blister your bottom."

He wouldn't, of course. It was just a threat meant to intimidate her into cooling her outrageous behavior. Being twice her size, he didn't need to resort to physical cruelty to subdue her. A man who would debase himself by striking a defenseless woman was no man at all.

Thwack!

Jonas yelped as her "defenseless" foot made violent contact high on the inside of his thigh. All prior thoughts of chivalry flew straight into the pain that crawled up his leg to settle in his gut.

"I should have done this an hour ago," he snarled as he dragged her across his lap.

Acadiana set her teeth to keeping from screaming in outrage as the blow struck her bottom. Her back arched momentarily with the second slap, the need for vengeance flooding her like red-hot plasma. With a graphic oath, she dipped her head and took a savage bite out of his leg. Gritting his own teeth against the pain, Jonas jerked to free himself, then raised his arm again. Though his mind argued that she well deserved any punishment he deemed necessary, and the throbbing in his groin and his leg testified to that fact, he wouldn't strike her again. He sensed that he could beat her to death and it would do no good; she would never submit docilely to this kind of treatment. He would have to find another approach.

"You son of a mule . . . you wretched oaf . . . you . . . you . . . *Oooh!*" Acadiana cried when his hand dropped lightly this time on her backside.

"Will you run?" Jonas demanded, holding her squirming body across his leg in the most humiliating position Acadiana had ever found herself in.

"Just as far as I can go!" she hollered. "Why, y—" Her words sliced in half when his fingers began to drum playfully on the leather skirt.

"Will you run?" Jonas repeated in a softer, silky tone.

"Let me up!" Acadiana pleaded. For the first time in ten years, she was truly afraid. Not so much of his superior strength, but of a less tangible power. It was that glimpse of unleashed passion she had seen in his eyes that had her quivering like a trapped animal. The strength of his iron-hard legs was unyielding against her slight body, and she knew there was no escape. At least not now in this undignified position.

"Will you run?" he asked again. He slipped his hand

beneath the skirt and began rubbing her posterior in a meaningful gesture that brought a horrified gasp from his offended victim.

"Non! I won't run," she cried, retreating emotionally in utter humiliation. What followed was a sting of curses in several different languages, only a few of which Jonas could understand. The gist of them, however, was not lost on him.

"Would you lie to me?" he teased, making no attempt to remove his hand. His other hand brushed back her hair from her shoulders. His mouth dropped to the sensitive back of her neck and he began to nibble at her exposed skin. His breath, warm and heavy from exertion, danced along her flesh from the base of her ear to her spine, sending a deluge of shivers to her toes. His teeth nipped at her skin, then his tongue soothed the tiny hurt until Acadiana thought she would scream from madness, but her breath was lodged in her throat and she could do nothing but whimper in helpless anger. Her back arched again as his mouth closed over the strained tendon in her neck to suck lightly and his hand moved in indecent, mind-spinning circles over her thighs. "Would you lie?" he asked again, his breath curling around her ear.

"An Indian never lies," she dissembled, hanging her head in temporary defeat. She commanded her mind to stop its chaotic whirling, forced herself to ignore her undignified position. She was too highly disadvantaged now, but as soon as she could get loose . . .

"You're not an Indian," Jonas said, amusing himself with the feel of her fleshy backside. "You just look like one." He didn't know her game with that falsehood and didn't care as his fingers trailed in heated exploration across the taut but silky skin. Acadiana's muscles bunched with the awareness of those calloused fingertips, and Jonas had to stop himself from kneading her buttocks into soft acceptance.

"Let me up, please! I won't run, and I don't lie. *Please!"* Acadiana's entire body burned with the impropriety of the situation. Her cheeks flamed in embarrassment as his hand splayed wide to roam down her bare thigh. She shrank from the expert fingers that were stroking gently, their light touch much more devastating than his rough manhandling had been. Sudden chills crawled across her skin, raising gooseflesh and making her voice quiver in loud protest. "Let go of me!"

Jonas struggled with his own raised flesh. The time of toying with her was at an end. He couldn't concentrate on the purpose at hand with her delicious body tempting him beyond good sense. There was a pulsating need growing within him that had nothing to do with desire for her land. How easy it would be to turn her over and douse the heat in his body within the heat of hers.

Jonas released his hold on her suddenly and sent her sprawling to the ground at his feet. There was a glint of restrained triumph in his veiled eyes as he hauled her back up, yet it was the hunger there that sent a shiver of renewed fear through Acadiana. She shut her eyes briefly to protect herself from the raw desire kindled there.

"That's better," Jonas mocked, checking her subdued expression.

Acadiana had never wanted to slap someone so badly. She coiled her fist at her side and wondered if she dare strike the insolent face towering over her.

"Don't do it," he warned her. "I'm not certain exactly what is churning through that pretty head of yours, but your eyes look devious."

Mon Dieu, he was perceptive. Acadiana stared at him coldly, waiting, pondering his next move with stony resistance on her set and defiant face. Jonas stared back at her for a long moment, assessing her mood, then said frankly, "I'm starving. I've not eaten since yesterday. Is it possible that I smell food?"

Acadiana gritted her teeth before she spoke. "It's over here, and I hope you choke on it." Wishing she had her dagger and relishing the thought in explicit detail of cutting his heart out, she led him over to the fire.

"Stew?" Jonas asked. He glanced into the pot to see onions, carrots, and potatoes bubbling round and round chunks of tender white meat. "You made this?"

"Do you see anyone else here, imbecile?"

"Curb your tongue," he grunted. "I came here to make peace, not to endure insults. That's very unladylike."

"As you can plainly see, Jonas, I am not the *lady* you so mistakenly thought I was. So, you may get back on your horse and inform Uncle Grayson that you cannot possibly marry a heathen savage. You won't be the first one to cry off." Acadiana lifted her chin in sassy style, and her eyes seared him with a blaze of violet that only strengthened his determination. "So sorry to have shocked your Creole sensibilities, Jonas *dear.*"

Something in her words gave him pause. He began to realize that her hauteur carried more defense than depth. The way she was dressed, the ability to care for herself in these adverse conditions said something about her past. Gently bred young ladies simply did not go around half naked and riding astride bareback horses. She looked like an Indian, but Jonas knew that wasn't possible. In past years she must have had some association with them, which accounted for her free-spirited nature and the four missing years no one would talk about. If she had, indeed, lived among the natives, he could understand why she was so defensive about her past. If he felt sympathy for what she must have gone through, it didn't alter his own plans to gain her land in any manner he could.

"I told you, Acadiana, I am not leaving without you. I have no intention of calling the wedding off either. And as far as my so-called sensibilities are concerned, I am quite enjoying the shock." He was smiling now, and that lecherous grin grated on her far more than his words did. "You may not consider yourself a lady, but you play the part well when you deem it necessary." He continued with a determined edge in his voice. "You can hide behind that wall of indifference where other men are concerned, but I see

through it. Call yourself a lady or not; it makes no difference to me. You are certainly more woman than I have laid
eyes on in a long time." Jonas finished his oration by bowing low.

"Mais non," she scoffed, "you are no gentleman, so do
not bother."

"Precisely." He nodded. "We should do well together. At
the risk of sounding presumptuous, we were made for each
other."

Acadiana shook her head in disbelief at the arrogance of
the man and took a deep, fortifying breath. She was going
to have to hit him. It would probably hurt her knuckles, but
as long as she took a few of his teeth, it would be worth it.
And damn the consequences. He could beat her black and
blue . . . he could tear her limb from limb . . . he could
. . . She couldn't think of any more clichés, and it wasn't a
beating she was afraid of but the other ways he touched her.
Even as she balled up her fists she knew she would have to
change strategies and another thought surfaced.

"Very well," she said. Her look was smug, as was her
tone of voice. "I concede defeat for the moment. How will
you explain your marrying an Indian to your family? Introduce me as your squaw?"

"I don't have to explain anything to them. I care naught
for your lineage, but I know your family. You are no Indian."

Her self-confident look turned bitter and challenging, as
if she would force him to listen, to understand. *"Non?*
White trash then. It will make little difference in their
minds what they call me, the feelings will be the same."

"You're not trash either," Jonas said flatly.

"Then you give it a name," she said in scornful amusement. "I was raised near the Caddo for four years. I know
their language and their customs. I walked among them as
one of their own, wearing deerskin and buffalo clothing—
not silks and satins. I learned about warfare and ceremonial
rituals—not stitchery and mixing sweet-smelling creams. I

know how to plant corn and gather thatch, how to hunt and fish and survive. But I do not know *anything* about being a wife to a wealthy Creole planter!" She stopped to see if her words were having any effect at all on the imperious man. Jonas merely nodded indulgently for her to continue. "You cannot change that!" She thought to disgust him with her words, but his expression never wavered. It was disconcerting to find him so immovable, but there was more to disclose, more she could tell him if it became necessary that was certain to disgust him.

"I wouldn't change anything about you, love, except your feelings for me," he said. So, what he suspected was true. Raised for even a portion of her life as a Caddo would have made her an outcast to some of the more uppity Louisiana settlers. It explained her family's reluctance to talk about her past and her ability to fend for herself in the wild. Jonas suspected she had been ostracized by other men, which explained the aloofness he had seen her direct toward the fools at several of the parties they had attended. But if she thought such a declaration would sway him, she was sorely mistaken. He wanted her land no matter what he had to do to get it. If that meant marrying a spitfire to obtain it, he would do it. And enjoy taming her in the process.

Acadiana's eyes narrowed as she glared at Jonas's passive face. "You will be snubbed," she warned. "Treated like a pariah."

"As you were?" he said, and watched her face blanch.

He didn't know, didn't realize the full extent of what he was saying. She had lived among the Caddo as a daughter, laughed with them, learned with them. She had watched them build their mounds and guard the sacred fires in their temples. She had visited their conical houses with grass-thatched roofs and traveled the river in their dugouts. She had even been on fur-trading expeditions with the *taovayas* who acted as middlemen for the *coureurs de bois*. She had returned a stranger in white society, and this stubborn man was acting as if none of that mattered.

"You are a fool," she said flatly.

"Possibly," Jonas replied unemotionally. "Let's make peace, Acadiana. I'm famished and tired of all this arguing. Your past makes no difference to me, so get that through your head. Peace?"

"Oui," she said slyly, but he did not know all of it. "Make no mistake, *m'sieu,* I find no peace in your proposal, and neither shall you. I will fight you to the bitter end."

"Warning taken, Acadiana, but we shall yet see the victor," he stated. The gauntlet had been cast, and he was only too eager to pick it up. "Do not underestimate me, love. I shall win everything—even your affection."

"I am not your love," she said forcefully even as a look of doubt crossed her violet eyes and she stared into his determined face. Her voice was low, but heavy with irony. "Even if you succeed, Jonas, you fail. For everything won there is always something lost. Even if you win . . . you have won nothing!"

Jonas stared at her for a brief moment and chose not to dignify her statement with one of his own. She stood there so cold and unapproachable that she almost repelled him. He was forced to wonder what he had gotten himself into, and if he would be saddled with an icy witch for the rest of his life because of his obsession with the land and lack of foresight in the matter. No, he thought not. Fire could melt ice, and he certainly had fire burning inside of him where this saucy female was concerned.

Acadiana resigned herself to the temporary stalemate and began to dish up the stew. Nothing would be accomplished by their constant bickering, she reasoned as she handed Jonas a bowl and sat down resolutely. They ate in almost companionable silence, and as the sun reached its zenith then arched in slow descent, an underlying peace seemed to settle about the camp. The day was bright and warm, the sky cloudless; a cool breeze radiated from the steam, bringing with it a false sense of well-being.

Jonas finished his meal and admitted a grudging respect

for the beauty he knew so little about but who stirred him
in ways almost incomprehensible to him. He stretched his
arms behind his head and leaned back against a tree to
watch her, ever mindful that she would bolt given the
chance. She moved about the camp gracefully, like a sleek
wild animal as she cleared things away and banked her fire.
He sat up abruptly when she rounded a grassy hill and
disappeared from sight, but she returned soon with a
roughly carved spear and proceeded to the stream. He followed her to the edge of the bank and watched as she
stepped into the cool, clear water. She stood there frozen,
like a Greek statue of timeless beauty. Jonas paused as the
breeze lifted her ebony locks and sent them drifting over
her shoulder, and eternity stood still, motionless and waiting, as he was suddenly caught in a tangled web of peace
and passion.

In one fluid motion, Acadiana hurled the spear down. It
pierced the water silently, striking the target. She'd had to
hunt for food often while living in the wilderness; it had
meant her survival. It was more a game now, a pastime, and
her skills were rusty. She quickly brought the spear back
over the bank, careful not to lose her prey. Jonas smiled at
her efficiency as she flopped a wiggling catfish at his feet
and resumed her frozen stance.

"If you want to eat later, you had better string the fish
with the thong attached to the rock over there," she whispered over her shoulder.

"Bossy little thing, aren't you?" he whispered back in
amusement.

She speared another fish and attempted to sling it at his
smiling face.

"En garde." Jonas chuckled, ducking out of the way. He
strung both fish and lowered them back into the stream.
"Why are you doing this? There is plenty of stew left for
supper."

"The stew is for tomorrow," she murmured, tossing another fish on the bank.

"Tomorrow!" Jonas shouted, startling her. "How long are you planning to stay here?"

Acadiana sent him a scathing look over her shoulder. "Until I am ready to leave! If you do not wish to eat before your journey back, so be it, but hush! You frighten the fish." Missing the slippery prey now swimming out of range, she threw her spear down and spun around to rebuke him.

Jonas cut her off with a clipped reply. "Come on, we have enough." He offered his hand to help her out of the water.

Acadiana glanced up at that arrogant stance and knew there was nothing solicitous in the gesture. He was ordering her out. Her eyes made a broad, insulting sweep of his body from head to toe before she took his hand firmly. She shouldn't . . . she knew she shouldn't . . . but this was just too tempting. She took one step forward, braced her foot against a rock, then pulled back with all her might, throwing Jonas off balance and sending him sprawling headlong into the shallow water.

Acadiana scrambled up the slippery bank and ran straight to the hut. Giggling uncontrollably, she tried to gather her things but ended up sitting back on her heels, laughing so long and hard that she finally had to hold her aching sides. She tried holding her breath to stifle the hurt in her ribs, but the remembrance of Jonas's startled face sent her into fresh peals of laughter. She had flirted with danger before but never with such satisfaction.

She looked up suddenly when drops of water began puddling around her bare feet. She smothered another rush of convulsing snickers by throwing her hand over her mouth when she found a thoroughly soaked man before her. Her eyes grew enormous and the laughter died quickly when he began stripping off his clothing.

"M'sieu!" She gasped as he made no move to discontinue.

"What did you expect, love? That I would stand here dripping wet all day?" he asked, one insolent eyebrow raised.

"Non . . . I did not think . . . did not expect . . ." She gulped.

"That's obvious" came the sarcastic reply.

"Jonas, do not!" She squealed and would have made a wild dash for the entrance but the half-naked man was barring the way. She covered her eyes as he started peeling off his trousers.

"Never let it be said, my dear, that I was alone with a beautiful woman in a state of greater undress than myself. I am just equaling things up a bit. A situation, I might add, brought on by yourself." He paused, and Acadiana could hear a rustling sound. She concluded that there was now a fully naked man barring her exit. "If you desired seeing me like this, Acadiana, all you had to do was ask. You will find me a most accommodating fellow."

"Oh, you . . . you . . ." she started, then clamped her mouth shut. She just couldn't think of anything vile enough to describe him at the moment.

"Yes, love? Is there something you wish to say?" he taunted, pulling her hands away from her face.

Acadiana kept her eyes tightly closed, shame rising crimson on her cheeks. "I am not your love. Don't call me love!" she said shrilly as she snatched her hands back.

"You could be," Jonas teased. "Good heavens, woman, you are blushing like an innocent virgin."

Acadiana's head shot up. Her eyes flew open and she glared at him with undiluted hostility. "I am a . . . I am one!"

Jonas's deep laughter seemed to ricochet off the walls to echo in her ears. Acadiana pressed slender hands to her hot cheeks, realizing she had been goaded into doing exactly what he had intended. Jonas had wrapped one of her blankets around his hips and was mocking the relieved expression on her face at seeing him thus.

His laughter subsided finally to be replaced with a puzzled expression. She didn't seem to find discomfort in her own lack of clothing, but all he'd had to do was start taking off his shirt and she had gone into a frenzy. Jonas's avid gaze traced every line of her exposed flesh, making Acadiana want to shrink back and cover herself. His eyes stopped their roaming and rose to meet hers.

Acadiana glared back at him with unabashed loathing, knowing exactly what he was thinking as if he had spoken it aloud. It had been normal for her to be around meagerly clad Indian males, she thought defensively, and she had been much younger then. It was different now. She had never seen a white man unless he was fully clothed. It wasn't at all proper for him to disrobe in front of her for any reason, even if he *had* been soaked from neck to heel. Besides the breach of etiquette, the sight of Jonas's magnificent bare chest and arms was doing terrible things to her insides. *Mon Dieu!*

Jonas ignored Acadiana's glowering look and sat down to face her. She tried staring back at him but found she had to divert her eyes from such a open display of flesh. He began asking questions about her elusive past, drawing her out of the angry shell she had wrapped herself in and into a life long past and fraught with memories both painful and pleasant.

Acadiana was so startled that he wanted to know about her past, she forgot he was only partially covered. The other men she had known were repulsed and embarrassed to learn where she had spent four years of her life. Jonas would be too when he learned the full extent of her time away. She felt compelled to explain, to make him understand that they would never be suited to one another.

"I was on a trip with my parents," she replied. Her eyes filled with sadness, and it was with great effort that she continued. "We were going west to see some of the new unexplored land my mother's relatives had written to us about. Months before we planned to leave my brother, Matthew, was killed. He was only sixteen at the time. We all took it badly, but it was hardest on my mother. She cried and cried for months, and I think my father feared for her health. He decided that she needed to get away for a time, to distance herself from the things that reminded her of her son. For some reason *Maman* did not want to leave, but Papa insisted.

"We were almost out of Louisiana when our wagon was attacked, and my parents were killed. The Indians found me hiding and took me back to their camp."

"Good God," Jonas said. "You were held captive by your parents' murderers for four years? How did you escape?"

"Men." Acadiana grimaced. "They always choose to think the worst." Jonas raised his eyebrows but said nothing. "I did not say that the Indians did it. My parents were killed by bandits. The Indians found me hiding in the wagon and took me in." She lifted her eyes to face him with the full and final truth. "A trapper, Jean Baptiste, came to their camp that year. He knew me, had known my parents well. And I went with him. For four years I stayed with him living the life of a *taovayas* on the fringes of the Indian settlements. I regret very little of the years I spent with him, only the circumstances that brought me to him."

She braced herself for his reaction, steeled her emotions against his loathing, but his face remained impassive. "Did you hear me?" she asked.

"I heard" was his only response.

"I *lived* with him! He is not my father, or brother, or even kin!"

"Did he use you?" Jonas asked quietly, and it was impossible to ascertain his gut reaction. His face was closed, but his eyes intense.

"Non!" Acadiana gasped, then realized what a fool she was to admit it. It was that very idea that had repulsed her other suitors. She called herself an imbecile and an idiot, but knew she would not call back the words even if given a choice. She would never lay such scandal at Jean's door.

Jonas felt a twinge of her grief as he witnessed the hurt shadowing her eyes. He could well imagine the discrimination she received upon her return to civilized society. He was left to wonder how truly civilized men were that they could shun a helpless orphan so easily.

"I am sorry, Acadiana. I didn't realize your past was so painful," he said, but knew it was little consolation.

"I am all right," Acadiana said coolly. She stiffened inwardly at the sympathetic look on his face. She didn't need or want pity from this man. "My parents' death happened a long time ago. It will always be in the back of my mind, but I have put it behind me. We all must go on," she continued with more conviction. But the malice in her voice gave her away, and although she was always so careful to rebuild the towering wall of indifference that kept the hurt out, she was not successful in erasing the pain from her face.

"Why did this Jean return you to your uncle?"

"When I was about fourteen, I . . . ah . . . started maturing, you know—" Acadiana shrugged, blushing.

"Yes, I know." Jonas smiled. "I can see that you 'matured' quite well."

"*Non,* I . . . oh . . . stop looking at me like that!"

"I'm sorry, go on." *Liar.* He wasn't sorry at all to be sitting there studying her rosy cheeks and long golden limbs.

Acadiana shifted uncomfortably and stared off at the farthest corner of the small hut to keep from studying the broad chest in front of her. A thick, intriguing thatch of sable hair covered the muscular torso, so unlike the Indians' sleek . . . *Mon Dieu,* what was she thinking!

"There were some things that happened, and Jean thought it time I consider returning to my uncle."

Jonas heard the pain and longing so evident in Acadiana's voice. It was obvious she loved this man she had spent four years with, and it made Jonas wonder what had happened that he would make her leave.

"What sort of *things?*" he asked.

"Nothing of importance to you," Acadiana said with a cool stare and note of finality that told him their conversation was over.

Jonas decided to respect her secrecy for the present and felt a strange tugging at his heart for the courageous maiden. For whatever the reason, he felt compelled to comfort her, but she didn't seem to want it, and he had held so little room in his life for such feelings. He liked and respected women, had always enjoyed their company on a detached level—either through friendship or desire for momentary satisfaction. But his real passion had been for the land, and now he felt very inadequate and incapable of dealing with this unfamiliar emotion.

"It must have been hard for you to adjust to the trapper's way of life," he ventured, picturing a small, courageous child trying to adapt to a new culture.

"Ha! Not nearly as hard as adjusting to society again," she said seriously. "Can't you see, Jonas? I am not like the other girls. I am not equipped to handle your way of life. I would end up disgracing you as I have Uncle Grayson so many times." She drew a raw, heartfelt breath and looked deeply into his eyes. "I do not want to marry you!"

Jonas chose to ignore her last statement and the pleading in her voice. "You didn't want to return to your uncle's family?"

"*Oui,* Katherine and I have always been like sisters. It was just that when I got back . . . things were different . . . *I* was different. Jean accepted me as I was, the Indians were at least tolerant. Society was not so compromising." Acadiana's eyes took on that look of defiance that Jonas was beginning to recognize as a defensive front. "Wild and untamed, they called me when I returned." Among other things.

Although he wouldn't say it, Jonas thought the name fit her perfectly. Much more apropos than her more recent sobriquet, ice maiden. He had seen the chilling looks she turned on other men to disguise the hurt within her, but with him . . . Ah, there was a fire in her eyes that could not be cloaked. Jonas cleared his mind of the seductive thoughts and continued to question her.

"Why did you stay with your uncle instead of returning to Jean? You are obviously not afraid of going out on your own."

"Jean returned a year later with a wife, but even if he had not my place is with my family. They love me, even if they do get put out with me at times." She laughed softly.

It was the first relaxed emotion to cross her face since Jonas's arrival. He was eager to continue the camaraderie that was slowly developing between them, to watch her face light up, to see her violet eyes sparkle in genuine gaiety. The protective barrier was beginning to weaken and the wall of ice was melting around her, allowing the warmth to shine through. Jonas found her silvery laughter provocative and compelling. Too provocative. Too compelling.

He needed to turn his thoughts away from the pressure in his lower region. It was damn near insulting how his body so easily betrayed him when around her, as if he were sixteen again and in the throes of his first real passion. "Do you miss the other life?"

"At times," Acadiana said wistfully. "I was free there. Everything changed when I returned. There were different rules of behavior and an unbreachable code of ethics to live by. No freedom. I no longer take the liberty for granted."

Her passionate words made Jonas cringe inwardly. If she loved her freedom so much, would marriage vows be enough to hold her? "Will you ever go back to that life?" he asked coolly.

She shrugged, noncommittal. "There is nothing there for me now. I have a dream to finish, the dream my parents started. Life was so simple then, the work of day-to-day survival hard, but real and satisfying. There were no social fronts to contend with, just one's own dignity to uphold." She cocked her head to the side in a guilelessly innocent gesture that sent a kick to Jonas's gut. "Can you see an Indian maiden or the wife or daughter of a trapper worrying about what dress to wear or how many times she can dance with a certain beau before she sets the widows' tongues to wagging?"

Jonas grinned at her comparison. He too had felt the bite of the stringent and strict Creole society. "What about your heart, Acadiana? Where does your heart lead you now?"

"My heart lies with many things. Uncle Grayson and his family, Jean Baptiste, but mostly my heart lies with the land," she said softly. Her gaze rose slowly to meet his. Every plane and angle of his face spoke of power and confidence, the width and breath of his shoulders cried strength, and in his eyes was definitive purpose. Acadiana shuddered suddenly, realizing she had just spewed her life's story to the man who wanted to destroy her dreams.

"The land." Jonas sighed. "Our dreams are the same whether you want to admit it or not. You know you can't develop it without me, so why are you fighting this marriage?"

"I am not ready to get married," she almost pleaded. "But when I am it will be because I am in love with the man."

"Christ!" Jonas scoffed, throwing his hands up in exasperation. "Another hopeless romantic."

Acadiana ignored the slur. A mockery of love was exactly what she would expect from this arrogant beast. "I cannot believe you are willing to give up your freedom for the land," she said heatedly.

"Because you aren't?" he taunted. "Obviously I want it more than you do, Acadiana. Aren't you willing to marry me to keep the land you profess to hold so dear?"

"I will find another way!" She rose quickly to her feet to still his questions and comments.

"Where are you going?" Jonas asked, rising to follow her. She was a tempting sight stalking away, hips swaying in the soft animal skin.

"To gather wood," she threw back over her shoulder, sulky. "I need it for cooking, and it gets dreadfully cold up here at night." Their easy conversation had been spoiled along with her good humor. How foolish to have let her guard down and to have forgotten the very reason he was here.

"I am well aware of the merits of a fire," he called, thinking of his prior night on the trail. Then his thoughts took another direction and a slow grin spread across his face. "We will certainly have to do all we can to stay warm tonight."

Acadiana came to a jarring halt in midstride and spun around to face him. Her mouth was set in a grim line, and her finely arched eyebrows were knitted in a bewildered frown. She took two steps toward him then stopped and stomped a bare foot.

"We? Aren't you going back?" she asked, stunned.

Jonas leaned toward her defiant stance and said calmly, "I told you, I am not leaving here without you."

"Well, you may have a long wait!" she stated, throwing her hands on her hips.

"How very enjoyable," he teased, watching the violet in her eyes darken.

"You can't stay here," she said in a low, menacing tone.

"Why not?" he asked, daring her to challenge him.

"It would not be proper!" she wailed. "Uncle Grayson would . . . would . . ."

"Would what?" He chuckled insolently. "Make me marry you? Force me to see that your honor is upheld? Really, Acadiana, what can he do that I have not already set into motion myself? Besides, if you ran around dressed like that for four years, I'm not sure you have any honor to protect."

Acadiana gasped. "I was a child . . ."

A stinging pain gripped her chest. She felt as if the breath had been knocked from her like the time she was caught by a low-hanging branch and swept from Shawnee's back. Tears stung her eyes as she stared at him. How dare he question her virtue? Was she so crude in her behavior that she invited such accusation? Acadiana grabbed her leather pouch and fled from him in shame.

Jonas felt no triumph as he watched her hurry away. He had seen the tears spring forth in her eyes as his words had struck a telling blow. Maybe she was and maybe she wasn't chaste, but he had taken unfair advantage with his tawdry words. He left the hut slowly, chafed by his own insensitivity. He would find her and make amends, he decided. Having told her he wanted peace, it was peace he would have if he had to cut his tongue out to insure it.

He found her in a wooded area gathering twigs and small sticks, and watched her for a moment before approaching. She bent to add another broken limb to the pile near her feet, and Jonas could see the sleek curve of her buttocks where they joined her thighs. Her legs were gently muscled from riding yet soft to the touch. He remembered too well the feel of his hand on that tender spot and shifted uncomfortably as he continued to watch her. She could tempt a saint, he wagered as he sought to cool his rising desire. But he was no saint and certainly not used to tamping down his passions.

Noticing her tear-streaked face, Jonas approached her cautiously, feeling as guilty as an errant schoolboy. Damn her! She drove him to anger one minute, then had him panting with lust the next. Never had he been so affected by a woman, and he was having a hard time adjusting to the mixture of emotions she created. Acadiana saw him coming but ignored his presence and continued to gather wood as if the entire world were in need of a warm fire. Jonas grasped her shoulders and turned her to face him, running his thumbs soothingly over her delicate collarbones.

"You have enough wood." The words were spoken softly but his voice sounded loud to Acadiana, shattering the serenity she had sought in the forest.

She jerked back to free herself from his grasp. Keeping her head down, eyes averted from his piercing stare, she kicked at his shin. All her helpless rage and hurt erupted in fury of righteous anger, and she lashed out at him again. Jonas picked her up under the arms and held her dangling in the air. Though she knew from experience her efforts were futile, she writhed and squirmed in his masterful grip. She would not stand by and be tormented by this hateful beast. With her feet rendered helpless, she struck out at him with hands clenched into tight little balls. Jonas threw his head back as her fist swung close to his nose.

"Acadiana, stop this," he warned while trying to dodge her wild blows. "I came here to apologize."

"I do not want your apology, *m'sieu,*" she snarled. "I'd rather lay you low!"

Jonas hung his head back and laughed at her preposterous statement. Finding her tears too unnerving, he was determined to spark the return of her anger. That emotion he could deal with. With a leering grin, he slung her over his shoulder and patted her backside in a lascivious manner, causing her to shriek in outrage at his intimacy.

Jonas had donned just his wet breeches, and Acadiana pummeled his bare back with flailing fists, mauling with all the rage of a crazed person. Jonas subdued her kicking legs and allowed her to pound out her frustration there, sincerely hoping that she would be spent by the time he got her back to camp.

Acadiana beat at him for most of the way. But when her attack proved ineffective, her anger finally abated and she hung limply over his shoulder, exhausted from more than the physical exertion.

"You were wrong," she said weakly. "In the summer the Indian women we lived near wore less clothing than I have on, and children under the age of ten wore nothing at all. I was very well covered by their standards." She didn't know why she was telling him this. It irked her just to put forth the effort, but she would not be ridiculed for a way of life she loved and respected.

"I was wrong, Acadiana, but unless the trappers and braves were blind, I'm sure they found you as alluring as I do," Jonas said as he lowered her slowly, sliding her the full length of his body to the ground.

"That was a long time ago," she said, loathing the hard, masculine strength that seemed capable of dismantling her willpower by his sheer presence. Her senses flared at the provocative contrast of dark bronze skin against golden, muscular arms encircling more slender limbs. Her pulse began a mad race toward some unknown destination, and she leveled her palms against his chest to push away from him. Fine, springy hair coiled around her fingers, a heartbeat pounding as madly as her own thumped against her palms. Her breath strangled in her throat when she realized her efforts to shove him away only served to press her hips closer to his rigid groin. Awash with embarrassment, she stopped abruptly and flashed him a mutinous glare.

Jonas eased his crushing embrace, but left his hands on her shoulders. He lifted one finger to brush the hair back from her face. "Maiden," he whispered, his voice heavy with teasing and something darker. "Do you carry the memory of some young man in your heart?"

Jonas found he was unprepared for the answer when she raised a lofty chin to face him. Her words were soft but direct when she spoke.

"I carry many memories."

She refused to say anything more, and Jonas was left wondering how many broken heathen hearts she had left behind.

6

The remainder of the day was spent in preparation for the evening. Wood was hauled, fish cooked, and more ingredients added to the stew. The sun was sinking fast when Acadiana returned to camp after cleaning the sunbaked clay supper dishes. Keeping an ever wary eye on her, Jonas finished tending the horses, then returned to the hut to study the inimitable young woman. He reclined against the packed dirt wall, welcoming the coolness that comes with evening, and watching her graceful movements inside the hut. She was lean and lithe, efficient in her preparations for the night. She was in her element here, he thought, well suited to each task.

"I'll be hard-pressed to forgo hiring kitchen help after eating your cooking," he commented.

"Assuming that I will be there to cook for you," she said, slinging her pouch into a corner before sitting down cross-legged to face him. Nightfall was upon them, and Acadiana had to figure out some way to rid herself of Jonas Courtland. She would appeal to his ethics as a gentleman if she thought he had any, but knew by his previous behavior that that approach was lost to her. As she could not pit her strength against his, she hoped logic and the dagger con-

cealed beneath her hands would be enough to convince him
to leave.

"Assume nothing, love, it's fact. You will never escape
me now," he bantered lightly.

"Do not underestimate me, Jonas. I am not your love,
and I am very adept at escaping," she said with a calmness
that belied her turbulent feelings. "You would not have
found me this time if I had thought to be more careful. My
mistake." Her eyes glittered strangely. "I will not make
another one."

Jonas drew one knee up and leaned on it while he
watched her closely. She was hiding something, formulating
some plan. There was a tense quietness about her that was
too conflicting to ignore, and he knew he would have to be
cautious, alert. "You cannot run the plantation by yourself.
There's nothing there but an old cottage and some land. No
supporting facilities, no animals, no equipment. Nothing."

. . . *an old cottage . . . some land.* The words struck
Acadiana like a blow. Those things meant nothing to him,
everything to her.

"I happen to know that there's also no money," Jonas
continued. "How will you start fresh?" He reached out suddenly and took both her hands. That's when he saw the
dagger, gleaming wickedly in the dying sun as Acadiana
fumbled for it. Pinning her hands with one of his, Jonas
picked up the weapon, held it up for her inspection, then
tossed it behind him. He need not accuse her; her intent was
deadly clear.

Acadiana watched her only means of protection settle in
the dust and sent Jonas a stare as cold and sharp as the
blade lying just beyond her reach. "I told you I will find a
way!" she said, snatching her hands back, feeling the weight
of his words press down on her, squeezing the very life out
of her, leaving her cold and empty. She knew his words
were true, but she didn't have to recognize that fact. Not
here and now when she was so far from the land itself. She

was of a double nature, a dreamer and a realist, and her dreams better suited her hopeless situation at the moment.

"You have a way, Acadiana. You will not only be marrying a Courtland; you will be marrying Courtland money. Think of it this way: You won't really be losing the land, but given a chance to develop it."

Greatly offended, Acadiana stiffened. "I would never stoop so low as to marry a man for his money."

"Don't be so Puritan. It's done all the time," Jonas said bitingly. "At least we are being honest about it. I will marry you for the land, among other things, and you will marry me for the money to keep your land."

Acadiana's eyes narrowed with suspicion and interest. "A marriage of convenience?" she asked. Most marriages were arranged for political or financial gain. She had previously abhorred the concept, but now found it more appealing than her present option. "A marriage in name only?"

"Hardly." Jonas scoffed, dashing her hopes. "A marriage not consummated can be annulled. I won't risk that fate or my sanity. I could hardly look at you day in and day out, not to mention share a bed, without touching you. I'm having a devil of a time right now with you dressed this way."

Jonas broke into sudden and hearty laughter when Acadiana scrambled to retrieve a blanket to cover herself. "Nay, love." He chuckled, pulling it from her. "It's a little late for that. You won't deny me the one pleasure to be found in this godforsaken wilderness. You must admit, sweet, there is little else to occupy us."

Acadiana was not amused by the turn their conversation had taken. Jonas was beginning to make her very nervous. There was something about his eyes, a strange look that she could not quite fathom, but she had seen it before. It reminded her of the look he had given her the night of Charles's party just before he had . . . had . . .

"Oh!" she gasped, startled by the revelation. "You are not going to try to kiss me again, are you?"

Jonas couldn't deny that the idea had been running a

dangerous course for most of the afternoon. He had tried to steer clear of such intimate imaginings, but since she had brought it up. . . . "At least that, love. Least of all that," he said in a low, demanding tone. He was stunned by the startled look on her face, having expected some acerbic, indignant reply. Not fear. Lunging forward, he grabbed her wrists when she tried to back away. "Don't fight me, love," he teased in an effort to bring back her spunk. "I mean you no harm. Quite the contrary."

Acadiana almost climbed the earth wall in an attempt to put distance between them. Her back scraped up against the crude barrier impeding escape, and she knew she was trapped. Jonas was stunned anew by the stricken look on her face. It annoyed him that she had taken his teasing to heart and thought he would actually hurt her. Grabbing her slim ankles, he pulled her back to the center, then held her hands against her sides as she tried to scramble away.

"Easy, love," he said. "I'm not—"

"I'm not your love!" Acadiana found herself flat on her back and quickly drew her knees up in an attempt kick Jonas off her. Her feet slammed against his stomach, but other than a grunt of pain, there was no indication that she had fazed him. Jonas angled his torso sharply when she pulled her knees up again and slung a rock-solid thigh across her legs, pinning her to the dirt floor. Holding her immobile, he stared down into her wary eyes. Her hair flowing around her like a bolt of black silk, her nostrils flaring and chest heaving from exertion, Acadiana stared back at him with angry, fearful determination.

Jonas reached out and gently stroked her cheek, his intent to ease her mind, but something happened when their flesh made contact. Desire kindled beneath their clothing and scalded where skin met skin. As Jonas's tall, able-bodied frame pressed down on her slight curves, the fire that had leapt out in her uncle's parlor rose again to sear him. Every nerve ending was taut and alive from the combustive force of passion tasted then denied. All thought of gentlemanly ethics rapidly burned to ashes and lay in smoldering cinders in Jonas's mind.

His breathing slowed, his eyes narrowed, almost feral, he lowered his face and said gruffly, "I've wanted to do this the right way, no blasted interruptions, since the first day I met you."

Jonas bent his head farther for the kiss, softly brushing his lips against hers then pulling back. It was to be a gentle kiss, one that would not frighten her, but his senses reeled with only the barest touch, then spun out of control as his mouth plunged back down to hers. It wasn't enough to have her firm, unresponsive lips beneath his, would never be enough, and he began to move over her mouth, slanting and molding it to better accommodate him.

Acadiana jerked her head from side to side to avoid his ruthless and relentless pursuit of her. "Bastard!" she hissed, cursing as much his greater strength as she did the man. She strained away from him as his lips grazed her cheek and jaw then worked down the delicate column of her neck before returning to maraud her mouth. "Cur, *vaurien!*" she swore against his lips, thrashing beneath him in a feckless waste of energy. The sleek flesh of her arms, midriff, and thighs writhed against him, alternately pressing then retreating in a maddening abrasion, creating the impetus that fanned the flames of Jonas's desire until they burst into blaze. "Whoreson!" she railed in impotent fury.

Jonas braced Acadiana's arms beside her head so that she could not turn away and lifted himself a fraction above her. "My mother would be offended." He smiled slowly, before his mouth captured hers, captured the vivid and useless threats she hurled at him. The pressure of his lips, the full, heavy length of him was daunting. The unspoken command to surrender vibrated loudly in the still, dusty air, until she was forced to yield to his demands just to draw breath. Her lips parted slightly and the kiss turned scorching, even more exacting as Jonas pillaged the tender inside of her mouth, determined to break through and tear down her barriers.

Acadiana cried out at the touch of his tongue and stared at him, stunned, her eyes growing rounder with the pressure of his lips, with each dip and swirl as his tongue parried and thrust then parried again with hers. The grittiness of the earth beneath her sensitized her skin as effectively as the hard strength above her. Both were immovable and unwelcome.

"Cease, *je vous en prie!*" she pleaded against his lips, even as her heart began lurching in uneven thuds and her breathing grew unsteady. His body surrounded her, enslaved her, thigh to thigh, chest to breast, the shadow of his beard abrading her cheeks and chin. She had no weapons with which to fight his strength, no appeals for his conscienceless ears. Swamped by the heat, the constant besiegement of mind and body, her treacherous limbs weakened then dissolved, deserting her in time of need. Her lashes fluttered in hopeless agony, then drifted down to shield her from the glow of possessive fire in Jonas's eyes.

"Sweet," he whispered, his breath furling around her ear in a warm vapor that seemed to infuse her entire body.

Her muscles betrayed her and went slack, her mind too numb to renew the struggle. Acadiana managed only to moan in misery before Jonas's tongue darted out again and began searching her mouth.

Encouraged by the sudden quietness of her body, he gentled the attack, lightly flicking her lips until they softened, then delving deeper to tantalize her tongue. She lay still, lax, neither fighting nor participating as he teased her for endless, suspended fragments of time with his mouth and tongue until his teeth caught her lower lip and tugged. A faint tingling shimmered in the pit of Acadiana's stomach, then seemed to stretch and grow, spreading fiery tendrils down to the inner recesses of her body. Her breath hitched on a moan, then she stirred beneath him, stunned, afraid, yet caught up in the moment, unaware that her own frantic movements were not now struggles but a result of the tide of passion that washed over her.

The sound shot through Jonas like cannon fire, pulling him beyond the tether of his control. He shifted his body to cover hers completely and met her fervor with unleashed aggression. His hips bore her deeper into the earth, grinding out an ancient rhythm that shouted loudly his need. Startled by the fierce, full weight of him, by the hard, swollen length moving against her, Acadiana gasped in fright and tried to pull away. Jonas captured the sound with his mouth, and his tongue plunged even deeper as his body imitated the action.

Acadiana was losing herself to the smothering kiss, to the suffocating heat of awakening passion. She felt Jonas's hand on her inner thigh, the stroke of his fingers as they moved in erotic spirals higher and closer. His other hand snaked up her rib cage, drawing nearer her breast, then closed over it completely. Some inwardly primitive force tightened the muscles in her stomach and caused her inadvertently to arch against him. But when he began kneeing her thighs apart, and his hand moved in unerring circles on her breast, it was too much. Her innocence warred only briefly with the naked yearning within her before it won. She jerked her mouth away, strained wildly with her imprisoned body.

"Non! You must not!" she cried, bucking suddenly then twisting beneath him, her fingers digging into his upper arms. She tried kicking and pitching, anything she could to push him away.

"Be still. I won't," Jonas soothed, and slowed the movement of his lower body. His hands took possession of hers once again, intertwining their fingers and pulling until they were over her head. He fought his own turbulent need, which was heightened by every twitch of her body, by every whiff of her purely feminine scent, and commanded himself to go slowly. He resumed the seduction by pressing lazy kisses along her neck and collarbone, stopping only to nip the rounded part of her shoulder. Spurred by the shiver that rippled throughout her body, he quickly lost the battle for self-control, and returned to her mouth with feverish intenity, his lips sliding softly as the flutter of a butterfly's wing on some spots, with the scorch of burning coals on others.

His hand slid along the length of her arm, his fingers curled over the supple leather binding her breast, and the fleeting contractions now surged across Acadiana's abdomen and were almost painfully gripping in their urgency. Her free hand tunneled through his hair, gripping the sable locks as if they would stablize her even while a desperate moan emerged from the depths of her soul at the compelling forces that caused her body to burn and tighten in a profusion of shame and anger and unwelcome longing.

The sound stirred Jonas beyond the bounds of reality, where some hedonistic nature reigned, and he became aggressive in his pursuit of keener pleasures. He nibbled and tasted and trailed downward over her heated cheeks and neck, going lower and lower until hampered by the soft leather hide. He released her hand and began to tug on the offending straps that laced the wrap together as he sought to free her loveliness from the restriction.

Slammed back into reality, Acadiana knew the ultimate terror of being alone with this man. The implication of his actions panicked her along with the renegade feelings that began to evolve and grow within her, awakening her to a realm of womanhood that was so new and strange it made her feel as if she were ablaze.

"Jonas, stop," she cried weakly, struggling against him in halfhearted confusion. She pulled on his hair, her legs moved fretfully, rubbed against him from thigh to knee, unknowingly compounding her danger.

"Shhh," he breathed, unwilling to listen. He continued the assault, running a lean bronzed finger over the curve of flesh swelling above the binding. And his eyes bore into her with the all-consuming need that rode him hard, urged him to press on despite her resistance. It was lust but something more—the thing that drove men to capture the elusive, to tame that which is wild. Obtaining possession of the land had driven him for a year. Now he was driven by another

force. A needy, obsessive force. He wanted to possess no
only the dormant fields but their elusive owner. He woul
have them both.

Acadiana felt none of these emotions. There was a natu
ral longing in her for a husband and children, but it was
vision for the future. The yearning this man stirred in he
was in the present, and it frightened, angered, and confuse
her.

"Jonas, do not." She gasped, wedging her hands unde
his palms to cover herself as she tried to inch away.

"Stop squirming, Acadiana," he whispered darkly. "
won't . . . yet." He raised a little to look at her face, hi
smoldering blue eyes sweeping the length of her, then re
turning to rest on her stormy face and pinched mouth
"What are you afraid of?"

"Nothing!" she said. She caught her bottom lip betwee
her teeth and clutched the wrap as she tried to will he
racing heart to slow down.

"Then why stop?" His voice was laced with irritation, hi
body too stirred by the tempest of desire and need to hol
back, too aroused to want to.

"It . . . it is not decent!"

"It's going to happen sooner or later. I would much pre
fer it happen now," he stated bluntly, as if it were inevita
ble.

He was no longer a youth, content with teasing love-play
and frustrating nights. A competent and generous lover, he
pursued only those women willing to enjoy and return affec
tion. Acadiana's rejection was as new for the man as it wa
frustrating. He refused to let the idea enter his conscious
ness that a night spent with a woman as beautiful and allur
ing as this one would not reap the bounty of a joining and
sharing of intimacies. They had gone too far, much too far,
to stop now.

He could well understand her reluctance, even if he
didn't want to accept it. It was expected as a flirtatious
practice, widely used by the most discriminating ladies

Most wanted, needed to be wooed, and only the most brazen of females abandoned the pretense of innocence. So let her play her games if she must. The outcome would be the same.

"Non!" Acadiana cried again, frightened by the sapphire eyes that glittered down at her boldly, so confident and self-assured, as if they knew secrets of which she was unaware.

Jonas's eyes narrowed marginally. "It won't matter to me if you're not a virgin, if that's what you are worried about." But even as the words surfaced he knew that he had lied.

Her reaction was explosive. "How dare you!" she ground out. "Of course I am a . . . a . . . how dare you!"

"Then I will be gentle," he coaxed. "It won't be bad, if you will relax—"

Acadiana shrieked.

Jonas flinched as the shrill sound assaulted his ears.

"I can't . . . *I won't!*" she said, outraged. She swung her fist to strike his face, but he caught it deftly and held it firm.

"You can, and you *will* if we stay in this isolated place much longer," he said. "You cannot expect me to play the uninterested fool when I want you more than any woman I have ever had the misfortune of being alone with."

Misfortune? "I did not ask you to come here," she said, hurt by that one, unfeeling word. "And it doesn't matter how long I choose to stay here! You don't have any right to—"

"I will have *every* right in a few days. A few short days, Acadiana. If I am forced to stay here to prevent you from running off again"—he let the words linger a moment—"I'll exercise my rights early."

Her quick, indrawn breath assured him that his threat had not gone unheard. Dilated amethyst eyes glared at him defiantly. *"Oui,"* she said. "We will return first thing in the morning, but promise me that you will stop this . . . this . . . assault . . . tonight. We cannot travel safely until daylight."

Jonas had the advantage, if it could be called such, for he

was as captured by the sexual tension between them as she was frightened by it. He pressed on quickly. "And when we get back? Will you marry me gracefully? Without a fight?" He nibbled her shoulder, then dropped to the soft mound rising above the hide.

"I . . . I do not know. I cannot promise . . . *Stop that!*" She squealed when he began tugging on the strips of leather again.

"Yes, love? Did you say something?" he said as the first strap pulled free.

"Stop it, Jonas! I mean it!" She groaned, fighting with her free arm.

She pushed with her hand and jabbed him with her elbow in a futile attempt to subdue his ardor. Jonas quickly pinned both of her wrists over her head and held them with one of his hands while the other resumed the attack.

"Give up, love. If this keeps on, you'll have to marry me anyway. Your maidenhood will most certainly be compromised."

"Well, I never!" She gasped.

"I know, love. I am trying to remedy that as fast as I can." He sighed. "If you would only cooperate. . . ."

"Oooooh! You vile, despicable creature! You . . . you are the most uncouth man I have ever known."

"Will you marry me?" he asked sweetly. "There is only one strap left."

"This is blackmail!" she argued, kicking her feet up and down beneath him in vain.

"Exactly." He grinned crookedly.

"That's not fair!" she wailed, turning her head to bite the arm holding her captive. "If I had my dagger, I would stab you right through that coldblooded heart of yours."

"Half a strap," he warned.

"*Non!*" she yelled.

"Here is your strap, love," Jonas said, dangling it in her face before burying his head in the loveliest valley he had ever explored. Her skin was like warm silk, inviting, fragrant, tempting him almost past the point of seduction to brutal invasion. He lifted his head slowly. Moonlight spilled over her golden flesh, and the sight of her, full and round above a slender rib cage and belly, athletically firm, femininely soft, was nearly his undoing. She might never forgive him if he took her like this. In truth he might never forgive himself, but he was aroused to the point that he was almost willing to risk it.

Color burned Acadiana's cheeks and flooded down to the nakedness her entrapped arms could not hide. And it was terrifying to be so open, so vulnerable. "Uncle Grayson will . . . will . . ."

Jonas raised his eyes from Acadiana's delectable flesh to stare at her coldly. "Will make you marry me twice as fast if this keeps up." He was angry. Angry at her and at himself for his unruly and insane passion. He had never *ever* had a problem controlling himself. Had never even had more than a passing interest in a woman who had not wanted him first. But he had set a course with this woman, and right or wrong, he would see it through. "Make no mistake, you have only two choices, Acadiana. Sell me the land or marry me. Since I can't force you to do the first, I'll accept the second." His head dropped suddenly, his mouth closed over her bare nipple and he tugged once, forcefully, then released her.

Jarred by the impact, Acadiana's body jerked, a soundless cry died in her throat, and she could do nothing more than stare up into his dangerous, determined eyes.

"I *will* compromise you if that's what it takes," Jonas said, each word hard-bitten with such resolution that it acted like a shower of ice on her defiance.

"Oui," Acadiana conceded in a strangled whisper. *"Oui,* Jonas, I will marry you, but . . . but I will not like it. And I swear, you will regret that you ever forced my hand!" Her teeth gnashed in frustration, and a single tear slid down her cheek. *Mon Dieu,* defeat felt wretched.

His thoughts were hooded as his thumb brushed the tear

from her cheek. "You don't have to like it." He sighed, releasing her arms but reluctant to drag himself away from her supple body. "But given time, you may learn to love it."

"I will never love anything about you," she cried, tears of anger falling freely now. "And I won't do *this* after we are married either! I will marry you in name only . . . for the money to rebuild my plantation."

"You'll do it," he promised. "You may marry me for any reason you wish, but it will not be in name only. In the first place, Acadiana, I want children. Second, I won't live like a monk in my own home. Is that understood?"

"You are abominable," she said, covering her naked breasts with her arms.

"That may very well be true," he said dispassionately. "I am also very tired." He rolled from her roughly then spread a blanket over the both of them. "Go to sleep."

Frustration. He'd never known such aching, overpowering frustration. Jonas fixed his eyes on the thatched roof overhead, though he couldn't really see it now in the darkness. His manhood had been sorely tried this night, his civilized upbringing furiously at war with his baser instincts. It didn't help to recall that Acadiana had responded to his kiss somewhat, that he was beginning to melt the ice when she balked. Her uncle was trusting him to bring her back unsullied, but Jonas wasn't sure he could comply with those wishes if he had any further contact with her.

The savageness with which he wanted her still stunned him. Never had he been so driven to take forceful measures with a woman. Even now, with her body curled away from him and the sounds of her soft weeping filling the strained silence in the hut, it took every ounce of control within him to stop himself from flinging her on her back and spreading her thighs to plunder her softness like some lunatic. The fact that she incited him so toward purely lecherous intentions enraged him. Damn her soft, delicious body and startling violet eyes. Damn her refusal of him. But the ultimate victory would belong to him. His ruthless pursuit of her land would bring her to heel, and he would have them both. Her land to cultivate at will, and her—*at will*—in his bed.

His victory was short-lived, however, when her tremulous voice cut through the darkness, causing him further discord.

"You would force me?" she pressed, unaware of the battle he waged against his desire.

"I would," he said cruelly. "I'd rather you come to me willing, but have no doubt, I will have you either way. Now, go to sleep before I prove the point."

Acadiana turned back on her side in a huff. Taking an angry swipe at the tears that were tripping over themselves in a cascading frenzy, she mumbled depraved curses on Jonas, his horse, his line of ancestry that challenged his connection to the human race, and finally the impossible situation she found herself in.

Jonas took note of her restless movements and sighed in the darkness. She could not possibly be more uncomfortable than he was. Arms propped behind his head, he listened to her indecent oaths with wry amusement, then turned on his side and slung his arm around her waist to draw her buttocks against him. Acadiana snarled at his caress and tried to scoot away, but he wrapped his arm more securely around her middle and pulled her hips toward him until he was nestled against her softness.

"You sound so unhappy, love," he explained, nuzzling her behind the ear. "I thought you might need comforting."

Acadiana growled something deep in her throat, but did not open her mouth. She didn't dare risk stirring his anger or his ardor. Alarmed by the contact of his body against hers and the tremor of apprehension that shuddered through her as he fitted himself to each curve, Acadiana resigned herself to spending a perfectly miserable night.

The hours crept by as she lay stiff and sullen, listening to Jonas's regular breathing and the soothing calls of the night creatures. Eventually, her eyes grew strained from peering into the darkness, her lids too heavy to remain open, and she fell into a fretful, troubled sleep—a sleep plagued with nightmares of the past. They were the same horrifying visions that had recurred with frequency for the past ten years.

She was a child again, racing along at an alarming pace, the wagon she was in swaying drunkenly as great billows of dust rose from the horses' thundering hoofs. Her father's face, contorted in agony, kept looking past her as his hands gripped the reins, and he continued to slap the backs of the horses unmercifully. *Maman* was there, soothing her, cooing sweet words while pushing her down below the ledge that served as the wagon seat.

"*Non, Maman!* Don't put the bundles around me. I can't see! It's dark, *Maman,* I can't see!"

Light streamed in through rough wooden slats, and the golden rays eased the confused child's mind for a moment. Then two men rode up beside her father and snatched the reins from his hands. Huddled in her cramped hiding space, the child could see the dreadful balding man, his eyes bulging with hatred, and the thinner dark-skinned man with the strange voice.

"Don't hurt my *maman!*" the child cried shrilly, but there were other screams now to hide the pitiful wail. There was so much blood the child couldn't look. Sticky and red, it poured forth until she shut her eyes and mind against the horrors. But she couldn't stop the sounds. Her mother's screams reverberated in her ears over and over, buffeting her like hurricane winds. The sound echoed loudly in Acadiana's mind until her own cries mingled with those of her dream.

Her eyes flew open. Her breathing was ragged as she frantically searched the darkened hut, trying to discern where she was. Jonas was there, holding her, whispering soothing words of comfort until she relaxed again. She lay still a minute, trying to sort out reality from fear, then eased herself into a sitting position. She shook her head to clear the sleep from her mind. Jonas rose with her and drew her back into his arms.

"What is it?" he asked, his voice a heavy whisper.

"Just a dream. It comes often." Acadiana sighed, rubbing her brow as if trying to erase the horrifying memory.

"You were calling for your mother."

"So I am told," she attempted to say reasonably, but the words erupted into an anguished cry. "It is always the same, always so clear, as if it were yesterday! I w-will never forget those men, their awful faces and voices . . . and the sound of my mother's screams." She took a shuddering breath and leaned forward, hugging her knees to her chest to insulate the churning in her stomach. Jonas's arms encircled her and pulled her firmly against him. "Do not," she whimpered, but she was tempted to bury herself there, craved the security of those strong arms as a bastion against the terrors of darkness. But he represented a new terror in her life, one that would not fade away with dawn's light.

"It's over, Acadiana. They cannot hurt you now. I'll never let anyone hurt you again," he said, folding his arms more tightly around her when he sensed her pulling away.

He stroked her hair as one would a child's and gently rocked her back and forth. Acadiana didn't have the strength to pull free and rested in his strong, protective embrace. Feeling warm and safe and shielded from the nightmare of the past, she repressed her fears for the future and was soon lulled back into a dreamless sleep by the security of his presence.

Jonas waited until he was sure that she was deep in the arms of Morpheus. After laying her down, he stretched out beside her to snuggle her soft, pliant body next to his. Pushing her hair back from her face, he stared at the gentle curve of her jaw, the fluttery rise and fall of her breasts in troubled sleep, and was forced to take a deep, steadying breath. He had never seen this side of her before. It was unnerving, unsettling, yet it comforted him to know that she could be vulnerable. He had seen the stormy face of a rebel flashing spitfire at him; he had seen the elfin innocence of a prankster. But here was a terribly frightened woman-child who had borne too many of life's cruel strikes. For all her stubbornness, he had to admire her resilience.

He had yet to tame her unruly nature, but he would enjoy that almost as much as he would her willingness. And she would be willing, he pledged. Of all the women he had known, he wanted this one in his bed most. If she brought half of that wild, carefree abandon to their lovemaking, a portion of that soft vulnerability, it would be a tolerable marriage indeed.

Acadiana awoke with a start at the lusty whack on her backside. "Lecher! Must you abuse me?" she said groggily as she rolled over to face her attacker.

Slumberous violet eyes glared at him beneath half-closed lids. Her dark tresses were tousled in a most fetching way as they spilled around her nude shoulders and breasts.

"Nay, love, I can think of much sweeter pleasures in your present state of undress," Jonas said, eyeing her with open desire. His eyes mapped the path of her raven locks where they swirled provocatively over her creamy shoulders to fall in splendor to her trim waist. One of her golden breasts peeked through the veil of ebony silk to tempt him unmercifully. He felt his hidden parts stir painfully, and wondered if he would ever know peace again, wondered how long a man could exist in a constant state of arousal.

Acadiana blushed when she peeked down to find the source of his blatant and heated perusal. She hastily crossed her arms over her chest, cast him a deadly stare, then proceeded to heap every vile threat that she could imagine upon him. No voodoo queen or witch doctor had ever conjured up worse afflictions than what were decreed to befall the man staring with open-mouthed astonishment.

"Cease, woman. Never have I heard worse from the most common sailor along the docks of New Orleans. Perhaps I am about to marry a wharf rat instead of the fair maiden I held so tenderly last night," he taunted, raising one cocky eyebrow in stern disapproval.

"Perhaps, sir, you would do better to seek a wharf rat to wed, for you will find no peace from my tender lips," she returned flippantly.

"Of that, love, I have no doubt," he chuckled. "And if we don't get moving soon, you will get to spend another night in my willing arms. I'm beginning to like this hut."

Acadiana scrambled to her feet, not mistaking his threat. She snatched up her dagger from where Jonas had flung it the night before, then grabbed her leather pouch and clutched them both to her chest modestly. "Leave!" she commanded.

Jonas merely stared at her, not in the least concerned with her timidity. It would be quite pleasurable watching her dress, though admittedly he didn't need the strain just now, and he wasn't foolish enough to let her out of his sight so she could hie herself off to some other remote hideaway.

Acadiana stomped her foot and again commanded him to be gone but knew there was nothing she could do to force him. When he only folded his arms over his chest and leaned back against the wall near the entrance, she knew she was once again beaten. She turned her back on him and pulled the ragged boy's shirt and breeches from her sack.

"Your modesty is misplaced," Jonas said. "I have already seen most of you and find it pleasing. I'll see the rest soon enough. What difference now or in a few days?"

"Go to the devil," she said, tugging on the pants with more haste than finesse.

"Ah, love." Jonas chuckled lightly, taking in the sight with more self-control than he thought humanly possible. "I went to hell and back last night. 'Tis heaven I seek now."

"I am not your love." She bit out each word with every button she fastened on the old shirt. "You will never know heaven or any happiness at all if you carry through with your plans." She spun around then to face him but found she had no more energy or inclination for verbal sparring. She felt tired, drained, defeated.

Jonas merely lifted an eyebrow and stared at her attire.

"Well, what did you expect?" she asked tartly. "That I would ride the countryside dressed as the Indian maiden?"

"Where you are concerned, Acadiana, I have learned, much to my manly regret, never to expect anything . . . normal or otherwise."

They rode hard the first few hours. Acadiana ignored Jonas for the most part until they reached the floodwaters of the Mississippi River. She stopped on a ridge and searched the sandbar below for the safest place to cross. She slid off Shawnee's back and led him down a steep incline of slippery mud and jutting roots. Twice she was caught dangling from a tree limb as her feet gave way. Shawnee hunched down and slid most of the way on his rump, and Acadiana scooted after him in much the same fashion.

Once at the bottom, she turned to see if Jonas was managing the precipitous ledge. He was nowhere in sight. She scanned the higher ground but could find no trace of him. She was awash with a sense of freedom and an eagerness to flee that was suddenly tempered by a gentler concern. There was no doubt in her own mind that she hated him beyond reconciliation, but underlying that was the grim realization that she did not truly wish him harm. Cupping her hands to her mouth, she called for him. Then again. Still she could not see him anywhere above her on the dangerous ridge.

"Miss me?" came a voice filled with humor.

"Oooh!" she squealed, spinning around. "Where did you come from?" Bemused by her own reaction, and unconsciously relieved that he had not met his doom in pursuit of her, Acadiana flashed Jonas a wry smile.

He pointed to a gently sloping hill farther down that led to the sandbar. "Do you always do things the hard way?"

"Forgive me," she said with cheeky insincerity.

"I might forgive you," he said dryly, "if you give me one small kiss to prove your worthy intentions."

"*M'sieu* Courtland," she said, instantly alert to the nuance in his voice and the glimmer of cunning in his eyes. The mere thought of his lips on hers sent a flurry trepidation spiraling clear down to her toes. "The last 'one small kiss' I willingly gave you got me in a heap of trouble with Uncle Grayson, something I am now certain you planned."

"Are you accusing me of dishonorable intentions?" he blustered as if offended.

"*Oui!* Were your intentions honorable, I would not find myself in this impossible situation," she said, lifting her chin in indignation. "And if I can find any way to get out of this marriage—"

Jonas pressed his finger to her lips. "You gave your word that you would marry me, Acadiana. Albeit unwillingly, you did agree," he said seriously.

"How binding is one's word given under duress?" she asked.

"There are other ways to insure your acquiescence," Jonas warned, moving to take her in his arms.

Acadiana ducked beneath his hands and skittered out of his reach. "Now, J-Jonas, *m'sieu,* behave yourself!" she said, feet braced apart, ready to run if necessary.

"I am behaving. The best way I know how." He grinned at her wary stance, which only made her madder. Realizing he would accomplish nothing with her defenses raised, his voice dropped to a cajoling tone. "Come back over here and we'll talk about it."

"I do not talk well in a supine position," she retorted, her mouth set in a firm line and an angry sparkle in her eyes.

"I won't seduce you here on the open sand."

"Your word," she demanded, leery of coming near him.

"I promise, now come here." He reached out a supplicant arm, and Acadiana began to walk toward him cautiously. As soon as she got close enough, Jonas swung her up in his arms and planted a devilish kiss on her lips. She kicked and squirmed, flailing her arms about wildly in an attempt to wiggle free.

"You are dishonorable! You promised!" she said against his mouth, her words coming out as more of a muffled rasp.

"A promise under duress . . ." he said with a grin.

"What duress?" she argued. Despite her helpless position, it was impossible to maintain a high level of animosity while looking into his smiling eyes. There was no threat there now, no heated desire, just brilliant laughing blue. *Devastating.*

Jonas tightened his hold. He liked the way she felt in his arms when she wasn't struggling, the lilt in her voice and the sparkle in her eyes when she wasn't overly furious.

"Just the sight of you, love. It makes all thoughts of chivalry fly."

Acadiana rolled her eyes at the ridiculous flirtation and sighed. "If you expect me to hold to my word of honor, then I must assume the same from you."

"Agreed. You will be most willing to marry me when we get back, and I will agree to leave you alone on this sandy beach," he said, placing her on her feet. He kept his hands on her shoulders and leaned forward to gaze into her eyes. "I will wait until we camp tonight to work my evil wiles on you."

Jonas backed away quickly as Acadiana wrenched herself from beneath his fingers and grabbed a piece of driftwood. He could tell by the gleam in her eyes that she was intent on using it as a club if he got within arm's reach of her. He tried to snuff a grin as he held up his hands in surrender and waited for her to relinquish the weapon.

Acadiana glared at him for a moment, assessing their situation, then spoke in a barely audible voice.

"I will ride all night to get back to Providence if you do not give me your word that you will not try to . . . to . . . you know what I mean."

"I know what you mean," Jonas echoed with as much sincerity as he could muster while watching her stand there as if she could take on a whole army all by herself—and win.

Acadiana propped the weathered gray stub of wood on her shoulder and glowered at him. The Mississippi churned behind her in murky brownish-gray swirls, and Jonas wondered which was more turbulent, the restless river or the rebellious beauty standing there so defiant, so determined to hold on to an innocence that she would lose in less than a week's time. He didn't understand that fierce loyalty to herself. She flaunted convention at every turn with her hidden life-style. She obviously had no great love for society-enforced restrictions. Why then was she so unwilling to defy those standards now? He had always taken his pleasure with women freely, with no regrets. True, he had stayed away from the innocents. They expected too much in return for a night of indiscretion. But he had offered Acadiana marriage, and he knew she was not unmoved by his touch. Although she had fought him with every ounce of strength, he had sensed her own desire rising along with his when he had tried to seduce her.

If he had to wait until their wedding night, he supposed he could stand it, but what if she didn't come to him willingly then? He would just have to continue to court and woo her until his persistence and the natural desires within her overpowered her resistance. He could play the attentive suitor if it afforded him the glorious commingling he knew would unite them.

He stared back at Acadiana then bowed elegantly before her. "I concede defeat. When we camp tonight I will be a perfect gentleman, attentive in every way except one. Of course, if you change your mind about that . . . uh . . . act, you will let me know, won't you?"

Acadiana felt her cheeks pinken and stubbornly refused to lower her eyes. When he made no move toward her, she shrugged her shoulders and let the weapon drop slowly to the sand. She had been at his mercy last night, and as horribly as he had behaved he had not pressed her beyond endurance. She didn't think he would now. She walked over to Shawnee and took her leather pouch from around his neck. Taking a deep, relieved breath, she absently rubbed the hide against her cheek, then took out her canteen and drew a refreshing drink. Jonas stepped up behind her and fingered the soft tanned bundle. He had noticed over the past two days how she coddled and cared for the pouch lovingly as if it were something of great value.

"This is special to you," he stated, wondering if she would divulge its contents and the sentimental attachment she felt for the simple object.

Acadiana just stared at him and tried to drag it out of his reach. Jonas tightened his grip and refused to relinquish it.

"Let go," she said coldly, daring him to deny her right of possession.

"What special meaning does this hold for you?" he asked, a touch of irrational jealousy stabbing him.

She would not accept him and all that he was offering her, yet she kept this wretched thing close to her side as if it held all the riches of the world within its weather-bleached folds. Jonas pulled more firmly on the leather thongs and slipped it from her fingers. He then raised it high over his head out of her reach.

Acadiana stared up at him for for a long, agonizing moment with a look so akin to hatred that Jonas wondered at the folly of his action. She stretched her arm to the sky, assessing the distance between her and the beloved pouch. Jonas towered over her, a hint of challenge in his smile. Her outstretched hand could barely reach the top of his head. She brought the inadequate appendage down to her side and backed away slowly, her eyes never leaving the dangling hide. Jonas watched perplexed as she took several long strides back, then stopped and scrutinized the water. After several seconds Acadiana tensed her lips and emitted a shrill whistle. Not the lilting melody Jonas had heard her whistling when she worked around the campsite, but a high-pitched skirl, an unintelligible cry for help.

Shawnee perked his ears at the command and flew toward Acadiana like the winged creature of mythology Jonas had once likened him to. The horse never slowed a step as he approached, and Acadiana ran apace then leapt onto his back as nimbly as a sprite. Guiding the mount with her knees, she directed him toward Jonas. In a fleeting motion, she snatched the baggage from his hand and sped down the sandbar.

Jonas stood amazed as she veered off through the woods, holding the leather pouch to her chest. He quickly mounted his sturdy companion and gave chase, but Acadiana was long gone by the time he reached the forest.

Stretched out on her bedroll, Acadiana stared at the stars twinkling in the heavens. Heat lightning streaked the sky at intervals, illuminating the wooded area momentarily in a hazy glow. She was lulled into a trance as she listened to the night sounds—a croaking bullfrog, buzzing mosquitoes, an occasional possum or armadillo rooting around on the ground. She loved the night sounds. They gave her a feeling of belonging, comforted and soothed her, took the edge off her jagged emotions. This was contentment, peace. She would never find this married to Jonas Courtland. He wanted to break her as he would a lively filly kicking its heels to the world. She might have to marry him to keep her land, but he would never break her spirit, she vowed.

She was Sun-Child, adopted daughter of the great chief, child of the Kadohadacho tribe of the Caddo. The Caddo farmed the land, acted as middlemen for many nations, and hunted the buffalo. Their spirit was hers, and she would never be tamed. She was Acadian, raised of the swamps, trapper, farmer, outcast of the aristocratic Creoles, child of the bayou. This too was her spirit, and it would never be tamed.

Acadiana snuggled down, a lonesome smile haunting her lips as she thought of the sapphire eyes and arrogant smile of her oppressor. He was a fine specimen of a man with his broad, muscular shoulders and tight, flat waist, but she had met many handsome men, and none of them had been able to turn her from her chosen assignment in life. This man would be no different.

She would reach Providence tomorrow. With any luck, she would be able to talk Uncle Grayson out of this insane idea of marriage, and go on about her life as before . . . wondering how she would find a way to rebuild her plantation.

Jonas found her like this, star-gazing, a bemused expression on her face. He tethered his horse and walked over to crouch by the fire, sorting through several thoughts that had occurred to him on the long ride to catch up with her. Did her misgivings about their marriage have something to do with someone else? Did she harbor an affection for some young man who had captured her heart in a way no other could? Jonas glanced over at small form huddled beneath the blanket. Whatever her reasons, whatever her past, her future was with him. The sooner she resigned herself to that fact, the better off she would be. He stared at the flames awhile longer before stretching out beside her. Acadiana cast him a wary glance, then reached beneath her blanket and pulled out her dagger. She pointed the sharp blade at him and spoke so softly he had to strain to hear her.

"If you make one improper advance toward me, I will not hesitate to use this."

Jonas chuckled. A deep sound that was beginning to infuriate her even as it stirred a dormant place within her. Everything about him was unsettling to her. He turned on his side and lightly touched the weapon. "Acadiana, you know I could disarm you, but I won't. If it makes you feel secure to keep the dagger, then hold on to it. Just make sure I don't roll over on it during the night."

She refused to rise to the bait. "Consider yourself warned," she said.

"Warning taken. Now go to sleep before I change my mind."

Acadiana huddled under her blanket, a blank expression on her face. She would be safe this night, but what of the next and the next and the next?

7

Grayson Hamilton was in a fit by the time his niece galloped into the yard. Never in her life had Acadiana been subjected to a tongue lashing like the one she received upon dismounting. Her uncle immediately set the wedding for three days hence and would not listen to her pleas for clemency. Nor would he comment on her allegations, almost graphic, about Jonas's untoward behavior. He couldn't. Grayson's eyes just got wider, his face grew redder, until Acadiana thought he was going to explode.

To compound the problem, Jonas stood by with a smug look on his face, knowing Acadiana's accusal would backfire. He didn't bother to deny a thing, which only strengthened Grayson's decision to see them wed. His eyes wounded and angry, the veins popping out on his neck, Acadiana's uncle declared that she was still his ward, and he would do what he thought best for her if he had to lock her in her room until the ceremony was over! The fact that she had spent two nights alone with a man had sealed her fate far better than anything he could have done to see her wed.

Frantic now, Acadiana searched the faces of her family. Aunt Elizabeth kept her eyes downcast; Katherine wrung her handkerchief. Neither would look at her nor offer their support. She could feel the desperation clutching at her insides. For her aunt and cousin, who had been raised by a strict code of behavior, it was a matter of what was proper now. No one would dispute her uncle's decision.

Grayson grabbed her shoulders. For all his ire, he was tender when he pulled her to him, but there was a pinched look around his mouth.

"I love you like a daughter, girl," he said in a constricted voice. His shoulders slumped, as if defeated, and his eyes were full of pain as he searched Acadiana's face. "But I can't control you. Mr. Courtland obviously can by the fact that he found you and brought you back. He has seen your temper and your unruliness, and he still wants to marry you."

"He just wants my land!" Acadiana cried. "Can't you see that?"

Grayson shut his eyes and closed his ears to block out her pleading. If he listened, he would give in. Maybe he loved her too much, for even knowing what was best for her, he couldn't bear seeing Acadiana so distraught.

"Charles has told me that Jonas is a good man and an honest one. Please understand why I am doing this, girl. I've got an obligation to your mother and father, and an obligation to do the best I know to do for you."

Acadiana glanced around her once again, struggled to force acceptance of her plight from her aunt and cousin. All was lost. By their silence, she knew that they supported her uncle's decision.

"Aunt Elizabeth? Katherine?" she whispered in a last, valiant effort. When they wouldn't comment or even lift their heads to look at her, Acadiana whirled to face Jonas, mutiny flashing from her violet eyes. "Tell them!" she demanded. "Tell them nothing happened!"

Jonas stood by in stony silence, but his eyes bore into hers. Sell the land to me, they glinted ruthlessly, and I will straighten this mess out for you. *Sell me the land!*

With a cry, Acadiana jerked free of Grayson's hands and

darted for her horse. Jonas caught her just as she meant to mount Shawnee and held her until her uncle reached them.

"I'm just going to Jean's!" she cried, struggling for freedom in her tormentor's arms while squeezing back the hot tears that betrayed her helplessness. "I swear it! I'll be back before dark."

Grayson nodded for Jonas to let her go before he spoke. "I have to believe you, child. You've done plenty, but you've never lied to me." Saying that, he turned his back in what Jonas saw as a foolish display of trust and forced his feet to drag him back to the house.

As Jonas watched Acadiana's slender form easily mount the skittish horse, he felt the first inkling of remorse for his part in the rift between Acadiana and her uncle. The older man's shoulders were hunched beneath his coat, his head bowed as he slowly made his way back to the house. Jonas let his gaze wander back to Acadiana as she set her heels to the horse's sides and galloped toward the woods. Her raven hair streamed out wildly behind her, her back rigid as the stately cypress trees that she approached with reckless haste. Jonas felt the sudden, burning urge, like a hot coal settling in the pit of his stomach, to follow her, to make sure she did not escape him despite the fact that her uncle so trusted her to return.

He was just turning to follow his inclinations when a small, delicate hand touched his sleeve. "Let her go," Elizabeth said softly, entreating him with liquid blue eyes and a sadly sweet smile. "Jean is an old friend of hers. Cade can confide things to him that she would never tell Grayson and me for fear of upsetting us." At Jonas's skeptical look she continued in a confident tone. "She will be back, you know. She has given her word."

Elizabeth could see that Jonas was leery of believing her, but she knew Cade as well as anyone could know her, wrapped up as her niece was within the decaying shroud of an ill-gotten past so that she was not apt to let anyone too close. She linked her arm through his and began a gentle tugging until he, unwilling to be rude to this gentle lady, began to walk with her back to the house.

He turned his head to catch the last glimpse of the slight figure before the trees swallowed her up like huge sentries standing guard over their mistress. In his mind there was remorse for cornering her and using her family to gain the land, but his body loudly proclaimed a need that had nothing to do with his desire for the fertile soil that was her inheritance. There would be a reckoning to pay, he knew, for forcing her to marry him, but in that instant Jonas knew he must have her at any cost.

A note was dispatched to Courtland Manor, announcing the wedding and subsequent arrival of Jonas and his new bride. As Jonas composed the note, he sincerely hoped Minette would have time to simmer down before meeting Acadiana. Things would be difficult enough without the added antagonism that was sure to erupt between the two headstrong women.

Acadiana rose dreary and sullen despite the day, which dawned bright and cheery. The staff of the Hamilton house had worked themselves into a fevered pitch getting ready for the wedding. It was to be a small affair, for Acadiana had insisted that the ceremony be performed at home with only the immediate family present to witness her downfall, but her aunt and uncle wanted everything to be perfect for their niece. Acadiana let them make all the arrangements. She wanted no part of the preparations, let alone the marriage.

She had spent the last three days in agony, devising then discarding plan after plan that might gain her release from this commitment. She could find no way out without destroying her relationship with her uncle, whom she loved fiercely even in the midst of her anger. Refusing to leave her room, Acadiana had seen nothing of Jonas, which was to his credit, for she was not sure she could contain the violent hatred that engulfed her every time she heard his voice drifting up like smoke from belowstairs to choke her.

By the third day, Acadiana had resigned herself to the fact that she must marry Jonas Courtland, but she would never be a wife to him. Never! With every ounce of strength within her, she would withhold those most vulnerable parts of herself from him. The love and devotion of a wife, the intimacies of the marriage bed that she would not, could not think about without shuddering, these would she withhold from Jonas in fear and retribution for forcing her into marriage. He would regret his ruthless determination to get her land, as she now regretted and cursed the day she had met him.

Acadiana sulked around her room and waited for Pearlene. She had been pampered, petted, powered, pulled, and pushed, and she had had enough! Having bathed herself for nigh on twenty years, she didn't need someone else to scrub her skin until it glowed and place fragrant scents in the most unspeakable places. If they presumed Jonas Courtland would ever get close enough to catch a whiff of those dainty areas, they needed to be educated to the contrary! She had finally forced everyone from the room with a most unladylike tantrum, proclaiming she didn't care how she looked for her mock wedding.

But it wouldn't be a mockery; Jonas had seen to that. He had insisted on having a priest preside over the ceremony, just in case she wished to expound later that it had not been legal in the sight of God. Oh, he was a wretched man! Never had she had to resort to schemes or playing on the emotions of her family to get her way, but he thwarted her contrivances at every turn. Nothing she could say or do would detour him from this wicked mission.

She flopped herself into a chair and waited for her wedding gown. In her present mood, she would just as soon marry in sackcloth. Aunt Elizabeth had promised a surprise to lighten her niece's spirits, but Acadiana thought no surprise in the world could lift her from the mire she had bogged herself in.

Well aware of Acadiana's glum mood, Pearlene stepped into the room tentatively. Elizabeth followed with a freshly laundered gown of antique-white silk draped over her arm. Acadiana peered at the gown in growing confusion at its vague familiarity. She raised questioning eyes to her aunt and rose to touch the soft folds.

" 'Twas your mother's, darling," Elizabeth said softly, "and her mother's before her. Do you remember when you and Katherine used to rummage through the old trunks in the attic?"

"Oui," Acadiana breathed. A look of longing passed her eyes, turning them a soft lavender. "I do remember this gown. I didn't know it was *Maman*'s."

"It is for you now, on this most special day," Elizabeth said simply. "It is time."

Acadiana contained her emotions while they helped her into the gown, but when her toilette was complete, she begged a moment alone. As soon as Elizabeth ushered Pearlene out of the room, Acadiana fell on the bed in a torrent of tears.

"Oh, *Maman,"* she cried, pouring out her anguish into the soft downy coverlet. "I should not be marrying in this gown! It is not right; this gown is sacred. Your life with Papa was based on true love, not some farce acquisition of land. I am so sorry for the mockery I am about to make of your most beloved possession."

Even as Acadiana poured her heart out, she knew her words were more self-pity than truth. No lifeless object had been the center of Elaine's life. It had been the people connected with those possessions that had held her love.

Acadiana dragged herself from the bed and went to stand before the window. Swaying gently, the curtains floated into the room and carried the smell of sunshine and Aunt Elizabeth's roses. Acadiana pushed them aside to see a blue jay chirping at its young one. A horse whinnied from the stables; the wind soughed plaintively through the trees. The sounds of nature—these had comforted her in times past. Not today. This day there was no relief for the girl about to pledge her life away to an arrogant, strong-willed man.

Acadiana turned to the full-length mirror and smoothed the silken dress with hands that trembled. It was a simple gown with none of the extravagance of the more modern fashions. It had a scooped neck and was cut with slender lines that tapered down to her hips where it ended in a V. The skirt flowed out over modest *panniers*. The delicate lacy sleeves were puffed to the elbow, then fitted with pearl buttons to Acadiana's tiny wrists. On her feet were eggshell satin slippers. Having no jewelry of her own, a borrowed string of Aunt Elizabeth's pearls graced her neck. Her sleek, dark hair had been swept up away from her face and hung in free flowing, wispy curls all about her shoulders, then tumbled down her back in silken waves. Small white flowers were woven throughout the coiffure, encircling her head in a wreath.

"This is so unfair!" she cried piteously to her reflection. "I should be marrying for love!"

Acadiana didn't know what married love entailed where one's feelings were concerned, but she knew it wasn't this resentment, this slow, consuming hatred. She spun away from the mirror and pressed the heels of her hands to her eyes to stop the insistent burning.

"I don't need the man that waits below. I need a partner, a companion, a friend! I need . . ." Her words died softly in a pool of tears as she thought of the fruitlessness of her yearning. Jonas would never be those things to her. He wanted to own her, to tame her, and in many ways he had already won, but in the winning he would also lose, for she would never sell herself for the price of her land.

She took a deep breath and set her chin in a show of defiance, then walked to the door to await her signal. The pianist was playing a soft tune as the family took their places. Uncle Grayson met Acadiana and took her arm.

She studied Jonas as she glided down the stairs. He was a vision of masculinity in his black formal attire, the long-tailed coat perfectly tailored to enhance his virile strength. The white ruffled shirt with its lace cuffs did nothing to soften the appearance of the stunning man.

Jonas watched as Acadiana descended the stairs with measured caution, the essence of gracefulness and beauty. He felt his body stir painfully until she drew closer and he could see the contempt that was directed solely for him etched along her piquant features. Coolly his gaze swept her with a critical eye for detail as he took in her dark curls, pale face, and slender yet ripe figure. They would have beautiful children, he thought without an ounce of the remorse he had been feeling over the past few days. A cynical smile curved his lips upward as he thought of the means toward that end.

Reading his thoughts clearly as she looked into his burning eyes, Acadiana's knees felt as if they would collapse beneath her as she approached him, and her mind whirled chaotically. What if she reneged? What if she simply refused to answer the priest? Uncle Grayson's shame would be unbearable. All his plans and hopes for her future, the years of tireless dedication to his brother's child. She could not do it—could not deliver the *coup de grâce* that would end this.

It was over. All her dreams for a future of her own making diminished. Like the feeble light from a swiftly melting candle, her dreams flickered bravely then died. Acadiana turned to face Jonas with one last, bleak stare that was more a plea for help before giving her attention to the priest. Jonas also turned to face the Father, and their vows were spoken clear and resonant before God and man. The dainty gold band, feeling as weighty as prison shackles to Acadiana, was slipped on her finger, sealing them together for a lifetime.

Jonas's kiss, pressed against cold, unresponsive lips as he stared into her equally icy eyes, promised more than Acadiana was willing to accept. His palm was flattened against her rigid back to keep her from jerking away, but she didn't move. She wouldn't embarrass her aunt and uncle before the parish priest, who undoubtedly thought this a happy occasion. Acadiana allowed Jonas's lips to move over hers with tender aggression while she remained frozen beneath his mouth and hands out of regard for her family. It would be the last kiss he would ever take from her, she vowed silently, and hoped she could fulfill that promise.

The reception following the ceremony passed in a numb sort of haze for Acadiana until Jonas walked up and took her arm. He had bided his time as patiently as possible, but the time was quickly slipping away. The journey ahead would take more than a week, and he didn't wish to tarry longer than necessary. Neither, he noted ruefully, did he wish to spend his wedding night under the watchful eyes of Acadiana's guardians. He made no mistake in assuming the night ahead would be filled with marital bliss. But with gentle persuasion . . .

He led Acadiana away from the others so they would not be overheard and whispered in her ear. "It's time to change. Do you need any help?"

"Go away," she said coldly. "You have what you want now. Why don't you just go and leave me here?"

"I don't have *all* that I want . . . yet," he said, his impatience to be gone overriding his compassion for the pale young woman standing before him. "What about you? Don't you want to see the land again that you've fought so desperately to keep?"

"Oui," Acadiana said slowly. "I do want to see it, but this price was almost too high."

Jonas cocked an eyebrow at her remark then motioned her toward the stairs. "Almost, *chérie,* but not quite."

Acadiana fled his presence and retreated to her bedroom to change. Katherine was waiting to help her slip into a high-waisted gown of eau-de-nil silk muslin with a small ruff collar of cream-colored lawn. Acadiana thought it a ridiculous gown for traveling, but Aunt Elizabeth had insisted on providing her with a trousseau befitting any new bride. She had worked day and night to complete garments she had already begun sewing for her niece and altering others lovingly donated by Katherine.

As she patted the gown in place, Katherine blushingly tried to reassure Acadiana that the first night with Jonas wouldn't be that bad. Acadiana listened to none of it. In her mind, there wouldn't be a first night—or any night, for that matter. Katherine finally threw her hands up in exasperation and went below to wait with her mother.

Jonas paced impatiently by the packhorse and carriage provided by Grayson and listened to the numerous farewells. He finally took Acadiana by the arm and settled her inside the conveyance before another spate of well-meaning advice could be given. The plantation roads would allow them to travel by carriage for portions of the journey, but mostly they would be restricted to horseback, then river transportation, as there were no suitable roads for wheeled vehicles. Acadiana pushed back the leather curtain and stared out the opening, her heart breaking as her family faded from sight. She found no comfort in the balmy morning or the man, now husband, handling the reins. She sank down in the seat, closing her eyes against fresh tears, and faded into a despondency.

Within hours, she felt hot and irritable cooped up inside the swaying carriage and was relieved when they left it at the last plantation to travel by horseback. Tired of Acadiana's glum mood, Jonas had said little to her since the noonday meal. He would rather brave her waspish tongue than this dark depression that seemed to be hovering over her.

The air was sticky and hung about Acadiana in layers. Perspiration trickled down her back, and tiny beads formed on her face. She pressed a handkerchief to her forehead for what seemed like the hundredth time, then tried to fan herself. This served only to stir up the already too-warm air.

She noted with resentment that Jonas did not seem to be suffering overmuch. How could he look so impeccably dressed even after discarding his coat—something a man never did in the presence of a lady, no matter how hot it was. Of course, she had already seen him in a lot less, and she had never been called a lady except by Aunt Elizabeth, who refused to see the bad in anyone.

Acadiana surreptitiously studied Jonas as he handled his horse. The muscles of his arms flexed beneath his cambric shirt as he gripped the reins, sending a tickle of fear along her own arms as she compared the meager size of them to his powerful strength. Her eyes drifted down to his superb waist and hips, his fit thighs as his body adapted itself to the rhythm of his horse's gait. She fanned her face more rapidly as the heat rose to her cheeks when she realized where her wayward thoughts were leading. She would not lie beneath that strong body and give herself to him in the way Katherine had described to her. The thought was reprehensible!

A man has needs, Katherine had said.

I will not live like a monk, from Jonas.

Acadiana could not stay with the stifling, slow-moving pace another second with only her blameworthy imagination for company. She needed to stop and stretch or to gallop full force into the wind, something ill advised since the horses had been traveling most of the day. She called to Jonas, and he pulled his mount to a halt.

"When do we stop for the night?" she asked.

"Wife," he teased. "I didn't realize that you were so eager for the bridal chamber."

"Beast!" she huffed, and, in a state of supreme agitation, kicked her horse forward.

Jonas chuckled as he caught up with her. "Would you like to stop this early?" Sapphire eyes glowed in the tanned face as they swept over his shapely wife. The glint of appreciation dimmed as he took in the miserable droop of her shoulders and the drenched handkerchief clutched in her tiny hands. His wife. The word ambled around oddly in his mind, finding no footing, had been odder still on his tongue. For all its foreignness, she *was* his wife, under his protection now. He frowned at the thought of her enduring the heat without complaint. He wouldn't treat his servants this way, yet he had let his temper override good sense by allowing her to sulk in silence. His eyes rose to meet hers, and he offered his hand to help her down.

Swallowing her pride, Acadiana ignored his outstretched arm as she scrambled down and headed for shade. She stood by a small lake, the surrounding landscape a blur of color that lifted her mood. The wind played through her hair, cooling the back of her neck and setting the expertly dressed coiffure in sad disarray. Abandoning all pretense of maidenly decorum, she shook the few remaining pins free and tied the rebellious curls back with a strip of lace from her petticoat. Her spirits absorbed the beauty of the earth and sky as her eyes roamed over fields of cotton stretching across the land in fluffy white splendor. The ground was rich dark delta soil nourished by the floodwaters of the Mississippi River. The only land of comparable value anywhere in the world was that along the Nile. Truly this was sacred ground that God had seen fit to bestow on farmers brave enough to tame the wildness of the territory. And she felt a part of it—heart, mind, and soul.

Tall pines stood majestically with their prickly needles carpeting the ground below. Sturdy oaks graced the water's edge, their gray beards of Spanish moss dripping from the limbs to tease a passerby. Their coolness beckoned.

Acadiana ignored Jonas as she wandered aimlessly. He was exasperated yet amused at her stubbornness, drawn to the rebellious spirit within her as a stallion is to a mare. In the heat of battle for supremacy and the continuation of the herd, the stallion usually won. Usually. But there were no hard and fast rules in this life that couldn't be altered. It would behoove him in the days to come, he felt, to go slowly with Acadiana, to give her time to adjust to her new life.

Silently he studied her as she reclined against a pine tree and turned a cone over and over in her gloved hands as if to study its making. The waning afternoon sun cast soft shadows along her delicate cheekbones and lingered there in mauve highlights that complemented the lavender glow of her eyes beneath her lowered lashes. She looked almost pathetically alone, her slender figure curled against the tree trunk, a look of sad longing on her face.

But Jonas knew all too well the fire the lay beneath that quiet exterior, a fire that would erupt without the slightest provocation. And the plans he had for the night ahead would give her provocation aplenty. He walked over and stared down at her pensive face to assess her temperament before squatting down beside her.

"We stop for the night in a few hours, love. Are you prepared for the evening?"

Acadiana lifted her head and looked at him in bewilderment for a second as she tried to dispel the melancholy dulling her senses. Like a slap in the face, his insinuation struck her full force. Her soft eyes darkened to a stormy violet and she fought to control her voice when she spoke.

"I will never be prepared for another night with you," she managed calmly.

"Nevertheless, will it be a night to remember?" A slight quirk twitched his lips as he tried to hide a smile.

"I think not," Acadiana said sweetly, a strange glow lighting her eyes and shadowing her smile, "unless the feel of cold steel against your ribs is something you wish to remember."

"Never that," he chuckled. His voice lowered, became seductive, compelling, as did the look in his eyes. "I would much prefer the feel of your warm flesh next to mine."

Acadiana gave a start at his boldness. Vivid scarlet flared across her cheeks, then settled to a dull red. With immense control she composed herself and stared back at him.

"Would you have the forest devour your screams of terror as my dagger pierces your black heart?" she asked softly.

"I think not," he taunted, mocking her own words. "Perhaps it will be your lusty cries of passion that are heard as I truly take you for my wife."

"Oh!" Acadiana exclaimed, aghast. Burning crimson rode high on her cheeks again, and her jaw tightened.

Smiling in the face of her outrage, Jonas lifted her chin with his forefinger to stroke her soft ruby mouth, then drew back when she swiped furiously at his hand. He thought of the meek, docile debutantes Minette Courtland had paraded before him. Never would they send such scathing looks his way as Acadiana was doing. They would have lowered their lashes in blushing response, and just as pliantly they would have yielded to him on the wedding night. He would get no such response here. Still, he goaded Acadiana, if for no other reason than to see her eyes flare with so much fire that it resembled passion.

"Careful, love, your temper is showing. I know you are anxious for my bed, even if you are too shy to admit it, but we should take advantage of the daylight for travel. Be patient until tonight. I promise it will be worth the wait."

Acadiana spat and sputtered explosively but could not manage to get the words out as Jonas strutted away arrogantly. She seethed for the remainder of the day. The miles truly seemed to fly by now as the time brought her closer and closer to the evening ahead. The thought of what was to come hung over her like an ever-present storm cloud, marking her passage with foreboding. Acadiana set her jaw firmly in determination. He had her land now; he would get nothing more. She had not sold herself for his night of pleasure. How could he expect her to fulfill that wifely obligation when there was nothing but animosity between them? It mocked all that was holy!

Too soon the sun began to drop below the treetops, bathing the land in a greenish glow as it reflected the embellished foliage. To make camp, Jonas chose a spot that was less overgrown than most of the surrounding area and near a small lake. Although it was not necessary, Acadiana gathered wood for a fire. She needed something to occupy her hands and keep her mind from wandering to the night at hand. Jonas tethered the horses near a lush cropping of grass before turning to the fire he had already started. He then cooked a pot of beans flavored with salt pork and warmed a pan of biscuits left over from lunch. The meal was simple yet filling as they ate in the solitude of the forest.

When Jonas was done eating, he strung twine between two trees and draped a blanket over the string. Acadiana eyes darted suspiciously between him and the makeshift wall.

"To preserve your modesty," Jonas said dryly. "Unless you're willing to strip down in front of me."

Acadiana stared back at him belligerently.

"I thought not."

"I will sleep in my clothes," she ventured bravely, although by now she was quite unsure of herself. What a wretched night this would be, garbed in stockings, chemise, pantalets, corset, petticoats, and dress.

"And will you bathe in your clothing?" Jonas asked with a sardonic lift of his brow as he pointed to the lake.

Acadiana knew a moment of indecision as she stared at the peaceful water that beckoned to her. Its glassy surface was broken only by the moonlight that streamed down in silvery rays across the still water. The lake looked so inviting, and she was so dirty . . .

"I can't . . . I . . ." she stammered.

"There is no one here, Acadiana. You are well protected."

"Who will protect me from you?" she asked caustically.

"I am your husband," he began, but seeing her obvious discomfort, he took a more lenient tone of voice. "You have that wretched hide with you. I assume you brought your Indian clothes. If it makes you more comfortable, bathe in them."

Acadiana lifted her chin haughtily. "I won't don the Indian clothes again until I am assured of escaping the white man."

Jonas began to laugh. He couldn't hold it back, even though he knew it would make her more furious. She wasn't as big as a minute but had more than enough courage to compensate for her slight stature. Her remarks, though biting at times, were a measure of her intelligence, which he had to respect.

"I will turn my head this time," he said solicitously. "There will be time for us later."

Acadiana glared angrily at his smiling face and stepped behind the blanket to remove her dress. She had a dickens of a time unfastening, unlacing, and untying, but never in a lifetime would she have asked for his help. Her task finally complete, she wrapped herself in a blanket and strode to the pond.

"Jonas," she called tentatively from the water, hating her forgetfulness more than him at the moment. "I forgot the soap."

"I am not supposed to turn around, remember?" he said playfully.

"I am covered" came a disgruntled reply.

"How regrettable," he murmured, then turned to hand her the fragrant bar. He stopped in amusement as the water swirled away from her shoulders, and he glimpsed a sodden chemise floating up. "Lord," he muttered under his breath, "she's bathing in her underclothes."

He tossed her the hand-rolled soap, then shook his head as she began lathering her arms and face. He turned his back to her again and pondered his situation. Somewhere between the ride back from the wilderness and the wedding, Jonas realized, he had lost the half-naked Indian maiden. Oh, the fire was still there, the savage defiance, but this maidenly modesty was something he had not counted on. It was a sobering thought and one he did not wish to dwell on.

Acadiana was soon finished. The night air was chilly as it

caressed her almost-naked flesh, and she wrapped the blanket snugly around her as she stepped from the water. She hurried back behind the partition, then stopped in dismay. What would she wear to sleep in? She could not possibly wear one of those filmy nightdresses Aunt Elizabeth had packed. She shivered under the blanket as she berated herself for bathing in her undergarments. *Mon Dieu,* you fool! The things that man caused her to do! He muddled her brain until even the simplest of things became monumental tasks.

Jonas, standing patiently on the other side of the blanket, noted her sigh of desperation, accurately guessed its cause, and handed over a soft flannel shirt.

"Will this do?"

"Merci," she said stiffly.

She quickly shed her wet underclothes and pulled the shirt over her head. The cuffs hung well below her fingertips and the tail reached to her knees, but it was warm and comfortable in the night air.

"Finished?" Jonas called.

"Oui," she mumbled, throwing the damp blanket around her waist to shield her bare legs—a ridiculous gesture in light of the fact that he had seen her in much less.

"Then I am going to bathe," he stated, lifting the blanket-wall to walk underneath. "I'll need that." He pointed to her wrap. "Oh, wife . . . you are welcome to watch."

Acadiana threw the blanket at his imperious face and scrambled beneath the covers of their bedroll. Jonas's deep, resounding laughter could be heard all the way to the lake, echoing through the silent woods until his head was well underwater.

Acadiana pulled the blanket over her head to block out the sound of his voice as he sang in a deep baritone the words to a tawdry barroom ditty. Not only was the man abominable, but he did not even pretend to be a gentleman! She clamped her hands more tightly over her ears. She had married a man who flaunted propriety at every turn. Much like herself, she had to admit, but above all else, she *acted* like a lady in the presence of others. She would not let him compromise her womanhood because of a few meaningless words spoken before a priest. She huddled under the covers and prayed that sleep would overtake her before he returned.

Jonas stared down at his wife and again the word *strange* came to mind in regard to her. She was not the sort of woman he would have chosen in his youth, when he used to think of such things. But then a wedding night spent under the stars with a reluctant bride were not part of his plans then either. He watched her for some time before slipping under the blanket. Acadiana's feigned slumber did little to sway his intentions. This was his wedding night, after all. He had every legal right to take her as he desired. But morally he wasn't sure just what his rights were. Where did legal ownership end and moral obligation intrude? The crux of the matter lay in the fact that the bride, whom he had promised before God to love, honor, and cherish, was definitely not willing to be a wife to him.

Jonas had not determined exactly how he would go about this, and for a shattering moment he felt as nervous as that callow youth who had entertained lusty thoughts as he grew to manhood.

"Damn," he swore beneath his breath as he gathered her in his arms and pressed her back against his chest.

Acadiana knew the moment she had dreaded had arrived, and wondered how far Jonas would go to claim the rights of a husband. Knowing her strength was no match for his, she could only hope that a firm denial would reach some part of his black soul to stay him. She kept her eyes tightly closed and tried to calm her rapid breathing, all the while holding her body rigid. Unable to accomplish that, she moaned fretfully as if in the throes of a horrid nightmare.

Jonas chuckled at her feeble attempt at deception, his breath warm against her ear.

"Good try, love, but even if you were asleep, it wouldn't do you any good."

Acadiana rolled to face him, her fist clinched, her voice cutting the darkness to rebuke him. "I am warning you . . ."

In a twinkling, Jonas grabbed her wrist and held it until Acadiana felt her fingers tingle with numbness, then covered her protests with a kiss that left little of his purpose to the imagination.

Acadiana jerked her mouth free and penetrated the night with a cold, hate-filled gaze. *"Non,"* she rasped out, her bosom heaving as she gulped air. "Would you have me scream this forest down around your head?"

"Who is there to hear your cries?" Jonas said in a voice that was calm but coldly confident. "You are my wife. You would not be the first timid bride."

Acadiana knew her situation was hopeless. She felt trapped, betrayed by fate, her life once again out of her control. She stared at her husband with pleading eyes that were rapidly filling with tears.

"Please!" she cried. "I will die of shame!"

"You won't die," he cajoled. Jonas dropped his lips to hers softly, then pulled back. "There is no shame in a husband and wife—"

"I will not be your wife," Acadiana said frigidly, her stiff body giving testimony to the truth of her resolve.

Jonas growled an obscenity and cast her a vehement look. "Listen, Acadiana, this is not how I would have planned for us to spend our wedding night, but it can't be helped."

"Please," she whispered again, trembling now from the force of his words, the determination in his voice.

Jonas grumbled something else beneath his breath, then gripped her chin and pulled her face within a hairsbreadth of his. "If you need time, I'll go slowly. I'll tell you what I'm going to do so there won't be any surprises—"

Acadiana was shaking her head, almost frantically, hearing his words but trying not to. Jonas's fingers tightened on her chin to still the restless movement. The night sounds surrounded her, mocking in their call. The ground was hard beneath her, a twig poking into her back, but his fingers were harder still on her face. "You are hurting me," she whispered.

Jonas released her lest he leave bruises then sighed deeply, angry and frustrated, at a loss as to how to handle her and this untenable situation.

"I give you the next few nights for the innocence you wish to maintain, but understand this," he said, his voice unyielding, each word deliberate as if he would pound them into her head, "we will soon spend the night at an inn. Resign yourself to the fact that it will be our wedding night in every sense of the word. Do whatever you have to do to settle the matter in your own head, but have it settled before we reach our destination."

Jonas threw himself back and propped his arms behind his head as he gazed at the stars twinkling overhead. Acadiana turned onto her stomach and buried her face in her arms. Weeping softly, more in outrage than sorrow, she mourned the lack of control in her life. She had lost her brother, her parents, the Indians, and Jean. Now she had even lost her cousin, aunt, and uncle. For her entire life, it seemed, anything that offered a measure of security was eventually snatched out from under her.

Here she was again, left dangling in a dark void to grope her way toward the light. All that was left now was the land. And even that was under her husband's control.

He wanted to plant sugarcane, she thought, crying harder, but what if she chose rice or cotton? There was absolutely nothing she could do about it! With no money of her own, she was still at the mercy of his decision. She dug her face farther into her arms before her weeping could turn into full-blown wails of self-pity. He wanted children; she did not want him touching her and feared she would have no say so in that matter either. There would be no one to stop him when the time came. As her tears seeped through the arms of the flannel shirt, she thought of the house she had painstakingly designed and hoped to build one day— another dream dashed, like so many others of home, family, and a life of happiness. They were best forgotten, those dreams, lest they tear at her mind as they were doing her heart.

But Acadiana was not one to give up. Her dreams had been the life-sustaining force that had held her together over the turbulent years. With a last good sniff for the travails of womankind, she dammed the flood and rubbed away the evidence. She would find a way to gain back control of her life, she swore. She must!

Jonas listened to what seemed to be an endless rash of weeping and felt compassion for Acadiana despite his anger and frustration. He felt like the culprit of some evil deed perpetrated upon an innocent victim when all he truly wanted was to show this woman tenderness, to build a normal life with her. The land, which had been so important to him, now acted as the bane of his existence. It would ever be between them, he reasoned, because he had wanted it first. Foolish man that he was, he should have practiced the gentlemanly form of deceit and courted her and won her heart. Then the land would have been offered to him graciously, and the wife willing. But he would have her, he vowed. This unwillingness of hers was just one more obstacle to overcome, one more barrier to break through before he could reach the deep, passionate heart of her.

He waited until Acadiana's crying subsided, then gathered her back in his arms. Emotionally spent, she had no strength left to fight him and rested her head on his shoulder as she waited for him to speak. She knew something was forthcoming and hoped he had not changed his mind about this night. Jonas only sighed and waited for the sleep that eluded him. Finally he turned to face her and cupped her chin with strong but tender fingers. She shrank at his touch and fought to shake his hand away, but Jonas remained steadfast.

"What are you afraid of?" he asked, measuring each word carefully. "Is it me? Are you afraid that I will hurt you?" Even as he spoke, he knew his words were hollow. She had lived a rugged life for four years, suffering much worse hardships than what he had in mind. "Why do you fight me?"

"You don't love me," she said flatly. "It would be a mockery and a lie to pretend that things are as they should be. I would be selling myself for a piece of land."

"Don't be so childish, Acadiana. Love has little to do with this. We are married; that is enough."

"Not for me," she said, and rolled over onto her stomach.

"Soon, Acadiana," he warned, staring through the darkness at her stiff back. "If it's love you seek, then rest assured, I plan to love you well into the night."

Frustrated to the point that he feared he wouldn't be able to hold to his word until they reached an inn, Jonas turned away from her and attempted to block out her presence with sleep.

Acadiana rode beside her husband, yet absent, in no mood to brave his lighthearted wit or joking smile. But even when the heat grew stifling and the act of breathing seemed like a chore, she felt chilled to the bone for what lay ahead. Jonas stopped trying to tease her and draw her into conversation, but let her work the misgivings from her mind as the days wore on. It was best she come to terms in her own way with the life they would share.

Acadiana's spirits were brighter during the daylight hours as they traveled south toward Natchez. The trip was much more comfortable without the confinement of a hot carriage, so they disdained further use of them, and she began to recognize different landmarks in each area they passed through. For days they followed Indian trails as they crossed the countryside, Acadiana silent during the day, lying stiff and sullen beside Jonas at night. Although he had not tried to touch her again except to hold her as they slept, she could not shake the dread that overwhelmed her when she thought ahead of the night when their accommodations would not be limited to the stars and ground.

As they neared a settlement on the Mississippi, the bluffs of Natchez loomed across the river, threatening Acadiana with their overwhelming presence as did the husband who rode beside her. There would be no escape now. The settlement was a trading post and boasted an establishment where travelers could spend the night.

They ate dinner in silence in the dining room of the inn. When the last dish had been cleared, Jonas rose and sent Acadiana a look that reached deep down to wrench her heart, then summoned a servant to fetch water for her bath. She would have to face this thing sooner or later, but she burned with the pain of her helplessness and vulnerability, with the fear that her strength would not be enough.

To her surprise, Jonas retreated after escorting her to their room, leaving her with greatly appreciated privacy. But she bathed quickly, afraid that he would walk in any minute. After briskly drying herself with a rough towel, she donned the "special" nightgown she had been saving just for this occasion. She had rummaged throughout the slave cabins for just such a discarded masterpiece, finding it in the plantation storage shed. She smiled with revenge when she viewed herself in the full-length mirror. The gown, which resembled a sack, fastened high beneath her chin and extended down in tremendous folds to the floor. It was cut from a bolt of thick rough cloth that would have braved even the coldest winter's night and chafed her bare skin atrociously. She pulled her ebony curls severely away from her face in a bun and giggled at the awful transformation.

This is sure to stop him, she thought as she sat down primly to await her husband. Without a doubt, she looked more like a rejected spinster than a newly wedded bride.

8

Jonas returned in due time after having bathed elsewhere. A deep frown creasing his strong features, he placed two crystal goblets and a bottle of red wine on the bedside table. The wine was a gift from the innkeeper who, after taking one look at the bride's pale face, had told Jonas quite frankly that the small courtesy would not be amiss. Jonas had strangled back an angry setdown for the man's impertinence when visions of his ill-fated wedding night suddenly flashed before him, and he graciously if a bit stiffly accepted the gift. Turning to view his new wife, he stared aghast at the sight that greeted him.

"Damn you, Acadiana. What is *that?*" he growled in disgust, pointing an accusing finger at her apparel.

"What?" she asked, a wide-eyed and chaste look on her prim face.

"That . . . that thing!" he fumed, his eyes darkening to indigo at the sight. Jonas knew immediately what she was up to, but even with her hair pulled back like some elderly maiden aunt and her shapely curves hidden from neck to heel, she couldn't hide her eyes. They had captured him from the first and could not escape him now.

"This is my nightdress," she replied sweetly, fluttering

her lashes the way she had seen Katherine do countless times.

He leaned one shoulder against the bedpost and crossed his arms over his chest. "I did not marry a nun, and I am not taking one to bed. No, not even a nun would dress for bed in that wretched thing!"

"I do not know what you mean, *m'sieu*," she said pertly. Acadiana tilted her chin at an angle and stared at him with wide-eyed innocence.

Jonas's eyes narrowed to predatory slits, and his voice was low and threatening as he spoke. "You know exactly what I mean. Take it off."

"*Non,* I will not! It's not decent!"

"That degrading thing is not decent," he countered. "I mean it, Acadiana. Take it off, or I'll remove it for you."

"You wouldn't!" She gasped, her eyes growing into even larger amethyst orbs as her plan began to backfire.

"Just try me," he warned, walking toward her.

Acadiana sprang from the chair and dashed to the other side of the room. Slowly, patiently Jonas advanced until she realized she was about to be cornered. Cautiously she moved this way and that but he continued to sidestep her, preventing escape. She felt trapped as he slowly stalked her around the room. The more she backed up, the closer he moved. She rounded the table in the center of the room, her eyes wild, her heart hammering in her chest, and Jonas steadfastly followed.

With Acadiana's hands tracing one edge of the wooden obstruction between them and Jonas's on the other, they circled the table with slow, measured movements, their eyes glaring at one another, their breathing labored, each for different reasons. Unable to stand the tension building with each step, Acadiana darted behind a chair for protection, but it toppled as Jonas threw it aside and continued to advance. Panicked now, she ran for the door. Jonas cut her off and lunged forward, catching her around the waist in a grip of steel. In one sweeping motion, he tossed her onto the bed and threw himself on top of her.

Acadiana began to fight in earnest now, lashing out with arms and legs, her eyes flashing violet fury and fear. His weight atop her was suffocating, pressing her down into the sheet covering the feather-filled ticking until her blows were mostly ineffectual. Jonas avoided her strikes with a barrage of more intimate strategy, pinning her thighs with his, catching her delicate wrists. His hands moved over the rough fabric of her gown to suppress each thrashing curve, each misguided kick. His attempts to protect himself and subdue her finally resulted in his ripping the hated gown down the middle, sending hooks hurling across the room. After jerking the garment from her quivering frame, he tossed the offensive sack to the floor. Following that, amid more violent kicking and screaming, were the pantalets and chemise she had kept on underneath.

Acadiana's entire body convulsed and she drew herself into a tight ball to hide her nakedness. The pins in her hair were slung free in the struggle, and her ebony tresses spilled across her golden shoulders and the white bed linens, while her eyes flashed anarchy.

Jonas shook his head ruefully at her timid pose. The fight ebbed from her eyes, replaced by fear; her body trembled as she hugged her knees close to her chest to hide herself from him. The candlelight played over her shoulders and wild hair, causing Jonas's blood to flow hot and certain through his veins. He wanted to taste each sun-touched inch of her golden flesh, to clutch her rigid body to him and stroke each taut muscle until she lay pliant beneath him, to drink in the fresh scent of her still-damp hair where it curled invitingly about her slender hips. The fright on her face penetrated his drugged senses to lash his conscience, and it took every ounce of willpower that he could gather from the tortured edges of his mind to drag himself away.

He rose, never taking his eyes from hers lest she bolt and they have to begin again, to fetch the wine decanter and goblets. Returning to the edge of the bed, he sat down and poured her a glass.

"Drink this," he ordered as he stood to remove his own clothing. "You look like you need it."

Acadiana scrambled beneath the covers, then took the glass with trembling fingers. His frock coat was discarded as his eyes bore into hers; the waistcoat and shirt followed, revealing the broad, tanned shoulders that had haunted her since she'd seen them in the wilderness. When his strong hands reached for his breeches, Acadiana quickly averted her eyes from his magnificent physique and downed the wine in three gulps, then poured herself another glass. She drank the second just as quickly and reached for the bottle again. She had it raised to her lips when Jonas slipped the crystal from her fingers.

"Enough. You only need enough to calm your nerves, not addle your beloved brain," he rebuked. "Too much of this" —he waggled the glass in her face—"and you won't even remember this night."

Acadiana peeked at him from beneath her lowered lashes. His naked form seemed to drift and sway in and out of her vision. *"Mais oui,* I don't want to remember it," she said.

Never having had more than a few ounces of champagne in her life, she was unprepared for the effect of the spirits. She felt giddy and a little light-headed, as if she might float off the mattress. She clutched the covers more tightly to her chin as Jonas slipped into bed beside her.

Pressed next to her, his naked body felt lean and hard. The unfamiliar warmth of flesh meeting flesh sent shivers up her spine. She trembled involuntarily as he took her in his arms, pulling her toward him until she was lying on her side facing him.

"Cold, love?" he asked softly against her neck.

Cold was not how Acadiana was feeling at the moment. A fire burned through her veins, heightening the color of her cheeks. "How silly," she said, somewhat dazed, "to have a fire burning in the hearth this time of year."

"There's no fire, love, except in this bed," Jonas whispered as his mouth dropped to hers. Her lips were soft and incredibly sweet with fragrant traces of wine, her body sleek and taut where they touched. His fingers tensed, gripping her shoulders as he clamped an iron hand on his rampaging hunger. Slowly, go slowly, he commanded himself as his mouth moved over hers.

Acadiana pulled her lips free, pointing a slender finger at her assailant. *"M'sieu* Courtland, behave yourself." She blinked her coal lashes several times to stop his face from swimming before her.

"I am." He moaned. His senses were fired by the feel of her naked flesh pressed against his, her bare breasts pressing into his chest as she arched her head back to escape his lips. Hungry flames were licking their way down his spine to settle in his groin, too fast, too consuming for him to be gentle as he knew he must. He had waited for this too long, had lain beside her too many unfulfilled nights. He prepared his mind and body to meet her denial, her inevitable struggles, but he realized her slender legs weren't kicking as he had expected, but lay sleek and firm where they tangled with his. The hostility in her eyes had been replaced with a disoriented dullness. "I fear you've had too much wine."

"Non, I can still see you," she snapped.

Dazed but not undone, Jonas thought with satisfaction. Curiously he did not want to add trickery to further compound his manipulation of her. She would have grievances enough to hurl at him before the night was through. He disregarded her slight intoxication and began to attack slowly, savoring the touch, feel, and sweet smell of her. Her skin was like silk, smooth and rich. He wanted to wrap himself up in her, to feel her enfold him with arms and legs, to take him into the womanly heart of her where he could bury himself until she cried out with the same burning passion he was feeling.

Acadiana felt a heady anticipation as Jonas burrowed his face in her neck and his skillful fingers began kneading her shoulders, then worked their way down to the small of her back. His kisses were light on her throat and jaw as he worked his way toward her mouth. His tongue flicked her lips until they parted in denial, then absorbed the protest and invaded the moist inner warmth. His tongue retreated and he molded her mouth to his own, his strong white teeth nipping and tugging at her bottom lip until Acadiana's unconscious moan and the curling of her fingers against his chest caused him to plunder the sweet inside of her mouth again.

Acadiana knitted her brow in bemused consternation; this wasn't at all what she expected being ravished to feel like. This was soft and sweet and infinitely stirring. She didn't wholly like the way it was affecting her, all warm and liquid and draining. She opened her mouth wider to order him to cease, and he deepened the kiss until her mind was awhirl with new and strange sensations. She was left struggling within herself for a denial that seemed wont to go skittering away, just out of reach, though her mind grabbed for it. Her body moved restlessly beneath him, and the kiss deepened further still, until she seemed lost to do anything but return it out of curiosity, fitting her mouth to his and allowing his tongue to swirl around hers in a rhythmic dance that made her want to move her body in the same swaying tempo. She found herself becoming increasingly alarmed by the feelings his tongue and fingers were creating. A strange excitement fluttered within her breast, then surged deeper, making her heart skip and the innermost places of her body thrum like the plucked strings of a bow.

Slowly, insidiously the drugging effects of his kisses mingled with those of the wine to dissolve the last of her will and inclination to fight. His lips held her prisoner, demanding yet solicitous as they controlled hers, unyielding yet gentle, confusing her mind and body until she made a small strangled sound of pleading down deep in her throat.

Jonas ignored the sound, not wanting or willing to listen to her protests. He continued to kiss her possessively, chipping away at the years of armor with which she had surrounded herself. Generous in his giving and taking yet also subtle, he lightly began to run experienced hands over her flushed body, gently touching, stroking with agile fingers down her side, over her slender hip then back up again. Then carefully, because he knew beforehand that she would balk, he pulled her more closely to him and slid his hand up over her midriff to cup one rounded breast. His thumb rubbed back and forth across the rosy peak, teasing it until it answered his command and stood rigid.

Acadiana gasped in surprise as her body was jarred by sensations that coursed through her, so intimate, so fiery. Her fingers instinctively reached out to curl around his forearms, alternately pulling, then pushing at him as her confusion grew. Jonas dipped his head to take the source of her pleasure and chagrin into his mouth. Acadiana cried out and shied away instantly from this strange occurrence, twisting her upper torso and releasing his arms to push against his head. His sable hair was sleek against her hands, threading through her fingers like watered silk, almost robbing her of the desire to yank his head away from her breast. But she did pull as Jonas's tongue flicked and circled the tip. He reached up to stay her hands and began a gentle tugging, fitting his mouth to the puckered flesh and sucking until all Acadiana could do was sigh in heated wonder. His gentle but sure actions drew a sound from deep within her, and she moaned with newly awakening desire for something she could not fathom, could not grasp even as her fingers reached out to dig into the flesh of his shoulders.

The sound spurred Jonas on, the bite of her fingernails bringing more pleasure than pain. He left the boundaries of gentle persuasion and his kisses became hot, more demanding as hungry desire washed over him. His lithe fingers caressed her quivering body from the rapidly beating pulse at the base of her throat, drifted across her creamy breasts still moist from his mouth, and finally down to a more intimate region where he plied her womanly folds with insistence.

Her head swirling, almost mindless from the force of his seduction, Acadiana's eyes flew open at the invasion, and she was suddenly startled back into awareness. Her arms and legs went rigid; her fingers stopped their caress of his shoulders to grip his wrist, and she began tugging at his hand. Noting her reaction with dismay, Jonas quickly covered her body with his, his knee parting her thighs. Acadiana's eyes grew wide and she stiffened further as she felt him searching, probing for entrance. Panic surged through her at the thought of what was about to happen. She neither wanted him to continue nor, oddly, could she bear for him to stop.

"Jonas, wait!" she cried breathlessly. She didn't want to beg, but the frantic words escaped her mouth, born of a fear more deeply rooted than the new and langorous burning that had been ignited by his caress and even now consumed her entire being. She twisted her head to the side to escape his kiss, which, she sensed, would lead to the final and total possession of her. "Wait!" she cried out again.

"Nay, love," he said gruffly yet with compassion. "It's time."

"Jonas, please!" The words were ripped from her in a strained whisper as she realized the moment was at hand and she had not been able to stop it. She felt so torn by the traitorous conflict of body against mind. How easy it would be to accept her plight, to let him have a husband's way with her as was his due. The thought sent rebellion burning throughout her to replace the fires of passion he had ignited. He was not her husband by choice but by trickery, and his desire for her now was the base lust of a man for a woman. His real passion was for her land. This last she could understand; the other she would not tolerate, not while there was strength within her to fight him.

"Acadiana, relax," Jonas breathed against her frozen lips. "I don't want to hurt you. Let me be gentle." His hair-roughened thighs pushed steadily against the silken inside of hers, and the mere chafing of his flesh there sent a quickening through his loins that was more powerful than any he had ever experienced. It was all he could do to hold back the primordial urge within him to take her now, without soothing words or gentleness.

"Non!" Acadiana cried as she felt her legs widen. She began pushing violently against his chest, her entire body straining against him to stop the invasion. "Please wait . . . don't . . . we must talk about this!"

She was frantic now. Jonas cupped her cheeks and stared down into her panicked eyes. "Do you need for me to explain things to you?" he asked tenderly, concerned that part of her fear lay in innocence. "Explain what will happen between us?" Acadiana shook her head wildly, unable and unwilling to discuss such with him. Jonas traced her delicate cheeks, soothed the hair back from her face, then captured her hands to halt their mauling of his chest and arms. Lord, he'd have scars by morning. "Then there is no need for talk," he whispered, and pressed a provocative kiss on the corner of her trembling lips.

Acadiana felt trapped, suffocated in a sea of turbulent fear, anguish, and longing, swayed by the light touch of his lips and caressing words from her previous determination to keep him from having her this way. "Don't I have any choice in the matter?"

"Certainly. You may choose to enjoy it or not," he said warmly, passion turning his eyes a stormy blue.

"I won't . . . I'm . . . not ready," she stuttered.

"Just relax and you will be," he coaxed, smothering further conversation by renewing his conquest.

"Never!" she cried. "I'll never be—" But the words were strangled in her throat as he began again, kissing, touching, tantalizing until Acadiana felt her entire body melt into a boneless mass of sensation beneath him. Jonas released her arms and dropped his head to kiss her throat, moved down to her breasts, then lower, while her arms moved fretfully, not knowing whether to push him away or clutch him to her. His cheek turned into her belly, his tongue darting out to circle her navel. Her skin was feverish beneath his mouth, her stomach muscles jumping and tightening in erotic spasms that sent hot shards of desire shooting through him until he wanted to dip lower, taste deeper, dissolve into the very essence of her. But, daring not to go farther on this first night, he retraced an urgent, upward path to her mouth.

Acadiana gripped at the sheets then his shoulders, the sound of her own harsh breathing tormenting her as it mingled with his. Her nails dug into his back as if to maintain balance, allowing his tempting love play if it deterred him from the other more frightening path. But unknowing in her innocence, it served to further ignite the fire in her husband. The wine she had consumed was a heady buffer against her anger, a stirring stimulus for passion. She was floating now beneath the expertise of his mouth and hands, drifting farther from reality into the impassioned nether realms where time was measured only in heartbeats and whispers, and kisses so powerful and sublime that they blocked out all else save the two whose bodies were straining to become one.

Jonas moved back between Acadiana's thighs and she stiffened again. Not merely because she was frightened, but because with the removal of his lips, she was being hurled back into reality where guilt and resentment would follow in the wake of broken dreams, where her vow of a marriage in name only would be shattered.

Jonas was riddled with a desire more overwhelming than any he had known, consumed by a passion that was almost damning in its force. He could wait no longer. He grabbed her lush hips firmly and pulled her to him. Acadiana dug her heels into the bedding and tried to stop his progress, twisting and turning as she attempted to squirm away. A whimper broke from her throat, a cry of fear, confusion, and passion.

"Do not—"

Jonas captured her words with his mouth, unwilling to comprehend her refusal, rationalizing it as maidenly fear to ease his own mind. He made vain efforts to soothe her with words of comfort and encouragement as he searched again for entrance. His aching body begged for release but found its passage made difficult by her virginity. He probed gently at first, then thrust harder to break the maiden barrier. Acadiana released a startled, angry cry at the entry.

"Easy," Jonas soothed, clutching her, desperately trying to control his movements against the dictates of his desire. He knew he must give her time to adjust and endeavored to deflect his thoughts away from the writhing body beneath him, to think of something, anything to cool the raging flame of passion that licked his insides and urged him on. It was impossible when each twist, each turn of Acadiana's taut body created an exquisite friction that devoured him.

"Stop . . . moving," he ground out, but Acadiana either didn't hear or his words fueled her rebellion further, for she struggled harder now, wildly, making it worse for herself and his fleeing good intentions.

Her thrashing was awkward, angry, yet it moved him more powerfully than the most experienced courtesan could have. His iron control slipped a notch as he tried to hold her still, then another as she writhed against him, unwittingly burying him deeper within her.

Control was gone as passion won out, and he pressed deeper still with smooth, thrusting movements. Acadiana whimpered at the burning sensation his motion caused, and tears squeezed out between her closed eyelids as she struggled against the pain and indignity of the act. Over and over Jonas moved within her, his hips grinding against hers in a timeless pattern of pleasure and pain, not even allowing her the blessed numbness of feeling nothing.

The burning eased to a dull throb, and Acadiana gave up fighting to clutch his sweat-slick shoulders as she tried to find that place of sweetness and light where there was more than just the physical mating. But her rebellious need for self-control clashed with her woman's passionate yearning, and she could neither escape his possession of her nor recapture that blissful outer world.

With a final, powerful lunge, Jonas lay still. His head dropped to the warm hollow of her neck, his heartbeat thunderous as he spiraled slowly back to reality. His body shuddered once more, echoing the spent waves of hunger and passion that had, for the first time in his life, pushed him beyond the levels of self-control. Still joined to his wife —now truly his wife—he felt the warmth and tightness of her surrounding him, heard her muted sobs against his shoulder. He grimaced and drew a ragged breath at the memory of his rough severing of her maidenhead. An undercurrent of pride rippled through him at the sure knowledge that she had known no other man, but it was quickly dashed by the sinking realization that, although not permanently injured, Acadiana was certainly angry, and there would be hell to pay for his brief touch of heaven.

When his breathing eased, he shifted his weight and bent to kiss her. Acadiana quickly turned over and buried her face in the pillow.

"Acadiana, look at me," he entreated softly.

She shook her head adamantly and refused to lift her face. She couldn't bear to see him gloat over her defeat and shame. He gently but firmly turned her over amid much resistance and kissed her pert nose.

"It will be better next time," he said carefully, then braced himself for her reaction.

Acadiana wailed, adding several foreign curses while covering her burning face in her hands. "There won't be a next time—"

Jonas pried her fingers away and gathered her into his arms. She struggled to get loose, but he sensed she needed to be held and cinched his arms tighter. He fought to assay his guilt by remembering her earlier passionate responses, but in the end the passion had been his alone. His mindless need of her had clouded his reason until he had blocked out the knowledge that she had not wanted him. The fact that she was his by legal and moral right was little comfort now in the cold aftermath.

"I'm sorry," he whispered against the top of her head.

"Non, you are not!" she accused, childlike.

No, he wasn't, not in the way she meant. "For hurting you. I never wanted to hurt you."

She wanted to scream at him for a liar and a thief, but could not gather the strength for another confrontation. She felt achy and beaten, hurting much more in spirit than flesh. Unable to escape her husband, Acadiana buried her face in his chest and angrily sobbed out life's injustices there. She pounded weakly against the arms that held her, feeling invaded and used, but he only held her tighter. And when the rhythmic rise and fall of his chest said sleep had claimed him, and his arms went slack around her so that she could pull away, she stayed. Weary and hurting, she stayed, strangely and inexplicably unwilling to abandon the security of his embrace.

Acadiana awoke the next morning to soft kisses being pressed against her ear and throat. Her head was pounding, her tongue as thick as cotton in her mouth, and her stomach promised revenge. Her eyes, blurry from the effects of wine and fatigue, flew open as the memory of the night dawned on her.

"Morning, love," Jonas teased in a husky voice as his kisses trailed lower.

"Stop," she said hoarsely as she tried to force her mind to clear. Her senses returned rapidly as his hand began stroking her naked body. She evaded his caress with a quick, deft movement and scampered off the bed out of arm's reach. Jonas caught a fleeting and too-tantalizing glimpse of her golden shoulders and slender round backside before she dropped from sight.

Acadiana hurriedly scooped her nightdress—little good

that hateful thing had done her—from the floor and pulled the torn material on, holding it together at the waist. The rough fabric chafed her tender skin unmercifully, but at least it covered her nakedness.

"Acadiana, get back here," Jonas demanded, frustrated by her timid manner. Knowing how tender she would be after her first time, he had awakened feeling extremely considerate of himself for not taking her again in the middle of the night, as was his desire. So much for chivalry.

"Non!" she refused with an adamant shake of her head that sent her black curls spilling gloriously across her shoulders. "I can't . . . we can't . . . Jonas, it's broad daylight! *Non!"* she cried again in embarrassment at the glow of appreciation in his eyes when she stomped a tiny bare foot, causing sundry parts if her body to bob up and down, much to his enjoyment.

"The time of day has absolutely nothing to do with it. Now come here," Jonas coaxed. He shifted over and patted the bed beside him.

Acadiana stared in horror at the flecks of blood on the sheet—bold evidence of her lost innocence. She backed away slowly, her stomach rolling and churning with each step. It wasn't the passion she remembered in the brutal light of day, but the pain and the power he held to pull her outside of herself. She would not do that awful thing again if she had to murder him in his sleep!

Jonas watched with regret and prepared to leave the bed to seize her if he must to return her to the nest. He wouldn't let her go on thinking that every time would be like the first. He threw back the covers and swung his legs over the side of the bed. His powerful body, boldly revealed in the light of day as he stood, sent the blood draining from Acadiana's face. But his forward movement was halted by a knock. Relief was paramount on Acadiana's face as her eyes darted to the door, then back to her husband, who was gathering the sheet around his waist as he sat back on the bed. She grabbed a traveling gown and hurried behind the dressing screen as Jonas growled an obscenity before bidding entry.

A serving maid labored under a breakfast tray laden with a delicious assortment of food. There were eggs soft boiled and fried, ham steaks and a slab of country-cured bacon with a pungent odor, and fluffy biscuits dripping with freshly churned butter. The maid set down small crocks of heavy cream, honey, and a varied assortment of jams, jellies, and marmalade on the table.

"Mr. Courtland, your horses will be readied within the hour as you requested," she said, keeping her eyes on the food instead of the striking man in the bed sporting an angry scowl. He looked ready to devour something, and it was not the food she was serving.

"Thank you, that will be all," Jonas said stiffly, cursing himself for planning an early departure and wondering what he could have been thinking.

Acadiana stepped from behind the screen as soon as she heard the door close. She was fully dressed from the tips of her soft black boots to her slightly sassy grin.

"Woman, must you gloat?" Jonas asked, chagrined. She was stunning in a claret-colored riding dress that hugged her figure to her waist like a second skin. The smart military style had an open standing collar that was tied at her throat with gold ribbons. Below this was a striking insert, a chemisette of white silk trimmed with horizontal strips of gold braid, that enhanced her bosom to perfection. There was also gold braid on the epaulettes and sleeve ends.

"If we are to leave shortly, you had best eat," Acadiana said with a satisfied lift of her chin. She sat down demurely and picked up a napkin.

Jonas thought she looked just a bit too smug. He climbed from the bed and strode toward the table completely naked. Acadiana gasped, shut her eyes instinctively, and took a convulsive gulp of air.

"Jonas!" she rasped in shame, her cheeks turning the dark red of her riding dress.

"Wife," he taunted, "you look as shocked as an innocent virgin."

"I am a . . . I am . . . I . . . *Le bon Dieu!*" She wanted to die! There should be a canyon nearby that she could throw herself headlong into and end this perpetual torment.

"Tsk, tsk, how soon they forget." Jonas shook his head soberly and proceeded to sit down.

"Jonas, I can't possibly eat with you dressed . . . ah . . . undressed like that," Acadiana stammered, her eyes still tightly closed. *"Mais non!* It is not dignified!"

"I can always think of something else for us to do, love." He smiled wickedly.

"I'll eat," Acadiana said quickly, stuffing a biscuit in her mouth. "I won't look, but I'll eat," she finished in a whisper.

After Acadiana's third attempt to spear her eggs blindly, Jonas rose, wrapped a sheet around his hips, and returned to sit down. He might as well satisfy his ravenous hunger for food; his other appetite would have to wait. "Wife," he said blithely, "I've never been known to maltreat women. I'd rather not start now by starving you to death."

Acadiana opened one eye then the other when she saw that he was partially covered, but finished her meal quickly, not truly tasting what she was eating. She had no appetite under his amused gaze and rose to remove herself from his scrutiny.

She wandered around the room, picking up clothing and toilet articles to pack them away. She stopped when she reached the bed and once again stared at the dots of blood marring the sheet. Shuddering unconsciously, she moved to the mirror where she inspected her reflection. Her dark hair was swept up in the same simple style she always wore when she fixed it herself. The riding dress was as impeccable this morning as it was the day Aunt Elizabeth ordered it, hoping her niece would give up the ragged boy's breeches she loved to wear. Violet eyes stared back at her in the same way they did every day of her life. No newfound knowledge of men and women seemed evident there. Except for the considerable soreness between her thighs, she felt no different. Acadiana heard a sigh directly behind her and spun around.

"You don't look any different, love," Jonas said as he wrapped his arms around her waist and pulled her to his chest. Sunlight danced off her ebony hair in sparkling tribute but reflected a sadness in her eyes, a lost look that Jonas silently cursed. He would rather see fire there, the rebellion he could spar with. The haunted look reflected in the deep violet was a place he could not touch. He turned her in his arms until she faced the mirror again and propped his chin on her shoulder. "No one will ever guess that you just spent a passionate night in my arms, unwilling of course," he added, "except the maid who changes the bed linens."

"Oooh!" Acadiana growled. Her eyes flared with the anger Jonas welcomed now as she struggled out of his arms. She sprinted across the room, intent on stripping the sheets from the bed.

Jonas followed, laughing outrageously, and dragged her away. "Don't," he rumbled, his whole body shaking with mirth. "There are too many women who can't claim such innocence. 'Tis an honor to be the first."

Cheeks burning, Acadiana clenched her fists and spun around to face him. She struggled with a scathing retort but mere words failed her, so she seethed inwardly at her deplorable state. Stomping away, she grabbed her treasured leather pouch and clutched it to her chest. With a huff she sat down to wait for Jonas to get ready to depart.

He watched her from the corner of his eye as he dressed. Huddled in her chair like an errant child, she speared him with angry shards of violet ice. He wondered again what the bag held that was so precious to her that she must watch over it like a mother hen. No, more like a tigress, he corrected.

"What have you there, wife? Memories of the past?"

"Humph," she grumbled, trying to ignore him.

"Show me," he requested.

"Non."

"I could take it from you," he ventured, watching as she clutched it tighter. The stormy mist that clouded her eyes was the only indication that he was touching a tender nerve. "You have no secrets, remember?"

Acadiana gave him a disgusted look but her chin wobbled when she lifted it. "You have taken everything from me. My land, my body, have I nothing now that is sacred?" Jonas took another step toward her. With a violent oath she tossed the hide to the floor at his feet. "Amuse yourself, *m'sieu,*" she sneered, "then do not ask me about it again."

Jonas picked up the weathered pouch slowly and emptied its contents onto the bed. There were several bright feathers tied together with a thin strip of leather, three arrowheads carved with different points, and a strange, flat circular piece of leather with an image of the sun burned into its face. Last was a rolled-up parchment, which Jonas disregarded for the moment as he turned the leather piece over in his hands.

"What is this, a talisman?" he asked, holding it up for her regard.

"It . . . it was to them," she said haltingly. She was hurled once more through time to see Jean and the Indian chief sitting around a campfire fashioning the charm with the utmost care. Chanting a mysterious melody, the chief called on the spirits to endow it with magical powers to protect the wearer from harm. Acadiana shook her mind free of the haunting scene. "For me it is just a token of their love and concern."

Jonas put it down to pick up the scroll of parchment and noted that Acadiana flinched when he touched it. Her hands reached out as if to take the paper, then drew back weakly. Jonas unrolled it and stared dismally into the face of a young man. Dark eyes stared back at him with cold, cruel strength, and the mouth, although grim, held a hint of humor. The artist had captured the youthful face with savagery yet softness, and Jonas grunted when he noticed that the sprawled signature said *Cade*.

"A friend of yours, madame?" he said quietly with an undercurrent of tension in his strained voice as he tossed the parchment on the floor at her feet.

Acadiana bent to pick up the paper with loving fingers and stared back at Jonas, silent, her thoughts unreadable.

"Who is that?"

She ignored him and stared at the ceiling. She could feel the pressure mounting around her, like storm clouds gathering.

"Who?" he nearly shouted.

"None of your business!" she threw back at him. She bolted suddenly from the chair to face him. Although he towered over her, she was not intimidated but stood her ground with open contempt.

"What is he to you? Does he hold a place in your heart?" Jonas asked coldly, jealousy rearing its ugly head to strike him.

"Oui," she said softly.

"Did you love him?" Jonas demanded.

"Oui," she said again slowly, quietly. "I always will."

Jonas marched over to where she stood. So cold, so unapproachable, he thought. He grabbed her forearms and pulled her to his chest.

"I will make you forget him!" he said forcefully, shaking her as if to imprint his words into her consciousness.

"I have no desire to forget him," Acadiana said calmly. Too calmly. A storm was brewing behind her amethyst eyes, threatening to erupt any second in a shower of angry sparks.

"I was the first, Acadiana," Jonas ground out, "and I will be the only one! The sooner you realize that, the better our life together will be. You are my wife! He will never have you."

Acadiana stared at Jonas in wide-eyed bewilderment.

Didn't he think she knew that? *Mon Dieu!* Her body still ached from the consummation of her forced marriage. The man had gone mad; there was no other excuse for it. She waited silently until he released her, then placed her beloved possessions back in the pouch. She walked to the door, intent on waiting for him outside, but turned instead to face him.

"You say that he will never have me," she said coolly, "and that is true. But neither will you, not really. Do not seek to control my affections as you control all else now, Jonas. However ancient or past tense, they are mine to hold. My loyalties run deep."

"An admirable trait," he said, sneering, "as I said once before. But remember this. You had damn well better leave your 'loyalty' outside our bedroom!"

His caustic remark caused Acadiana to flinch. Her heart thudded painfully in her breast at the brutal look on his face, and the color slowly ebbed from her face, leaving her with a look of stunned bewilderment. She spun on her heel and left Jonas standing there alone and angry at a distant ghost, a figment of her past. His small victory of the night paled at the memory of the hard young face that must mean a great deal to her if she would keep his portrait ever close to her side.

But he was her husband. No man, however much loved by Acadiana, had ever touched her the way that he had, and Jonas vowed that he would replace that phantom to occupy a place in her heart. It never dawned on him in that tortured moment to question the reasons why he wanted it thus.

The day proved to be another scorcher. Acadiana sent a resentful look at the glaring sun, then hopped to straddle Shawnee, momentarily revealing beautifully shaped calves and ankles to a gaping innkeeper. She was not appropriately clothed to endure the heat and could already feel a prickle of sweat forming at her temples. Jonas rode up beside her and nodded his head politely. Acadiana contemplated the change in his mood for a lingering moment, then shrugged her shoulders wearily. Who could fathom the workings of a man's mind? She certainly could not.

The travelers were silent as they rode to the river and boarded the flatboat that would take them down Louisiana's main waterway. Aptly named for its flat bottom and squared ends, the flatboats were used to transport freight on inland waterways. Though not far in land distance, the trip on the winding Mississippi stretched many river miles. After days of traveling on the river then more days of crossing dry land, they were finally within a few hours of their destination.

Acadiana dangled her bare feet lazily in a pond and basked in the peaceful surroundings. She had spent most of the day wondering what her life would be like now that she was going home. Not to *her* home exactly, but she would get to see her land eventually. What would life be like at Courtland Manor?

"Where are you, love?" Jonas asked, giving her a quick peck on the cheek.

"I'm not your love and what do you mean?" Acadiana asked irritably. "I'm in no mood for riddles."

"You look rather tense and faraway. What were you thinking?" Jonas eased himself down to sit beside her.

Acadiana skipped several stones across the placid surface of the water and watched tiny waves ripple out in a circular motion. Not answering his question, she queried, "How long before I get to see my land?"

"Tomorrow if you like."

"It's that close?" she whispered, a little amazed.

"Of course. Where do you think I live?"

"You said you live in New Town," she returned. "My land is in New Iberia."

"New Iberia, New Town, Nuevo Iberia, it's all the same place," Jonas said drolly. "I assumed you knew."

"Undoubtedly I am too ignorant to know such things,"

she said tartly. Jonas watched as she clutched another handful of pebbles and sent them skimming one by one across the water. He shouldn't have teased her, he realized too late. She'd been in a pensive mood all day, and he had been trying merely to relieve some of the tension. "Why did they change the name?"

"I'm not sure. Everyone seems to use whichever name he prefers. Now, what else is bothering you?"

Acadiana stared at him with rising pique. "You mean other than the fact that I was forced to marry you, forced to do disgusting, unspeakable things with you, and have lost my land, the *only* thing in life that I owned?"

"Other than that," Jonas said.

Acadiana fell silent, wondering if she should confide in her husband, if she should voice her fears. Not that she was really *afraid* of anything she told herself, but something had been nagging at her. She grabbed more small rocks and let them sift slowly through her fingers. "What will your family think . . . when you come home with a bride?" she asked, concern shadowing her delicate features.

"I sent a message ahead. They will be expecting us," Jonas said evasively.

Aggravated, Acadiana threw the rest of her rocks down and turned to face him. "You know what I mean, Jonas! How will I be received?"

"All right." He sighed. "My brother will be infatuated with you immediately, and . . . well . . . my mother will be outraged . . . to say the least."

"I knew it! Oh, how will I face them?" she cried, putting her face in her grimy hands.

Jonas's brow shot up in amazement. "Where is the she-cat who almost tore my head off when I tried to buy her land? Where is the Indian maiden who can fish and ride as well as a man and threatened me with cold steel should I trespass on her innocence? Good Lord, Acadiana, don't tell me that a tiny, middle-aged woman with an abominable temper frightens you!"

"Stop, you're teasing me," she said with a halfhearted smile. "What right does she have to be outraged? What have I done?" She rubbed at the dust on her cheeks, making a smeared mess.

"You? It's not you, love. It's me," Jonas replied. "She likes to have things her way, rule the domain. She wanted me to marry from her pick of young ladies."

"Why didn't you? Couldn't you find one who would have you?"

"Hardly that." Jonas chuckled. "I just never found more than one woman who cared for anything but silly gossip, Sunday teas, and acquiring a fortune."

"I am no different. I also married you for the fortune it will bring me," she said.

"You are different," he said cynically, taking in her dirty face and hands. Very different, he thought.

"Who was the one woman you referred to earlier? Why didn't you marry her?" Acadiana asked.

"Ah, that one is special," Jonas said warmly, "but I met you before I could ask her."

"Oh." Acadiana pouted, pricked by his careless words. Jealousy crept over her, but she pushed it aside as frivolous. Why should she care? "Would that you had asked her before coming to Providence," she added flippantly to hide her annoyance. "I suppose she was your mother's choice?"

"She was," Jonas teased, noting the telltale signs that had affected him of late. So, the little hellion was not as unaffected as she would have him believe. Somewhere beneath those guileless eyes was a woman with the same passionate longings as all women, and the same weaknesses—in this case, jealousy. "Beware, Acadiana, my mother is very much like you. She is a tiger. Be careful that she doesn't scratch your eyes out."

"The old bat! I'll snatch her bald-headed!" she said, angry at being rejected before being given a chance, and insecure in the knowledge that Jonas's mother had already selected a suitable bride for her son.

"I knew my little squaw was still in there somewhere," Jonas laughed. " 'Snatch her bald-headed?' You're threatening to scalp my mother? I'll have to warn her to wear a cap at all times." Acadiana balled her fists up, scarlet patches coloring her cheeks. She was going to throttle him if he said another word. Heightening her mortification was the sound of his rich male laughter, which stirred some empty place within her. Jonas choked down his mirth when he took in her tight fists and snapping eyes. He sent her a repentant smile then wet his handkerchief and began wiping her face. "I shall savor every minute of watching you two best each other."

Acadiana allowed his ministrations until his words slowly began to sink in. Suddenly she slapped his hands away. "You are really looking forward to this meeting, aren't you?"

"Immensely, love. I've been trying to get the upper hand on that battle-ax for years. You're just the one to do it."

Acadiana rose abruptly and dusted off the back of her skirt with angry swishes as she walked away. Jonas felt the now familiar tightening in his loins as he watched her and wished *his* hands were doing the dusting. As they lacked proper privacy in the roughly constructed shacks abroad the flatboat and had spent the previous few nights on the Indian trails, they had not been intimate since their one night at the inn, and Jonas ached with the unfulfilled desire to sate himself within her softness, to hear her cry out with the same passion he had felt but had not been able to draw from her.

They rode in silence for the remainder of the way home. Acadiana was nervous and agitated. It put her at a disadvantage to be presented in such a disheveled state, and she wished she could freshen up before meeting the "battle-ax." Well, she might try to rule other people, thought Acadiana with conviction, but she won't rule me! I'll give her back in full whatever she tosses my way. If she crosses me . . . *Mais oui,* she just better stay out of my way!

Jonas watched with amusement the fine temper his wife silently worked up, then the staunch look of determination that eventually settled across her face. This would be a homecoming to remember. At a firm nod from him, they spurred their horses on.

9

The afternoon sun was waning when a weary couple turned their horses down the carriage lane to Courtland Manor. The first thing Acadiana saw was a white-washed fence that stretched for endless arpents across the front border of Courtland land. Brick columns supported the broad gate that gave entrance to Jonas and his new bride. A black man in green and gold livery rushed to the gateway with a startled expression on his face.

"Master Jonas, welcome home, sir! We weren't expecting you for another week." The servant tipped his hat and bowed as they walked the horses through the gate.

Acadiana stared in awe at the beautifully sculptured lawns. The drive leading through the grounds was lined with colossal live oaks draped with gray Spanish moss. The soil was of a mellow hue and fertile beyond reason if the luxuriant growth surrounding her was any indication. Trees bearing aromatic blooms grew in clusters, adding color and fragrance. Acadiana spied azalea and camellia growing in profusion. When in bloom, the camellia's showy pink flowers and elegant dark green, laurellike leaves would grace the plates of dinner guests entertained at the manor.

She could smell the perfumed magnolia blossoms as

surely as if it were already late winter and the large white flowers had unfolded to foil the waxy green leaves. In this conglomeration of color—somber browns, vivid greens, subtle yellows—Acadiana's senses vibrated with the breathtaking beauty. Wisteria vines formed tunnels as they crept over iron arches, lending an air of intricately designed architecture. Deep within the greenish haze of reflected sunlight were romantic palm gardens nestled in secluded spots. Their wrought-iron benches seemed to call a mysterious melody meant for lovers: *Steal away, partake.*

Acadiana snatched her mind back from the seductive song as she ambled along beside her husband and used the leisurely pace to absorb the abundance of common foliage and to question that which she did not recognize. Jonas was quick to point out the strange exotic plants that had been imported to decorate the lavish plantation. In the warm, humid climate, the vegetation grew splendidly, and the gardens would have been quickly overgrown had they not been so carefully tended. Although unbidden, resentment crept in to press itself on the young woman as she moved through the opulent greenery. Never had she been a part of such wealth. She felt the subtle lure and feared she would be dissolved into this life and lose sight of the dreams that had been the measure of her existence for so long.

The feelings were intensified when the plantation mansion came into view, looming before her like a gigantic mirage. It was so hauntingly familiar in design that Acadiana had to catch her breath before moving her horse forward to the steps that graced each side of the main portal. She was certain she had seen this elegant home before, but whether in her dreams or in reality she could not determine. The first-floor gallery extended the length of the house in the front and swept around each corner to the back. Huge semicircular staircases swept up each side of the front door, leading to the second-story veranda. Curious black faces peeked out of the curtains billowing in the warm breeze from the dormer windows on the third floor. The murmur of excited voices, muffled giggles, and the scurry of bare feet followed small slave children as they darted beneath the porch to watch the master's approach. Acadiana strained to catch a glimpse of the grinning mischief-makers, but her view was obstructed by the narrow double columns before her that held the pitched roof over the whitewashed brick structure, creating an elaborate framework of sturdy, graceful beauty.

She sat still and dazed until Jonas put his hands around her waist and helped her dismount. The spell the lovely grounds had cast was broken, and Acadiana despaired at having to meet his family face-to-face. It was inevitable, of course, but she didn't think she was ready to brave his mother's rejection right then when the rest of her life was in such turmoil. She took one last look at Jonas before ascending the front steps that would lead her into a future slowly spiraling out of control.

Just as they walked into the foyer, they were met by a loud, piercing screech. It so startled Acadiana that she unknowingly latched on to Jonas's arm. "Oh, Lawsey, it's Mast' Jonas! You's home, boy! I didn't hear no hoss ride in." Dark brown eyes narrowed playfully as they caught sight of Acadiana, and the Negress's voice lowered to a drawl that was as slow and rich as warmed molasses. "What you got with you, boy? This sweet-looking thing marry the likes of you? Girl baby, you don't know what you done, taking up with this here outlaw!"

Acadiana was immediately enfolded in two of the biggest arms she had ever seen on a woman. She was too startled to do anything more than smile warmly at the merry face that seemed as large as the woman.

"Acadiana," Jonas said with obvious affection, "this is Mattie. She runs the place with an iron fist. Mattie, my wife, Acadiana Hamilton Court—"

"Hamilton? You be kin to the Hamiltons what used to live near here?" Mattie rushed on, giving Acadiana no chance to answer. Her whole body rippled with merriment as she jabbered delightfully about her "boy chile's" return. "Ooowee, Mast' Jonas, she be too pretty to take up with you." Hands on her generous hips, the Negress shook her head and eyed Acadiana up and down. "Um-hum, looks like we gonna have to fatten her up a bit; she be a mite small. Been needing a girl baby around here, sho has. Y'all go on in the library. Baby Boy be in there, and he gonna be surprised to see you here already."

Baby Boy? Acadiana giggled, recalling that Jonas had mentioned he had a younger brother who was twenty-five years old.

Jonas shot her a sideways grin, then turned to Mattie with a wary look. "Where is Mother?"

"Humph!" the maid grumbled. "She upstairs. She been ranting and raving around here for most the week since getting your letter. Lawsey, Mast' Jonas, you sho better watch your backside. I know she figures you ain't too big to whup. I'll go fetch her directly, if you promise to protect this here girl chile."

"Don't worry, Mattie," Jonas assured her. "Acadiana can take care of herself."

"She sho gonna have to," Mattie said, her jowls flapping with each shake of her head. "She sho is."

Jonas escorted his wife into the library to meet his brother. Their sudden appearance so startled the younger man that Edward jumped up and almost knocked over a silver service resting on the mahogany sideboard near him.

"Well, welcome home. I didn't expect you for another few days." He extended his hand to his older brother only to leave it dangling in midair as his eyes met Acadiana's. His mouth split into a broad, comical grin. "Well, well, well. Don't tell me, this is your new wife." The words were apparently for Jonas, but Edward's eyes never left his sister-in-law's face. "How in heaven did you manage to capture this enchanting young woman?"

"Heaven had nothing to do with it," Jonas snorted. "This woman put me through hell before agreeing to marry me."

Acadiana was reserved as she extended her hand, but Edward's eyes, not in the least threatening, held only welcome. Her guard slowly lowered and she broke into a soft smile for the young man who looked so much like his older brother. His hair was lighter, a bit more sun-streaked, he was just a few inches shorter, but the family resemblance was unmistakable in his dark blue eyes.

"Mais non, he blackmailed me," Acadiana said with a flippant turn of her wrist, "to get my land."

"Good God." Edward laughed, somewhat taken aback by her boldness. "Don't tell me this is Abe Hamilton." He looked her up and down with anything but brotherly interest, then sent her a roguish wink. "You sure don't look like an Abe to me."

"Non." Acadiana smiled demurely, but there was a pert gleam in her eyes and a hint of mischief dancing around the edges of her mouth. "Acadiana Belizaire Hamilton, to be precise. At your disposal, *M'sieu* Courtland."

Edward liked the way the French and some other accent whose origin he couldn't detect rolled from her tongue with a spicy snap. She was thinner than he usually liked his women, but her eyes were the sharpest, most entrancing shade of—

"Acadiana," Jonas broke in, noticing the glow of appreciation on his brother's face. "This is my snake of a brother, Edward. Keep your eyes in your head, Baby Boy, and your hands off."

Edward grimaced at the nickname Mattie had coined at his birth and pointedly ignored his older brother as he took Acadiana's hand. "Miss Hamilton, or I should say Mrs. Courtland now, I am honored to make your acquaintance." He made a great show of bowing gallantly and kissing her palm, much to the annoyance of his older brother. "Your appearance here is quite a surprise, but a welcome one."

"The pleasure is all mine," she drawled sweetly, enjoying the playful exchange. Her fragile peace of mind latched on to the hope that she had captured at least one ally in this household.

Edward cocked his head and gave his brother a lazy grin. "Blackmail, Jonas? That's a twist."

Jonas returned his brother's indolent smile. "One must do what one must. By the way, Edward, how is Mother?"

"Ha! Don't mention that barracuda's name to me. You sent that note and left me here to put up with her all week. I'll get you back for that one, Jonas. And dare I add that you'll pay dearly?" Edward didn't bring up the absurdity of his brother marrying a Cajun. The mere thought made him shudder at the idea of such a social blunder. Most considered the Cajuns to be an unruly bunch, backwater trash without the aristocratic heritage of the Creoles. Edward felt honor-bound to rearrange his thinking now that his brother had married one of that breed. He knew how much Jonas wanted the land. Under different circumstances he would have thought his sibling had gone too far to achieve that goal, but after meeting Acadiana, he was better able and quite willing to understand.

A door slammed upstairs that shook the whole house and brought the conversation to a jarring halt. Acadiana's head jerked up, and both tall, strapping men cringed visibly.

"Jonas, you hide the girl! I'll get the pistols!" Edward shouted dramatically, sweeping his arm about the room in feigned search of a hiding place.

"Brace yourself, madame. The queen approaches!" Jonas said humorously, taking Acadiana's hand for support. He wouldn't allow Minette to bully his wife on this first meeting.

Acadiana winced with each click of the monster's heels as she could be heard crossing the marble tiles in the hallway. Minette stormed into the room with a regal presence, ready to do battle. The sight of her flashing eyes and stern visage would have cowed the bravest regiment of soldiers.

"Jonas Royale Courtland!" she raged.

"Mother!" Jonas interrupted forcefully, daring her with

his stern look and tone to continue her tirade. He lowered his voice to a more amiable level. "May I present my wife, Acadiana Hamilton Court—"

"Cade?" Minette gasped. "Cade?"

Acadiana stood as if frozen, all color draining from her face. Her world began to spin crazily, and she croaked a harsh rasp as she sought to drag a breath of air from the suddenly stagnant room.

"Grand'mère?" she managed to whisper, afraid to move lest the phantom disappear.

"Oh, Cade! It *is* you!" Minette cried, rushing to enfold the girl in her slender arms.

"Grand'mère!" Acadiana cried in return as the spell was broken. She fell into the older woman's arms, tears springing forth to trickle down her face. "Oh, *Grand'mère*, I can't believe it is you! I have missed you so much!"

"And I you, *ma petite"* was the tender, heartfelt reply. Minette smiled, brushing back her own tears of joy. She pushed the girl at arm's length only to clutch her back to her breast. "You have grown up, *bébé*. What has happened to my little girl?"

"How did you know I was coming? Who told you—"

"Ah, my precious, I live here." Minette interrupted the rush of words while caressing Acadiana's face with perfectly manicured fingertips. "I have the dubious honor of being this ungrateful son's mother."

"I did not know . . . I never asked." Acadiana laughed between soft sobs. Embarrassed, she brushed at the drops on her cheeks and searched the lovingly familiar face.

"You are well?" Minette asked softly. She looked deeply into the amethyst eyes that were so recognizable, so familiar, so very dear to her.

"I am fine, *Grand'mère*, just fine now that I have you again," she replied. "What of you?"

Acadiana searched with her eyes, touched with trembling fingers the beautiful face that was so much a part of the past life she wanted to remember. She *had* recognized the house, although she had been here only a few times as a child. Now it was to be her home, and all the fear of a life spent within its walls seemed to vanish with the vision of the woman standing before her.

Jonas stared at the two women in stunned silence. He rolled his eyes at Edward who had the same gaping look on his face, then turned back to his wife and mother.

"Ladies, ladies, please," he ordered, vexed. "Would someone start explaining immediately?"

"Jonas, you ingrate!" Minette snapped. "You have married my Cade. Pooh! She is too good for you!"

Edward had watched the exchange with astonishment and was now more confused than ever. "Hurumph!" he sounded, clearing his throat to gain the attention of all present. "First Abe . . . then Acadiana . . . now Cade . . . Jonas, who *is* this woman?"

"Jonas, take your babbling brother off somewhere!" Minette barked in a tone that said she was used to being obeyed. "Cade and I must have some time alone to talk. Now, off with you!" She waved her hand imperiously at the men to shoo them away.

Hands resting negligently on his hips, Jonas leaned forward to glower at the dowager. "No, Mother, you are not sending us anywhere. It has been a long, tiring journey. I see that my wife and I have much yet to discover about each other, and," he added slowly, suggestively, "we are still newly married."

Acadiana paled, then blushed. "Jonas, please, I must speak with your mother. It has been so long."

"No, little one, your husband is right," Minette said kindly, eyeing the pair with a shrewdness acquired over many years. "You must go rest now. I will have Mattie send a tray up to your suite. Tomorrow morning, first thing, we will slip away for our talk, yes?"

Minette kissed Acadiana's cheek and gave her a loving pat before handing her over to her husband. "Jonas," she said, her voice quivering with a depth of feeling he rarely saw in his mother, "you have done well for this family. I could not be more pleased. Your father too would be very proud." She turned sharply and crossed the room, then took her other son's arm. "Now, Edward, come see! We must have a long talk about *your* future."

"Mother." Edward grimaced as she dragged him out the door.

Acadiana whirled to face Jonas, insult written all over her otherwise beautiful face. "Tiger! Battle-ax! Jonas Courtland, how could you? You ought to be ashamed of yourself! Your mother is the sweetest, most wonderful person in the world. I have known her since I was a child."

"No doubt, love, your childish vision was blurred by innocence all those years," he mused aloud, drawing a withering glare from his wife. "Come, I've a need to see our bedchamber." Jonas chuckled as she stiffened her shoulders and reluctantly followed him out of the library. He intended to remove himself and his wife to the privacy of their own quarters before solving the mystery of the unexpected relationship between Acadiana and his mother. Minette would have some explaining to do later, for Jonas was certain she must have known who the heir to the Hamilton property was all these years, but for now he wanted to give all his attention to his new bride.

A Creole feast awaited the couple upstairs in the sitting room that joined Jonas's bedroom. Spicy jambalaya, crawfish étouffée, and a cucumber salad were served with fresh-baked cornbread and delicate rice. A colorful bowl of cantaloupe also graced the round oak table in the center of the tastefully decorated room.

Long, tall windows opened onto the second-story gallery. Although vivid scarlets, greens, and golds were the commonly used colors of the decade, this room had been done in soft blues and yellows. Delicate floral paper adorned the walls from the wainscot to the bolder pattern bordering the top edge. The colors blended nicely to give the room a bright, airy feeling.

Acadiana stepped through a large archway and found herself in the bedroom. An area rug in the traditional scarlet and ivory covered the cypress-planked floor. The colors were repeated in the heavy damask draperies that were tied back to allow the breeze. On one wall was a huge four-post tester bed. Three steps led up to the fluffy, moss-filled mattress, which was covered with an intricately handmade counterpane. Mosquito netting draped the bed on iron rods and was tied back at each carved post with ivory satin ribbon.

Acadiana ran her hand over the wooden roller on the footboard, which was used to smooth out the mattress each morning. Never had she been a part of such luxury. Even Uncle Grayson's home, though elegant, was modest when compared to this. A cherry-wood commode with a wicker seat was placed under one window, and a matching side table stood next to the bed. A massive wardrobe stood on one wall and a smaller linen press on the other.

The bed was large and inviting, beckoning to her weary body. But she would not be allowed to sleep there alone. Even if she were allowed her own quarters, which Jonas had adamantly refused to grant her, it was expected that the newlyweds would spend two weeks locked away, even taking their meals in the bedroom. On that point Acadiana found some relief. She and Jonas had already been married over a week, and he had said his neglect of his plantation duties would not allow him that luxury. Still, the nights would be spent with him.

Acadiana shivered at the thought and whirled away to stare at the opposite wall. A wood-and-marble mantel graced the fireplace before her. Unused in June, the hearth was blocked by a delightfully painted fireboard depicting an eerie swampland. Massive cypress trees draped with beardlike moss stood in the murky, still water. Marshes were surrounded by an abundance of green foliage. Palmetto, palm, and creeping vines grew in riotous mass along the water's edge. A lazy alligator floated among the cypress knees like a rotting log. The scene looked vaguely familiar, and she turned questioning eyes to her husband.

"That was painted to resemble an area down along the bayou where your land borders ours," he said.

"*Mon Dieu,* it's so close!" she whispered. Acadiana shook herself free of the lethargy settling about her and turned back to Jonas, her voice trembling. "It has changed, *oui?*"

"Not too much," he said. If he wondered at the melancholy expression on her face, the faraway, almost sightless look in her eyes, he did not comment on it. "We cleared some of the land about an arpent from the border for a boat landing to haul cargo from the river."

Acadiana gave him a brusque nod, then turned abruptly as if the scene were forgotten and marched back to the sitting room.

Jonas seated her at the table before asking the obvious question. "*Grand'mère?* As far as I know, my mother is not anyone's grandmother yet. Is there some grave family secret I should be aware of?"

Acadiana acknowledged his confusion. The tension left her face and she laughed softly, a rare tinkling sound that captured Jonas's imagination whenever he heard it. Few were the times since their acquaintance that she indulged in such gaiety, and he would have her laugh more often.

"When I was very small," she began dreamily, remembering only Minette and not the reasons she was here, "your mother used to come visit at our house. She and *Maman* would sit for hours, telling me stories of my grandparents and the way life was for the struggling people that I was named for. The Acadians had been exiled from their homeland in Nova Scotia, or Acadia as they called it, and had fled to this territory to make a new life for themselves. Our mothers used to recount tales of legend and folklore in whispered French that made it all seem so exciting. I told *Maman* on one such visit that I wanted to see my grandmother. Your mother told me that Marie Hamilton was in heaven now, but she would be *Grand'mère* to me if I wished it."

"My mother is French Creole. What did she know of the Acadian people?" Jonas asked.

"They were neighbors." Acadiana shrugged casually though she could feel her spine stiffen. She knew the real question underlying his casual one. "Your family was wealthy, mine was not. That did not seem to be a problem for *Grand'mère* as it is for many of the other Creole families. I have always respected her for the friendship she shared with *Maman*. They were very close."

"If so," Jonas said, a skeptical lift of his eyebrow, "why did I never meet you?"

"I imagine, as you were older, that you were away at school most of the time. *Mais oui,* we did meet once." Acadiana's eyes narrowed at the recollection. "It was either you or Edward. Some nasty, half-grown boy was trying to throw my kitten into the bayou."

Jonas glared back at her, remembering the incident with the feisty kitten well and stunned by the realization that he had met Acadiana a long time ago. For a stretched moment they glowered at each other, then Jonas burst out laughing at the absurd memory of a grimy little girl with angry violet eyes and a mass of tangled black curls. "And you bit me, you little viper! I still have the teeth marks on my leg."

"You were being hateful to an innocent little kitten!" Acadiana said defensively.

"I only wanted to see if the little pest could swim," Jonas replied.

"Cats don't like the water; she would have drowned."

"Rest assured, madame, I never tried that again. My father was certain a rabid animal had attacked me. From the look of that bite, he was sure I would start foaming at the mouth and go mad. Mattie fussed over me for a week with the most awful-smelling concoctions."

"You never told them what happened?" Acadiana giggled, picturing the reckless youth.

"Ha! I was too embarrassed to admit to being accosted by a five-year-old brat." He scoffed derisively. "I endured in silence with a malicious intent to get back at the little imp one day."

"Jonas, it couldn't have been that bad. You are exaggerating the incident."

"Would you like to see the scar?" he asked, rising to unfasten his pants.

"Non!" Acadiana squealed, covered her eyes, then added in a more contrite tone, "I believe you. Please sit back down."

"I'll show you later," he promised, the tone of his voice promising much more.

The meal was soon cleared away and bath water hauled in. Jonas dismissed the servant and made no move to leave the room when Acadiana got ready to disrobe.

"Jonas!" she said, arms akimbo, foot tapping nervously.

"Yes, love?" he asked. Oh so casually, he tipped his chair back against the wall, stretched forth his long legs, and crossed well-formed arms across his chest.

"Leave!" she demanded.

"Why?" He grinned.

"I need to bathe, and I can't with you here."

"Why not?" Watching her wrestle with this phase of married life, Jonas wondered how she'd go about trying to extricate herself. "I'm your husband."

"I know, but . . . I can't . . . I mean, not with you watching. I just couldn't!" she cried. "Will you please leave!"

"No."

"Why?" she pleaded.

"Because, Acadiana, you are my wife. This is my house, and I have a right to be here. You'll just have to get used to it. Besides, I'll derive great pleasure from watching you bathe, and I've never been one to deny myself any of life's little pleasures."

"You may have the right, but I just can't do it!" Acadiana

cried. "Someone should have denied you the pleasure you seek at my expense. Maybe then you wouldn't be so callous!" She was pacing now, arms folded over her chest, legs taking lengthy, agitated strides. After the second pass, she whirled to face him. "Have you no decency?"

"None where you are concerned, pet. Do you need some help?" he offered. Rocking forward on his chair, he rose to his feet and moved toward her.

"*Non!* Jonas, don't!" she squealed, backing up.

"You say that an awful lot, love." He sighed, closing the distance between them.

"Stop! I don't need help," she wailed. "Do you want me to scream?"

Jonas stopped dead still, his eyes as cold and rock-hard as the sapphires they resembled. "You had better not," he warned. "I won't have my family upset because of your shyness. Get used to it, Acadiana. We'll be spending a lot of time together."

Get used to it? Non, *she would never get used to this!* "Will you at least turn your head?" she said, almost in tears. "Please!"

"You're a cruel woman," he said with exaggerated woe. "As much as I will regret it, I'll turn my back this one last time. You are too beautiful for me to deny myself the sight of you."

"Pooh!" she huffed. She threw her arms up in the air, more angry now than modest. "I am not beautiful! You are just a degenerate toad with no more decency than a . . . a . . . Jonas! I'm sorry!" she shrieked when he started walking toward her again. "I said I was sorry!" she cried when he slipped his hands behind her and began unfastening the gown.

Acadiana bit her lip to keep from crying out as he slipped it from her shoulders. Oh, why did he have to be the son of one of the women she loved most in this world! She wouldn't upset Minette with her problems, and he knew it.

It was embarrassing enough to be in this situation, much less bringing someone else into it.

"Jonas, please, I regret my hasty words. If you will please turn around, I'll try to do better." She forced herself to speak in a meek tone of voice, but it riled her to have to humble herself before him.

"Unlikely, love, with your temper," he said dryly, not convinced in the least by her submissive attitude, "but I will give you the benefit of the doubt."

He turned his back and Acadiana shucked her clothing in a matter of seconds. She fairly flew to the tub, afraid he would turn back before the soapy water could conceal her. Jonas's shoulders shook with laughter at her haste. He spun around without warning and caught a glimpse of gently rounded breasts sinking beneath the water. Walking slowly toward the tub, never taking his eyes off hers, he divested himself of his clothing. Acadiana stared back in horror, first at the broad, tan shoulders, then the narrow, firm waist. Finally, manly thighs stood next to her and she had to shut her eyes to keep from looking elsewhere. Leaning forward, his arms on either side of the tub, Jonas grinned at her horrified expression.

"Jonas," she choked out, almost drowning herself when she inched down under the water, "what are you doing?"

"I am going to bathe. Surely you don't expect me to wait until you are finished. The water will be cold by then." His eyes roamed over her devilishly as the water swelled away from her bosom, teasing him with a rosy glimpse every few seconds.

"I'll be through in a second," she murmured, scooting down more and keeping her eyes shut. "If you will just turn your back again . . . I will—"

"Nay, love," Jonas said softly as he stepped into the tub and picked her up underneath the arms.

Acadiana's eyes snapped open, as did her mouth, when he pulled her on top of him until she lay across his hard body. She pushed her hands rigidly against his damp chest, putting him at arm's length, then realized to her utter dismay that she had fully revealed her upper body. Jonas's hungry stare wandered over her nakedness with unabashed desire from the slim column of her throat, arched back now in retreat, to her creamy shoulders and delicately muscled arms. He released his hold on her to slide his hands down her rib cage, then caressed his way back up over her stomach to reach the mounds of flesh so near his face.

"Jonas Courtland! This is just plain indecent!" she cried in embarrassment.

"I know." He grinned, skimming his wet hands over her slick, ripe breasts.

Aware of his unseemly intentions, Acadiana flopped herself down suddenly onto his chest, sending a spray of sudsy water into his face. The unexpected weight caught Jonas off guard, and he was momentarily unbalanced. Acadiana countered by rising before he could recover and pressed a dainty foot to his midsection, then sprang lightly from the tub.

Jonas let out a "whoof!" as the breath was knocked from him by her well-placed aim. Acadiana grabbed a towel as he spit and sputtered soap bubbles along with a few choice obscenities. She was just about to don the nightdress Mattie had laid out for her when Jonas grabbed her about the waist and spun her around.

Locked in an iron embrace, all Acadiana could do was grapple with her nightclothes while staring up at her husband. His eyes were hot, his intentions clearly written there. *"Non,"* she said viciously. "You will not do this again. Have I no rights here? This is my home also; you saw to that!" She struggled with her anger and helplessness, and her eyes were fiercely stubborn as they blazed into his. "You may reap what you have sown, *M'sieu* Husband!"

Jonas's mouth was set in a grim line, but understanding played around his eyes, softening his harsh features. "Let us hope the harvest is bountiful," he said, and lowered his lips to hers in a long, devouring kiss that sent the world spinning out from under Acadiana with a swiftness that left her hanging on to his neck for support. He pulled the night-gown from between their bodies, the soft cotton like burning coals as it grazed Acadiana's skin, leaving her open and vulnerable in her nakedness. Scooping her up in his arms with ease, Jonas carried her to the bed with total disregard for the water dripping in puddles on the floor and bed-clothes. He placed her on the soft coverlet and shielded her body with his before she could seek refuge.

Acadiana squirmed beneath him, trying to cover herself with something besides the long, hard length of male above her, but it was all to no avail. His body, sleek and wet, pressed her into the counterpane as his hand reached up to scatter the pins that held her hair. The thrashing of her head from side to side unwittingly aided him, and her ebony locks sprang forth to flow over the bed linens in shimmering glory. Jonas's heavy legs locked with hers to stop their kicking, his elbows pinned her arms close to the sides of her breasts as his hands cupped her face, his thumbs tracing the high curves of her cheekbones. Her wild writhing stilled and Acadiana stared up at him. The look in his eyes was predatory, hungry, frightening. Her voice was a weak, breathless whisper when she spoke.

"What are you going to do?"

"Make love to you, of course," Jonas said.

"But you already did that."

"And I hope to again and again," he teased, not realizing her fear.

"Not again. I won't have it!" But her voice broke, her words dissolving into a tearful plea. "Jonas, please."

"Acadiana, what is it?" he grumbled, startled and irritated by the fearful expression on her face. He had expected her reluctance, but not this whimpering. "You're acting like a scared child. What's wrong? You knew this would happen."

"You hurt me!" she said, angered now by his cold-hearted treatment along with the inevitable changes taking place in her life that she couldn't stop or condone—this progression toward wifehood that she wanted no part of. She tried to turn away to hide the tears that were now falling unheeded.

"Acadiana." He sighed, feeling some of his frustration evaporate in light of her tears and confusion. His hand went to her cheek and he tenderly brushed away the drops. "It's that way the first time. You brought a lot of that on yourself with your resistance. It wouldn't be so bad if you wouldn't fight me. Relax," he whispered. "Let me prove to you how gentle I can be."

"I don't want to know how gentle you can be. I don't want to do that! It was the most horrible, awful, hateful, disgusting—"

Jonas put his hand over her mouth and held it there until her lips stopped moving. When she appeared docile, he raised his hand a fraction of an inch. "Some would disagree with you." Acadiana opened her mouth angrily, and Jonas replaced his hand. She mumbled something forceful beneath his palm that told him she didn't believe anyone could find what he had in mind agreeable. "You are wrong," he said softly, and eased his hand away.

"You will force me?" Her eyes were huge, luminous pools of violet as she stared up at him.

His frustration returned full blown, and Jonas flung himself away from her desirable body and onto his back where he slung one arm over his eyes. "No, I won't force you!" he replied, angry now. "It shouldn't be this way, and I'm tired of your resistance. If you won't be a wife to me, I'll seek my pleasures elsewhere."

"Non!" Acadiana gasped.

Jonas swiftly turned on his side to face her. "And why not?" he asked coldly.

"I would be shamed, disgraced if people knew—"

"Knew what? That I took a mistress, or that I did so because my own wife won't sleep with me? That's what is disgraceful, Acadiana. A wife turning her own husband away from his bed. And I will seek another," he warned viciously, "if you refuse me. I won't play the martyr, enslaved by my marriage vows, if you won't honor yours as well. But know this: That is the only reason I would turn to another, Acadiana. I am not like other men who would keep their wives at home bearing their children, while they find greater pleasures with a quadroon mistress. I want you, only you. But I won't play these silly games. If there is to be shame, then know that you have brought it on yourself!"

Acadiana's eyes had grown wider with each word of his heated declaration. She had heard of the beautiful part-Negro women of New Orleans who were raised from birth to pleasure men in a sort of half-marriage arrangement. Once she had found out from Katherine about the intimacy of marriage, she had not understood the wives who would put up with such defection from their husbands. To think, by her own hand, that Jonas too might turn to just such an arrangement made her quiver with uncertainty.

Jonas watched the emotions—fear, anger, and insecurity—play across her pale face. Was she so repulsed by him then that her decision was so difficult?

"If I must, then do it!" Acadiana growled between set teeth, startling her husband as she turned her head away.

She shut her eyes and threw her balled fists out stiffly. Jonas almost had the urge to laugh as he looked at her, but with great effort he refrained. Her arms were spread wide but her knees were clamped tightly together. Her whole body was as rigid as an oak tree. Out of his amusement evolved a tenderness within him for her sacrificial pose. She would offer herself to him, if it could be called such, rather than see him turn to another. There was in that offering the tiniest of beginnings that he could build on and a new hunger that was not so much born of lust but of caring.

Acadiana was tense with waiting and wondering why he didn't hurry and get it over with. Hadn't she agreed? She opened one eye cautiously, then the other. She didn't know what she had expected, but what she saw was Jonas's handsome face staring down at her with the most amused expression.

"Well?" she asked irritably.

"Acadiana," he chuckled. "You look like a statue. If this is your willing stance, I think I prefer you the other way."

"Well, what am I supposed to do?" she asked, offended to the very center of her soul.

"Just relax a little, I'll do everything else," he coaxed.

She snarled in reply and let her arms go limp but covered her breasts. Her only hope was that this would be over fast. She didn't think she could take too much of this as often as he seemed to need it. "Jonas," she whispered, shy and uncomfortable and dreading what was to come. "Blow out the candles."

"Why? I've seen all of you and you must know it is all to my liking."

Acadiana blushed hotly at his bold words and made her request again. Jonas reluctantly nodded, but when his lean, naked body left the bed, Acadiana thought of the foolishness of her request. He was completely revealed to her, powerful and strong, frighteningly beautiful. She closed her eyes against his superb masculinity, shivering when he again claimed his place beside her.

Jonas began by placing soft whispery kisses on her eyes, mouth, and throat. He continued the slow, patient assault until he felt her rigid pose soften. Running his fingers lightly over her arms and shoulder, he decided to stay away from the more intimate areas until he felt she was ready. His lips traced a path over her collarbone back to her mouth, where he kissed her more passionately now, probing with his tongue. He continued with tempered aggression until she began to respond. At first shy, then with a curiosity born of inexperience, she began to experiment more freely, kissing him more out of desperation than passion. For reasons unknown to her, Acadiana could not bear the thought of Jonas with another woman, touching, kissing, whispering endearments to someone else the way he was doing to her. Whether vain ego or insecurity, she couldn't say, but her mild response to him held startling surprises for her almost virginal body.

Her lashes fluttered open and she stared up at him with wide, dazed eyes, noting the way his dark sable hair curled against his temples and his brilliant sapphire eyes burned into hers. And when his gaze dropped to wander over her full, slender length in nothing but the muted cast of moonlight, she cupped his face firmly to stop him, embarrassed by being displayed before a man who, no matter how aggressive his pursuit of her, did not love her. Jonas saw her expression cloud over with a pain he did not understand and his mouth plunged down to recapture hers, to rekindle the fire that had begun to burn, if only briefly, in her eyes. His lips melted away her rising resistance, leaving her susceptible to the sweet ecstasy that overpowered her senses and sent her heart, soul, and spirit spiraling out of control and her mind fighting for logical ground. But there was no logic to be found within the iron-muscled arms of her husband, no solid ground on which to gain her footing when she was soaring to a place even higher than the clouds could touch.

Her blood was racing through her veins now, coursing in burning pulses to sensitive nerve endings. She squirmed beneath him, uncomfortable with the strange feelings that began to churn deep inside of her, making her breathless and hungry to cling to him. She didn't like the forceful urgings that were pulling her away from reality into the hinterlands whose boundaries she sensed were limitless.

Jonas's capable hands continued to roam her body, deriving exquisite pleasure from each soft curve, each noble crest. His moan echoed Acadiana's gasp when he fondled her breast, his fingers cupping then kneading the firm mound until his lips craved their share. A warm sensation spread over Acadiana and grew torrid with each pull of her husband's lips. Tiny sparks ignited in the pit of her stomach and trembled down her thighs. She marveled at the feelings his touch stirred in her, but fought to suppress the foreign urges that threatened to overtake her. Jonas continued touching and caressing her, moving his hand lower and lower until he found her secret place. Acadiana flinched then stiffened, suddenly aware of the searching fingers that sent hot shivers throughout her body.

"Acadiana, hold me," he commanded softly.

"I can't," she moaned.

"Shhh," he whispered, kissing her mouth.

Acadiana lay tense and afraid as he brought her arms up to drape his shoulders. She was amazed by the sleek feel of his muscles as they rippled beneath her fingers, could picture them in candlelight, and the memory sent new prickles of discovery shimmering down her body to unsettle her. Jonas wedged his knee between hers and began kissing and caressing her with more urgency. Acadiana moaned beneath him, unable to stop herself. Her body was at war with her mind, searching for a release that she knew nothing about but could sense, and she was afraid if she gave in to this sweet agony, her mind and soul would be shattered. She would lose herself.

She clasped Jonas's back tightly as he began to enter. She no longer feared the pain that his possession would bring but welcomed it, welcomed the clarity of mind that was sure to follow that hot, ripping invasion.

"Non." The whimper broke from her throat, despite her determination to hold it back.

"It's all right," Jonas soothed, reining his passion just barely before it rampaged all out of control. "I know you're tender. I'll be gentle, please relax."

He slipped inside, holding her firmly, allowing her body to blossom and accept him. The pressure she felt was more filling than painful, and Acadiana almost regretted the ease with which he took her as she lay deathly still, more afraid of the unknown than of what she was actually feeling.

Tight! She was so tight, it was an excruciating effort to remain calm. But Jonas began a slow rhythm, whispering encouragement as he coaxed her to love him in return. But Acadiana blocked out his seductive words as the tempo increased, carrying her over wave after wave of cresting emotion. On and on he continued, and it seemed that he would never end the slow, confusing torture that caused tingling sensations to build with each hard thrust. Attempting to act on its own, her body arched to greet him, and she fought against the power he had to make her heartbeat thunder against her breast as his was doing, her body to move with the motion of his. A part of her cried out and searched for fulfillment before she subdued her impassioned movements in confusion and fear, holding the innermost part of herself free from this total possession.

Jonas sensed her withdrawal and tried to hold back the blazing fire that lurched within him, but he had gone too far, come too close. He thrust deeply several times, unable to control the aching pulses any longer. His breath caught and struggled in his throat as he reached the ultimate peak, then was released as he plummeted back to earth.

Acadiana felt him shudder within her. The burning throbs seemed to echo throughout her own body for the merest second, a tingling so faint and undefinable that she wanted to grasp it, to hold it within her until the frustration that even now in the aftermath trembled throughout her body could be put to rest.

Jonas took a long, deep breath and lay quiet, still joined to her intimately. The heat that flowed through him was quickly dissipating, leaving him spent yet empty and disappointed. He didn't understand Acadiana's detachment at the last, not after her fervent responses earlier. She had slipped away somehow, retreating within the protective shelters of her own making to a place he could not touch. Never had he experienced so agonizing a frustration after such an explosive climax—the heights of passion he had reached alone. A liberal lover, he had never taken women without a care for their own enjoyment. But this woman he could not reach.

He raised himself on his arms and searched her blank face for answers, tried to delve into her thoughts and the reasons behind her withdrawal. The moonlight played over her arresting features, deepening her wide amethyst eyes and the golden tone of her skin. Her hair, black as midnight, was a vivid contrast to the white bed linens. Jonas wanted to wrap himself up in those silken tresses, to press his lips to hers again until she was mindless with passion and he could erase the haunted look in her eyes.

"Did I hurt you?" he asked, concerned by the vacant expression on her face.

"Non," she replied, shaking her head then covering her inflamed face with both hands.

What would he think of her? She had tried to lie still, but her body had acted like some treacherous marauder, plundering her will to steal the very breath from her lungs and leaving her as shaky as a newborn foal. She despised the weakness that engulfed her when she was in his arms. For a frightening moment she had been poised on the edge of a vortex of heinous depths that promised to sweep her uncontrolled into some dark void. And for that same fleeting moment, she had wanted to go there, to allow her body to be sucked into that whirlpool until she drowned in it. And that fatal want was what frightened her the most.

"Are you sure?" Jonas asked, trying to fathom her withdrawal. "Look, Acadiana, if I hurt you, I'm sorry. I tried to be gentle." He was certain she had begun to enjoy his love-making and just as certain that she would not admit it. Yet near the last she had retreated into that closed-off world he had begun to recognize as her place of defense.

"Non, you didn't hurt me," she groaned. *Mon Dieu,* why didn't he just shut up!

"Perhaps you enjoyed it?" he inquired.

"Non!" Acadiana gasped much too quickly. Her eyes flared in shame and on her face was written the obvious. She abruptly turned away from him to salvage her pride.

"Look at me." He smiled. He had to turn her over twice

before she would lie still on her back and look at him. "I wanted you to enjoy it."

"Non!" she denied. It was unthinkable. She had behaved like a wanton. Or at least that's what she *thought* one of those passion-ruled women would act like, all hot and squirming inside.

"Yes," he teased. "That's the way it should be."

"But I thought . . ." she started but could not go on.

"Let me guess—making love is a wifely duty to be endured but certainly not enjoyed. Right?"

"Perhaps," she said, eyes downcast lest Jonas see the tangle of emotions there. She didn't actually know what she was supposed to think. She had not had a mother to discuss it with, had been too embarrassed to listen to her aunt, and the conversation with Katherine had been flighty at best. Sex, when spoken of at all, had been mentioned only in whispers, as if it were something evil or humiliating, something to be ashamed of. And she knew her heated reaction to this man who did not love her was certainly shameful.

"Puritan ideas, love," Jonas said, assessing her thoughts as accurately as if she had spoken them aloud, "that have no basis in this relationship."

"Oh," she said, burying her face in his chest because he wouldn't release her, and she couldn't look into his eyes while he spoke so blatantly of such things.

She wasn't sure whether she believed him or even wanted to believe him. Her body ached for something she didn't understand, and lying naked next to a man who was equally unclad, she just couldn't think clearly. She would have to dwell on this later, she reasoned tiredly. She was wrapped within his arms, enveloped by the male scent that was becoming all too familiar to her. He shook her peace with those strong arms, yet there was also a feeling of security there that could not be denied even by the most angry heart of her. She wanted to cry out her frustration, to lash out at the man who had caused the upheaval in her emotions. But her arms and legs were heavy-laden with exhaustion and her mind dulled by conflicting thoughts. Her face pressed against the soft hair on his chest, Acadiana listened to Jonas's heartbeat for what seemed like hours before she was eventually lulled to sleep.

Jonas tried again during the night to recapture the intimacy, but Acadiana's confused whimpering was as effective as an angry denial to his manhood. Despite her rejection he tried once more, but her numbed, sleepy submission as she lay beneath him so disgusted his passionate nature that he turned angrily away to find solace in sleep. And yet sleep eluded him, and the darkness tortured him with visions of what marriage should be, of things he had never needed or thought he wanted—talking, sharing, and loving—until in quiet desperation he gripped Acadiana's shoulders and shook her until her eyes opened, wide and startled. His voice cut through the blackness like a steel-edged knife.

"Why do you hold yourself from me?"

Time hung still and motionless around them. The very air seemed to have been sucked from the room as Acadiana stared back at him with deep fathomless eyes. Her whispered response when it finally came held the fierce and fatal sound of one doomed.

"You would have my soul!"

Jonas could not deny it.

10

The first hint of sunlight was stealing through the window. Tiny specks of dust were dancing in the golden beam that stretched its muted rays to the floor. Acadiana rested in the stillness of early morning, watching the little motes drift and sway, and had the sudden urge to flash her hand through the sunbeam like a child to watch the motes scatter then resettle themselves.

Easing up on her elbow with the utmost care so as not to awaken him, she studied her husband. Even in sleep, his face held a troubled look. The bold light of day sent vivid pictures of the night past chasing through her mind to heat her cheeks. The scenes were not something she wished to dwell on, and she slipped out of bed before Jonas stirred, afraid his passion would rise if he found her still beside him. She wasn't yet ready to face the conflicting feelings prompted by their coupling.

Acadiana didn't think there was real meanness in her husband, but he had acted quite awful in the middle of the night. Imagine wanting to do that again, she thought with growing unrest. It was truly beyond her to understand such behavior. She began to wash and winced at the soreness that brought the night's activities even more clearly to mind. Did men suffer no such ill effects after the deed? Jonas must not, she thought resentfully, pursuing her as he had even in the wee hours of the morning.

Her uneasiness grew as he stirred in the bed, and she dressed quickly in a high-waisted sprigged muslin gown trimmed with bottle-green ribbon. Disregarding the matching bonnet because of further movement from the bed, she hastily stripped the ribbon from it and tied back her hair while inching cautiously out the door. Once reaching the safety of the hall, she went in search of Minette. This was one person she was not the least confused about. A flutter of sheer excitement raced through her with the knowledge that she would be a part of this woman's life again. Acadiana found her outside on the first-floor veranda awaiting breakfast.

"Good morning, *Grand'mère.*" She beamed. Her entire being radiated with a happiness, the like of which she had not felt for over ten years.

"My precious Cade, you are a breath of sunshine," Minette said warmly. "Come see."

Acadiana sat next to her, basking in utter bliss at being reunited. The sweet aroma of rose, honeysuckle, and jonquil surrounded them. Not far from the house a faint breeze stirred the palmetto and the weary bayou trudged onward, rippling sluggishly against its grassy bank. No words were necessary for the moment, and Acadiana stared lovingly at Minette, content to see that time had served only to enhance the beauty of her aristocratic face. She was a small-boned woman with fine, sharp features, and her dark hair held not a touch of gray.

Born in this country to parents of French nobility, Minette had fallen in love with Jonas Edward Courtland, a struggling planter of French and English descent. Mostly French, Minette would proclaim, the English being too far back to be considered applicable. Together they had built an empire of sugar, timber, and indigo, based on hard work, dedication, and a reverential fear of God.

It had never been easy—not then, not now. The duties of a plantation mistress stretched far beyond the idealized view of the genteel woman sipping lemonade on the veranda. Minette was required to manage the household economically, from furnishings to domestic supplies. She was responsible for teaching the servants special skills in cooking, nursing, dying, weaving, and clothing care. Many hours were spent supervising the Negro hospital and presiding over all the affairs pertaining to the welfare of the servants. She had total control over the operations of the main house and its supporting facilities.

As the plantation mistress, she also took on the duties of her husband when he was away on business. In Minette's case, as with so many of her friends, her husband had fallen prey to one of the common swamp fevers. She had become a widow early in life and had been forced to take over her husband's duties of managing the plantation with the efficiency and effectiveness that her beloved spouse had.

For the last thirty-two of her forty-seven years of life, Minette had risen each day before dawn, managing all the social affairs for friends and business guests. She had arranged countless services for Negro weddings and funerals, also attending birthings and illnesses. The household help, under Mattie's guidance, had been picked for honesty and steadfastness. There had been no reason for Minette to keep food stocks and supplies under lock and key, as so many other plantation owners had to do. And thankfully now she had two grown sons to help with the manly duties.

Life was hard at Courtland Manor, but it was as rich and rewarding as life at any court of England or France.

Minette took in the radiance and freshness of the girl sitting across from her, but her eyes grew sad when she asked the question that could no longer be avoided.

"What of your parents, Cade? They are dead, no? When your family did not return, we feared the worst. Later we heard so many conflicting reports. We were never exactly sure what had happened." The words were spoken with sadness, and concern was etched across Minette's classic face. Though she had grieved over a decade ago for her dear friend, the agonizing loss had returned full force last night when Cade had appeared but had offered no word of her parents. Prayers that in the past had petitioned God for Elaine's safe return had been offered last night for her soul. But mingled with the sadness was a new elation that the child born of Elaine and Armand's love was now truly a part of her family.

"Oui, they are gone," Acadiana said softly. But not forgotten, she vowed to herself, and the dream that had been theirs would one day live through her.

"I thought as much. So, little one, tell me of your life for the past ten years. There has been more sorrow, yes? I can see it in your eyes. But not too much. No, not enough to dampen your spirit. You have the same determined look of your proud Cajun mama."

"Life did indeed deal a few cruel blows, *Grand'mère,* but I think it has served to strengthen me," Acadiana said in earnest.

"I would have expected as much from you, Cade." There was pride in Minette's voice as she spoke, and a warmth in her eyes that only a mother would have for a daughter. "Now, you will tell me everything, yes? And, Cade, do not hold anything back. I will understand."

Acadiana embarked on the long journey back in time. She told Minette everything, from the death of her parents at ruthless hands, to her years with Jean near the peace-loving Indians. She recounted her difficult adjustment back into society and even her marriage to Jonas, based solely on his acquisition of her land.

Minette listened intently, sometimes laughing, other times crying, reliving the past with Acadiana in pain and pride. Only at the last did she become silent and thoughtful, smiling softly at Acadiana's rendition of the reasons for the marriage.

"Do not let your troubled mind play games with you,

Cade. Jonas wanted the land, that much is true. I will admit that he has thought of little else for the past year. But never would he compromise his freedom for the sole purpose of acquiring your property. You must not argue this point," Minette said as Cade began shaking her head. "I know my son. Remember, I raised him. He sees something in you that he wants. The land was just his means to get it." The older woman's expression was introspective as was her secret smile. "I am not sure that even he realizes it yet."

"I wish I could believe that, *Grand'mère,* but he told me he was marrying me for the land," Acadiana replied, hurt and confused by the feelings that surfaced with her confession.

"You wanted this marriage?" Minette asked, skeptical.

Acadiana's eyes were downcast, her fingers twisting in the folds of her gown. She could not, nay, would not lie to this woman. *"Non,* I fought it at every turn."

"Yet you expect Jonas to profess love when you have none to give?"

"Non!" Her head snapped up. "I want to love . . . I mean, I could . . . I mean . . ." Her breath came out in a deflated groan, and she squeezed her eyes shut. "I don't know what I mean."

"I thought so." Minette smiled in understanding gained from years of experience. "Listen, Cade, love takes time. It must be nurtured; it is a growing thing. Anything else is just infatuation and does not last." Her words were smooth, like warmed honey, and they served to ease Acadiana's battered emotions. "Love between a husband and wife must be developed over a period of time with trial and patience. If both persons are willing to weather the storms, and there *will* be storms, love will find its way, and time will see it out."

"I hope so, *Grand'mère,* I truly do," Acadiana admitted slowly. Had that not been a part of her dream also? The love of a husband and children? But her resentment of the man who was not a dream but her husband in truth sent anger burning through her mind. She could not picture herself devoted to the man who, with his high-handed ways and greed for her land, had forced her into marriage. Her rage, too close to the surface now, showed in the heated timbre of her voice. "Jonas seems interested in only one aspect of marriage." The words were out before she could stop them, and Acadiana lowered her lashes in embarrassment.

"Of course, *bébé.*" Minette laughed softly. "It is that way with a newly married couple. It is part of getting to know each other." Her voice dropped to a mischievous whisper. "When Jon and I were first married, we could never get enough of one another. We would sneak off at every chance and got almost no work done." Her smile was faintly reminiscent of bygone days. "Disgraceful, were we not? We settled down over the years, but we never lost the joy of those first stolen moments. I have been tempted many times since my husband's death to take a lover, just to fulfill those basic desires born to every woman, but my firm devotion to God and respect for myself would not permit me to be so immoral."

Acadiana squirmed, uncomfortable in the face of Minette's honesty. "You enjoyed your husband . . . his advances?"

"Enjoyed?" Minette laughed. "No, Cade. I craved him, longed for him as a starving man does food. Oh, I am sorry if I have shocked you, child."

"Non, I wanted to know. It is just hard for me right now to . . . you know . . . accept Jonas." She couldn't imagine anyone craving that act and wondered for a brief moment if they were talking about two entirely different things. The color of her cheeks was heightened by the sudden memory of the night past.

Minette took pity on the girl who was squirming so uncomfortably before her. Although she could sympathize with Acadiana's plight, she also had a son to consider.

More than anything in the world she wanted the two of them to find happiness with each other.

"The way you two have started out, that is no wonder. But if you will permit me to give you some advice?"

"Oui, anything."

"Jonas is a passionate man like his father was. Men of that nature do not do anything without a full commitment, and what they possess, they hold dearly. You have not been together long, Cade, but try to give yourself freely to your husband. This intimacy is not everything in a marriage, but it is a very important part. You will find a joy you never knew existed. As much as a mother hates to admit it, I know my son is not inexperienced in the ways of love. He will teach you, if you are willing."

"I will try, *Grand'mère,"* Acadiana mumbled, mortified by their conversation. "All I can do is try."

They were interrupted as the object of their discussion walked up with an irritated scowl on his face. "Good morning, ladies." Jonas nodded curtly, affording his mother only the barest courtesy before turning to his wife. "Acadiana, shall I forever be wont to find you out of my bed when I awake?"

"You knew I was meeting your mother early," she replied, undaunted by his stern voice but very much affected by his manly appearance. He was casually attired in a white linen shirt and tight-fitting fawn breeches that disappeared inside his tall Hessian boots. Even disdaining the proper coat and cravat, he was striking, his commanding presence sending an involuntary shiver down her spine.

"It is a sad day when a man's wife takes a preference to her mother-in-law over her own husband," he returned in the bored voice of one annoyed but not angry. His eyes lazily swept his wife's figure and settled on her glowing cheeks. Her eyes gave none of her thoughts away, but at least there was no martyred look there.

"Cade and I have had a lovely chat," Minette said. "Be a good boy for once and join us for breakfast."

"Thank you, Mother, but I have come to fetch my wayward bride. I have an inkling she may want to accompany me over to her property."

"Oui!" Acadiana gasped, jumping to her feet. "Excuse us, *Grand'mère.* It has been too long since I have seen it."

Jonas almost had to run to keep up with his wife as she neared the stables. He had ordered the horses saddled before locating her, and they set out at once. Acadiana was anxious to put her dreams to sight, and rode with reckless haste through the woods until she caught sight of her former home. She skidded to an abrupt stop, her heart throbbing wildly with equal portions of grand elation and devastating pain. It was a tangible thing, that pain, choking off her air while her throat worked in spasms to hold back the tears. She moaned softly, soaking in the view that rushed back happy memories of love and laughter. She fought back useless tears as Jonas helped her dismount, feeling so empty, yet so right—home again.

Although badly in need of repair, the Hamilton cottage stood as she remembered it, nestled between towering oaks. The roof was high-peaked and had a gable at each end. The front gallery ran the full width of the house and was recessed underneath the main roof to become known as the *galerie intérieure,* or inside gallery. She had watched her mother stand there so many times smiling from the porch to welcome guests or to greet her father when he came in from the fields. Elaine was forever scolding him to remove his muddy boots before entering, and Armand would tease her back to good humor. Such a trivial memory, a paltry thing to bring such a burdensome ache to Acadiana's chest.

She walked slowly toward the house, drawn by the memories yet repelled by the pain that crossing the threshold would bring. It was almost a relief when Jonas took her arm to guide her around to the back.

"Where are we going?" she asked, pulling away. "I want to see the house."

"I have something to show you," he said, gripping her

arm more firmly to pull her down a path. Reluctant, she followed him, casting furtive glances over her shoulder at the cottage every few feet as if to make sure it was still there.

But the cottage soon faded from sight as she was pulled along through the woods. They passed wild azaleas, huckleberry bushes, blackberry brambles, and other wild foliage growing alongside the narrow path—until they stepped into a clearing. Acadiana caught her breath when they rounded a familiar magnolia tree.

"Your wedding present," Jonas said.

"A gazebo," she said, stunned. She stared in awe at the whitewashed structure, a replica of the one in her painting, fitting perfectly in the tranquil setting. It looked just as she had known it would, just as she'd planned it over the lonely years when she'd been surrounded by people yet belonged to none. And a softening crept in, slowly at first then more poignant, salving the wounds that seeing her old home had resurrected. "Oh, Jonas, I don't know what to say." She shuffled the toe of her slipper in the dirt, self-conscious, feeling awkward and uncertain . . . and grateful. After much consideration, she lifted her head to look at her husband. *"Merci,"* she breathed, and tentatively placed a kiss on his cheek.

"I will build you a hundred," he said, dazed.

"It is wonderful," she managed, blushing. With dreamy-eyed reverence she took in the cozy eight-sided room with benches lining the walls, overwhelmed that this staunch, overbearing husband of hers could be so thoughtful.

Jonas led her up the steps, hard-pressed to keep her still long enough to walk in safely. Acadiana strolled gaily around the circular structure three times, stopping each lap to grace him with a whimsical smile, the first genuine warmth she had shown him. It was with childlike excitement that she did so, he knew, but enjoyed it nonetheless. Jonas finally halted her after the third trip, begging her to stop lest she make them both too dizzy to stand.

"This is truly the finest wedding gift a bride has ever received," she said, and meant it. There wasn't anything that he could have done, could have given her that was more personal, more suited to her than this, lest it be the house itself. "But I have no present for you."

"I can think of one," Jonas said, the blue of his eyes darkening as he enfolded her in his arms.

"What?" she asked innocently, then gasped when she realized the clever way he had turned her words and gratitude to his favor. "Here?"

"There is no one but us. It is as private as our bedroom," he coaxed.

"You are teasing me." She grinned shakily, because she feared that he wasn't. Still, she couldn't possibly imagine that he would want to follow through with what his devouring expression suggested.

"I would never tease about that."

"You can't be serious, Jonas!"

"I've never been more serious."

Acadiana wanted so badly to ignore Minette's advice, but she had promised she would try. But out here, in the open, in the daylight, she would die of shame! *Non,* she probably wouldn't die, and that would be worse. She stared into Jonas's eyes, her own filled with mistrust and uncertainty. "Please don't ask this of me."

Jonas cupped her chin, his fingers lightly caressing her cheek. "And what if I do ask?"

He already had. If not in so many words, the request was in his eyes, in each stroke of his fingers, in the deep clarity of his voice. Acadiana wondered if he was truly giving her a choice or only prolonging the moment before he would demand it.

Give yourself freely to your husband. . . .

Oh, *Grand'mère,* you cannot know how hard that would be for me! Acadiana shrugged, feeling overwhelmed but resigned, then summoned every ounce of courage and abandon she could muster and smiled at Jonas shyly.

Her arms were crossed protectively over her breasts and her head was shaking no, but the words that crossed her lips said, *"Oui."*

"Somehow I had a feeling you would say th—"

Jonas's words skidded to a halt out of shock and disbelief. It took him but a moment, however, to recover. Everything about her stance was crying an emphatic negative, but he was willing to test the waters. He lowered his head and kissed her lightly, expecting her pull away any second. When she stood docile before him, neither accepting nor rejecting, he pulled back and stared at her flushed cheeks, her deep violet eyes. He knew this would be more than difficult for her, knew also that if they crossed this milestone one more barrier would fall, he would be one step closer to demolishing the entire wall. His hands traveled lightly down her arms, unhurried, until his fingers threaded through hers and he pulled her arms away from her body. He lowered his head again, brushing his lips along her hairline to her ear.

"If you're going to pull away, do so now," he whispered. "I won't be able to stop later. I want you to understand that."

Acadiana shivered as his breath curled around her ear, down the side of her neck, purling through the blood in her veins until it thickened into a heavy thump in her chest. She felt sluggish, weighted down by the heaviness of having to make such a decision. And she almost wished he had not asked it of her, had just taken what he perceived was his right, so she could be justified in her resentment. "I have agreed," she said.

Of course, she had not. He knew it no matter how she verbalized it. But it was more than he had expected, and he would play it to the end, whatever the outcome. He kissed her deeply, without caution now, and she returned his kiss with as much fervor as she was capable of. She pressed her slight body to his larger one, molding her feminine softness to his steel strength, for there was nothing else to give her succor from the heavy emotional baggage of the past that clung to her like a ball and chain. Her senses spun dizzily as emotions swelled within her, whirling through her racing heart and plunging below, making her knees weak.

Jonas pulled her tightly into the circle of his arms and drank from her as if he would drain every drop of inner resistance, soothe the past hurts, rekindle the joy she had found in his gift. His lips glided over her cheeks and neck, lingered on the frantic pulse in her throat as he glanced quickly around the gazebo and damned himself for not supplying the place with cushions, which his logical mind knew would mildew in a day's time. He drew back slightly, his breathing escalated as he ran his fingers over her shoulders until they rested on the upper fullness of her breasts. Then he stopped and waited.

Acadiana's heart skipped with anticipation, then stalled when nothing more happened. Her eyes fluttered open, brimming with confusion and something more as she stared back at him. His fingers flexed then slid lightly over her bodice, testing, then moved to her back where he fumbled with the fasteners of her gown. One button pulled free, then another and another until the gown went slack on her shoulders, and still his eyes did not leave hers. Acadiana made a sound, indefinable to both of them, as he slid the gown and chemise from her shoulders, baring her to the waist. She dropped her head to his chest, hiding without physically turning away, unable to meet his appraising stare. He touched her everywhere, softly as the wind did on her exposed flesh, without aggression but with a sureness that sent a hot kick of alarm through Acadiana and jolted her into action.

She lifted her head and pulled his face back down to hers to resume the kiss. *Mais oui,* she could get used to this kissing, if she just didn't have to do the other! Jonas's hands caressed every inch of exposed skin, and she had to fight to squelch the desire to cover herself. She was quickly losing the battle when he suddenly scooped her up. Her arms went around his neck for balance and she clung to him as he walked to a bench and sat down, settling her on his lap. His desire for her was boldly evident beneath her bottom, and Acadiana squirmed in embarrassment, which ripped a deep groan from Jonas and caused her go still as a stone.

"Do that again," he said, and the color flared brighter on her cheeks. "Do you know how utterly charming you look with your face all pink, your eyes round as saucers"—his eyes dropped lower—"your pretty br—"

Acadiana couldn't respond, just lowered her lashes as she attempted to burrow her head back into his chest, but his fingers caught her beneath the chin and tilted her head back.

"Don't hide. There is nothing wrong with us being here like this." She could hear the smile in his voice, not teasing but reassuring.

"It feels wrong," she said.

"I know, love, but it shouldn't." His lips dipped playfully to hers. "Smile, I'm not going to ravish you." *Not just yet.* She didn't smile but gave herself up to the kiss, the seductive calling of his deep voice, the gentleness of his restraint. His tongue entered easily between her lips and danced along the inside of her mouth before touching hers. She evaded him at first, but he was relentless in the chase, growling in mock frustration as his arms tightened around her, and the kiss became a playful exchange of wills. Her squirming and twisting gave rise to real frustration, and Jonas squeezed her until she gave a muffled cry for air and finally allowed him to have his way.

The ravishing of her mouth seemed to bathe the rest of her in a warm glow, almost contentment, so paradoxical to the feelings more deeply seated in the heart of her. A strong, sly hand began a lazy journey beneath Acadiana's petticoats, up her calf, past the inside of her knee to her thighs. She gasped and wiggled in protest, locking her legs tightly together. Jonas echoed her gasp, not in protest but intense pleasure as her delectable backside grazed him repeatedly.

"You agreed," he said against her lips, and she knew by his tone that he was grinning.

"You are despicable," she said, but she too was smiling, if reluctantly, as his hand struggled to edge its way between her legs.

A tender battle began that eventually toppled them both to the floor, leaving Acadiana gasping and giggling as she scrambled on hands and knees to evade him, and Jonas thankful that her thoughts had been deflected from painful memories of her past as he caught her around the waist and spun her beneath him. She called him a rogue and a scoundrel, and he proved it by nipping at one of her rose-tipped breasts, which caused a matching color to splay across her cheeks. His eyes, hot as the sun's revealing rays, roamed her with a directness that made her want to shield herself, but each time she tried he buried his face in the hollow of her breasts, rubbing his sable hair back and forth until she cried mercy, while his hand did outrageous things below.

Her skirts were bunched up near her waist, Jonas's hand insinuated between her thighs, her humor lagging almost as quickly as her dignity. She squealed anew when his fingers began a daring foray over areas, at least in her own mind, better left alone. His knees parted her legs farther, his fingers finally finding what they had so avidly been seeking, and he began to stroke her with a constancy that made the heat rise and plunge within her. Acadiana gasped, her back arching involuntarily, her eyes widening with wonder, then growing heavy-lidded with the deluge of sensual feelings. He did deliciously wicked things with those fingers, tantalizing her humid flesh until unrest sizzled through her, and she arched again to meet him.

A blur scampered past them, and Acadiana's startled cry had nothing to do with desire. They both twisted sharply to see a squirrel scurry across the floor and dart to the rail.

With a jaundiced eye it perched there and chattered angrily at the couple below.

"Mon Dieu," Acadiana said in dismay.

Jonas rolled his eyes at her tone. "It's not as if it knows what we're doing."

But that's what it felt like to Acadiana, as if they had been caught at something illegal. "I think we are invading its new home," she giggled nervously, then rolled to her knees and clutched her gown to her shoulders in modesty. Her color ran high as an errant child's in mischief. "Maybe we are not welcome here."

Jonas cursed silently but nonetheless violently. "It is the one who is not welcome," he stated.

Suspiciously he looked back and forth between his wife and the animal as if they were in league together, then rose and helped Acadiana to her feet. He gave an exasperated sigh as he turned her around to fasten the gown. His hands lingered on her bare back only a second, for she had gone all stiff and anxious again. The moment had passed, but Jonas was left with a burgeoning ache and just a touch of bitterness that everything had gone awry.

"Maybe we should wait for a more appropriate time, like winter, when *it* is in hibernation," he said soberly.

"Do squirrels hibernate?"

"This one had better, or it'll end up in Mattie's dumplings," he warned.

Feeling somewhat braver now that her bodice was closed, Acadiana gave her husband an awkward smile. "I guess I will have to find another time to thank you properly for the gift."

"I shall count the minutes," Jonas promised as he escorted her down the steps.

Acadiana walked slowly up the stairway leading from the gallery into the *grenier*. Each step was labored, each sight a painful memory of all she had lost. The attic had been used as a loom room for spinning and weaving when she was much younger, then had been turned into a *garçonnière* for her brother, Matthew, to sleep in when he reached the prestigious age of fourteen and was considered a young bachelor instead of a child. How proud he had been that day when their father had made a big to-do about moving everything out to make room for Matthew's things. And how jealous she had been because he was so grown up and she was still a child. Acadiana had thought things would change between them, but they hadn't. Matthew had not acted any differently than he always had. For the first time in her life, Acadiana was glad he had not lived. She wouldn't have wanted him to see the destruction of his family's future.

Acadiana lifted her head, and Jonas could see the tears caught in the tangle of her thick lashes. He wanted to comfort her, to wipe away the hurt that clouded her vibrant eyes. But he did not know the words that would erase the pain. Only time would heal the ache. He followed his wife back down the stairs and into the kitchen. Acadiana wiped away another tear as she stood by the window and ran her hand over the *tablette.* The shelf was built to extend outside the house, forming a table to wash dishes, for cutting vegetables, or for Elaine Hamilton to do other kitchen chores while keeping company with her children as they played outside. It had also served as a convenient place to quickly cool the freshly baked custards, pies, and cakes that her children loved so.

Once a much smaller cottage, additions had been made by adding another house of identical design and size alongside the old one, gable to gable to make room for another bedroom, sewing room, and small sitting area. And for the other children Elaine had not been able to conceive but had mourned in her silent, accepting way.

Acadiana smiled sadly as she wandered silently through each dust-caked room, fighting the pain while cherishing the memories. She remembered the music and dancing of the Saturday night *fais dodo.* Everyone from the neighboring farms would gather for the fun. Musicians had stood in this very room, members of the community skilled in playing the fiddle, accordion, and the triangle, or "ting-a-ling," as she had called it. When she was small, Acadiana had been confused by the term *fais dodo,* which she knew was baby talk for "go to sleep." Her mother had explained later that the event usually lasted throughout the night, and the adults could not start their dancing until the children had been put to sleep and were out from underfoot. She recalled fondly how her mother used to rock neighboring babies, cooing softly to them until their little heads would drop to her bosom.

After the initial shock, the morning was blissful in some ways for Acadiana as she explored the grounds and the house. Jonas took note of needed repairs as she searched through childhood memories in the form of possessions left behind. She laughed and wept with every room, and Jonas felt a heady satisfaction watching her, laughing with her over some small treasure, consoling her over articles too painful to bring joy.

She stopped at noon, glanced up at her small home, and her breath caught on a sob. "I do not think I want to live here again," she whispered fiercely, defensively.

Jonas pressed her face to his chest. "I would never have let you," he said soberly.

They returned to Courtland Manor in a quiet mood. Acadiana still clutched an old ragdoll she had retrieved from a toy chest. The simple homemade object had prompted more tears than the rest of the house combined. Jonas had wrapped her within his strong arms, stroked her hair, and let her weep until the ache had eased. And for the first time Acadiana had gone willingly into those arms and, for the moment at least, had felt a security she had not known in over a decade. Jonas helped her dismount when they reached the manor house, then kissed her forehead as he eyed the doll pressed to her breast.

"You must put the past behind you, love. Come, let us go forward."

Giving him a tearful smile, Acadiana nodded her head, determined to do just that. Jonas followed her into the house, steering her up the staircase toward their bedroom. He had grand delusions of rekindling the ardor of the morning before they had been interrupted by the squirrel. Mattie's voice rose sharply to halt their progress.

"Mast' Jonas! You get that chile back down here! She ain't had no lunch, and it be nigh on to six hours since she ate breakfast. She didn't eat enough then to keep a bird alive. Just mosey your fine self back on down to the drawing room and I'll bring y'all something good in." Jonas leveled a murderous warning at the maid that turned almost pleading when she returned his stare. "Go on now! Don't be looking at me in that sassy way, boy. I'll take a strap to your backside. Ain't gonna starve that girl baby in my house, sho ain't!"

Acadiana, grateful for the timely interruption, hid a giggle behind the ragdoll as she followed her husband back down the stairs. Jonas wondered at what point he had completely lost control of the manor that a servant could talk to him so—and he allow it! Alas, he realized he had never really had it. Mattie had been running the place alongside Minette for longer than he could remember. He sighed, accepting the fact that the sweet interlude he had planned would have to wait for another time.

Acadiana ate in silence, thinking of all she had seen at the cottage. The pain was almost unbearable as she thought of everything she had lost. How in the world had she thought she could forget the hurt? The protective wall she had been building for so many years had come tumbling down around her when she stepped into the cottage. Its unique design had been imbedded in her memory for so long, she never dreamed it would bring so much pain with the joy that washed over her upon seeing it again.

Acadiana shook her head, pushing back the hurtful memories as she stared at the bouillabaisse. The highly seasoned stew was made with several kinds of fish and seafood. The

aroma steamed up, making her stomach grumble in anticipation, and easing her mind from the cottage.

Edward asked Jonas to accompany him to the mill after
lunch. Unable to think of a plausible excuse for staying in
the house during the middle of the day, Jonas grudgingly
went with his younger brother, cursing himself for not hauling Acadiana off somewhere else for a few weeks to get
acquainted.

Acadiana retreated to her bedroom, glad to have some
privacy to gather her thoughts about her family and time to
grieve once again for her loss. Thoughts of Jonas came unbidden to her troubled mind, visions of his kindness at the
cottage and his generosity in having the gazebo built. She
did not welcome the thought that he could be as kind as he
could be overbearing. It was too hard to hate the man who
had held her tenderly and allowed her to cry out her pain,
too hard to associate him with the man who coveted her
land and had forced her into marriage.

The solitude of the elegant bedroom suddenly became as
uninviting as the thoughts of the man who shared it with
her. Acadiana walked over to the wardrobe and withdrew
the satchel that held loving memories of another life. A life
that was filled with so much hard work toward survival that
it had washed away the hurt for a while, leaving no room
for anything but day-to-day living. All those years with Uncle Grayson's family she had been able to escape back into
her world when she felt the despair creeping up on her. But
now she could not run away and hide. Now she had to
make a new life. A life with Jonas.

She opened the hide and took out each article with reverence. She savored the smell and feel of each object, as she
had done so many times before when in this mood. She
almost laughed aloud at the expression of shock and indignation that would plant itself on Mattie's face should she
walk down the grand staircase in her Indian garments. She
could imagine the scolding she would receive when the Ne-

gress finally found her tongue. There were few who would tolerate her need for freedom, fewer still who understood it.

She unrolled the drawing and ran her fingertips over the familiar face. "You would understand," she whispered. "I wish so much had not happened, *mon ami,* and you could be here to tell me everything will be all right."

She placed everything back in the sack and slumped down on the bed. *Grand'mère* would know how to console her, but Acadiana was a grown woman now and should not need to seek comfort in a mother's arms during these feelings of desperation. Desperate? What was she desperate for? The love of a family lost in childhood? Or another family, one little understood by the civilized white man? Or of a man, now her husband? Would he give her the love that had already been twice lost to her a lifetime ago?

Acadiana wiped at a stray tear that rolled down her cheek. *"Mon Dieu."* She sniffed and angrily swiped at another drop. For almost a decade she had been unable to cry. With everything that had happened over the years she had not shed a single tear. Now it seemed as if that was all she ever did. She didn't understand but felt so strongly the need for comfort from her troubling thoughts that she almost went in search of it. But where would she go? Who would offer her ease?

She wondered if she could seek shelter in her husband's arms as normal wives did, as her mother always had, as Aunt Elizabeth did. It seemed the way of things, for a wife to give and receive comfort from a husband. But that option was not open to her with Jonas. She knew he desired her, but that was not enough. Right now she felt she would go off in a screaming rage if he mocked her feelings. *Non,* she could not take the chance of losing her self-respect, of laying her soul bare before the man who only compounded her problems.

She tossed fretfully on the bed, ill at ease in the strange house, in the bed she shared with a stranger. Nothing registered in her troubled mind until she forced herself to lie still and quiet. The voice came as clear and undiluted as if the chief were standing before her.

"Remember, Child of the Sun, you are strong. As the corn gathers strength from the sun, your strength lies within. Draw from that spirit."

The words spoken so long ago drifted back to haunt her. Words that had brought comfort in the past now seemed sadly lacking. "But I am not strong," she whispered brokenly. "I am weak and uncertain. Everything seems so lost and out of balance." Acadiana cried herself to sleep long before darkness put the land to rest.

Jonas climbed the stairs slowly, thinking of the woman who would by now be waiting in his bed. He'd had to deal with numerous problems facing the mill—most of them due to the fact that he had been gone for so many weeks.

Acadiana tossed restlessly as he walked in and lowered his weight to her side. She looked so innocent yet troubled, not at all the fierce vixen he knew she could be. Her face was pale against the inky black of her hair, her small fist alternately gripping then releasing the coverlet. He wondered if her thrashing was another ploy to repel him, but pushed the idea aside as the stirring in his loins gave rise to other thoughts. He gathered her into his arms and tenderly kissed her sleepy eyes, hoping she would not turn away from him this time or try to struggle out of his grasp. Her mild responses earlier in the day had left powerful urgings within him to return to her, and the hope that she was finally willing to be a wife to him.

Acadiana sighed, restive, but did not awaken as his nimble fingers unlaced her gown. She gave a startled cry as Jonas pulled it over her head, thinking through the layers of sleep that she was trapped. Jonas braced himself for the confrontation ahead as he sought to claim his bride by right of marriage. This was not the way he wanted things to be, always the conqueror of an unwilling foe, and wondered if her mild acceptance in the gazebo had only been in his imagination. No, damn her, she was willing then, why not now? He looked deeply into her eyes and searched for the answer. He half expected to face that rebellious, defiant look she had leveled on him so many times before, but what he saw was relief. Relief?

"Jonas!" she cried, throwing her arms around his neck. "I was having the most awful dream! I was being chased by outlaws again, just like before. *Mon Dieu,* it was the most terrifying feeling to be trapped with them bearing down on me." Her body trembling, she clamped her arms tighter around his shoulders and pressed her cold cheek to his warm chest, inhaling the masculine scent of leather, sweat, and the clean, fresh smell of the land.

"You are safe now, love." Jonas chuckled.

Her head snapped back, the look of defiance he knew so well returning to her delicate face. "You think it is funny, *m'sieu?*"

"No, Acadiana." He laughed softly, drawing her closer as she tried to push away. "I was not laughing at you, just at myself. I was afraid that you were refusing me again. After our . . . enlightening morning at the gazebo, I had great hopes of a willing bride for once."

"For once! Ha!" she railed. "I will never be willing. How can you think it after blackmailing me into marriage?" The small bit of abandon she had been able to muster in the gazebo had come hard for her, and now he was tossing it back in her face. How dare he tread all over her feelings! However irrational the observation, it consumed her. Unable to free herself from his grasp, Acadiana raised her head and bit into his shoulder with savage determination.

"Acadiana, stop that!" Jonas yelped, pushing her back down and pinning her to the bed. Even with the pain in his shoulder, he was having a hard time keeping the mirth from his voice as he spoke to her. "Now listen to me! I told you I was not laughing at you. I was laughing at myself. I had such wonderful and wicked thoughts about us the entire afternoon. All day I tried to get away from the mill to come back to you. When you cried out in your sleep, I thought you were fighting me again."

"I was fighting you," she lied, embarrassed by her outburst but outraged by his patronizing smile.

Used now to her mercurial moods, Jonas ignored her and dropped a kiss on her nose. "I laughed because I was overjoyed that it was a dream that made you act as you did."

Acadiana listened reluctantly to his explanation, but gave no quarter as he lowered his head to kiss her pouting lips. She didn't respond, just lay limp, trying to ignore what she knew he was going to do to her.

"Do you need instructions?" he asked near her ear. His warm breath, the scent of the land clinging to him, sent anticipation curling through her entire body despite her resolve.

"Non," she answered, but the denial lacked conviction as his teeth nibbled a path down her neck.

"Put your arms around me," he commanded.

Acadiana shook her head, but his mouth dropped to the valley of her breasts, and her arms went up instinctively to protect herself. Jonas nuzzled his way between her hands, and the feel of his back, sleek and firm beneath her fingers, the rough shadow of his beard on her tender breasts, mingled to create vivid images in her mind that the darkness hid. Restless, her hand began exploring the muscles from his bare shoulders down to his firm hips, and her body seemed to take on his heat, a slow blaze that radiated from the center of her and spread to each of her tingling limbs. Her nerve endings seemed to expand, come alive, with the hard press of his broad chest against her. His shoulders and arms, well developed from working the land, enfolded her in a crushing embrace, and she could feel herself being caught up in the passion that seemed to rule him when they were together.

"What *do* you need, Acadiana?" he whispered darkly, and her fingers curled into the small of his back as she fought to hang on to a passive attitude, to hold herself aloof from this sweeping away of her control. Jonas groaned in hungry ardor when she ran her fingernails up his back and caught his hair at the nape as she tried to jerk his lowering head from hers. She was awed by his passionate reaction to the rough gesture and quickly removed her hands. Jonas reached for her wrists and pulled them back around his neck.

"No," he murmured against her throat. "Don't push me away, Acadiana. Don't deny the both of us."

He began kissing her then with unhurried, heart-stopping gentleness, with an ease that told her she could pull away at any time. But that same gentleness was an unbreakable cord that stretched taut between them, enslaving her more thoroughly than his brute strength ever could. She returned his kiss out of a longing deeply rooted in her need to feel loved for herself. She wanted to feel his love, to pretend that it existed though she knew better, to know that he wanted her, not just in bed and not only for the land, but for a lifetime. Tremors of heat and tension wound their way through her body, and she arched against him then sighed in weary acceptance of the fact that her body would betray her again. Her breath mingled with his as his tongue slid into her mouth, and even her rebellious mind could not deny the glory of it.

Their bodies meshed, their arms and legs tangled in a gentle war as they strove for victory, her breasts throbbing against his hair-roughened chest, their heartbeats pounding out a cadence of mutual desire. She longed to give herself up to him, to cling to him as a saving line, to lose herself within the dark fires of a passion that she had forbidden herself, but she could not risk the hurt. If he ever grew to love her, she would consider letting down her guard. Until then she would be safest wrapped inside her lonely cocoon.

Jonas frowned at the sight of Acadiana sleeping peacefully beside him and wondered at the shyness that engulfed her whenever they were in bed. There was so much of the savage, free-spirited maiden still inside this woman, but with the intimacy of lovemaking, she became aloof, withdrawing to that remote corner of her mind, as if she were afraid to unleash the passion sleeping within her. His mind searched for a logical explanation, but found no sane reason that would not unman him for her withdrawal. She was a passionate woman. That much had been evident in her writhing body and the way, for a time at least, she had returned his impassioned kisses. Had his hunger for her so blinded him that he could not see that her desire did not match his own? No, she wasn't artful or guileful enough to feign the passion that had consumed her—a passion she denied.

Could she not understand that when she denied herself, she also denied him the bounty of so rich a joining? Or did she understand that all too well? She could not withhold him by strength, but could keep herself emotionally and spiritually detached. If that was her plan, she had done well. Even the sight of her now sleeping beside him, curled into a protective ball as if she would shield herself, made him want to wake her, to break through that invisible barrier and bury himself within her until he could feel her hips rock against his as they strove together to capture that unearthly place. The hardening of his body brought home the realization that he was not sated as he should be, would never be satisfied until she traveled that passionate road beside him.

It was little consolation that she had come willingly tonight, little warmth in the meager semblance of passion that had been his for the briefest moment in time. But a woman with the inborn strength of this one, with a love for the land that equaled his own, could not forever hold herself apart from him. Though he was not proof against such speculation now, it was a desire he could build on, an assurance that would carry him until he could finally crumble the barriers and touch the deepest, most hidden part of her. His determination would win the day, but how long? How long would it take?

Jonas ran his hands lightly over her naked flesh, sighing at the exquisite beauty of her. He thought of how her violet eyes had turned smoky for a fleeting moment before she had retreated inside herself, and he remembered the thought he'd had upon first seeing them. A man truly could drown in those eyes. He had. The devil take her, he wasn't going down alone.

11

$\sim$ $\sim$

Acadiana was immediately thrown into a whirlwind of activity. A wedding reception would be held in two weeks. Minette was eager to show off her new daughter-in-law and would tolerate no resistance to her lavish plans.

The celebration would start with a *boucherie*. A group of men would gather together at sunrise and butcher a prize hog. Another group would work together throughout the day, cooking roast and chops, making sausages, *boudins,* and cracklings. That evening there would be a seafood buffet. All available servants were sent with nets and lines to catch the enormous amounts of crab, crawfish, and shrimp necessary for the gumbo, jambalaya, bisque, court-bouillon, and piquant.

Cuisinières were borrowed from other plantations to help with the pastries and the hors d'oeuvres, but gumbos, served at every occasion, were always the secret recipes of individual plantation cooks. The gumbo was always began with a *roux,* seasoned flour browned in oil. Added to this was the soup made from ham, oyster, chicken, okra, herbs, and any number of different types of seafood. A liberal sprinkling of filé, powdered sassafras leaf, was used to thicken the soup.

Draperies were washed, carpets aired, and silver polished. Minette gathered dress designs and imported fabrics, and the sewing was done in record time.

Acadiana was giddy yet exhausted at the end of each day. Jonas rejoined Edward in the cane fields and at the mill. Absorbed into his demanding responsibilities, he had little time to spend with Acadiana. She, in turn, was much too busy to notice—at least during the daylight hours. But at night when Jonas would drag his weary body into bed beside hers, would gather her into his strong but tired arms, she would grow tense with waiting. Would this night mark the one that would see the demise of her defenses? Would he finally succeed in his ruthless breaking down of the last hold she had on her resentment and anger, leaving her spiritually naked and vulnerable?

Of late he would merely stare at her in the darkness, piercing her with those questioning sapphire eyes that asked that which she was not willing to give. She didn't even know what it was he craved, just that most nights he would turn away from her in frustrated anger, leaving her to stare into the darkness, feeling alone and isolated though he was scant inches away. She had not wronged him! she would remind herself as guilt crept in unbidden to flay her conscience. He had no right to make her feel as if she had committed a mortal sin against him, when it was her freedom that had been bartered for the land. Had she denied him his husbandly rights? *Non!* She had not, but had lain submissive beneath him on those nights when the hunger seemed to ride him so hard that he would roll her over with a strangled curse and have his way until she was brought panting and wanting to the edge of . . . of what? She knew not what was beyond or what she feared, knew not what it was that she wanted. There was something, some intangible force that she longed to capture and hold within her until the torturous feelings inside could be put to rest, but she feared that in the taking she would be the one captured, forever trapped in a web of her own making.

And so the weeks passed in a sort of guarded surface peace, the exhausting labors during the day the only thing making the nights bearable.

The day of the party finally arrived, dawning bright and beautiful, but with the promise of sweltering heat to come. Acadiana donned a day dress of starched white muslin that billowed out airily over a stiff petticoat. Rosy satin ribbons bound her tiny waist and light, puffy sleeves gathered above her elbow. Delicately embroidered batiste bordered the low decolletage. The effect was stunning yet innocently fresh. Her dark hair, swept up to the side and falling in soft, dainty curls, was adorned with fresh pink flowers. She was a vision of loveliness as she floated gracefully down the stairs to join her husband on the front gallery.

Jonas watched her, mesmerized. He had known many beautiful women in his life, but not one could match the grace that came from within this woman and spilled generously to the surface. She was like a rare exotic bird that had been captured, he thought. The fact that she had not yet been tamed had a heady, challenging effect on him. She blended well with the surroundings as if born to that splendor, but Jonas felt as if he were keeping a secret from all those who would view her as merely another appealing face. As innocent as a child, yet as fierce as a savage, to him she was the epitome of womanhood. He felt pride and no small amount of longing swell within him as she stood by his side to greet their arriving guests.

Acadiana must have been introduced to nearly a hundred people by early afternoon—quite a feat since the settlement could boast fewer than two hundred land owners. But they had come from the surrounding areas as well to see who had captured one of the area's most eligible bachelors. Jonas was never far away, offering moral support, shielding his new wife from amorous men, and acting as a buffer for the snide remarks thrown out viciously by enterprising mothers.

The snobbish Creole families were appalled that one of their own had linked himself to someone of Cajun heritage. The Courtland brothers were considered the supreme catches by social-climbing parents and those well established alike. Now that the older brother had been caught in the bonds of matrimony, their attention would be centered on Edward —a fact that Jonas found very amusing and Edward very upsetting. He had watched Jonas dodge them for years; now he would have to beware of giggling virgins and homely spinsters out to secure their futures.

The tactless remarks and sly glances did not bother Acadiana a whit. She and Katherine had had to parry them for years. There was only one female whom she dreaded meeting. Only one who struck a tremor of insecurity through her.

Mary Beth Clayton.

Mary Elizabeth Clayton, to be exact. Acadiana had heard that name spoken often in familiar, loving terms by both Jonas and Edward since her arrival at Courtland Manor. Everyone seemed to acquire the most absurd glow when they talked of her, as if she were a candidate for sainthood. Acadiana had discovered from Mattie that the Courtlands and the Claytons had considered an alliance between their son and daughter as inevitable, a match Minette apparently had favored.

Acadiana had no misgivings about her relationship with Minette, but what of Miss Clayton? Would she be a sullen, hateful female offended at being set aside for another woman? Worse, what were Jonas's feelings for this person?

"They was practically engaged," Mattie had told her. How could Jonas be so uncaring? Acadiana wondered. For two weeks she had fretted over her inevitable meeting with this Clayton woman and had come close to demanding an explanation from Jonas. But that would make her look as if she cared what his feelings were for another woman, and of course, she did not care! Not at all . . . not a bit . . . not . . . But hadn't Jonas threatened to find pleasure elsewhere? Her heart sank until it was a dreadful weight in the pit of her stomach. Jonas's glowing remarks about Miss Clayton certainly made her sound like a paragon of virtue. He no doubt found something very pleasurable about her.

Acadiana began to chew her thumbnail nervously as the object of her tangled thoughts pulled up in an elegant carriage. As soon as the Claytons' driver halted the matched team of horses, Jonas slipped from Acadiana's side and strode to the carriage like a gallant knight to help Beth down. Acadiana watched as the woman's bright green eyes lit up when his hands went around her waist and he lifted her, then lowered her to the ground. She felt her heart slowly sink to her toes as Jonas hugged the delicate beauty and placed a light kiss on her cheek. Beth returned his kiss sweetly, whispering something in his ear that brought a hearty laugh from Jonas. From where she stood on the porch, Acadiana could detect the undisguised affection in her husband's sapphire eyes, and something in her chest twisted brutally.

Acadiana had never felt so inadequate or so unlovely as she did at this moment. She watched in dismay as Jonas led the pale blond, angelic-looking creature toward her. Alabaster skin, shapely figure, and the loveliest emerald eyes she had ever encountered. A lump rose in her throat as he introduced Miss Clayton with as much pride as he had used when introducing his wife all morning.

"Mrs. Courtland, I am so glad to finally meet you. The town has talked of little else since your arrival," Beth said with genuine warmth. "Papa sends his regards. He isn't feeling well today and is unable to attend."

"Miss Clayton," Acadiana said with reserve, "I am honored to make your acquaintance." This woman was either an accomplished actress, or she was truly pleased to be meeting Jonas's wife.

"Acadiana, now that I have you in capable hands, I will see to our other guests," Jonas said.

Acadiana gave a start then stood motionless, smiling frigidly at her despicable husband as he strolled off. She wanted to put a hole through his arrogant back as he walked away, leaving her at the mercy of this petite beauty. Stiffening her back, she turned slowly to face the woman who was close to her height but more shapely and delicate. If they were going to have to stand there making polite conversation, she might as well get to the point and put nagging suspicions behind her.

"You are good friends with my husband, Miss Clayton?" Acadiana opened, leery of the forthcoming answer.

"Please call me Beth, Mrs. Courtland. Yes, Jonas and I are very best friends. We have known each other such a long time, Mrs.— may I call you Acadiana?" At Acadiana's nod she continued. "Jonas has been my friend, ally, and confidant for a number of years now. I care for him like a brother."

Acadiana felt the foolish defiance slowly drain from her body to be replaced by humiliation. "A brother?" she asked weakly.

"Well, yes. I don't have a brother, of course, but if I did, I should hope he would be just like Jonas." Beth laughed. She stopped and eyed Acadiana closely. "Are you all right, Acadiana? You look a little pale."

"A brother?" Acadiana repeated. She had done all that worrying over someone who viewed her husband as a brother?

"Surely you didn't think—" Beth began, then paled also. "Oh! I can see that you did . . . that we were . . . oh, my." Beth turned an embarrassing beet-red. "I can assure you, A-A-Acadiana, Jonas is my best friend in the world, but that is all!"

It was Acadiana's turn to blush now. "I am sorry, Beth, but I thought your parents wanted—"

Beth interrupted quickly, her expression contrite and uneasy. "They did press for an alliance, and Jonas and I almost consented out of obligation, but we are much too good friends to become romantically involved. We love each other, as friends, but we are not *in love* and never could be. Please believe me when I tell you that I am relieved and happy for the both of you. It . . . it would have been quite . . . awkward to marry one's best friend."

It was awkward to marry someone one detested also, but Acadiana didn't say that. She was relieved by Beth's declaration. Jealousy was a new emotion to her, and she didn't like at all the way it felt. Still, to know that Jonas would have married out of obligation rather than love only reconfirmed her determination to shield herself against future hurt should she one day succumb to his charm. There was no threat of her weakening now. She was trying to be an acceptable wife, more for Minette's sake than her own, she admitted. She didn't want that beloved woman to know that her resentment for the son still ran high, especially when mixed with the newer, passionate urges he was creating in her.

"I hope we can be good friends too, Beth," Acadiana said, determined to put the other thoughts aside for now. "My best friends call me Cade."

"Very well, Cade, I would be honored," Beth said with a genteel curtsy.

They strolled the lawn together at a leisurely pace. Beth acquainted Acadiana with interesting facts about each of the families they passed, giving her a little background about the ones she knew personally.

"Uh-oh." Beth suddenly stopped. Her delightful expression changed and she looked as if she was pondering some dire question. After much consideration she finally turned to Acadiana with a frown. "Here comes Merrill LeBeau. I'm not sure that this will be pleasant for you. She's furious that Jonas has taken a wife."

"Oh?" Acadiana whispered.

"She's a widow. Her husband left her with a failing plantation to run. She had hopes of capturing Jonas's affection and his money."

I also married him for his money, Acadiana thought unhappily, but she wouldn't say that either. "A mistress?" she asked bluntly.

Beth's eyes widened at the indelicate remark. Unmarried ladies were not supposed to know of such things, much less discuss them, but of course there were many forbidden things she and her friends had whispered about over their growing years. "She has been very discreet," she said lamely, "but when it was rumored that Jonas and I were considering an engagement, she was quick to hint that there was something of a romantic nature between them. And there was nothing courteous about the way she put it. Be careful, Cade. She is a spiteful, vengeful witch."

"*Merci,* Beth," Acadiana replied softly, feeling Beth's embarrassment and realizing the courage it must have taken for her to discuss such a thing. But she could handle Mrs. LeBeau's type of woman. It was Beth's type she was concerned about. "What about Edward? Will she be after him now that Jonas is taken?"

"She had better not!" Beth said angrily. "I . . . uh . . . oh, bother. I'm afraid I'm not very good at being coy, am I?"

"You and Edward?" Acadiana said with a mischievous sparkle.

The color quickly dissolved from her cheeks and Beth's face took on a stricken look. "No, Cade! No, not Edward and me, just me," she said, deflated. "I've held a secret affection for him for some time now. He doesn't even know I'm alive."

"How can you say that?" Acadiana asked. Who wouldn't be beguiled by such a sweet person? she wondered. "Maybe he just thought that you and Jonas . . . *Mon Dieu,* here comes Mrs. LeBeau. Our conversation will have to wait."

Merrill strolled forth regally, eyeing both ladies with disdain. She was taller than Acadiana had expected and much more beautiful. She had rich auburn hair and ivory skin. Darkening sea-green eyes glared at both women with contempt as she sashayed toward them in a striking morning gown of apple-green and turquoise taffeta that floated around her in shimmering glory. Acadiana felt quite colorless next to this green goddess.

"The new Mrs. Courtland, I presume?" Merrill said with a sweetness that belied the malicious look on her face.

"Mrs. LeBeau," Acadiana returned with the same false attitude. "There is no need for introductions. Your reputation precedes you."

Merrill raised her eyebrows and a sneering grin found its way to the surface. So, Jonas Courtland's new wife could not be so easily intimidated.

"And sweet little Miss Clayton. You must have been devastated to find out Jonas had married," Merrill drawled.

"Just devastated!" Beth returned dramatically, throwing her hand to her brow. "But I find Acadiana so charming, I simply cannot hold a grudge, and I have decided to go on with my life."

Acadiana threw her hand over her mouth to stifle a giggle threatening to disgrace her. Merrill eyed her suspiciously, feeling the brunt of some private joke, and it infuriated her to be bested by these two infants.

"Run on along, Miss Clayton, and let us chat," Merrill said imperiously, then turned her back in rude dismissal. "Acadiana . . . May I call you that?"

The hair rose on Acadiana's neck along with her defenses at the spiteful command. "Stay, Beth!" she whispered. "My very best friends call me Cade, Mrs. LeBeau, but you may call me Acadiana . . . or Mrs. Courtland. Whichever suits your fancy."

"How quaint," Merrill said coldly. They eyed each other openly, each assessing the qualities she saw in the other that she knew she did not possess. Acadiana felt like a child next to this elegant, worldly woman. Merrill, on the other hand, saw a youthful innocence she could never recapture. "I must say, we were all so shocked to hear that Jonas had married."

"Some of you more shocked than others?" Acadiana asked. She knew she was being hateful but couldn't seem to stop herself from rising to the bait.

Anger burned within Merrill, but her composure never wavered. "I do declare! It is just too funny that Jonas would fall so hopelessly in love, almost overnight," she said with sarcastic sweetness. "I just can't imagine him doing that. It's simply not his style. There's not some other reason, is there?"

"Don't be so Puritan, Mrs. LeBeau. Jonas married me for my land," Acadiana replied.

"Your land! The Hamilton property? Of course, he has been after that for some time." Merrill's eyes narrowed as she stared at Acadiana. Oooh, the little twit was bold, but she was by far the more experienced of the two and would not be undone by this fledgling. "Why didn't he just purchase your silly old land?"

"I wouldn't sell." Acadiana smiled, gritting her teeth.

"I see," Merrill said in a silky-sweet voice. "So, you lured him with your property. Very convenient, isn't it? Jonas is quite wealthy."

"Quite," Acadiana agreed, relishing her own form of subtle vengeance.

Unable to shatter the younger woman's icy composure, Merrill lashed out with the one thing she knew would deliver a stinging blow. "If that's the case, my dear, you certainly won't mind if Jonas and I resume our little . . . ah . . . *affaire d'amour*?" She had already invested too much time in Jonas to let him go without a fight. She could not be his wife now, but maybe she could retain a place as a well-provided-for mistress—discreetly, of course.

Acadiana had had enough. Her relationship with Jonas was shaky at best, and she did not need to be reminded that there were other ways he could obtain sexual fulfillment. As anger and insecurity rose within her so did her voice. "Contrary, Madame Wasp! If you come within two feet of my husband, I will take great delight in snatching you bald-headed!"

"Wasp?" Merrill took one startled step backward before her temper flared. She bore down on the younger women, shaking her finger directly in Acadiana's face. "How dare you, you little twit! Don't you ever threaten me again. You are way out of your league, sugar, and you'll find yourself in grave circumstances!"

"No graver than yours if you make another advance toward my husband!" Acadiana warned.

"I'll make advances toward whomever I please, you bothersome little pest!"

"I'll make you think pest when you are wearing a cap this winter to cover your naked scalp!" Acadiana's voice was a vibrating crescendo that rose, then fell ominously. "Provided I leave your scalp!"

Lips pulled away from perfect white teeth, nails curled into claws, Merrill took a menacing step forward. "It is quite obvious that Jonas has married well beneath his station in life," she said with a snarl. "You disgusting Cajun brat!"

When things began to heat up, Beth had departed quickly to find Jonas. She knew Merrill for the conniving witch she was but did not know about Acadiana's volatile temper. Jonas did, and he arrived just in time to hear the last of their conversation and to catch his wife in midflight as she lunged toward Merrill intent on doing bodily harm.

"You are wrong, Merrill," he stated, holding a squirming Acadiana around the waist. Her arms and legs flailed in the air as Jonas ignored her protest. "I married a genteel southern lady equal to or surpassing my so-called station in life, and certainly well above yours. I don't know what prompted this catfight, but I won't tolerate any rudeness to my wife on my property—or anywhere else, for that matter. Is that understood?" he asked silkily.

"Let me go!" grated Acadiana. "I can fight my own battles!"

"Genteel? Lady? *Are you crazy, Jonas?*" Merrill asked in furious shock.

"Hush, Merrill, or you will be requested to leave," Jonas said firmly. "Now, Acadiana, will you behave if I let you go?"

"Certainly, darling," she drawled saucily. "I promise not to scratch her eyes out . . . yet!"

"How dare you!" Merrill screeched.

"I'm the wife, that's how!"

Acadiana cloaked her rage in hauteur as her feet touched the ground and she strolled away, her bearing graceful and seemingly confident, leaving Merrill standing with her mouth gaping.

Gossip spread like a brushfire, making the party considerably livelier. What had promised to be an elegant summer social was turning into a gala jamboree with females whispering and tittering the scandalous news like buzzing bees and the gentlemen placing bets on the outcome of the uproar. Some wagered fisticuffs by sundown, while others had the ladies dueling at dawn. It proved to be sumptuous affair for the gossips, an abomination of good taste for the dowagers, and a riotous amusement for the gentlemen.

Acadiana enjoyed each and every minute. Even Jonas's stern looks could not quell her lighthearted view of the whole affair. Merrill, on the other hand, had sulked off to the house, nursing an agonizing headache.

By evening, things had settled down to a dull roar. Mrs. LeBeau was once again able to show her face, masking indifference. Acadiana was on her best behavior, and the soiree turned out to be an unqualified success.

Later that night, Acadiana turned away from Jonas's ardent pursuits. "What is that Merrill creature to you?" she asked, green-eyed.

"A business acquaintance."

"Ha! I've never had a fight with your lawyer, Henry Smith! Was she your lover?" Acadiana asked, turning onto her stomach to escape his questing hand.

"In a manner of speaking," he said cautiously.

"What manner?"

"I haven't been celibate, Acadiana, since I was sixteen."

"Or very discriminating either!"

"I married you." He chuckled, trying to turn her over.

"Don't touch me!" she cried. "You were almost engaged to Beth, your name was linked with several other women, and you had an affair with Mrs. LeBeau. How many more are there?"

"None lately," he assured her, and began inching her gown up to stroke her bare bottom.

"Don't touch me!" Acadiana all but shouted, clutching the edges of the mattress to keep him from turning her over.

Jonas wedged his knees between her legs and bent to kiss the small of her back. "I guess this position is as good as any," he murmured.

Acadiana's head shot up. "How dare you!"

"I'm the husband," he replied.

And proceeded to prove it.

Acadiana's breathing was deep and ragged as she tried to still the pounding of her heart. Lying in the quietude after their wild coupling, her mind spun with the craziness of what had just happened. Theirs had been a frenzied, almost savage, joining, with none of the honeyed words or teasing caresses she had grown accustomed to. She had been angry and jealous, bringing those powerful emotions to the forefront when Jonas claimed her. Her eyes had blazed at his, her nostrils flaring with each hard thrust, until her body had bucked wildly beneath him as if to prove that she could not be taken but would match him stroke for stroke. But in the end he had been the victor, flooding her being with such sweet torture that she had withdrawn, had lain docile and afraid, lest the fire that engulfed him reach out to consume her also. And she had come away feeling as if she had barely survived.

Never would she let such jealousy for another woman take hold of her. She had been a mindless, groping creature, bent on striking the woman's beautiful auburn hair and voluptuous curves from her husband's mind. And she didn't even know why! Why should it matter that her husband, a man she had not chosen, might seek out another for the fulfillment she did not even wish to give him? But it did matter, and Acadiana cursed herself, then the man who held the power to make her feel that way. In the end she had not been victorious but conquered, almost swept away by the glory of her husband's passionate lovemaking until only her determination to maintain her self-control had kept her from dissolving with the raging heat. Never would she be caught so unaware of her own dangerous feelings again!

12

Life settled down once again at Courtland
Manor. If anyone noticed the silent war between the newly
wedded couple, no mention was made of it. Everyone went
about his normal duties, and Acadiana began to learn daily
the great responsibilities Minette carried as mistress of the
house. She wondered if she would ever be able to handle the
demands of running a plantation as smoothly and efficiently
as the older woman, wondered too if she would ever be as
suited for domestic life. The challenges were there, but they
were different from the excitement of drawing life from the
land. Acadiana tackled each day with a fresh determination
to learn everything she could about the duties that would
one day fall to her.

Toward the end of the week Jonas decided that he and his
new wife needed some time alone, even if it was just for an
afternoon. Acadiana had not quite forgiven him for the
night of the wedding reception and hadn't spoken to him
much over the past week but had thrown herself into other
activities. Jonas hadn't had much time to make amends
because he had been busy getting the mill ready for the
harvest.

He didn't want to back down from his intimate demands,

but realized he should be more gentle in easing her into something she wasn't ready to accept. God, she had been angry that night, but with that anger had come a passion he had never before experienced in a woman. In the ensuing days and nights Acadiana had become even more remote, hiding her innermost thoughts and feelings from him. Jonas knew if he didn't spend time with her and win her over now, his wife would become more and more distant as the demands of the mill took an increasing amount of his free time.

The success of sugarcane on the lower Mississippi had caused interest among the planters in this area. Since Etienne de Bore, a planter living near New Orleans, perfected the granulation process in 1795, most of the plantations along the Teche were turning to sugarcane as their main crop.

Although a number of American planters had come to the region, they were not usually as successful as the Creoles. Native to the soil, the Creoles were frugal and industrious, and like the Courtlands, they were nearly all stock raisers, which added to their growing wealth. Scattered among the herds of cattle were the famous Creole horses, the best and largest selected for the horse-powered sugar mills.

But this would be the last year that Courtland Manor Plantation would use horse power to mill the sugar. The steam process was too new and daring for most planters, but Jonas felt the lure of progress, could see the potential in sugar production on a much larger scale than some of his friends who continued to stick with the lucrative cotton crop. But from the moment of planting through harvest, which would take them on through the winter months due to Louisiana's semitropical climate, the work was unremitting, requiring meticulous attention during every phase to yield a profitable return. Several crops a year could be produced, so it was a never-ending cycle, some phases seeming to overlap the others. Combined with his work overseeing the running of the estate, the steam conversion would take up most of Jonas's waking hours over the next year, and he needed to grab what little extra time he could with his wife.

He knew where he'd find her, for life had taken on a predictable monotony. Jonas always awoke at first light to find Acadiana's side of the bed empty. The first few mornings after the party had shaken him somewhat. Thinking she had flown, he would tear through the plantation for sign of her passage. Always he would find her near her parents' cottage. The first time he had caught her cleaning out years of accumulated dirt and trash and had been moved to send servants over to take care of the chores. The next day he had discovered her on her hands and knees digging a garden.

There had always been a plot of ground for vegetables, she had tearfully and resentfully told him when he had tried to pull her away. It just wasn't seemly that the wife of Jonas Courtland be scruffling around in the dirt like a common servant. It had taken hours of what had eventually ended in a shouting match to convince her that her labors were needless.

Since then, Acadiana could always be found sitting behind the manor house on the bank of the bayou, her bare toes curled in the mud, a fishing pole in her hand. Jonas would sit atop his horse, swathed in the early-morning mist, and watch from a hidden place among the trees. Many a daybreak before his work began, he pondered about this woman he had taken for wife. She looked every bit the bedraggled orphan in her old shirt and faded breeches. A score of gowns hung in the wardrobe, but these she donned only at night for the evening meal, or when informed there would be guests visiting.

She was like a night wind—elusive, obscure, but ever there. Sometimes quiet, no more than a whisper through the trees. Sometimes violent, with enough force to be destructive.

Most days he did not approach her. Jonas would turn

away in silence, his mind burdened by the sight of her looking lost and alone with her chin propped in her hands, eyes staring vacantly at the water.

The nights took on the same sort of tenacious routine. Acadiana was passively reluctant in their bed. She never fought him outright or denied him a husband's privilege, but neither did she fully give herself to him. When the passionate responses he artfully drew from her reached a plateau of unbearable heights, she would hide within herself, completely lost to him.

Jonas suspected that most nights left her aching and wanting, for it was much the same for him. His body could attain physical relief, but the spiritual man yearned for more than she was willing to offer. Angry and reduced to the level of coaxing for her favors had so unmanned him that Jonas had vowed finally he would not touch her again unless she came begging *him.* There was a woman lurking beneath that protective shell, he knew, who would have a woman's needs someday. He just hoped when she emerged it wouldn't be too late.

His pompous avowal had been destined to backfire the moment it left his mouth. She would never come seeking him, Jonas realized, and after a few sleepless nights of not giving in to his desire when her soft, luscious body was unknowingly cuddled next to his own heated one, the freshwashed fragrance of her ebony curls spilling between them like a river of fine black silk, it was too much even for his control.

He had stared into the gray shroud of early-morning fog, his body aching, his mind tired of the constant turmoil she caused there, and had decided on a new course of action. Starting today, he would play the aggressor, but only to the point that she willingly accepted his advances. If she shunned him, he would not press her. Though his thoughts shied away from that possibility, he forced himself to consider it. There were other more willing and experienced women to be had, he thought with a vengeance born of frustration, yet he craved no other. He knew now with the fatal realization of a man doomed by his own hand that he wanted no other woman but the little amethyst-eyed hellion who absorbed his waking moments and plagued even his dreams with her cold, untouchable heart.

Although she tried to suppress it, Acadiana felt giddy as she rode alongside her husband, remembering their first visit to her land and his thoughtfulness in having the gazebo built. He had surprised her with this outing, and a wave of happiness washed over her as they turned the horses down the lane that led to the cottage. Returning here lifted her spirits, and they soared free of earthly restraints until she couldn't recall why she was supposed to be angry with him. She thought she should feel calmer now that he had stopped his nightly forays to control her physically, but she was actually feeling oddly out of sorts these days and more confused that ever. She told herself repeatedly that she was relieved. It was, after all, what she wanted. Was it not? She searched her mind for reasons of her disquietude and disappointment, but could find no sane explanation. Lurking within the darker corners of her mind was the heart-wrenching fear that Jonas's abstinence might mean he was seeking pleasure elsewhere. The thought jolted her upright in her saddle, and she shot a quick look in her husband's direction.

He didn't look like a lecherous adulterer as he sat his horse with a manly grace that caused her heart to skip a beat. *Non,* he looked tired, she thought with a sudden twinge of compassion, the usual cocksureness of his sapphire gaze faded now to one of introspection. Acadiana knew he had been working hard to prepare the mill for the harvest; he had had no time for unholy pursuits.

She felt a measure of her earlier happiness return, and gratitude for his bringing her home again replaced her depressing thoughts. She looked again in his direction, a smile hovering about the corners of her mouth as she sought to

gain his favor and dispel the troubled look in his eyes. He
continued to gaze into the woods ahead, a solemn expression on his features, from the firm set of his lips to the
rigidness of his shoulders and back as he cantered on.
Acadiana felt piqued at being ignored, and it suddenly, if
irrationally, became a contest to see if she could reclaim his
favorable attention.

"Jonas," she said tentatively, unsure of how to proceed,
"I want to tell you how much I appreciate your keeping up
the grounds all these years."

They had reached the clearing surrounding the cottage,
and Acadiana hopped off her horse before Jonas could help
her down. Before he realized what was amiss, the scamp
had turned a very beguiling smile on him and was gone.
After the initial shock, he took the bait and started down
the path after her in a dead run. Acadiana ducked behind
the huge magnolia, then darted for the gazebo. Jonas
caught her on the second step and slung her over his shoulder, giving her backside a healthy smack.

Acadiana squealed in indignation and squirmed to free
herself. Jonas let her wiggling body slide slowly, intimately,
against his as he lowered her to the cypress-planked floor.
Alarms went off in Acadiana's brain as she was struck with
uncertainty over her actions. She could feel Jonas's body
harden against hers and wondered if it had been wise to
tease him. Before she could contemplate the folly of her
actions, he deposited her on the top step leading into the
gazebo. Taking her face in his hands, he began kissing her
in a manner that dissolved all protest.

"Now, what was it you wanted to thank me for?" He
grinned, encouraged by the breathless giggle that followed
the kiss. "If you owe me a debt of gratitude, I'm here to
collect."

"Stop," she said shyly. She wiggled nervously, pushing at
his roving hands. "As I said, I want to thank you for keeping up the grounds of Bayou Oaks all these years."

"I'll keep up anything you want, love, if you'll quit slapping my hands away."

"Jonas, I'm trying to be serious here," she said.

"I *am* serious."

"Jonas!"

"All right," he grumbled, withdrawing his hands and pulling her down to sit beside him. His earlier resolve was crumbling miserably around him, provoked only by one flash of a teasing smile. "Now, what is a Bayou Oaks that I am being commended but not compensated for?"

"My land. That was my father's name for it. Thank you for taking care of it."

"Sorry, love, you have the estate trust to thank for that," he muttered, trying to kiss her ear.

"Jonas, don't tease me," she scolded. "You know there isn't enough money in the trust for the upkeep, much less all this grooming."

"Look, Acadiana, all I did was have the gazebo built after you agreed to marry me," he said. "This place has been cared for since a year after your parents left. Gardeners report once a month in the winter and at least once a week the rest of the year. Maybe your uncle had it arranged."

"Non." She shook her head vehemently, obviously more annoyed than he had been giving her credit for. "He would have told me. He knows how much it would have meant to me."

"Settle down, love. Someone has been caring for this place, and that's all that matters. Right?"

"That is not all that matters!" she said heatedly. "Someone has been seeing to this place for almost ten years, and I want to know who. Moreover, I want to know why! Why would someone spend that kind of money for so long?"

"Maybe they thought they would own it one day." He shrugged casually, but uneasiness gnawed in the back of his mind. He had never given the continual upkeep of the land any thought, assuming it had been provided by the owner, then by Grayson Hamilton, once he had discovered that Acadiana held the title.

"*Mais oui,* you did it." She laughed. "I should have known."

"No, Acadiana, I give you my word."

"Then who?" she asked earnestly.

Jonas raked his finger through hair in agitation and sent her a slanted look. "I'm sure I don't know, and I don't know why you are getting all disturbed."

The afternoon was not going at all as he had planned. Remembering their first visit to the gazebo, he had harbored visions of a replay with a better conclusion. A foolish idea on his part, no doubt.

Only in her frequent outbursts of temper did he ever get a glimpse of the half-naked Indian maiden he had wanted to know so well. Since their marriage, Acadiana had always played the prim and proper lady-wife, as if she thought that was expected of her. At times she met him halfway and passively allowed his advances; at others she fought him like a demon. At all times, even when she almost gave herself over to the pleasure of his touch, she remained emotionally remote. Slowly, though none too patiently, Jonas had been trying to draw her out of the shy, puritanical shell she had encased herself in. He had noticed a softening in her before the issue of the land had been brought up, and he was ready to put this conversation to an end.

"The gardeners will be here tomorrow," he said, eyeing her forlorn expression. "I'll ride over and find out who the mystery financier is."

"I'm coming with you," she said firmly, then with a stubborn and infuriating lift of her chin marched back to her horse.

A visit with the gardeners at Bayou Oaks the next day only proved to frustrate Acadiana more. They either didn't know or wouldn't say who their employer was. Jonas was certain it was the latter. They admitted nothing Acadiana didn't already know, but they did look surprised when informed that she was heir to the property. Nothing she could say would persuade them to divulge anything else except that they must be about their work.

They rode back to Courtland Manor in tense silence, Acadiana frustrated and Jonas thoughtful. He had considered it unimportant—until now. After talking to the gardeners, he was growing very curious. The land was, after all, his concern too. He found himself extremely interested in finding out more.

Little more than a week later, Jonas had even more reason to be concerned.

It was Acadiana's twenty-first birthday. She had requested a small family gathering with the addition of Beth Clayton. They had become close friends, and secretly Acadiana was certain she could promote a match between Beth and Edward.

"I am so glad you could come," Acadiana welcomed her friend as she walked down the stairs.

"Hurry, Cade, everyone is in the library waiting for you. Wait until you see what just arrived!" Beth said.

Caught up in the excitement that had Beth fairly bursting with delight, Acadiana rushed behind her. Commanded to close her eyes, she allowed Beth to lead her into the room.

"Now!" Beth said with glee as she swept her arm aside with a dramatic flourish and stepped back to reveal the surprise.

The smile on Acadiana's face froze instantly as she stared at the lavish arrangement of delicate pink roses. Her mouth went dry; she squeezed her eyes shut to block the vision, but the flowers were still there when she opened them again. Warning bells sounded in her head, but she subdued them and attempted to find more logical reasoning.

"Jonas, how did you know?" she asked nervously, her violet eyes wide, almost pleading, as they spied him seated on the French provincial settee. The simplified rococo design with its graceful curves and dainty elegance seemed too fragile to hold the man with the grim mouth and icy reserve in his sapphire eyes.

The words sounded stilted even to her own ears, Acadiana thought when Jonas's expression never wavered. *Mon Dieu,* it has happened again. She winced and shut her eyes once more. Don't be ridiculous, her inner self scolded, it must be a coincidence. Open your eyes! She took a deep breath and summoned a smile.

"Happy birthday, Acadiana. How did I know what?" Jonas asked with a pleasantness that belied the cold look on his face.

"How did you know that pink roses are my favorite?"

"I didn't," he said. "They're not from me."

"Grand'mère?" Acadiana said shakily. "You remembered?"

"My gift is right here, *bébé,"* Minette said, patting the brightly wrapped box on her lap.

"Edward . . . Beth?" she almost pleaded.

They exchanged looks and shrugged. "Not us."

"Well, for heaven's sake, Cade, read the card!" Beth said. She didn't like the look on Acadiana's face—it had changed from delightfully rosy to ashen.

"I don't have to," Acadiana said, drawing the words out gravely. "I already know what it says . . . 'Happy Birthday, Cade, much love.' "

Jonas snatched the card in jealous anger and tore it open. He read the inscription then tossed it to Acadiana.

"Who sent this?" he demanded.

"I don't know!" she spat back, offended. She sank slowly into the nearest chair and added weakly, "I have never known."

"Explain yourself, madame," Jonas said tersely.

"I don't have to explain anything to you," she retorted.

"Oh, but you do," he said in an ominously quiet voice.

"Jonas!" Minette snapped.

"It's all right, *Grand'mère,"* Acadiana intervened. This was not the place to start something with her stubborn husband, not in front of everyone. "The roses have been coming every year on my birthday for about six years. For a long time I thought they were from Uncle Grayson, then I thought maybe I had a secret admirer . . . but here . . . now. Who would send them here?"

"That's what I would like to know," Jonas stated in a bored, insulting voice.

"Jonas, please! Don't look at me like that," Acadiana implored, noting the uncomfortable looks on the faces of the people around her. "I don't know who they are from. The card is always the same: 'Happy Birthday, Cade' . . . Cade! No one calls me that except my family and dearest friends."

"And your mystery man?" Jonas ventured in a bitter, accusing tone.

"Non!" Acadiana rasped. The insult was supreme and fed her anger to gigantic proportions. She lashed out at him without regard now for the others present. "You jealous fool! You know so little about him. The *man* in that picture was just a *boy.* And he is dead!" Her words ended on a small sob, but she stubbornly refused to let the tears fall.

Beth stared in awe and embarrassment at the outburst. Minette and Edward exchanged glances at the much-deserved putdown, and Jonas was forced to face them all. He had not meant to lash out, but the thought of someone else sending his wife a gift, however well intended, sent dark images racing through his mind.

"Something else came for you," he said, holding out a small, jeweled box.

"There has never been a gift with the roses before," she said, confused.

"Open it," he ordered.

"Non!" she stated defiantly. "I don't know anything more about this than you do! I won't open it. Just throw it away!"

Jonas slumped back in his seat and slanted his wife an indulgent, apologetic look. "I'm sorry, Acadiana, but how do you expect me to react? Someone sends you roses and an expensive gift. How would you expect me to feel? Please open it. You might as well see what's inside."

Hesitantly Acadiana took the box and lifted the lid. Her eyes opened wide in horror and her breathing stalled as she brought out an antique locket . . . and promptly fainted.

Beth screamed, Jonas jumped to his feet to catch his wife before she tumbled to the floor, and Minette hurried to fetch smelling salts. Edward stood in shock, not knowing what to do, and decided that comforting Beth was the best he could accomplish at the moment. Jonas carried Acadiana to the settee and lowered her gently. She was so pale, he had to fight back the wild surge of fear that threatened to overtake him. Never had she appeared so frail, so vulnerable.

Acadiana awoke as a horrible smell invaded her senses and stung her eyes. She sat up shakily, searching the worried faces surrounding her, and unconsciously her dazed eyes searched for Jonas.

"Th-that . . . locket, where did you get it?" she stammered weakly.

"It came with the roses. Remember?" he asked softly. "What is it, Acadiana? You look as if you've seen a ghost."

"I have," she whispered, putting a shaky hand to her lips. "The locket . . . it was my grandmother's and her mother's before her. It goes back as far as my family lineage is known. Marie Labiche Hamilton, Papa's mother, had no daughter of her own and gave it to my mother on her twenty-first birthday. *Maman* said it was to be mine on this day." She began trembling and her voice rose shrilly. "Jonas, where did it come from?"

"I don't know, love," he said soothingly, helpless at the shock and confusion in her eyes. "But, rest assured, I will find out."

"Here, Cade, drink this," Minette said softly, handing her a glass of amber liquid.

Acadiana's hands were shaking too badly to hold the

crystal, so Jonas helped her take a few sips before questioning her.

"Acadiana, where has the locket been all this time?"

"I don't know. Maybe *Maman* had it when we left, or maybe she left it behind. I just don't know, Jonas. I don't . . ."

"It's all right, love," he said, taking her in his arms. "Who knew about the locket? Who knew that it was to be yours on exactly this date? Your aunt and uncle maybe?"

"I don't . . . maybe . . . I mean, they knew about it, but they would have given it to me before now if they'd had it. *Non,* they couldn't have had it anyway. Everything not left behind was taken by the outlaws when they attacked the wagon."

"Think back, Acadiana. Who else knew about the locket? There has to be someone," Jonas prodded.

"No one. No one else outside the family knew about it." Acadiana sighed, laying her head on Jonas's shoulder. Her head was pounding, her stomach rolling with nausea. "I mean, as far as I know. *Le bon Dieu,* I was only ten when we left. How much can a ten-year-old know?"

"All right," he said, patting her hand comfortingly yet determined to get to the bottom of the matter. He would not have his wife hurt by these mysteries, and did not favor the idea of some unknown person sending her gifts to disrupt the small amount of harmony they had achieved over the last week since visiting the cottage. There was also the business of the care that had been given her property after the Hamiltons left. "Who in your family knew about the locket? What about your mother's family, the ones west of here?"

"We had very little contact with them over the years." I doubt they would know anything about it."

"Katherine?"

"Who is Katherine?" Beth whispered to Edward.

"Her cousin in Providence," he returned.

Acadiana smiled softly at Jonas's question. "It could not be Katherine. She could never keep a secret."

"Anyone else?" Jonas asked.

"No one. Just *Maman,* Papa, Matthew, and Coffee, and they are all gone now," she said sadly.

"Who are those other people?" Beth whispered once again.

"I think Matthew was her brother," Edward said. "According to my mother, he was killed six months before her family left here. I believe Coffee was a sort of nursemaid or mammy when they were children, although the Cajuns aren't generally slave owners. She died when I was still a boy. I remember Mattie bringing several of Coffee's children here to raise."

"Poor Cade," Beth whispered.

Everyone watched Acadiana as she turned the locket over and over in her hands as if searching the treasure for answers. It was a startling piece of work. Of silver inlaid with niello, it had animals interspersed with rosettes and human faces around its border. The faces personified the Five Senses, with Sight in the center. It appeared to have once been a brooch, a gold pin remaining from the original fastening to a shaft of ivory, but a silver back had been added along with a delicate filigree chain. Acadiana's eyes, full of sorrow and fear, rose to meet her husband's.

"Jonas, the outlaws—"

"Wouldn't have known it was to be yours. Besides, if they had stolen it, they would have sold it, not given it back to you. I suspect it's quite valuable."

Minette rose slowly and walked over to Acadiana. She sat down and took her hand, smoothing it lovingly. "Maybe this is not the time, Cade, for so many questions, yes?"

Jonas eyed his mother suspiciously. He knew her much too well to be deceived by her dismissal of the incident. "I think now is the perfect time for *your* questions, Mother."

Minette sent him a curt, negative shake of her head. Nonplussed, Jonas continued to stare at her. If it was to be a battle of wills, by the look on his face Minette knew she would lose. Given no avenue for escape, she turned to Acadiana for permission.

"Oui, Grand'mère?" she said, raising eyes brimming with sadness and confusion to Minette's sympathetic face.

"What do you remember about your life the year before you left with Armand and Elaine?"

"Not too much." Acadiana sighed. "I think I blocked a lot of it out. It was probably the worst year of my life."

"How so?" asked Jonas. He could sense his mother was trying to get at something, or avoid it.

"Bébé, it brings you so much pain. There is no need to go into it now," Minette began, but Jonas cut her short with another lethal stare.

Acadiana missed the potent exchange and began to explain. "Things kept happening. I remember Papa being so worried all the time and *Maman* crying. She cried so much that year. And fires, there were fires, lots of them. No sooner would Papa get the flames out in one field than another would start to burn. Over and over it happened. There were other things too—strange, horrible things that I didn't understand. A trusted servant would disappear only to be found later floating in the bayou. Others would just run off for no apparent reason. I really can't remember it all."

"How was your family life during this time?" Minette asked.

"Matt was always the same with me, playing, teasing, making me laugh," she said wistfully. "But with *Maman* and Papa, he was different. They were always fighting. He and Papa would yell at each other and *Maman* would cry."

"What were they fighting about? Do you remember?"

"Not really, but I know it had something to do with what was going on, the fires and all. Matt was always telling them to give up, quit fighting the others. He said they were too big, too powerful. Then he told them that he wasn't going to wait around and watch them die. He would do something. I don't know what he planned, but he never got the chance. He died a few months later, drowned in the bayou just like the others."

"What do you know about this, Mother?" Jonas asked suspiciously. "It's obvious, Acadiana, that someone was trying to run your family out."

Minette sent Jonas a frozen look, a warning. But it was too late, the words were already out.

"Why?" Acadiana asked incredulously. "Why would anyone want to do that?"

"I don't know for sure," Jonas said. "Mother?" Minette turned on him with a biting glance and refused to say anything, so he continued. "I can only speculate, Acadiana. Your land is prime property. It has the best soil and is in the best location in St. Martin Parish. The whole Attakapas region was once a part of the parish, but in 1811 it was divided into St. Martin and St. Mary parishes. The way our village is growing, we will one day be the parish seat of yet another division. That is why my grandfather regretted selling the land. It was registered as *terre de la première qualité*. He knew what a foolish mistake he had made."

"I still don't understand," Acadiana said in anguish. "Who would do such a horrible, wretched thing? It almost sounds as if your grandfather. . . ."

Minette gasped and Jonas stared at his mother accusingly until she finally spoke. Merciful God, she wished she had not stirred up this potential hornet's nest! "It was not Jonas's grandfather, Cade, I swear it. Your parents never knew for sure, but they suspected other, shall we say, men of importance."

"What men?" Acadiana cried, whirling to face Minette, icy hatred in her voice. "Tell me! I have a right to know whom they suspected. They made our life a living hell that last year. You must tell me!"

"Cade, please do not distress yourself," Minette pleaded. "It is over now. There was never any proof. Let the past lie, child!"

"*Non,* I will never let it lie," Acadiana stated in slow, measured tones. "It was not right, not fair! My parents worked so hard to build a dream! Do you know what it is like to work for something only to see it destroyed before your very eyes? Do you? Have you ever watched a strong, confident man fall apart as his world crumbles around him . . . seen a tender, loving woman turned into a weeping shell . . . just trying to keep what was already theirs? I will not let it lie, not now . . . not ever!"

"Stop it, Acadiana," Jonas commanded. He didn't like the wild look in her eyes, the distraught, almost frantic, expression on her face, and he finally realized Minette was being evasive for a purpose. Whatever the reason, he could find that out later in private. "Acadiana, you will make yourself sick if this continues. We will do everything to find out what happened eleven years ago, but not now, not to-night. For tonight it is over."

Rebellion flared within her and Acadiana could not be stilled. "But it's not over! Can't you see that?" she cried. "And there is still the locket. Where did it come from?"

"I don't know"—he sighed—"but you are pale and shaken. I think we will retire early. If everyone will excuse us?"

"Jonas—"

"No excuses. All this is too much for one day."

Jonas took her elbow and led her out of the room despite her feeble protests, but he stopped when he reached the door and turned back to look at his mother. By his uncompromising stare, Minette knew that this conversation was far from over. There would be too many questions to answer later—skeletons she had absolutely no desire to dig up.

Jonas led his wife to the bed, gently picked her up, and placed her in the center. Brushing her hair back from her pale face, he let his fingers linger on her cheek, then sat down beside her. "Do you need help with your gown?" he asked, and there was nothing at all sexual in his tone. But

there was tenderness and concern. It bathed Acadiana's
battered emotions like a soothing balm.

She nodded and sat up. Jonas worked the buttons at the
back and pushed the gown off her shoulders, then over her
hips. Her petticoats and stockings followed, but her chemise
remained as she crawled under the coverlet. Jonas disrobed
and climbed in beside her.

"Why would someone want to hurt them?" she whispered hollowly, staring at the mosquito netting overhead.

"I don't know, love. Men are greedy, fate is cruel. Must
there always be an answer?"

"*Oui,*" she said, tired and hurting. "In this there must be
one. I will find it. I won't rest until I do."

Neither would he. There was vengeance in her tone. Mingled with despair, it could prove a dangerous combination.
Jonas gathered her in his arms and put her face to his chest,
stroking her hair in soothing, rhythmic sweeps. "Let it go,
Acadiana, just for tonight. I'll help you find the answers,
but for now I want you to rest before you make yourself
ill."

He held her until she slept, then calmed her when the
nightmares came, and all the while his mind churned with
unexplained facts, unanswered questions, and the beginnings of an unreasonable and inexplicable fear.

Despite Jonas's warning, Acadiana did indeed manage to
make herself sick. She brooded continuously, waking in the
mornings in an unresponsive, often angry mood. The nightmares continued in full force, plaguing her nightly with
the tormenting screams of her mother. Acadiana felt better by
midday only to become dreary again toward evening. Jonas
comforted her as best he could when she cried out in the
dark, her body racked with spasms, her eyes sightless with
fear. But even though she would eventually calm down, he
knew he wasn't getting through to her, could not make her
realize that she was safe.

She seemed to spend her days in a state of semialertness,

helping Minette with the making of myrtle wax candles or soap, both time- and energy-consuming chores, collecting feathers for stuffing mattresses and pillows and fashioning the quills into pens. There was always an unending amount of blankets and clothes to be made for the slaves before the winter months arrived, and fruits and vegetables to be put up. Acadiana went about these duties without complaint, and with about as much verve as a zombie.

After weeks of her withdrawing farther and farther into herself, Jonas finally gave up trying to pull her out of her depression. Instead, he forced a meeting with his mother. As headstrong as her son, Minette had avoided all conversation that had any connection with Acadiana's land. Jonas was certain she knew more than she was willing to disclose, but had not been able to convince her to confide in him until now. His marriage was suffering, and he wasn't willing to give it up just yet.

Against her better judgment, Minette finally consented to meet with Jonas privately to discuss everything she knew. The past was dead; she preferred it remain buried, but she could not avoid him forever. She sat in the library, her usual composure shattered, wringing her hands and waiting for him to make an appearance. She knew the man Armand Hamilton had suspected of trying to run him out, and she also had a suspicion about where the locket had come from. There was a dreadful feeling in the pit of her stomach as she heard her son's footsteps ringing in the hall.

Jonas never made it to the library. He was halted by Mattie as she came screaming down the stairs.

"Mast' Jonas! Mast' Jonas! Come quick! It's Miz Cade! She dun fell out! She just lying there, white as a sheet! Hurry up, boy!"

Jonas flew up the stairs, shouting at Mattie to send for the doctor. When he burst into the bedroom, he found Acadiana struggling to sit up on the bed where Mattie had placed her.

"Don't, love. Just lie down," he said softly.

"What happened?" She moaned, a hand pressed against her forehead. "I was coming down to speak with you. I just feel so terrible about the way I've been acting lately but, Jonas, I just haven't felt like myself. I don't know what's wrong with me."

"It's all right, Acadiana. Mattie is sending Cain for the doctor. Just lie still." He brushed errant strands of ebony hair away from her ashen face, aching at how frail and spiritless she looked. Cupping her face with one hand, his thumb caressed her pale cheek with tenderness as he repressed the urge to take her into his arms, to bring life back to her wan features.

A flash of her old defiance sparked suddenly within the depths of her violet eyes. *"Mon Dieu!* Not the doctor, Jonas. I hate doctors! I'll be all right, really. I just need to rest."

"You've had plenty of rest lately. Just let him take a look at you." His voice was firm yet compassionate. "You don't have any choice, love. That's an order."

"You, sir, are no gentleman." She smiled weakly. "Forever forcing a lady against her will."

"Why, madame." Jonas grinned, pleased with her weak return of spunk. "I was under the impression that my unwilling bride was beginning to enjoy my advances."

"Oh, *non,* sir!" she replied saucily. "Perhaps you dreamed it. Would a genteel lady welcome the advances of a scoundrel?"

"My lady, were you not ill, I'd be forced to prove my point," he returned loftily.

"Were I not so ill, sir, you would have a hard time catching me."

"Prepare yourself, love." Jonas grinned. "When you are well, we shall see."

They continued their light banter until interrupted by the doctor. He was ushered in by a flustered Mattie, who was determined to leave nothing to chance. She didn't put much more stock in doctors than Acadiana did, but she had known Dr. Loreau a long time and trusted him as much as she did any of them.

Jonas was asked to leave the room, so he retreated to search for Minette. More than ever now, he was determined to find out everything she knew about the past.

13

Jonas stared at his mother in disbelief. It was not conceivable, this thing she had told him. It was ludicrous even to think it could be true, but he believed it nonetheless. Running his hand back and forth across his chin, Jonas slumped back in his chair and expelled a deep sigh. He knew his mother had not told him everything, but what she had said was enough to cause him to stop asking questions for the present. The lines that furrowed his brow didn't ease a whit as he began to speak.

"Acadiana must be told, Mother, but not yet." He tapped his fingers impatiently on the arm of the chair—an outward gesture, Minette knew, of internal decision making. "It looks like I'll have to make an unexpected business trip to New Orleans. But first I'll have to decide on an acceptable excuse to give Acadiana."

"Do you think that is such a good idea?" Minette asked. "Maybe you should leave it alone, yes? Look at what kind of condition she is in now."

"I can't leave it alone, Mother, you know that. What if she found out later?"

Minette shook her head. "A chance to take, yes?" Jonas refused to answer her hopeful plea, and Minette's voice rang out loudly in frustration. "She is strong, Jonas! She will recover from the fainting spell. But this . . . what will this news do to her? I cannot even be certain—"

"That is the chance I have to take." Jonas sighed.

Minette lapsed into aggrieved silence. Her son was so worried about Acadiana's health and preoccupied with the information she had just given him that there was no reason to continue, at least for the moment. She wasn't foolish enough to believe that the subject would not be brought up at another time. She still had not told him everything, but the other could wait for a more appropriate time—hopefully never. Grateful for the interruption, she turned as the doctor came into the room.

"Congratulations, Jonas," Dr. Loreau said, smiling. "Your wife is resting comfortably now. I am sure if she is extremely careful for the next couple of months, she will carry the baby to term. There are complications though—" The doctor's bushy gray eyebrows shot up over his spectacles. "Jonas . . . Jonas?"

Jonas, who had risen to his feet when the doctor walked in, had sat back down suddenly when his knees buckled. "Baby?"

Minette's troubled face softened, then brightened, and she reached over to pat her son's hand. "A child, Jonas. Our Cade is going to have a child!"

Dr. Loreau sent Jonas a dubious look. "I brought you into this world, son, but must have smacked you too hard. I thought you were smarter than this. Didn't you suspect?"

Jonas grinned lamely. There was just so much information a man could digest in one day. He was certain he had reached his limit. A baby! Thank God! That explained her ill health and moodiness. Dazed, he tried to focus on what the doctor was saying, but his mind was blurred by thoughts of Acadiana carrying his child. It filled him with elation and pride and no small amount of concern as the reality of the inherent dangers began to penetrate his foggy senses. Women often died in childbirth or from complications afterward. It was a matter of public record that women in the South were twice as likely to fall to that heinous end as were their northern counterparts. Jonas felt his jubilation ebb as Dr. Loreau's words only emphasized his concern.

"I must warn you, she is showing signs of difficulty. Nothing too serious, perhaps nothing at all, but she will have to be very careful for a few months. No overexertion, no horseback riding, and she should not lift anything heavier than a dinner fork. Which, I might add, she should be lifting a lot more." The doctor's eyes suddenly pierced Jonas with the same no-nonsense look he'd used when the Courtland boys had gotten into scrapes and he'd had to patch them up. "I would also advise you, Jonas, to exercise self-control, if you know what I mean."

Jonas grimaced faintly at that news, wondering if Acadiana had prompted this part of the conversation. Catching Jonas's dark scowl, the doctor hastened to explain.

"Just for the next few months, until we can be sure. I believe everything will be fine, but only time will tell. I will be back in about a month to check on her, unless you need me sooner. Now, if you will excuse me, I have other patients to tend. Minette, see me out. You can tell me your plans for this new generation of Courtlands before you tell the rest of the world."

Minette squeezed her son's hand once more, then accompanied the doctor to the door. Jonas, still operating under a heavy cloud of startling information, ascended the stairs to see his wife. Acadiana was propped on pillows in the middle of the big bed, glowing with the awareness of her newly discovered condition. She found it very strange and inspiring to be expecting a child, truly wondrous—and frightening. Her hands flitted down to her flat stomach, but there was no visible evidence to give proof to the doctor's words, nothing but an inner stirring more in the region of her heart that told her it was true. She should have suspected, she supposed. She had not had her flux since her marriage to

Jonas. Jonas! A blush stained her cheeks at the thought of telling him. Having a baby seemed such an intimate thing to share with one's husband. But then, intimacy had gotten her to this point. How would she tell him, approach the subject in a matter-of-fact manner?

"M'sieu Husband, we are to have a child!"

Never! This was not a common occurrence, at least not to her. Her entire world had just risen to new heights. Nothing would ever be normal or matter-of-fact again.

What of Jonas? Would he be pleased, or bothered, or indifferent? Not indifferent! Please, God, not indifferent! She could not endure casual acceptance from him right now. But she didn't know him well enough to guess what his reaction would be, didn't know him at all beyond his arrogance and stubbornness and . . . at times, tenderness. Protectiveness welled up within her, and her fingers splayed across her abdomen as if to conceal the fact, to keep the secret deep within her until she could be sure of his acceptance.

She thought of her parents, how Elaine could anticipate Armand's moods without so much as a word between them, how her father would usher the children outside at times, saying their mother was feeling poorly, when she and Matt had seen nothing of it in their mother's cheerful manner. There had always been a sort of silent communication between her parents.

Acadiana knew so little of Jonas, so little of the real man inside that brutally handsome exterior. She had only seen pieces of the emotions that made up her husband. There was anger—*le bon Dieu,* he could get angry with her when she defied him. But there was humor too, she admitted, thinking of his playfulness on the sandbar that time in the wilderness, and more recently in the gazebo. There was passion, but she could not think of that without her cheeks heating up, and there was even affection. He had held her tenderly at the cottage, soothed her with words and gentle strokes while she wept from the pain and loneliness of her parents' death. But what about love? Could they raise children, nurture them by God's design, without love?

Her parents had loved each other, and with slow, dawning awareness Acadiana realized they had shown many of the same emotions. Acadiana could remember her mother scolding her father for tracking mud on her clean floors, and Armand gentling her with affectionate words until Elaine's face would be wreathed in smiles and their laughter would ring out in the small cottage, letting the children know that all was forgiven. Though they never showed passion openly, Acadiana knew it must have existed, for two children were born of their love. Maybe the only difference in her parents' relationship and theirs was that her parents *knew* they loved each other. Maybe one day she and Jonas would find it in their own lives.

There were things about him that she already liked. She had to admire the way he ran his life, organized, efficient. He was kind and dealt with the workers on the plantation not in the manner of master and slave but in a fair and compassionate way. He treated her gently—well, most of the time. *Oui,* perhaps one day they would see love in their lives too.

Suddenly, fiercely, it became very important to Acadiana that she and Jonas have the sort of marriage that her parents had. There was more at stake here now than her own life. The gift within her, however begotten, was innocent of the turbulence that overshadowed her marriage. She was willing, *non,* determined to change things now for the child's sake, and prayed Jonas would be also. With this hope growing, Acadiana waited with equal portions of eagerness and trepidation for her husband.

Jonas stepped quietly into the room and smiled at his wife. His very beautiful, very pale wife. His heart swelled to an almost painful level as a protective feeling overcame him. Thick ebony locks spilled over her shoulders in delightful disarray, and her fingers fidgeted with the coverlet. He had not noticed until now that her breasts were fuller, more womanly. A pulse fluttered at the base of her throat, and he realized that she was nervous. His conscience was flayed by the sight, and he felt somehow guilty. Tenderness for her made his heart race and his body to heat up in a way that had nothing to do with desire or lust. The emotion felt so strange that he almost laughed . . . or cried. He didn't know what his heart and mind wanted to do. He sat down on the edge of the bed, and Acadiana smiled shyly up at him.

"Congratulations, love." He smiled in return, running his knuckles over her wan cheeks.

"You know?" she asked. His face gave away none of the emotions she was searching for. He was smiling, but he did that often. For a fleeting second she wanted to throw the cover over her head so she wouldn't have to look at his face when he declared his feelings on the matter. However, he spoke before she could retreat.

"The doctor told us." He grinned. "I'm sure Mother would be up here now fussing over you, but she felt the need to spread the news far and wide first, and she wanted to give us a moment to ourselves."

"You are pleased?" she asked carefully.

"Pleased? Don't be absurd, woman. Ecstatic maybe, but pleased? That is much too simple a word to describe the way I feel. I've never pictured myself as the proud papa, but I think I'm going to like this. I told you a long time ago that I wanted children."

"I am glad you are happy." She sighed in relief.

"Was there ever any doubt? Fie on you, madame! You discredit me immensely." Something in his heart twisted at her uncertain tone. That she could doubt for a second the joy he felt made his heart hurt in a way that he had never experienced. Was their relationship so tenuous that she could not see the pride that so enveloped him?

"It is wonderful." She smiled then sighed, her amethyst eyes darkening. "But it doesn't change the other."

"I know." Jonas took her hand and pressed it to his lips.

The gesture was simple yet compelling for the young woman whose world had just been spun around. "I will take care of it, Acadiana. I am going to undertake the investigation myself. I assure you that I will use every means available to find out what happened eleven years ago and about the locket also. But for now you will rest and protect my child."

It was a priceless moment to Acadiana, cloaked in the warmth of his soothing words and gentle smile, her fingers pressed to his lips, sharing the glory of creating life and the promise that held for the future. For the first time in a decade she did not want to resurrect the past, to have its haunting refrain mar the melody of the lifesong whispered between them. His tender gaze had held concern as he issued the command "rest and protect my child," and Acadiana basked in his concern for her and the child . . . *their* child. With a jaunty smile, she answered his command in a way that she knew would erase the worry she detected on his handsome face.

"Aye, aye, Captain!" she returned, saluting him with a pert wave of her hand.

Jonas grinned devilishly and returned her haughty stare. "You're a smart one, protected now by your condition, but I think you know who the master of this house is," he said sternly. "On this matter you will obey."

"Of course I do," she replied sweetly. "Mattie is."

Jonas merely smiled, that mocking, knowing smile, then kissed her hand again. "I think it's time I set out to find a manager for your plantation." The excuse was a legitimate one now, and he would use it to go to New Orleans without her suspecting any other motive. "I thought we would repair the cottage and build your dream house to raise our children in."

Acadiana's breath caught, hope dawning brightly, hope that had been so easily dashed in the past. "Do you mean it? You will build the house in the painting?" She stared intently at him, drinking in his every expression, looking fearfully for some sign that she had misread his words. It was too much to believe in, but she wanted—oh, how she wanted—to believe just that. Courtland Manor was his inheritance. By right that was where they should live for the rest of their lives.

"Of course I mean it," Jonas said wryly. "Maybe *there* I'll be master of my home."

"I wouldn't count on it." She grinned broadly, relief bursting within her until it flooded her entire body with warmth.

"We'll see about that," he chuckled, leaning over to kiss her. Instinctively her hand went up to cup his strong, tanned cheek, to lengthen and savor the moment before his mouth took control of hers. Her eyes fluttered closed as his lips drew nearer, and a surge of passion rushed through her so keenly it made her gasp. The sound was swallowed by his groan in the second before their mouths meshed and forged a bond so strong that it intimidated Acadiana with the strength of it. But instead of pulling away, she dissolved into him with a languor that made his arms encircle her limp body more firmly. Her head dropped back when the kiss ended, and her eyes flickered open to stare at his hawkish features.

"It will be a wonderful house to raise our son in." She sighed wistfully.

"Daughter," he corrected, "with your eyes."

"Son," she repeated, stirring within his irrepressible arms to gather her equilibrium. "Every man wants a son. What do I know about raising girls?" The thought of someone of her unconventional past life-style raising a precious little girl made her shudder.

"The son can come next," Jonas said against her lips as he tried to recapture the moment. "Right now I want a daughter."

Acadiana pulled away from him. "Well, I want a son!"

"Daughter!"

"Son!"

"Dau . . . are we going to fight, love?"

"Not this time." She giggled, and snuggled closer to his hard body, burying her face in the crisp linen shirt to hide a secret smile. She marveled that the endearment "love" did not rankle as it once would have, but sent hope singing through her veins. One day, she vowed, he would mean it.

The household was hard-pressed to make Acadiana behave. She was happy as a child at Christmas when she thought of the baby—which was always. If she let her mind wander to the locket, she became depressed as thoughts of her parents' tragedy came creeping in to destroy her joy.

Mattie gave up trying to coax more food down than Acadiana could hold. Minette pleaded with her constantly to be more sedate as befitted a woman in her condition. Jonas merely raved, *continuously,* placing her in a rocking chair that had been moved to the back gallery every time he caught her doing more than he thought she should.

"Rock my daughter!" he shouted for the third time that morning. This last time he had found her running through the house after a stray puppy. Acadiana had come to a skidding halt when he appeared, but it was too late. Before she could mouth a protest, he had picked her up and was heading for the door.

"My *son* will be seasick when he is born if you continue to make me stay in this infernal chair!" she shouted back.

"What did she do this time?" Edward asked with a chuckle as he stepped up onto the porch.

"Absolutely nothing!" Acadiana replied. Her head snapped back and forth as she vented her anger on the rocker.

"Stop rocking so fast!" Jonas yelled.

Violet eyes narrowed to challenge the bold sapphire ones looking down at her. "Make up your mind! First you tell me rock, then you tell me to stop!" Acadiana crossed her arms over her chest and drew a disgruntled breath. She was tired of being guarded constantly by the entire household.

Didn't they realize she would not do anything to hurt her child? She tried to get up but found herself imprisoned.

"Edward," Jonas said, ignoring his wife's attempt to get free by keeping his hand planted on her shoulder. "I think it's time I made that trip to New Orleans to locate a manager for Bayou Oaks. I want operations to be under way before the baby is born. I have to find a man who can handle the new steam process before we can complete the renovation.

"Of course," Jonas continued, giving Acadiana a stern look, "I can't trust my wife out of my sight for two seconds. Do you think you can keep her safely occupied while I'm away?"

The horror-stricken look on Edward's face made Acadiana roll her eyes even as she suppressed a giggle. "It would be easier to tame an alligator!" he said. "How can you do this to me?"

"Traitor." Acadiana pouted. She turned liquid eyes to her brother-in-law and sent him her most endearing smile.

Edward melted. "I'll go plead with Beth to spend a few days here to entertain you and keep me off of Jonas's bad list."

"That's the best idea I've heard for weeks," Acadiana said, jumping up from the despised chair.

Jonas grabbed her in flight and gently shoved her back down again. "Maybe Beth will be so kind as to teach you the more genteel art of sewing so our daughter won't remain naked after she's born."

"Grand'mère is already sewing, and Mattie has all of your and Edward's baby clothes washed and pressed. My *son* will be quite well clothed."

"Daughter," reminded Jonas.

"Son."

"Daughter!"

"Son!"

"I'll go find Beth." Edward snickered, leaving them in the same confrontation he had been hearing day after day.

Jonas left Acadiana in Mattie's capable hands and went in search of Cain. As on most plantations, when Jonas was a child he was allowed to have a selected Negro playmate. His early relationship with Cain had molded a close friendship that would last throughout their lives. Having a black man as an overseer was virtually unheard of, Jonas knew, but he would have no other man than Cain. His family was too old and well established in the area for anyone to oppose them openly. If they did so in private, it mattered not at all to him. He could trust the big, brawny man and needed Cain to accompany him to New Orleans.

Acadiana stood at her bedroom window, squinting in the predawn darkness to catch the last glimpse of her husband as he left the plantation. She could feel the old despair creeping up on her as he rode away, and fought back angry tears of loneliness. She had pleaded with Jonas to let her accompany him, but he had adamantly refused, blaming her condition. But it was more than that, she knew, by the hooded gaze that had accompanied his declaration. It had caused the old insecurities to build within her, and their parting had been shadowed by angry questions and hurtful replies. *Mon Dieu,* he was mean and hateful, domineering and arrogant and . . . Acadiana slunk away from the window and collapsed on the bed in a fit of tears because she missed him already, and didn't want to, and wholeheartedly regretted their angry parting.

The men left at dawn, traveling by barge down the river. The trip would take three days, and Jonas chafed under the restriction, disliking any amount of time that would take him away from his wife. Memories of their ugly leave-taking disturbed him without quarter over the ensuing days and long, lonely nights. Acadiana with her eyes flashing the familiar violet fury. Acadiana in the savagely alluring Indian clothes. Acadiana with her haughty smile or girlish giggle. Acadiana with heart-rending, tearful eyes pleading with him to take her along. But most of all, Acadiana with her midnight-dark tresses glimmering in the candlelight as they flowed across her bare shoulders, and eyes the soft hue of amethyst smoke as they darkened with a passion that she inevitably subdued.

His memories were more fanciful than real, Jonas admitted, for Acadiana always snuffed the candle flame before she would undress. But his mind through touch could see what his eyes could not in nothing more than feeble moonlight, and she always slipped into a nightdress before dawn. But each caress of her silken skin allowed his imagination to take flight, and he didn't need the glow of candlelight to know every inch of her. Or to conjure up that vision now as the barge rocked gently down the river taking him farther and farther from her.

To pass the long, gloomy days and torturous nights, Jonas used the time to formulate a plan. Finding a manager was not his primary purpose for this trip, and he would save that for last. No, he had a more important mission. First, he would try the shops on Royal and Chartres streets that served as outlets for smuggled goods, or the St. Phillip Street forge and workshop, also a secondary business to cover smuggling operations. All meetings and transactions pertaining to the business of contraband took place there. With any luck, he would be able to arrange a meeting with the infamous pirate Jean Lafitte, who along with his brother, Pierre, were leaders of the Baratarian corsairs, one of the largest and strongest army of pirates ever to travel the waterways of the world. If he could make contact, Jonas knew Lafitte would agree to meet with him at the buccaneer's home on Grande Terre that he shared with his mistress, Catherine Villars. There Jonas could find out if what his mother suspected was true.

He had met Lafitte through leading New Orleans citizens, lawyers Edward Livingston and Pierre Morel, and had rubbed shoulders with him on several occasions while attending social functions. Lafitte had an ostentatious list of acquaintances that included painter Jean Baptiste Sel, soldier of fortune Baron de Saint Geme, and legislator Louis

Louaillier. But in March 1813 Governor Claiborne had proclaimed the Baratarians "banditti" and had ordered them to disperse. By July Pierre had been arrested and charged with being a pirate and a notorious smuggler, and Jonas wasn't certain he would now be able to locate either Lafitte.

Thankfully, Jonas located Dominique You, alleged to be another of Lafitte's brothers, on Bourbon Street, and the arrangements were made that evening. The next morning he was escorted out to the lands surrounding Barataria Bay, about forty miles south of New Orleans near the Gulf of Mexico. Grand Terre Island and Grand Isle were the major strongholds and were highly populated with pirates and other seamen who had settled those communities to form a center for the buccaneering operations.

Jonas had never visited Lafitte on Grand Terre and was impressed by the pirate's home. Although the island consisted mostly of wind-swept grasses, sinewy weeds, and a thin drift-speckled beach, the house itself was nestled among dense groves of oranges and gnarled oaks. The largest on the island, it was elegantly furnished with rich carpets, silver, glassware, and many other fine items taken from raids on Spanish ships. This was a kingdom ruled by Jean and Pierre. They bestowed princely hospitality on their guests, whether the visitor be a dignitary, businessman, or as in Jonas's case, friend.

Jonas was met in an elegant sitting room by a slim, well-built man over six feet tall with prematurely graying hair. Lafitte was dressed in a coat of black superfine, matching breeches, and tall Hessian boots. An expert with the foils and the pistol, Lafitte was popular and daring, a man of adventure, but it was with sophisticated grace that the thirty-two-year-old man welcomed Jonas into his home. His features were cast in a handsome, classic profile, his glittering eyes, healthy teeth, and quick-witted charms attracting both men and women.

Although Jonas did not deal in contraband personally, most Louisianians enjoyed the tariff-free supplies Lafitte offered them at a greatly reduced prices, and readily welcomed him to their aristocratic world. A cultured man, Lafitte fit in superbly, patronizing the opera and frequenting many other social events, the New Orleans quadroon balls being one of his favorites.

Jonas was seated and offered refreshments before their small talk turned more serious.

"What brings you out here, *mon ami?*" Lafitte asked with a ready smile but wary glint in his eyes gained from years of dealing in the forbidden.

"Information, Jean. I need information on one of your leaders," Jonas replied. He shook his head slightly as Lafitte gestured at an intricately carved cigar box.

Lafitte's hooded gaze belied the casualness of his words. "If there has been trouble, Jonas, I will see to it personally." It was well known that Lafitte always disciplined offenders quickly. Taking control of the rowdy buccaneers was what had gained him acceptance by the people of New Orleans.

"No, Jean, no trouble. It's a long story, but I believe one of your men may know something about what happened to my wife's family many years ago."

"I see," Jean said slowly. He withdrew a hand-rolled cheroot and lit it leisurely, his eyes shrewd and intent over the flicker of his match. "As disreputable as they seem, there is a code of honor among my men. What do you want from this man . . . *if* he is one of mine?"

"Only to talk to him, Jean. I assure you, nothing more. My wife does not even know I am here. If the man does not want to speak with me, I will honor that decision."

"*Oui,* I will agree to that. Now what is the name of this supposed colleague of mine?"

Although Jonas didn't know his quarry's alias, he gave the man's given name. He searched Lafitte's face for some sign of recognition, but the pirate's thoughts were carefully concealed, and his eyes showed nothing more than casual interest.

"I will do some checking, Jonas. If this man is one of

mine, and he wishes to see you, I will have him meet you
back in New Orleans tomorrow at the Café des Réfugiés on
St. Phillip Street. You know the place, *oui?*"

"Of course." Nothing more was necessary.

"Good, I will send someone to make the inquiries, and
we shall enjoy this day getting reacquainted. It has been too
long, my friend."

Jonas did indeed enjoy the afternoon, listening to tales of
adventure and daring from this man who thrived on risking
his life. But more startling was the information he received
just before departing. Lafitte had it from reliable sources
that since Napoleon had been defeated, the British could
now throw all their resources against the United States, and
it was rumored that they were planning to attack New Orleans.

"Ah, *mon ami.*" Lafitte sighed, stretching his tall frame
then slumping back in his seat. "The British have offered
me a large sum of money and a naval captaincy if I will
gather my army of pirates and fight with them. A tempting
offer, *oui?*"

"What does Governor Claiborne say?" Jonas asked, recognizing the danger to Louisiana that such a proposition
would pose.

"Claiborne wants my hide"—Lafitte chuckled—"but he
knows if the British capture New Orleans, they will hold
the key to the entire lower Mississippi Valley and its rich
plunder of sugar, cotton, and tobacco, among other things.
The British expect little opposition from the Americans and
none from the French and Spanish Creoles."

"They are too arrogant in their thinking," Jonas said in a
low, steely voice. "And they are wrong."

"My sentiments exactly," Lafitte agreed. "But they are
confident. The British are already concentrated at Negril
Bay, Jamaica. They have a fleet of fifty ships commanded
by Vice-Admiral Sir Alexander Cochrane and an army of
ten thousand men commanded by General Sir Edward

Pakenham. You know he is the brother-in-law of the Duke of Wellington."

The Iron Duke, stormer of the strongholds of Badajoz and Salamanca in the Spanish Peninsula, Jonas thought as he nodded. He was familiar with the name and recognized the danger that statement carried. "So, this is no idle threat then?"

Lafitte chuckled wryly. *"Non,* even I am amazed at their boldness! There are civil officials on board the ships now ready to take over the government of Louisiana, and their wives as well as wives of naval and army officers."

"Good God!" Jonas groaned before his eyes narrowed and he asked brazenly, "What will you do, Jean?"

"Contemplating calling me out now, *m'sieu?* The dueling field is always greedy for my blood." Lafitte laughed, then waved his hand as if dismissing the statement. "No need to worry, Jonas. I have written a letter to Governor Claiborne offering my services and assuring him of my willingness to discharge the duties of a good citizen. I have never sailed under any flag but that of the republic of Carthagena, and my vessels are regular in that respect, but the man does not trust me."

Well acquainted with the pirate's nefarious deeds, Jonas lifted an eyebrow and flashed Lafitte a wry grin. "And why, do you suppose, that is?"

Lafitte countered by shrugging his shoulders innocently. "I suppose it is because Claiborne offered a five-hundred-dollar reward for my arrest and I, in turn, offered fifteen hundred for his head." Lafitte's deep laughter rang out in the elegant room, and his eyes sparkled with the memory. "The gracious people of New Orleans loved it, but Claiborne did not take the joke well. It is my opinion that he will try to the very last to capture me. But the British numbers are too great. He will be forced to come around in the end or risk losing everything."

Lafitte sighed somewhat wistfully. "Louisiana has been good to me, my friend, but I feel my days of, ah, service, to her are quickly coming to an end. Many of my men wish to settle down and become respectable citizens. It is toward that end that I will request a full and complete pardon as payment for our participation. My friend Judge Dominick Hall and legislators Marginy, Roffignac, and Louaillier have agreed to meet with General Jackson and the governor on my behalf to propose that I join my forces with theirs."

"A strategic move, no doubt," Jonas commented. "I thought Jackson was still fighting the Creek Indians."

Lafitte shook his head. "He has just completed the Treaty of Fort Jackson and is on his way to Fort Bowyer at Mobile where it is rumored the British will strike first."

"Contrary to what the British may be imagining, Louisiana will not be taken without a fight," Jonas said with the hard determination that would soon affect all Louisianians. He stood then and offered his hand in parting. "Keep me informed, Jean."

"*Oui,*" Lafitte agreed, and rose also. "Perhaps, Jonas, the next time we meet it won't be under such strained circumstances."

Jonas returned to New Orleans after agreeing to wait for the man he was seeking in the appointed place between four and six o'clock. If the privateer did not appear by then, Jonas was to leave without further questions. Part of him hoped the man would present himself so he could finally put his nagging suspicions to rest, and another part of him hoped his journey would prove fruitless and he could return home having done his duty, and Acadiana's past could be buried. No, he corrected, she would never leave it alone as long as there were unanswered questions. Although he could not fault her that, he wasn't sure just what any new information he might uncover would do to her.

His first task complete, Jonas began making inquiries about possible plantation managers. He could hardly return home without one. It was difficult to locate anyone familiar with the new steam process, but by noon Jonas had the names of several men. He sent Cain out with instructions to set up interviews for the following day.

Jonas arrived at the Café des Réfugiés at half past three. He paced the floor impatiently as scores of rugged-looking characters and well refined alike came and went, giving him little more than a quizzical glance. There were flatboatmen, filibusters, French *révolutionaires,* and American army and navy deserters along with leading New Orleans citizens. Quite a menagerie, Jonas thought cynically as he nodded to Buluche, Nez Coupé, and Gambi, some of Lafitte's most trusted lieutenants. Still, the man he sought did not arrive.

As he watched the men come and go, he had too much time to wonder if what he was doing was all that good an idea. Perhaps his mother was right, and he should just leave it alone, let the past take care of itself. But he was here now, and he would see it through.

Jonas had no more time to ponder, for at exactly four o'clock the room suddenly became deserted. He was left standing alone as the door opened once again to admit a stark, imposing figure. His long ebony hair fell in wavy rebellion well below his starched white collar. Commandingly tall and whipcord lean, he exuded feral power leashed now in casual yet alert intensity. With his tall, shiny polished boots and glittering jeweled earring, he could have been any one of a hundred swarthy pirates hunting coastal waters and terrorizing maidens—except for the eyes.

Deep amethyst eyes set in the ruggedly handsome face gave credence to the fact that one Matthew Hamilton was very much alive!

The resemblance to Acadiana was striking—the hair, the eyes, the haunted look and determined set of his mouth. At twenty-seven and at least four inches over six feet tall, the pirate had to duck to cross the threshold as he swaggered into the room with a zesty grin that did not pretend to reach his hard, brilliant eyes.

"Mr. Hamilton, I presume?" questioned Jonas.

"Presume nothing, Courtland," the man said in a cold,

deep voice. "I am Hunter. Matthew Hamilton expired eleven years ago. State your business."

Rising to the challenge, Jonas grinned, but the look was neither pleasant nor humorous. "I believe you have been paying for the upkeep on my wife's property and you sent her flowers and a locket on her birthday?"

"If I did?" Hunter asked, eyebrows raised in hard insolence. He could tell Courtland was no man to play games with. But then, neither was he.

"How did you know how to reach her?"

"I have my ways," Hunter said casually. A network of spies, both government sanctioned and underworld, allowed him a multitude of otherwise unobtainable information.

"She thinks her brother is dead."

"Her brother *is* dead," Hunter replied with icy contempt.

"*Au contraire,* my friend," Jonas said in subtle warning. "You are very much alive. If you wished to remain incognito, why send the locket?"

"It is hers," Hunter said flatly, his face an impregnable mask of cool regard and even icier menace. There was a lethal quality about this man that would have cowed a lesser person.

"It almost cost her the life of our child," Jonas said lowly. His anger rose dangerously at the coldness of the arrogant buccaneer. If the man thought to intimidate him, he was operating under a fallacy. Jonas was not affected in the least by the man's superior attitude except to wonder how the same blood could flow through Acadiana's and this man's veins. While his wife's hauteur was an artifice, Jonas was certain this cold, dark reserve was very much an integral part of Matthew Hamilton, and he wasn't at all sure he wanted his wife to know that the brother she mourned so deeply was not the person she remembered.

"What are you saying?" Hunter asked, the first hint of emotion crossing his guarded face.

En garde, Jonas thought, taking the man's measure and

noting a slight weakness. "She is having a difficult pregnancy. That locket has upset her tremendously."

"Is she safe?"

"She is."

"Then what do you want from me?"

Jonas thought he saw a glimmer of pain cross Hunter's eyes, but whatever the emotion, it was quickly veiled, and the cool mask of indifference returned.

"Nothing. I think you have done quite enough," Jonas said.

The man rounded on him then with a flash of fury that so resembled Acadiana in a temper fit. "Then why are you here?" Hunter snarled. "To prick my conscience? You could have saved yourself the trouble, Courtland. What guilt I harbor over what happened to my family goes much deeper than you could ever imagine. It has eaten away at me daily for eleven years. I don't need you to remind me of what I've done! There will never be any semblance of peace in my life."

A sudden and poignant silence filled the small room as the two formidable men stared at each other, one taut and barely contained in his fury and guilt, the other in astonishment. Jonas saw clearly the crack in his opponent's armor and realized his brother-in-law was not so very different from his wife in erecting barriers to keep out the brutalities of life.

"Surely you don't blame yourself for what happened?" Jonas asked quietly.

Hunter's laugh was cold and bitter. "I should have been there. If I had stayed, my parents never would have left."

"You couldn't have stopped the land grabbers."

"What do you know about that?" Hunter asked, his voice stunned and reeking of hatred.

"Just that someone was trying to run your family out. What I want to know is why. Acadiana is also determined to find out who drove her parents from their home."

"Is that what she thinks happened?" Hunter laughed sarcastically. "That those men drove them out? My father was a strong man; he would have stayed to fight if I had not left and upset my mother so." His eyes narrowed to sharp slits. "How much does my sister know?"

"She doesn't know about you, if that's what you mean," Jonas replied. "I thought it better to confirm my suspicions before getting her all riled up again. Her condition is delicate. I don't know if she can take another shock."

"And now you have seen me," Hunter replied mockingly. "What would you have me do? Rise from the grave and expect her to welcome a notorious pirate with open arms? She was gently raised; the shock to her honor would be as devastating for her as it was for our mother."

"You know nothing of your sister," Jonas scoffed. "When your parents were killed, Acadiana was rescued by a band of Caddo Indians and—"

"Raised by Jean Baptiste for four years," Hunter finished. "I know her past. It . . . could not have been easy for her."

"Not as difficult as you might think," Jonas said. "At least not that part of her life. She can function in the wild as well as any man I know, and her infuriating temper would rock the decks of the lowest pirate ship here or abroad."

"Cade?" Hunter asked, angered by the indelicate accusation. "Watch your tongue, Courtland, you do my sister an injustice. She is just a child—"

"Hardly," Jonas interrupted. "She is a woman, and if she takes exception to your line of work, you would do well to guard your neck . . . if you wish it to remain permanently attached to your head."

"I can't see how that concerns me," Hunter stated.

"You will," Jonas said evenly, "if you choose to *see* her."

"I made my choice eleven years ago."

"Where are your loyalties?" Jonas snapped.

Hunter's sudden laughter was hard and biting, ending as abruptly as it began. "Don't you know?" he asked quietly, dangerously. "I have none."

Jonas fought the urge to strangle the man and ran his hands through his hair impatiently. "Your life is your business; you can do what you want. But she would never forgive me if I didn't tell her about you. I won't build the foundation of our marriage on lies."

"Ah," Hunter said, his smile tight, his eyes alert, "but you have already lied to *Capitaine*. What is one more?"

"No," Jonas said amiably enough, although his grin was also a barely controlled line on his face. "I told Lafitte I would not press the issue if you did not wish to see me, but you are here . . ."

He let the sentence trail off, letting Hunter know that his presence confirmed that he was more interested than he let on. Jonas dropped all pretense of politeness and faced the man squarely. "I warn you, when she learns of your existence, she will seek you out. It would be far safer if you come to her first. In her condition I don't want her unduly stressed. I fancy my child being born safely at home instead of on some seedy street corner as his mother rants and raves throughout New Orleans searching for a wayward brother." Jonas stopped and gave Hunter a piercing stare that spoke volumes. "If you are the cause of anything happening to her, I will come after you."

The threat in itself meant nothing, but the words convinced Hunter of Jonas's devotion to his sister.

"I have missed her," he said tersely. It was a fleeting emotion, but Jonas could again see a hint of sadness flicker across the man's face. "Will you tell me some things about her?"

Jonas sighed and relaxed a little. So, the man was not as cold as he had at first appeared, he thought with grudging respect.

Jonas was wrong. Matthew Huntington Hamilton was every bit as cold and unapproachable as a man could be, but there was one person in the world who could soften the hardened steel that rested in place of his heart. Hunter had always carried a weakness for his younger sister.

"She is beautiful," Jonas said, a faraway light in his eyes. "She looks like you, the hair and eyes are identical, but she is about a foot shorter. She has the temper of an angry boar, and I have yet to find anything that matches her determination."

Good God, Hunter thought with sardonic cynicism, the man's besotted in the worst way! And the most amusing part of it was he didn't think Courtland even realized it yet. For the first time since entering the room, Hunter grinned honestly. "She hasn't changed much. Does she ever mention me?"

"She tries not to," Jonas admitted. "There are parts of those years she wants to wipe away as if they never existed. The memories bring her too much pain. But when she speaks of you, it is in loving terms. Once she gets over the shock, I think seeing you again will provide a great inner healing for her."

Hunter could not picture Acadiana as a grown woman with a family of her own. He still saw a barefoot girl wading in the bayou with her skirts hiked up to her skinny knees, or tousled black curls framing a grimy face as it peered out the leafy boughs of a magnolia tree. Mostly, he could not picture Cade with a husband.

"This marriage of yours was rather sudden, wasn't it?" he asked conversationally. If he meant to throw Jonas off guard, the deadly gleam in his eyes gave him away.

Jonas knew he was being assessed as friend or foe. Hunter had a calculating look about him, and Jonas wasn't sure that now was the time to discuss the marriage.

"You might say it was love at first sight," Jonas evaded, his expression equally closed. "Your parents' land borders ours. That's what brought us together."

"I know who you are," Hunter stated. "Your mother was a friend to my mother. Is that how you found me?"

"Yes," Jonas replied, relieved that they had abandoned the marriage conversation. "We haven't told Acadiana anything about you yet. My mother wasn't certain you were still alive. There are several unanswered questions, in fact. The locket was one of them; the others will have to wait until I have some proof."

Jonas could see that Hunter struggled with some sort of inner turmoil, which he understood for he was combating his own. Jonas couldn't rightly say that he wanted a pirate for a brother-in-law, but he could not disregard the fact that Acadiana had a right to know her brother was alive and to make her own judgments concerning the fact. There wasn't a prejudiced bone in her delectable little body, and he knew she would probably handle the information better than he had. But he could not be absolutely be sure, and that ate at him cruelly. If she was hurt further by the fact that her brother had abandoned her in a sense, Jonas would be tempted to kill the man for his treachery.

Hunter knew Jonas waited, waited for the answer he had no wish to give, but he could not deny the lure of seeing those amethyst eyes again, eyes so much like his yet not tainted by wickedness and debauchery. Would they once again gaze up at him with the light of adoration and impish mischief that had been so much a part of the ten-year-old he remembered? Or would they blaze with horror, as his mother's had? Hunter didn't think he could take the chance, neither could he refuse. If Cade rejected him for his jaded existence, it was nothing more than he deserved.

"Don't tell her anything," Hunter requested. "I have some things I need to do first. You have spoken to *Capitaine* so you are aware of the threat from the British."

Jonas nodded. The breath he had been holding without realizing it slowly drained from him, and he could not believe how relieved he felt at Hunter's hard-won decision.

"We must all band together in this cause, else our Louisiana will once again change government hands. I'll do what must be done to preserve our freedom."

"Gather the support of the people in your area," Hunter said without reservation. They trod common ground here as men with a purpose even had Cade not been involved. "It will take every bit of strength we can muster from Creoles, Cajuns, Indians, freemen of color, the American militia, and —let us hope—paroled pirates. It is rumored that Andrew Jackson's Kaintucks, his men from Kentucky, will also fight with him. It will take every man to a number to bring about a defeat."

Jonas nodded, promising he would raise as many as he could from the Teche area, then brought the conversation back to his original purpose. "Now, will you answer a question for me?"

"Perhaps."

"Why did your mother tell everyone you had drowned?"

Pain once again seeped through Hunter's carefully masked features. Though quickly covered, the evidence lingered in the drawn eyebrows and clenched fists. "I left bits of clothing tangled in the cypress knees. It wasn't the first time someone connected with my family had disappeared that way. Don't look so appalled, Courtland. My mother knew exactly where I was going, but she had her pride. I merely left the clothing behind as an excuse for her friends. I didn't wish to cause her humiliation along with the pain of my leaving."

Hunter agreed to contact Jonas at Courtland Manor as soon as the trouble with the British was ended. It would take many months for him to be in a position to leave his Grand Isle fortress with confidence. Jonas bid him farewell, extending his hand in a show of guarded friendship and truce. There were two major issues to unite the men, and if Jonas didn't exactly approve of Hunter, he at least felt much better about him than he had initially thought possible. He left for his hotel, relieved to have accomplished at least half his mission.

Jonas met with Cain that evening to find that his overseer had arranged for interviews the next morning with Jonas wondered how Acadiana was faring with him gone. He knew he should be worrying about everyone else without him there to keep her out of trouble. Edward would have a devil of a time fulfilling his obligation, but Beth was there to help, and Jonas was grateful for the loving friendship between her and his wife.

He probably would have married Beth out of obligation and for the sake of convenience had not a spitfire of a little girl stolen his heart completely. Even in the midst of a stormy temper tantrum, she was his beloved. Beloved! The thought gave him pause. He didn't know when it had started—this loving. It had just sort of crept up on him, catching him unaware, yet it felt as if it had always been there.

Duty and respect—those were the important things, the lasting things in a marriage. Jonas reflected on the times in his life when as a young man love had played a role. There were girls he had thought he loved, and girls who had said they loved him. None of these relationships had lasted. Someone had always been left empty and aching by the end. Loneliness and hurt had always followed; the rapture had not lasted.

As an adult he had watched for the danger signs and had avoided entanglements that promised emotional chaos. But this didn't feel dangerous, this loving Acadiana. It felt right, as natural as breathing, and as necessary.

You don't love me. It would be a mockery and a lie to say things are as they should be. The words she had spoken that moonlit night came back to haunt him.

Now he did love her, but the realization brought forth a feeling of vulnerability that Jonas didn't wish to explore. Maybe given time Acadiana would feel the same. She would have to, he vowed. There was no way to change their life path now. This entanglement could not be gotten rid of, for he would not let her go, not ever.

Jonas fell into a restless sleep that night, thinking of shimmering violet eyes and sleek limbs that were his and yet not completely. He hoped he would find a manager soon and get back home to his wife. His adorable, hard-headed wife.

Jonas interviewed half a dozen men before being introduced to Liam Connelly. Mr. Connelly was a middle-age Irishman with a small build and a large family. He had spent most of his adult life around sugarcane and knew as much as Jonas did about sugar production.

"Well, Mr. Connelly, I am looking for a manager," he said, "and I need one who can handle the new steam-powered mill we are putting in."

"Aye, gov'nor, I have to admit I knew that when I came here today," the man said with a nervous sort of boisterousness. "I came to these bonny shores to make a new life for meself. I hired on at sugar plantation, and I've been learning ever since. I kin do everything from planting to harvesting. I work real hard and my wife and the bairns are willing to do what they kin to help too."

"Mr. Connelly!" Jonas said, taken aback by the man's words. "I do not hire women and children! I've hundreds of arpents planted, and I'm here to get a manager, not slave labor."

Liam's weather-worn face fell. "Aye, I think I understand," he said dejectedly. "You be needing a man what kin hold a social position befitting your status. I know what's expected of them managers. I took a chance in coming here today, thinking you might not be having such a big spread, just getting started." He shook his head in self-derision. "I should have known better, that I should, by the fact that you're building the new stream-driven mill. A fine thing that! It's going to change the history of sugar-making, I can tell you that."

Jonas looked at the man in total confusion. Mr. Connelly was the most qualified person he had talked to all morning, yet he seemed reluctant to take what Jonas was offering.

"Are you telling me you can't handle the work?"

"The work? Oh, nay, sir, I mean, aye, sir." The man

looked positively flustered, Jonas thought. "I mean, everybody knows a plantation manager holds about the same prestige as the owner." Liam gave Jonas a rather tired half smile. "It ain't the work, Mr. Courtland, but I canna see where I'd fit in at some fancy ladies' tea party."

"Tea party!" Jonas hooted, just beginning to understand the man's worries. "Let me worry about the ladies' social affairs. Are you willing to take the job?"

"Oh, saints and mercy, sir, I'd be much obliged!" Liam fairly shouted as he leapt to his feet. He fumbled for an old kerchief, then wiped a tear from his weathered face in embarrassment. "Praise be the saints, Mr. Courtland, I got to go tell my missus. She'll be right proud, right proud indeed."

Liam took off in a dead run, skidding across the hotel's polished floor in his haste. Apparently changing his mind, he then turned and hurried back to Jonas's table. "Mr. Courtland, you aren't up to a bit of fun, are you? You'll no' be changing your mind?" When Jonas assured him he was quite serious, Liam let out another whoop, collected himself, then stared Jonas straight in the eyes. "Don't you be worrying none about those tea parties. My Maeve was raised proper like. Her family just fell on hard times is all, which is probably why she took up with the sorry likes of me. She's a fine lady, she is, and won't be shaming you none. I'll go fetch her straightaway. Oh, praise be the saints in heaven!" Liam shouted again as he rushed out.

Maeve Connelly looked like a worn-out china doll as she walked gracefully into the private salon with six children trailing behind. Her once-striking red hair was dull and lifeless, but her hazel eyes were bright with unshed tears. She was much taller than her husband and held her head high with a dignity that Jonas admired. Upon first glance Jonas could not help but wonder why a man would marry such a pitiful creature when he compared her to Acadiana, but after watching Maeve as she drew closer, he could see the loving way she looked at her children and the adoring glances she gave her husband. She wasn't as homely as she was undernourished, he thought. With all his money, he felt very poor in his relationship with Acadiana when compared to the richness of love he saw flowing between this family.

"I want ta be thanking ye, Mr. Courtland, for the honor bestowed on me family. Ye are a kind man ye be, and me Liam will be doin' ye proud," she said warmly, protectively, in a voice that didn't match her tired countenance.

"Your husband's credentials speak for themselves," Jonas said honestly. "I'm the one who is honored to be getting such a capable man."

"Ye are too kind." She smiled as six curious children peeked out from behind her patched and faded skirts. "Mind ye manners," she whispered, then picked up the smallest toddler and kissed his curly red hair.

"Please introduce me to your . . . uh . . . crew?" Jonas said, winking at the smallest girl who was giving him an impish grin. Her clothes belonged to an urchin, but her bright eyes and delightful smile were that of a princess. Jonas looked at the stair-step heads of flaming red hair, shaking his head and chuckling mildly. "And their ages, if you please. They all look about the same to me."

"You must not have children of your own." Liam smiled.

"Not yet," returned Jonas, amused by the little girl who was now sticking out her tongue at him while trying to imitate his wink. "Our first child is due this winter, and I am hoping for a little girl just like this one." He pointed to the elf and grinned, his thoughts drifting to a raven-haired beauty and the babe whose eyes and dark locks and yes, even indomitable spirit, he hoped would match her mother's.

"Congratulations," Maeve said warmly. "All right, troops, line up!" Her smile and voice were full of pride as all but the youngest child scrambled to get in line. She presented them one by one. "Brendan is eight, Shelagh is seven, Patrick is five, Timothy is four, Moira is two, and little Kieran here just turned one today."

"Today? Well, happy birthday, Master Kieran," Jonas said. He took an instant liking to the cherub faces surrounding him. "We should have a birthday party."

Liam and Maeve exchanged embarrassed glances that were not lost on Jonas. By the look of their shabby dress, a birthday party was a luxury long past. Jonas summoned a hotel maid and ordered enough French pastry and milk to feed an army. He thoroughly enjoyed the afternoon, watching bright faces and listening to giggling chatter that all sounded the same to him.

"Gracious," he muttered to no one in particular as he made his way back to his room. "I wonder how old they are before they learn to talk coherently."

His thoughts were filled with laughing amethyst eyes, his heart burgeoning with desire to set things right between him and Acadiana, for the sake of the babe—no, for his sake, he admitted, and for hers as well. God, he missed her! Missed her anger, her rebellion, her laughter, and even the soft side of her that showed tears. How would he ever be able to leave her again? Dark thoughts of the British confrontation ahead loomed before him to shatter his joyous thoughts of Acadiana. Leave her he must if the British threat proved reality, as it surely would. In that instant, Jonas hated the foreign foe that would take him away from his wife again—maybe even take his life.

Those thoughts lingered darkly in the back of his mind all that night and during the predawn hours as he prepared to leave New Orleans. Only the thought that he would be home soon and with Acadiana brightened his mood. Jonas and Cain left at first light after leaving money and instructions with the Connellys to be at Bayou Oaks within the month.

14

The molten summer sun waned heavy in the evening sky. As the brilliant orange ball approached the horizon, distorting the land in melting colors, Acadiana shielded her eyes and scanned the distance for riders. She saw only an old *calèche,* its wood and rawhide creaking as it lumbered on. She peered harder, as if to force the images she wanted to see, and was rewarded for her effort when two distinctive figures emerged from the sunset haze.

Jonas and Cain! A little tingle rippled up Acadiana's spine at the sight of them galloping toward the house. Her heart began to pound in an erratic fashion, her pulse to race, but she attributed these odd reactions to the suffocating summer heat combined with her delicate condition.

The silver-voiced coo of a mourning dove from the high bamboo hedges seemed to echo a sentiment within her, but Acadiana would never admit to anyone, most of all herself, that she had missed Jonas. If she could conjure up no resentment for a forced marriage, if she no longer shuddered at the thought of lying next to him, but reveled in the knowledge that this night would be spent in his arms, she would not admit it—not aloud. But her heart knew what her mind would not credit, and those feelings were reflected in the bright amethyst eyes that eagerly and anxiously watched him approach.

The last week and a half had been too long in passing. Acadiana had felt lost and lonely in the large, empty bed. Wherever she went, memories of Jonas followed her. She missed his anger, his concern, his teasing. Even during the most menial chores his face would appear, or a scent wafting gently on the hot summer breeze would send her head snapping around, her eyes searching feverishly for him. She always engaged in polite conversation with those around her, but never had she felt such a desolate oneness in a house full of people. *Mais oui,* she keened inwardly, *it would be good to have him back!* Her face split into a grin, and she started running when Jonas reined his horse in.

"Don't run!" he shouted, thinking of her condition as he watched her unbound hair flying wildly beneath the straw bonnet that had slipped back to flap against her shoulders. Its bright blue ribbons complemented her flushed face and bare shoulders above the simple muslin gown adorned with Mechlin lace. Blue and violet pennyroyals embroidered along the bottom edge bounced up and down with each hurried step that brought her closer to him. A flash of white petticoat and delicate ankle made his mouth go dry as the dust beneath his feet. "Do not run, Acadiana," he ordered again, not as harshly this time because he was having a hard time saying anything at all.

The command didn't rankle as it would have in the past, but sent a warm surge of contentment throughout Acadiana. The sternness on Jonas's face dissolved into a warm smile as his wife's arms went around his neck, and he was welcomed with a quick kiss.

"Hello, love." He smiled, startled. His arms gripped her instinctively, pulling her close for the familiar feel and tantalizing scent that was only hers. He buried his face in her neck to lengthen the moment, then raised sapphire eyes to devour her face. "Did you miss me?"

"Of course," Acadiana said. She blushed and backed up a

bit, idly smoothing the folds of her skirt while trying to cover her silly reaction. It would not do for him to guess at the emotions that were so new she didn't even understand them herself. "There has been no one here but Mattie brave enough to fuss at me. And she was so busy, even she didn't have time. It has been quite boring." Though she had shifted away, she did not brush off Jonas's arm around her waist. It felt too right there below the pounding of her heart, and she could pretend for the moment that she was truly as cherished as he made her feel.

"Acadiana," he said in resignation. "Have you been carrying on like a hoyden while I was away?"

Mon Dieu! "Whatever do you mean?" she drawled innocently, eyes downcast.

"What have you done?" he asked, tipping her face up.

"Nothing" came her cross reply, and a stamp of her dainty foot. But the warm strength of his fingers beneath her chin made her want to turn her face into that palm and rest in the welcome feel of him. "I didn't do a thing. Honestly, Jonas, one would think I need to be watched from first light to dark."

"Don't you?" He grinned.

"Non," she pouted prettily. Her fingers drifted along his forearm to the back of his hand where their fingers locked. Violet eyes lifted to regard him coyly beneath thick, midnight lashes, and a faint smile hovered at the corners of her lips, teasing, beguiling.

"Ah, you look so sweet, love, I *almost* believe you."

"I missed you," Jonas said, his voice as soft and low as the shadows swaying on the walls from the candlelight. His fingers ran down the sleeve of her nightdress, wishing they were beneath it.

Acadiana, curled on her side facing him in the bed that had been so lonely the past week and a half, smiled. "Then do not leave me here again."

But he would leave her when the confrontation brewing

with the British erupted. He did not want to speak of that this night when her welcome had been so warm, while her body was so warm and relaxed next to his. "Did you behave while I was away?"

"No one forced me to sit in the rocking chair." But she had sat in it, for hours, thinking of him and wishing he were home.

"You must have been good." He smiled in return. His hand drifted down to her hip and curled in the cotton fabric, inching it up her shapely calves.

"Non." She laughed lightly. "But they are all afraid I will dissolve like salt crystals if they yell at me the way you do." She could feel the night air on her thighs as the gown was pulled higher and wondered what he was about. Then his warm hand was on her bare leg and her breath lodged in her throat. His fingers climbed higher to grip her hip, then spread to lightly stroke her bare bottom. "W-what?"

"I just want to touch you," he whispered. "I know I can't do anything else." No matter how badly he wanted to. And he badly wanted to. He brought his lips to hers and lingered there, tasting, teasing without aggression because he dared not go too far lest he not be able to stop.

Acadiana sighed, her breath dancing with his, then felt his tongue begin a familiar exploration as he brought their bodies closer. She felt something else familiar, boldly familiar, against her tummy, and her fingers tightened on his naked shoulders. "We can't. . . ."

"I know." He moaned, grazing her neck with his lips and wondering if he had enough self-control to do more without doing too much. "I know," he repeated, catching her earlobe in his teeth. "I know I'm going to go insane if I can't have you soon."

Acadiana giggled at his gruff, needy tone. "You do have me, so you must have already gone insane, *m'sieu.*"

"I have," Jonas said with a growl, and rolled her atop him. He watched her cheeks pinken in the golden glow of candlelight as she struggled inwardly with what he was doing. And he wondered what it would be like to have her ride him this way, freely, unencumbered by her missish fears and shyness. She was further flustered when he pushed her to a sitting position astride him and grabbed her hips beneath the gown. The delicate white cotton pooled over his tanned arms so he could not see, could only feel that which he wished was revealed.

"I think you are very wicked," she said with a tremulous smile, feeling his body beneath her, so brazen it sent a flutter to her belly.

"You can't even imagine how wicked my thoughts are right now," he said. His teeth flashed white in the hazy darkness. "Want me to tell you?"

Acadiana shook her head and dropped it to his chest, burying her face there to hide her blush. He stirred beneath her, then groaned in abject pain and rolled her back to her side.

"I won't live until Dr. Loreau returns. I'll die in agony, a broken man. My stone will read, 'He died of horn—' "

Acadiana clapped her hand over his mouth and giggled outrageously. She'd never been more embarrassed or, strangely, more delighted.

Two weeks later a caravan of Courtlands, servants, and Beth headed for the Hamilton cottage. They had to get it ready for "all those bairns," as Jonas put it. Under his eagle eyes and unrelenting, often harsh expression, Acadiana rode in the carriage with Minette. She bounced along, silent and envious of Beth who was riding gaily between Jonas and Edward. Her eyes flew ahead to sear Jonas's back as he sat atop his sable stallion. He rode with masculine ease, sending a frisson of pleasure and warmth through her veins, and made her just that much angrier.

"*Le bon Dieu,*" she huffed, crossing her arms over her still slim stomach. "I do not know why I must suffer this carriage when I am perfectly capable of riding safely on Shawnee. A squaw wouldn't be caught dead acting lazy like this. I swear, they work as hard as ever until the baby is born, then go right back to work the next morning, sometimes the same day!"

"How many of them miscarry the first three months?" asked Minette. "Isn't that how it is? The strongest survive but the weakest—"

"I don't know," Acadiana said sheepishly, feeling suddenly as petulant as she must have sounded. "I'm sorry, *Grand'mère.*"

"Just a few more weeks, *bébé,* and the doctor will surely give you more liberties, no?" Minette soothed.

Liberty. Freedom for Jonas to do what he wanted with her under the cloak of darkness. The thought was terrifyingly exciting.

They worked on the house every spare minute over the next two weeks. It was once again restored to its former, simple beauty, and two more small bedrooms had been added. Someone was constantly assigned to Acadiana to keep her out of trouble. She had been very good for the last three days, ever since Jonas had caught her cleaning out a linen press in the *grenier.* She had gone up to the attic to look for some of Matthew's things and was standing on a rickety old stool, peering into the top cubbyhole, when Jonas walked in. He'd nearly thrown her into early delivery with his yelling as he swept her from the stool and into his arms, then had threatened to leave her at Courtland Manor.

Acadiana was now sitting regretfully but primly on the front porch, taking tiny stitches in a pale-blue baby gown. She had made more pricks in her finger than she had the delicate fabric and was now fit to be tied—a choice Jonas had not completely disregarded.

She looked up warily when a groaning old wagon spilling over with household goods and children pulled up. Jonas rounded the back corner of the house in time to greet Liam Connelly as he halted the tired, ancient mules.

"Liam, I'm glad you finally made it," Jonas greeted with a hearty handshake.

"Mr. Courtland, we dinna mean to impose on you here at the big house, all hot and dusty as we are, but we couldn't find no other dwelling around here by your directions," Liam apologized as he hoisted himself from the wagon seat.

"No mistake," Jonas said. "The main house hasn't been built yet. My wife and I still live at Courtland Manor, my mother's home. This is your house. We're just putting the finishing touches around back, but it's ready for you to move in."

"Saints!" Liam said, aghast. "This house . . . it's . . . I dinna ken what to say, sir. We've never had anything so fine." The Irishman's voice choked, his throat worked spasmotically as he sent a silent prayer of thanksgiving to heaven. "We've only dreamed of it!"

"You'll find this land full of dreams," Jonas said quietly, glancing at his wife.

Acadiana was drawn to the wagon full of tired children. She looked sympathetically at the face of their equally exhausted mother.

"Mrs. Connelly?" she asked. "Jonas told me all about your family. I am so pleased to meet you. I'm Acadiana."

"And I'm Maeve," she returned warmly. "I am pleased to be making your acquaintance also, my lady." Her tired eyes took in the petite, dark-haired woman whose piquant features were lively yet unassuming. She was as beautiful as Maeve had imagined after meeting the handsome and generous Mr. Courtland. Kindness was evident in the young woman's warm smile and soft violet eyes, and there was no trace of snobbery there to mar her lovely features. "Ye husband spake sa fondly of ye, I couldna wait to get here and meet ye for meself."

Acadiana smiled at Maeve's words and wondered just what Jonas had said. Her gaze shifted from the tall woman to the wagon bed. "The children look so tired. Can I help you get them settled in? We stocked the pantry so everything would be ready for you. We could just unload the necessities and get the other things out when you are more rested, *oui?*"

"Oh, ye be too kind," Maeve said tearfully as she stared at the house. It was like a fairy cottage with its fresh coat of paint and beautifully landscaped yard. A neat little porch ran the full length of the house—a perfect place for her Liam to remove his muddy boots at the end of a long day before coming in for a nice hot meal. There was a plot of ground for a garden, huge oaks and magnolias for the children to climb. Fruit trees and wild berry bushes for making the pies and jellies that her children loved, but that too often she could not provide. Maeve could already picture the desserts cooling on the little window shelf as she watched her wee ones play outside.

And flowers. Lord God be praised, there were flowers in every color and species imaginable! Like a loving wife and mother would plant to add beauty and richness to a real home. Her throat worked convulsively as she tried to get her words out. "Liam and me, we've never had so much hope for our future as we have right now. 'Tis going to be a wonderful home, a wonderful life for our children . . . all because of the good heart of ye husband and yeself."

Maeve sniffed softly and pressed a tattered kerchief to her nose. Exhaustion mingled with happiness made her unable to control the emotions overriding her usually composed demeanor. Acadiana fought back her own tears as she watched the woman gaze at the cottage with the same look her mother had always held—pride, fierce and protective. She turned away quickly to sort out the mingled emotions warring in her mind. She was jealous of Maeve's possessive glow, but deeper, more heartfelt, was the thankfulness she felt when she realized Maeve belonged here, would not be haunted by the violent past, and there would be laughter and love once again inside her former home.

She strode quickly to the wagon to busy herself and lifted a sleepy baby from the straw-filled box. Kieran opened drowsy eyes and began to nuzzle Acadiana's bodice.

Chubby little hands reached up to knead the linen fabric as his nose and mouth rooted around for nourishment. When none was forthcoming, he screwed up his face and let out an angry yowl.

"Oh!" Acadiana gasped as stinging prickles of delight shot through her breasts, causing the nipples to pucker. She laughed nervously to hide her embarrassment, and looked at Maeve in wonder.

Maeve blushed and held her hands out to take the child. "He's hungry. I should be weaning him, but there hasn't been enough food to go around."

Jonas stopped dead in his tracks when he saw Acadiana pick up the child. Her sweetly embarrassed flush when the babe pressed his face to her breasts sent the blood rushing to all parts of his body. He had never seen her with a child, and any nagging suspicions that he had secretly tried to suppress about her in the role of motherhood vanished with the sight of her soft smile and worshipful gaze. His arms hung limp by his side as he absorbed the Madonna-like picture she presented.

Something warm and maternal flooded Acadiana. Her voice was soft and constricted when she lifted her gaze to Maeve's. "There is plenty of food now. The pantry is full, and there are more dry goods stored. Come, let's get them something to eat before they collapse. They all look so tired."

Jonas turned away, gathering strength from the knowledge that there was still work to be done, but a quiet, languorous feeling followed him for the rest of the afternoon. The Connellys' meager belongings were put away in short order, the children fed and coaxed toward bed. It was no easy task with them squealing over and over as they ran through every room in the house.

"They are so excited," Maeve apologized, shaking her head as Brendan sprinted through the sitting room followed by Shelagh. "They've no' had such a fine place to be calling home before. Knowing how they are feeling, I kin hardly put a stop ta such joy. If I weren't so tired meself, I'd be right there with them."

His Irish brogue thick, Liam said prankishly, "And I'd be chasing right behind ye, Maeve, me girl!"

In a tone purely coquettish, Maeve's voice dropped to a whisper, and her eyes glittered playfully. "Would ye now? And would ye be gettin' us six more fine lads ta raise in the process?"

Brows raised, Jonas looked at Acadiana and wondered when she would feel that comfortable in their own relationship. Acadiana blushed to the roots of her hair at Jonas's wicked glance, and rose quickly to help with the children.

The day slipped away much too fast for the families joined in lighthearted conversation. Only when the talk turned to the impending confrontation with the British did everyone take a more serious tone, and that was only for a short time as everyone chose to keep to more pleasurable thoughts. The Courtlands bid farewell, feeling greatly satisfied with the new manager and his family.

Once inside their bedroom at Courtland Manor, Acadiana put her arms around Jonas's neck and placed a soft kiss on his stunned but willing lips. "Thank you," she said softly.

"For what?" Jonas asked suspiciously, wondering what she was up to.

"For hiring Liam, and fixing up the house, and being happy about our baby, and . . . just everything," she said warmly, looking deeply into his eyes.

"Acadiana," he pleaded. "Don't look at me like that!"

"Like what?" She sighed innocently.

"You know like what!" He grinned. "You know what the doctor said—"

"Charlatans, every one of them. What does a doctor know?"

"More than I do," he groaned. "I wouldn't take a chance with you or the baby, sweet." Oh, why did she have to try her hand at seduction now! She had been like this since his return from New Orleans—teasing, flirtatious, utterly charming. And oh so dangerous! He didn't know what had prompted the change from termagant to temptress, but now was not the time to find out.

Acadiana knew she was treading dangerous ground, but she couldn't smother the feelings she felt for this man right now. Her heart was full to bursting with emotions that needed to be gotten out. She had seen the way Jonas responded to Maeve's frankness, and had wanted to put that same glow in his eyes that Liam's had had. She was acting in a way that felt deliciously daring, but there was a small little voice in the back of her mind that assured her she wouldn't have to fulfill anything she might be initiating. She thought it safe to experiment, but the smoldering blue fire of Jonas's eyes told her his patience was quickly coming to an end.

"Jonas?" she asked cautiously.

"What!" he snapped, his nerve endings feeling as frayed and taut as his temper. He leashed the urge to snatch Acadiana to him and fling her on the bed to spread her thighs for a totally lecherous appeasement. Gathering his wits, he softened his voice. "I'm sorry. What is it?"

Eyes downcast, she twined her fingers one about the other, afraid to broach the question that had been nagging at her since discovering she was with child. She tried to formulate the words in her mind, but nothing acceptable would come, so she just blurted out, "Was . . . was this baby conceived in love?"

Jonas felt as if he had just been struck a blow to his solar plexus. He took a step back and raked his fingers through his hair. *Conceived in love?* Probably not, but then love had caught him from behind, like a gentle thief, and he didn't know where it began or ended, just that it completely encircled him now. "Why do you ask?" he said slowly. If he knew his own feelings, he certainly did not know hers, and there was an inherent need to protect himself, to go cautiously into this new and powerful phase in their relationship.

"I have to know," she whispered. She never should have asked, she knew that now. Jonas's eyes were hooded, his thoughts unreadable. Not knowing would have been better that this cloying sense of doom shrouding the very air about them.

"Why don't you tell me?" he said in a shadowed tone.

"I don't know!" she started defiantly, but there were tears in her eyes and her throat and she couldn't go on.

"Acadiana." He sighed. He reached out and pulled her to him. His determination to remain aloof crumbled in that instant with the tears forming on the surface of her dazzling eyes. Still, he could not voice the words that she sought, so he took a less treacherous path. "I have always had a place for you in my heart. Before I met you . . . after I met you. Always."

"Why?" she asked simply.

"I don't know 'why,' " he teased. He pulled her down to sit beside him on the bed and searched for some way to explain the things that had been so recently revealed to him. "When there is an emptiness in a person, he continues to search until the void is filled. When the land was my goal, I thought that by acquiring it that aching loneliness would be relieved, but then I found that I had to have you along with the land or it would all be for naught." He picked up her hand, studied the fine bones and soft skin with his thumb, then pressed her palm to his lips. "Our whole future is before us, love. We didn't start this marriage on solid ground, and I admit most of that was my fault for not courting you as you deserved. Even though marriage arrangements are common, and the people involved are forced to make the best of their situation, I want more than that for us. I see our child as more than just my duty and your obligation. She can be the bond that unites us, if we let her."

"Him." Acadiana sniffed.

"What?"

"Nothing," she said with a melancholy sigh. Nice words, she thought. Nice and empty, meant to placate her while he skirted the direct question. He had not said he loved her. When she could not put a name to her own guarded feelings, why was it so important that he declare his? The turmoil building within her sizzled to a dull, aching throb, yet she could not stop the despairing words. "I didn't come to you willingly," she said.

"I know." Jonas sighed, wondering why they were having this conversation, why now when his feelings were so new and raw within him. "But there was no hate or malice in your eyes, only fright and anger. I knew I could conquer that." Jonas cast her a self-deprecating grin. "I suppose I must be either infinitely patient or utterly arrogant, but I knew in time you would come to trust me."

"I do trust you," she said fiercely, honestly. "I may not know what else I feel, but I do trust you. It has been hard for me, though. It seems I have spent my whole life learning to trust the people I love only to have them pulled out from under me. One minute I would be safe and secure, then suddenly I would be uprooted again, adrift, and have to start all over."

Jonas's face registered shock and concern. "Is that how you felt when I took you away from your uncle's house?" Incredible! He had always known her to be strong-willed, rebellious, and defensive about her feelings, but he had never sensed that such bravado was rooted in insecurity. She had always seemed so stalwart in her opinions, reduced to tears only when his strength proved greater than hers. If he had only known of her fears, he would have done more to reassure her, been gentler in easing her into her new role as wife.

"I felt threatened at first. That's why I ran away. I had to be in a place where I could think. I felt like I was being torn once again from the security I had come to know. First my parents, then Jean and the Indians—"

"I thought Jean brought you back of your own free will," Jonas said, confused.

"He did. Sort of," Acadiana said slowly. "At any rate it was best that I leave because I was changing, growing up . . ."

"What happened, Acadiana?" Jonas asked, cautious yet concerned.

"A mountain man," she hedged. "He . . . he took an interest in me." Color throbbed in her cheeks. *"Mon Dieu,* I was such an imbecile! I didn't understand the extent of that interest until Katherine told me about men and their . . . needs. Jean was so angry when the man made covert advances toward me. I know now Jean was frightened by the life I was leading, by what might happen to me, but at the time I thought he didn't want me anymore. I was so hurt."

"I'm sorry." Jonas sighed softly against her temple. And he was sorry, at least for the pain she had suffered, but not for Jean getting her away. The man deserved a medal. His fists clenched involuntarily, but his tone remained passive. "Did you care for this mountain man? Is that why you married me reluctantly and won't give yourself to me fully, because you harbor affections for someone you can't have?"

Acadiana stiffened in his arms and her chin jutted out defiantly. *"Mais oui,* you can be exasperating at times!" She continued muttering in a guttural, completely incomprehensible language until Jonas shook her lightly to stop the tirade.

"Don't try to change the subject. And don't revert to that heathenish tongue. I like to know exactly how I'm being cursed."

"I didn't even know the man!" She sprang from the bed to turn her back on him in indignation. So much for his avowal of trust and making a future together. They couldn't get through a simple conversation without his insulting accusations interrupting the peace.

She felt his hands on her shoulders, firm but tender, turning her to face him. "You still carry a picture. . . ."

She felt the antagonism drain slowly from her to be replaced with a full and buoyant warmth. She smiled then dropped her forehead to his chest. "You are jealous."

"Exceedingly," Jonas said wryly.

"The picture is my brother, Matthew. Not a good likeness, I'll admit. I was very young when I drew it, but it's the only thing I have with which to remember him."

Jonas stroked her long black hair, strangling on the information he'd pledged to keep secret. He had no obligation to Matthew Hamilton, but he did to his wife. There were dangerous times ahead for all the men of Louisiana. He could not chance telling Acadiana of her brother only to have Matthew lose his life in battle. Not once but twice Matthew would be lost to her. No one should have to suffer that, but especially not his wife in her fragile condition. Still, withholding the information did not sit easy within him. They had talked of love and trust, and he was damned now by admission or silence.

He brought their conversation full circle to avoid his guilty conscience. "So, Jean brought you back to your uncle's."

"*Oui,* it was the best thing. I see that now, but it was so hard. The good citizens of Providence were appalled that I had been living with a man not my relative."

"They were fools," Jonas sympathized.

Acadiana giggled against his shirt front. "You are no more acceptable than I am."

"Thank God."

Her voice grew soft and serious. "I have never quite fit in, no matter where I was. And yet so many people have been good to me—the Indians, Jean, my uncle. Still, sometimes I feel I don't belong anywhere."

"You belong here, love, with me," Jonas said, holding her tightly, longing to do more, but knowing he must not. "Would you like to go back and see them all someday when our daughter is older?"

"Son." She laughed, burrowing her face into his chest

like a child. "The chief was here, you know." Jonas pulled back to look at her, confused, and she hastened to explain. "Not here really, but in Natchitoches. There was a large delegation of Caddo chiefs who met with *M'sieu* Claiborne there last October. Jean told me about it. The representatives asked about me . . . but I didn't get to see them."

Jonas's heart wrenched at the hidden pain in her eyes, the subtle longing in her voice. "They had work to do," he said. "Governor Claiborne was concerned even then about the British. I'm told he gave a rousing speech, trying to unite the Caddo with our American cause."

Acadiana nodded, understanding what he was trying to do and appreciating it. She sighed deeply then rested in his strong embrace. Their bodies were so close, she could feel his hardened need where it pressed against her quivering belly. Her own body cried out its yearning deep within her, making her long to nestle closer, to find and fill the aching emptiness.

"When do you see the doctor again?" Jonas asked a bit raggedly.

"Not soon enough," she murmured without thinking.

Jonas flinched and eyed his wife narrowly, certain that life had dealt him the cruelest of blows. Loreau had better give her more liberties soon, or he couldn't be held responsible for the savage thoughts that were sure to turn to action soon.

Although usually disturbed by his wife's plea to extinguish the candles before she undressed for bed, Jonas thought it a fine suggestion this night. His body was rigid with barely restrained desire as he claimed his side of the mattress and tried not to touch her. Acadiana was no help at all, snuggling close to him, inching her way between his arms and legs. His body burned with the need to crawl between her thighs and bury himself within her silken warmth. The restraint he was forced to use grew unbearable.

"Damn!" He moaned, pushing away from her. He untangled their arms and legs and sat up on the side of the bed, his face buried in his hands. "Perhaps I should go sleep in the guest room."

"You don't love me," she pouted, sitting up and pushing her long veil of ebony hair out of her eyes.

The faint scent of roses filled the air between them and Jonas groaned in agony. "I do! I want to love you right now! But we can't, so perhaps I should just sleep somewhere else until you see the doctor."

Acadiana was highly offended. "Don't you dare! If I can stand the wait, so can you!"

Jonas slanted her a sharp glance. He thought he must be hearing things. This was not the reluctant woman he had been married to for months. He stared at Acadiana suspiciously as if she might be enjoying some sort of heathen torture at his expense, but her large, jeweled eyes just stared back at him guilelessly. Too guilelessly.

"You're enjoying this, aren't you?" he accused.

"Not at all." She smiled like an imp. "But I find it hard to believe that you would obey Dr. Loreau when you never took *my* saying *non* to heart."

"That was different." He smiled in return, devilishly. "But mark my words, when the day comes, I will make up for all this time lost."

Acadiana sighed, a slumberous, contented sigh that nearly drove Jonas beyond endurance as she rolled over to sleep peacefully until morning.

He, on the other hand, had a wretched night, tossing and turning and cursing his confounded situation.

15

Life drummed on at a strained pace. The British threat was uppermost in everyone's mind, hovering like a dark shadow that refused to be pushed back. But no one spoke of it much. Silence seemed to keep the anxiety at bay while they went about their demanding chores. Everyone knew the danger they all faced if the British should invade Louisiana; there was no need to speak it aloud.

Jonas discovered that Lafitte's assumption had been correct. Governor Claiborne didn't trust the pirate, for on September 16, Master Commander Daniel T. Patterson, United States naval commander at New Orleans, led an expedition against the settlement on Grande Terre. He had captured Dominique You and about eighty men who had already fired their own warehouses and the village. About five hundred other pirates had escaped, and for Acadiana's sake, Jonas hoped Hunter was one of them. It was rumored that Jean and Pierre Lafitte were in hiding at Alexandre Labranche's plantation in St. Charles Parish, and those who had escaped capture were scattered around New Orleans. Jonas knew Lafitte would try again to offer his services to the United States and prayed that Claiborne would have sense enough to accept this time.

The Courtland fields had been planted in the spring, and now, in late September, everyone was anxiously watching the weather. Many a crop had been destroyed by the elements. Drawing a living from the soil was a gamble that farmers since the beginning of time had learned to accept, even expect, but Acadiana found it very disconcerting to be at the mercy of something beyond her control. Fortunes had been made, then lost with just a few bad seasons. Although careful management was imperative, it was not the end-all toward a secure future. Farming had been and always would be a necessary game of chance, and not the sort of livelihood for the lazy or weak-hearted.

Liam Connelly was busy preparing the Hamilton land for next year's planting; Jonas and Edward were getting the mill ready for the harvest; and Minette had her own duties to perform at the big house. Acadiana felt like an outsider. No one would allow her to help, so she wandered the mansion aimlessly, feeling bored and useless. At times she went down to the plantation quarters to see if she could be of service to the sick or the children, but she made the slaves nervous by her presence. They had been given strict instructions that Acadiana was not to do anything strenuous, therefore she was doubly cosseted and watched by their small community. Everyone on the plantation found her sweet and personable, and always ready to help—and therein lay the problem. No one wanted to take responsibility for the overeager wife of the master.

Jonas had completely banned her from the mill when he'd returned from town one day and found her trying to help with preparation for grinding. She had been bent over at the waist, listening attentively to the workers' explanations, her backside glaring at him provocatively. He had clenched his fists at his sides to keep from grabbing her, then barked orders that sent everyone scurrying for cover. He hadn't backed down an inch when she had argued with him about needing to learn the harvesting process. After listening to her querulous voice and watching her tantalizing breasts bob up and down angrily for thirty minutes, he had finally dragged her home, threatening dire consequences should she return.

His argumentative attitude was nothing new, Acadiana thought in rising resentment. He had been testy since . . . well, since forever, but especially since they had found out about the baby. He had been so gentle in dealing with her at first, but as the month passed, he grew more impatient and was always snapping at her and everyone else for no apparent reason. She couldn't imagine what she had done to make him so angry!

Acadiana couldn't know within the bounds of her inexperience that it was what she *wasn't* doing that had Jonas so on edge. The ache in his loins kept his temper raw, but Acadiana had always been too reserved for him to offer to teach her the things she could do to relieve his torment. The one night he had tried, pressing her hands to his engorged manhood, had left him worse for the attempt with her stammering and blushing in startled incomprehension as to what it was he wanted.

Minette and Edward recognized the signs, often exchanging raised brows and knowing eyes, but it wasn't their place to discuss such things with Acadiana. Jonas spent his days in frustrated ill humor, working himself into a bone-weary exhaustion to ease the agony of the long nights.

Feeling lost and forlorn, and unable to comprehend her husband's fickle temperament, Acadiana awaited Beth's visits. They walked daily along the bayou and discussed plans for a harvest ball, which the Claytons gave each year in the fall. This was something she was allowed to participate in simply because it took no physical effort to talk about the things that needed to be done.

The doctor had finally come. Satisfied with his examination, he had given Acadiana permission to resume normal activity within reason. She had never been called reasonable, she admitted, but would not take chances with her precious cargo. Jonas was working so hard at the mill during the day and attending political rallies in the evening that he did nothing more than collapse into bed each night, and Acadiana was becoming apprehensive waiting for the right moment to inform him of the doctor's visit.

She had just received another letter from Aunt Elizabeth, who had admonished her, as she had in all previous correspondence, to be "virtuous in all things. In mind, heart, and actions, darling, present to your husband a wife worthy to bear his name. Do not let your passions run a dangerous course, or your temper overrule good judgment, lest your husband put you aside as an embarrassment to him, but be meek and biddable in every way as befits a good wife."

Acadiana didn't know exactly what her aunt was trying to say, but blurting out to her husband that she could lie with him again would certainly not be considered virtuous. But if she didn't tell him, Jonas might think her deceitful. In any case, he had not asked, and that left her unsure.

With an air of resolve, anything to take her mind from the awkward issue, Acadiana threw herself into helping Beth plan the ball. The gala affair would actually take place before the harvest when the planters weren't too busy to enjoy the fun. Everything had been set for the following weekend. Acadiana worked all week readying formal attire for everyone in her household who would be attending. She also had to see that Liam and Maeve were suitably attired for their first formal presentation as Bayou Oak's new manager and wife.

She took several ballgowns from her own wardrobe for Maeve's inspection. Having never owned one, and finding them all so beautiful, Maeve could not choose. Acadiana selected one that could be easily altered and would catch the green in Mrs. Connelly's eyes and accent her now shiny red curls. Maeve had gained weight. She was becoming nice and round in all the right places. Where another man might find misery in the promise of his wife's abundant shape, Liam loved it. To him, it meant his precious Maeve wasn't going hungry. Acadiana thought her statuesque as the Irish woman spun gaily around the room in excitement.

"Saints preserve us," Maeve squealed, hands pressed to her racing heart as she did one more spin. "Just think what a grand lady I'll be in this beautiful gown. It's enough to go to a wee lassie's head!"

Acadiana laughed with her, feeling Maeve's elation and thinking the woman looked much younger now than her thirty-five years. How easy it had been to select a gown that would please her. Liam presented more of a problem. Jonas and Edward were too tall for his slight frame, but Mattie assured Acadiana that Naomi could alter something from the boys' younger days.

"Mattie!" Acadiana exclaimed, giggling yet horrified by the thought that had just crossed her mind. "Mr. Connelly won't show up in a short coat and knee breeches, will he?"

"Lordy naw, Miz Cade!" Mattie laughed. "Naomi be real handy with the sewin'. She'll have that man fixed up just right. She'll bring it over when she's through and tend them young'uns so the Connellys kin go with y'all."

"Merci." Acadiana sighed. "What would we do without you?"

"I sho be hopin' y'all don't find out." Mattie chuckled, shaking her head. "You git on now and see what's down in the kitchen to eat. You sho gonna have to put some meat on them bones . . . like Miz Maeve here."

"Mais oui, I do have a powerful appetite now." Acadiana giggled. "If I keep on eating like I have been, I'll be too big to pass through the door, *oui?"*

"That be all right, Miz Cade. Mast' Jonas kin just set you in that rockin' chair he's so proud of til the baby gits here."

The evening of the harvest ball finally arrived. The stormclouds that had been moving in over the week had suddenly disappeared, leaving the night clear and warm with just enough breeze to keep the mosquitoes at bay. Acadiana put the finishing touches to her elaborate coiffure.

Her midnight hair was swept up away from her face and fell in a cascade of ringlets to her golden shoulders. Wispy tendrils framed her face, and delicate diamond and amethyst earrings, a gift from Minette, dripped from her ears. A matching necklace dropped to her swollen bosom, enhancing the effect of her daring neckline. The only other jewelry she wore was her dainty gold wedding band.

Minette had created the gown to match her eyes. The dark violet silk looked like it had been sprinkled with stardust as tiny silver threads caught the light every time she moved. Acadiana looked like a shimmering angel as she plucked her puffed sleeves out, then patted the high-waisted gown in place. She was just about to reach for the purple satin ribbons of the high-crowned *Angoulême* bonnet when she sensed someone else in the room.

"You look ravishing" came a somewhat strained but familiar voice behind her.

Acadiana spun around, smiled invitingly, and gave Jonas a graceful curtsey. *"Merci,* so do you."

"A man does not look ravishing," he corrected.

"You do," she teased. "I would certainly like to ravish you." She shot him a coquettish look, half amazed at her own daring. Aunt Elizabeth's words flitted through her brain, but she ignored them as she had most of the rules that had not fit her purpose. Jonas was indeed magnificent in his dark gray trousers and claw-hammer tailcoat, his black velvet waistcoat a nice foil for his white silk shirt and cravat. But no amount of masculine finery could match the handsomeness of his sapphire eyes. Eyes that were now staring at her with burning intensity.

"We wouldn't make it to the party." He laughed wryly, then added more seriously, "Are you sure you should go tonight?"

"Oui, the doctor says I am fine."

"The doctor?" Jonas asked, scrutinizing her with one cocked eyebrow. "Has he been back?"

"Over a week ago," Acadiana murmured, turning her back to him to feign interest in the articles atop the dresser.

There, it was out. Would he demand a husband's rights or withhold his need as he had been doing? There was a part of her that didn't want to be pushed, that knew she would rebel the moment he tried to sweep her away to that place of oblivion where her mind and body were not her own. And yet there was a softer side, a woman's yearning, that longed to feel those strong arms around her, to see the fire of passion light his eyes, and to experience the tremor of desire spiral through her body in dizzying vibrations. Acadiana fidgeted with a silver-handled hairbrush and waited for her husband to respond.

"Why didn't you tell me?"

"You didn't bother to ask," she said crossly, defensively.

Recognizing the resentment and insecurity she was trying to cover with hauteur, Jonas crossed the short distance separating them and placed his hands on her shoulders. "Acadiana," he said, turning her to face him. "I fear I've been too busy lately to pay you much attention." *Liar! You've wanted to give her a lot more than attention lately.* "I will try to be more considerate, starting now. . . ."

He placed a long, loving kiss on her soft mouth, a mouth starved for just such affection. As his lips moved back and forth across hers, sensuously parting them to taste the warmth within, his arms encircled her, and his hands began kneading and caressing their way down her back to her rounded hips where he stopped to pull her tighter against his mounting desire. It was a gentle but unbreakable grip, his fingers digging into her gown to transcend layers of petticoats and tease the flesh beneath, but to Acadiana it felt more like a lifeline. She returned his kiss with a hunger of her own, drinking in the feel of him as if it were life-giving nectar. Her tongue flicked out to swirl with his, and began a mating dance that robbed her of breath and caused a groan to rise in her throat.

"Ah, Jonas," she whispered fervently as her fingers tangled in the nape of his sable hair. "I—"

Whatever she had meant to reveal in that impassioned moment was interrupted by a knock on the door. "Mast' Jonas, Miz Cade? Y'all ready?" called Mattie. "Miz 'Nette and the others be waitin' down to the carriage. They say for y'all to come on."

Jonas jerked free of the hypnotic trance induced by his wife's pliant body and breathy words. He stepped back to put some distance between them before he ignored their obligations and attacked her like some crazed maniac. What was it about this woman that aborted his good sense and left him wanting to grope and fondle her like an overeager lad? He took a deep breath and tugged on his cravat as if it were suddenly choking him. One smoldering look at her passion-darkened eyes and swollen lips almost chased his good intentions straight to hell.

"All right, Mattie. We're coming," Jonas struggled to say calmly while silently cursing the ball.

Acadiana blushed at her own abandon and thought she had better heed Aunt Elizabeth's advice from now on. Her husband certainly seemed agitated by the kiss she had so freely given him. She turned away from his irritated scowl and rushed to grab her reticule and fan, while Jonas muttered expletives beneath his breath as he prepared to escort her down. Acadiana peeked a quick glance at him over her shoulder, her bottom lip pushing out into a pout. It was his own fault, she thought rebelliously, kissing her like that and pressing her hips to his until her body flamed. How was she to remain "virtuous" in mind and deed when he swamped her entire body with such hot, sweet pleasure that she couldn't think clearly? *Mon Dieu, Aunt Elizabeth, you forgot to explain that part!* These rules for men and women did not make a bit of sense!

Her pique grew, swelling and expanding, shimmering like a soap bubble until it finally exploded and she spun around to face him. "What are you grumbling about?" she asked, her eyes widening at his further use of profanity.

He stepped nearer and leaned his head down to accommodate her height, bringing them almost eye to eye. A frown darkened the perfection of his handsome face. "We are going to build that dream house of yours, Acadiana." He pointed a finger in her face. "No one, and I mean *no one,* is welcome for at least two weeks! Is that understood?"

"Perfectly," she whispered, and turned demurely away to hide the smile that burst all boundaries to spread across her face. She nervously fingered the beads of her purse and asked softly, "Did you find my . . . ah . . . response to your kiss acceptable?"

"Acceptable?" Jonas snorted, before comprehension dawned on him. He pulled her around to face him and grinned, transforming his face into one of devilish charm that sent Acadiana's heart skipping delightfully. "Everything you do in the privacy of our bedroom is 'acceptable,' love. It is leaving this chamber that I find so damnably intolerable!"

Acadiana was having a marvelous time chatting with Beth and dancing with flirtatious planters on the ballroom floor of the Clayton house. She had met Beth's father, Robert Clayton, an exceedingly handsome man but much too reserved to have sired his bright, cheerful daughter. He had been strictly polite, but had stared at Acadiana as if sizing her up, she thought, deciding whether or not she was worthy to be Beth's friend. It was not unusual, she admitted, but there was something unsettling in his piercing hazel eyes.

Jonas leaned indolently against the wall, his eyes alert and watchful on his wife to make certain she did not become overtired. Her thickening waistline had been no deterrent for the amorous hands of inebriated merrymakers, but he allowed Acadiana to thwart them herself. She could very effectively quell the most eager foe with a cut of her cold violet eyes. Eyes that he would see softened in passion this night, he vowed, and bided his time in strained patience until he could take her home.

"Why, Jonas Courtland, I do declare, you are becoming quite stuffy as an old married man," drawled Merrill Le-Beau.

Dragging his eyes away from his wife with inhuman effort, Jonas turned to face Merrill as she approached, her hips swaying seductively.

"How so, Mrs. LeBeau?" he returned.

"You haven't asked little ole me to dance," she pouted.

"After our last encounter, I was certain our dancing days were over," he said dryly.

Damn your handsome, arrogant hide, Merrill thought. And damn your innocent-looking bride for taking you from me! With a conscious effort to appear nonchalant, she tapped his arm playfully with her fan. "Gracious, I've decided to forget that silly little incident. I'm sure I would be very protective of you if you were my husband." She batted her eyes coyly, but her smile lacked the warmth of affection and spoke more of aggravation. "That *is* why your wife acted that way, isn't it? Surely she doesn't act so heathenish and untamed all the time. No, of course not. I'm sure she was just jealous of our . . . past."

Jonas chuckled at Merrill's choice of words. "I don't know if Acadiana was jealous or not, but she acts 'untamed' most of the time. It's a virtue I find most rewarding." Pushing off the wall, he leaned close enough for Merrill to see her reflection in his vibrant blue eyes. "Fear not, Mrs. LeBeau. She is usually most cordial when she doesn't feel threatened."

Dropping all pretense, Merrill allowed the hurt and insult she was feeling to show in the inflection of her words. "It was unfair of you, Jonas, to lead me on, then marry someone else!"

Jonas frowned, recalling their brief but passionate liaison. "You never hinted at deeper feelings, Merrill. I never would have involved myself if you had given me any indication that you hoped for more than I was willing to offer."

"A woman never lays her soul bare before a man," she spouted self-righteously. Tears of anger and humiliation clouded her vision, and her voice dropped to a vicious snarl. "I am not a courtesan to be bedded then tossed aside. I thought you were a gentleman with a gentleman's intentions!" Jonas's mouth grew taut, and his eyes sparkled with sudden anger, but Merrill plowed on indelicately. "Why her? Was that land so important to you that you had to marry her? You are not as strong a man as I thought to let her trap you that way!"

Jonas kept his voice low to hide his ire. "My reasons are my own. Think what you like, Merrill, but keep your vicious ideas to yourself." With a curt bow, he walked away to discover Acadiana in a corner furiously fanning herself.

"What's wrong, love? You look ready to bite someone's head off."

"I am—hers!" she spat, pointing at his ex-paramour with her fan. "And don't call me 'love'!"

"Let's get a breath of fresh air," Jonas said, quickly steering her out onto the verandah. "It was just a harmless chat."

"Mais non! That witch is about as harmless as a coral snake!" Acadiana retorted heatedly.

"I love the way your eyes flash when you're jealous," he teased.

"Oh, stop it, Jonas! I would never lower myself to be jealous of that slippery, slimy creature. And you! You stood there talking to her like . . . like you know her!"

"I do know her." He grinned, amused and warmed by the jealousy she would not admit to. "Besides, I do business with her father and don't care to offend him by being rude to his daughter."

"Well, I don't give a hoot for the daughter, or your business arrangements."

"Neither do I," Jonas cajoled, "but I do care for you, and I don't like seeing you so upset."

"I'm not fragile," she snapped, feeling petulant and graceless and unlovely, but unable to stop herself. "I wish everyone would quit acting like I'm some breakable porcelain doll."

The breeze caught a lock of her hair, lifting it from her golden throat. Jonas's hand reached up, his knuckles slid along her cheek then neck and came to rest on her bare shoulder. "No, you are more precious than porcelain," he said softly.

Acadiana glanced up to see the rakish twinkle in his eyes and felt her anger slip a notch. "You don't mean a word of it."

"No?" His fingers drifted across her swelling bosom, pale in the moonlight, and in his eyes was the fever of desire. "Do you know what porcelain is made of? No? Kaolin, quartz, and feldspar." Spellbound, she watched and listened, as if this were the most important lesson of her life. His voice lowered, seductive, compelling, as his breath furled around her ear to send tingles darting through her body. "It's fired at high temperatures to create fine, translucent ceramic ware. That's what I'd like to do to you, fire you at high temp—"

"M'sieu!" Acadiana gasped, then giggled, her face flooding with hot color. "Cease, someone might hear you!"

His arms snaked around her middle and he brought her close into his powerful body. "Do you know what else I'd like to do?"

Acadiana shook her head against the fine linen of his shirt, unable now to look him in the eye. Her cheeks were burning along with other unspeakable places on her body. "Please, do not tell me."

"Scared we'll start a fire?"

Any anger left in her from seeing him with Merrill dissolved into a fit of giggles at his wholly disreputable words. "You are most evil, *M'sieu* Husband."

"Want to be evil with me?" he asked.

They were much too close to the house for this sort of private conversation. Acadiana pulled out of his arms and dipped into a graceful curtsey. "I want to take a walk."

"My pleasure, madame."

They strolled leisurely through the garden, breathing the aroma of fresh flowers and catching the faint breeze. Their senses were heightened by the enchanting surroundings. The fragrance of the flora, the moonlit night, the subtle song of nocturnal creatures all worked to dissolve their differences and to meld them into easy companionship that gradually gave way to more intimate words and stolen touches. Their conversation grew warm and suggestive, their sparring immersed in words and actions shared only by lovers. It began a season of awakening for Acadiana, and introduced a chance for the closeness Jonas had hoped for.

After a particularly sensuous volley of words that left Acadiana blushing and her husband walking stiff-gaited, Jonas decided it would be safer to switch the conversation to a more neutral subject. They talked at length about Acadiana's past and discussed plans for the new house. In a moment of playfulness, Acadiana skipped away and asked if Jonas cared to help her climb the nearest tree. He assured her in his firmest voice that if she dare even consider it in her condition he would spirit her home immediately.

"Promises, promises," she teased him as she skirted an oak and raced to another path.

Jonas shot after her, his voice rising with each word. "Don't run, Acadiana! *Do not run!*"

Ignoring the command, she slipped behind a leafy catalpa tree, peeked quickly through a cluster of whitish flowers and long thin pods, then darted in the opposite direction. Jonas caught sight of a flash of white petticoat and the chase was on. As wily as a fox, she slipped past a sycamore then a beech tree, knowing she would probably have to spend a week in the despised rocking chair to atone for her recklessness, but at this moment she didn't care. The thought of how her husband's arms would close securely around her when he caught her was worth any amount of scolding that was sure to follow.

At a last peek at him from behind a hickory, Acadiana fled into a open area where he was sure to see her. Jonas broke into the clearing only moments later, just in time to see his wife stop dead still, all playfulness gone from her lovely features. Even in the moonlight he could tell she had gone pale, and as he drew nearer he could see she was trembling.

"Ah, God!" he swore, and rushed to her. "Acadiana, what's wrong? Is it the baby?"

Acadiana pressed her hand to her stomach and looked up at him, dazed and shaken. "I saw someone," she said weakly.

"What?" he asked, concerned and confused. "Who?"

"No one. I mean, I don't know." Her trembling hand went to her forehead. "I don't how to explain it. I thought I saw someone or something just beyond the clearing, but when I looked again he was gone. I know someone was there, but it's more a feeling than anything else. I—I felt so threatened. Oh, Jonas, this sounds so silly!"

It did, but Jonas didn't say so. He was too concerned about his wife's wan features and dazed expression. "I think you've had too much excitement for one night," he said. "Let's make our excuses and return to the manor."

Acadiana nodded and walked with him back to the Claytons' house, but she darted a glance behind her every few seconds, feeling oddly disconcerted, as if there were something malignant out there watching her.

Jonas escorted Acadiana to their bedroom. Their sweet words of the evening past seemed lost now in the ensuing silence. He felt the aching need deep inside him as he helped her undress. He wanted to love her tenderly, passionately, savagely, wanted to push the self-absorbed look from her face, but she was already blowing out the candle, shutting herself off from him in darkness. He sensed that she would not respond to him as he would have her, with a desire that matched his own, and wondered if it was better not to have her at all.

He cradled her close to him in the bed, fearing only briefly for her sanity. She wasn't crazy; he wouldn't allow himself to even think it. She had an irrational temper at times, but not an irrational mind. If she thought she saw something, then she had. But why had it frightened her so? Why had she felt threatened when he was right there to protect her?

He wrapped his arms more securely around her, hoping she would seek him in her need for comfort, but she lay still, staring into the darkness as if it offered answers to questions that had not been asked.

"I want to make love to you," he whispered, running his hands through the black silk of her hair. Acadiana nodded against his shoulder, but he didn't think her heart was in it. "What do you want?"

"I want to be a wife to you."

"What is it, Acadiana? Why did seeing someone in the garden affect you so?"

"I don't know." She sighed. "I can't explain it, don't want to explain it."

"Why?"

"Because it sounds crazy." Jonas stiffened slightly. "See, even you think so."

He chuckled lightly to ease her concern. "No, you're too hard-headed for any craziness to enter that skull." She sent her balled fist into his shoulder but there was no force behind the blow. "Try to explain it to me anyway."

"I know it was a man, but his face was shadowed by darkness. He seemed so familiar yet not recognizable at all." She sighed again, deeply, bracingly. "And . . . and he was evil."

Jonas couldn't think of what to say, didn't know how best to console her. *No, Acadiana, you're not crazy. There was a man in the garden, and even though you couldn't see him, yes, he was evil.* Or better still, *Yes, love, you are crazy. There was no one there in the garden but a figment of your misguided imagination.* Damn!

He turned until they were side by side and he traced her jawline with his lips. His fingers flicked the buttons of her night rail until they slipped open one by one. "I don't want to think about tonight. I believe you saw something and it frightened you, but I'm here to protect you. Nothing can hurt you here." He pressed his moist mouth to the slope of her breast. "I want to make love to you; it's been so long. . . ."

Acadiana absorbed the careful thrust and ebb of her husband's body against her own, her arms clasped tightly around his back. His concern for her and the child she carried made his movements more fluid than powerful, less potent but more endearing than his savage thrusts. She clung to him while the tender storm within him raged, until its fury was spent and she was filled with the gentle rain.

She knew he was disappointed, knew also that he would never say it. And she wanted to weep for her inadequacies, for not being what he needed in a lover, for not even knowing what those needs were. If she were bolder, she might have asked him, but in the asking was a responsibility to fulfill. What if she was not capable of that?

She clung to him more tightly, pressing her face against the rhythmic drum of his heartbeat, wondering what feminine knowledge she was lacking. But mostly she wondered why she was so suddenly and inexplicably afraid.

16

Otis Johnson scooted off an old wooden box, flexed his short, squatty legs, and began to pace nervously back and forth across the Claytons' stable yard. His eyes were malevolent with paranoia, his mind murky with distorted images that seemed to meld the past with the present. The years merged finally, and a trace of obscure sanity returned.

"That gal seen me, Ezra. Of all the friggin' luck! I thought she'd been scalped by them Injuns what come up. But she's here, and married to that oldest Courtland boy."

"What you gon do, Otis?" asked Ezra, a short chunk of a man who was as square as he was tall. He was not particularly bright—he'd been put in the smokehouse as an infant to drive evil spirits away, and it had driven some of the oxygen from his brain—nor was he brave, which was why he had been coerced into doing Otis's bidding over the past few years. "Diablo ain't here to git you out of this 'un."

"Shut up, darky! You're in it too, now that Diablo got hisself killed," Otis returned wildly. His beady eyes scanned the old barn for eavesdroppers, a hint of renewed madness in their dingy gray depths. "I got to figure me a way to git rid of her. Soon!"

"Whoa, boss! I ain't takin' part in a killin'," Ezra said, as frightened of the deranged man as he was of the idea of murdering a white woman. "I did that other stuff for you, diggin' up that ground for nigh on three years now, but I ain't takin' no part in a killin', nawsuh!" He ran dirt-brown fingers across his brow and began shuffling his wide, flat feet on the straw-littered ground. He knew Otis was crazy—devil-possessed, his mama would say—and he was deathly afraid of the wicked man. He lumbered over to the empty crate Otis had just vacated and hunched down wearily. "Do Massuh Robert know that gal is Mistuh Armand's chile all growed up? Iffen he do, he be 'spectin' trouble, Otis. He sho is."

"Course he knows!" Otis screeched. "He got eyes, ain't he? She looks just like her mama come back from the grave." Otis laughed sadistically. "Couldn't take his eyes off the whelp last night, bet he wanted to plow her right then and there. Bet he weren't none too happy 'bout past mem'ries stinkin' up the place neither." Otis gave another eerie laugh that made Ezra's blood chill. Dirty fingernails idly scratched his bald pate as he began to plan. "I got to figure me a way to get rid of that gal real neat like, so's it looks like an accident."

"You better be careful," warned Ezra. "Massuh Robert—"

"Shut up! Just keep your big mouth shut!"

"I ain't sayin' nothin'!" Ezra jumped from the crate and backed away from the feverish light of insanity in the man's eyes. The next time his ma, the high priestess of the local voodoo rituals, gathered her followers under the cover of darkness to worship the snake god, *gran Zombi,* he would have her use her magic to make him an amulet that would protect him from this crazy white man. "Why don't you jest leave that little gal alone? She cain't prove nothin'. That wuz a long time ago. Maybe she left early cuz she wuz sick."

"Yeah, she was sick all right!" Otis cackled maniacally.

"Sick when she seen me. Naw, I ain't gonna leave nothin' to chance. I'll be glad to git rid of the last member of that meddlesome family."

Ezra backed farther away as he stared in frightened awe at the crazed look on the man's face. "You gots a demon, man. You stay away from me. I ain't tellin' no one. You stay away from me!"

Acadiana strolled anxiously back and forth across the damp morning grass. In the three months since the Claytons' ball her anxiety had not eased a whit. She could not account for it, could not accept it, so attributed it to the idiosyncrasies of the pregnant mind. Minette had told her that along with the changes in her body there would be changes in her perceptions and emotions. She hadn't warned her that they would be so severe.

Whenever she left the manor house she felt eyes on her, evil, watchful eyes lurking among the shadowy corners like furtive specters. They pierced her back like talons, clawing at her troubled mind. She did not fancy herself superstitious, but found herself staying closer to the house except when her restive spirit could not be contained and overrode her fear. She knew the foolishness of such thoughts but, like the recurring nightmares, couldn't seem to stop them. She confided in no one, fearing they would think her unbalanced. And perhaps she was, for there was absolutely nothing upon which to base her fears. The snap of a twig, a rustle in the bamboo hedges, the sudden caw of a blackbird in startled flight—nature's symphony in its most normal orchestration.

The political rallies continued and Jonas had made another trip to New Orleans to see what services were needed in aiding Louisiana against the British. Or so she was told, Acadiana thought resentfully. She didn't understand why a missive wouldn't have been sufficient for his purpose. But these doubts too, she decided, were the result of an overactive imagination and the aberrations of her mental state.

She made another aggravated pass across the back lawn, feeling jailed, imprisoned by her thoughts and restless energy. She glanced up at Minette and wished she could engage her in conversation about the past, but *Grand'mère* would not discuss it no matter how hard she pressed. Jonas stood by his mother in her decision, saying he didn't want his wife unduly stressed by things that had happened so long ago, things that could not be altered. Acadiana was frantic to know who had tried to run her parents off their land, but no amount of pushing, prodding, or pleading would get Minette to talk. Acadiana felt somehow betrayed, overly cosseted and smothered. To compound her irritation, Robert Clayton had insisted that Beth travel to a neighboring town to visit relatives, and Acadiana missed their daily walks by the bayou, missed having a friend in whom to confide her troublesome thoughts.

Minette watched from the porch, stitching a snow-white christening gown and humming to herself. She knew Cade longed for freedom and ached for her high-strung daughter-in-law who was heavy with child now. Minette remembered the fretful waiting that was a part of childbearing, remembered what it felt like to be smothered in attention. Jonas had forbidden his wife to go off alone. Until Beth returned or one of the Courtlands could accompany her, he wanted Acadiana near the house.

He had done it for her own protection, afraid that now, with her unwieldy shape, she might slip and fall when no one was near to help her, but Acadiana suspected that her husband didn't trust her to comport herself in a manner befitting a woman in her delicate state. While she faced an unreasonable fear of going off alone these days, she also chafed at her restrictions, the sum total of which caused her emotions to teeter like a seesaw.

"Grand'mère," Acadiana called, thoroughly bored and irritated with herself. "I am going to the mill." She braced herself for Minette's disapproval and was not disappointed.

"Bébé," Minette pleaded, placing her sewing aside. "You

know Jonas wants you to stay near the house. He'll do nothing but scold you when you get there."

"I won't get in the way," Acadiana cajoled, but she didn't care if he did fuss. She could stand anything but the monotony her days had become.

Harvest was upon them now, and the men were constantly needed in the fields and at the mill. Work crews were divided into three groups, working six hours apiece, but for Jonas, Edward, and Cain, eighteen-hour days were common. The narrow stalks of sugarcane were harvested first, the thicker ones later, and carried off to the presses as fast as they fell so the fragrant juice could be extracted and crystallization begun.

Acadiana hurried across the plantation grounds, feeling the familiar prickle of apprehension on the back of her neck. Nature was never still, she well knew, but the rustle of fallen leaves, the crack of an old limb, the thudding of small animals seemed to follow her from a distance, as if staying a pace behind and parallel with her direction. She darted a quick glance into the woods, as if to catch the culprit in spying on her, but saw nothing but her own foolish reflection in her mind's eye. Still, she quickened her pace, feeling silly and out of sorts, but nonetheless anxious.

A violent, impotent threat hissed from the trees and was swallowed up by the numerous sights and sounds of a mill in progress. The watcher hung back, thwarted, as Acadiana stepped into the clearing. She slipped quietly into the boiling house, staying well back from the five refining kettles. Each had a different name and function, all necessary for the process. Edward stood near The Grand, boiling the freshly extracted juice, while directing his crew at The Cleanser for second boiling. The air was stifling, the smells cloying. African chants rang out as the hot, backbreaking work droned on without ceasing. Acadiana felt her stomach turn over and placed her hand there, regretting her hasty decision in coming here.

Jonas, devoid of shirt, stepped near The Torch, the kettle

used for the first stages of purifying and thickening. Even in the cool of December, sweat poured down his back and chest, his muscles rolling with each movement, as he peered in, then crossed to The Syrup kettle and cursed roundly. At this stage the juice was supposed to obtain a syrupy consistency but almost never did, much to his chagrin. He swore again and had his crew transfer the juice to The Battery for the final cooking.

Perspiration trickled down Acadiana's temples in the suffocating heat, and although she was flushed, she felt pale and a bit light-headed. She fanned her face then plucked at her damp bodice. Edward, also shirtless, looked up and caught sight of his fading sister-in-law. He also cursed—a defect in Courtland genes, Acadiana decided in pique—and called Jonas.

"Traitor!" she said, and backed quickly out of the building.

Jonas caught up with her just outside the entrance, his expression stern, but Acadiana stared back at him in consummate innocence as if she were not two steps away from swooning with the tremendous heat and overpowering smells.

"*M'sieu* Husband," she said sweetly.

"Wife," he returned in warning. "I'm going to paddle you but good if you don't return to the house immediately."

Acadiana merely smiled with innate feminine knowledge. "You will not. I am *enceinte,* delicate, fragile"—her eyes sparked in sudden ire—"incapable of doing anything more than wile away the days like an invalid. I am going insane, Jonas!"

"And you're taking me with you!" he growled, but he was smiling in self-mockery. He grabbed her shoulders and pulled her to him, rubbing his wet torso against her bodice and protruding stomach. Acadiana wrinkled her nose at his sweat-soaked skin.

"*Mais oui,* you are hot," she said, and swirled the springy hairs on his chest absently with her forefinger.

"In more ways than one," he said wryly, feeling his need for her bloat painfully, inappropriately, within him. "What are you doing here?"

"I was bored," she said, studying the way his chest hair curled around her finger in tantalizing wonder. "I needed a walk."

"You came alone," he accused, but there was little he could do about it now. He could hardly spank her like a child for disobeying, especially in her condition, and knew it wouldn't do any good anyway. "You embarrassed Edward by seeing him indecently exposed," he chided, pulling her closer. Her nipples puckered against his chest, and the heat in the boiling house was nothing compared to the slow fire building within him. He dropped his lips to hers, hard, then drew back. "You offer a tempting diversion."

Acadiana blushed. She hadn't meant things to take this direction. They were surrounded by workers coming and going, hauling cane stalks while pretending not to see the master and mistress locked in an eloquent embrace. "I'll bring Beth next time. I bet she would like to see Edward indecently . . . oops. . . ." Her words trailed off in embarrassed silence.

Jonas lifted a cocky eyebrow and grinned. "Beth?"

"Shhhh!" Acadiana pressed her fingers to his lips, but he only nipped at them playfully. "I have divulged a secret, *oui?* She will murder me when she returns."

"Come with me into the woods," he said suggestively. "I'll protect you."

"Who will protect me from you?" she said, embarrassed and delighted and wholly uncertain about doing such a brazen thing.

"No one, that's the beauty of it." He began inching her away from the clearing toward the forest, but, flustered, Acadiana stood her ground. Pulling back a little, she glanced down at her rounded stomach. She would not, in the bold light of day no matter how diffused by the thick woods, allow her husband to divest her of her clothing!

Jonas was not a mind-reader, but it took little imagination to guess what she was thinking. "There are ways," he offered seductively against her ear, "of rucking up a lady's skirts against a tall oak tree so no one's the wiser. Except the gentleman and lady, of course."

"How would you know!" Acadiana said, her cheeks throbbing with heat and color at such a suggestion. Jonas thought it prudent not to explain how he had gained such knowledge and nipped playfully at her neck instead.

"Come, love." He began leading her—forcefully, she decided—toward the shelter of the trees.

"Jonas!" she whispered. "I do not think—"

"You rarely do," he chastised mildly, and continued tugging her inexorably forward. "In this instant it is not necessary that you think, wife, just obey."

She punched him with her free hand, giggling in spite of the embarrassingly wicked things he was planning. Cain called him then and Jonas muttered a mild profanity beneath his breath. He wrapped both arms around his wife and ground his body lightly against hers in aching regret. "Get back to the house, or this will get extremely embarrassing in another few minutes."

Her spirits revived by diversion, Acadiana gave him a sassy peck on the cheek and spun out of his arms. In a twinkling she was gone, but her fragrance and memory lingered long after she disappeared from sight. Jonas stood a moment more, a soberness settling about him. Along with the enormous strain of the harvest and his wife's advancing pregnancy, the messages he had received over the past five days had given him even more to worry about.

The British threat was now a reality, for on December 15 they had attacked Lake Borgne. Jonas knew it was only a matter of time now before volunteers would be needed to defend New Orleans and thus Louisiana. The only bright spot in the otherwise tension-filled days was the fact that Governor Claiborne had come around after all. On December 17 he had issued one of the most unusual proclamations ever made by an American governor. He invited the Baratarians to enroll themselves and to march against the enemy, guaranteeing them a free and full pardon should their conduct in the field meet the approval of Major General Jackson.

Christmas rushed in on Courtland Manor in a flurry of excitement. Exchanging gifts at this time was the only Anglo-Saxon custom from her husband's heritage that Minette readily embraced. The New Year was the most festive holiday of the normal Creole calendar, followed by Epiphany, which was a day for exchanging visits. By adhering to both English and French customs, this time of year offered a prolonged celebration for the inhabitants of Courtland Manor and was greatly appreciated by all during the harried time of harvesting.

The mansion was bedecked with holly and other Yuletide finery. The bright red berries of the evergreen shrub added color to every fireplace and doorframe in the house. A large, fragrant Yule log stood in the library, trimmed with winter greenery and lacy fans. Small lighted tapers stood in tiny silver holders on the outer branches, casting a warm glow. Jonas hung a cluster of mistletoe inside the entryway and caught his wife every time she stepped through. She secretly made more trips than necessary in and out of the library, feigning surprise with each amorous kiss.

Acadiana slapped Edward's hand away as he tried to shake the brightly decorated package she was placing by the Yule log. She had not put names on the gifts but used a technique of slow torture that her mother had invented. On each of the gifts from her, she had placed numbers. The household had been puzzled all week trying to discover which number belonged to whom. Jonas had threatened to no avail and Edward had resorted to bribery in an attempt to discover her closely guarded secret. There seemed to be no consistency to the order of numbers, as if they had been doled out at random. Acadiana assured her frustrated family that there was a method to her madness and they would just have to break the code.

"Merry Christmas Eve, all," Beth said brightly as she stood in the doorway, having just arrived.

"Merry Christmas, Beth," Edward said, a sly smile on his face. "Are you standing there on purpose?"

"Of course, silly." She laughed indulgently. She was not about to step into the room without removing her muddy overshoes.

Jonas pretended to offer Edward a merry chase as they both headed for the doorway, but Edward easily won when he bounded over an armchair, caught Beth off guard, and planted an extremely aggressive kiss on her stunned lips. Beth was a vision of startled high color at the unexpected passion of Edward's advance under his family's watchful eye.

Still holding her, Edward whispered, "If you don't hurry and move, I'll be forced to do that again."

"Is that a promise or a threat?" she asked flippantly.

"That is most assuredly a promise," he returned rakishly, then kissed her again.

Beth had fantasized about Edward kissing her for so long that she yielded unreservedly to the actual experience. His mouth moved with slow teasing over her pliant lips, then his tongue darted out to tickle and test her willingness. Beth responded immediately, her own tongue intertwining with his in a mating dance that sent shivers clear down to Edward's toes. Beth was feeling rapturous, giddy, and a little light-headed when Minette stepped into the room and cleared her throat, causing the couple to disengage themselves quickly.

"Having a merry Christmas, Beth?" Minette asked smoothly. "I see that Edward is."

Beth's cheeks pinkened; Edward stuffed his hands into his pockets, and Jonas exchanged a conspiratorial glance with his wife. Sympathizing with Beth's plight but grinning in spite of herself, Acadiana struggled to rise from the floor where she had been arranging more gifts. Jonas helped her up and patted her enlarged abdomen.

"Are you sure this babe won't be born for two more months?" he teased.

"I certainly am big," Acadiana said, seeing neither legs nor feet over her melon-shaped tummy. "Perhaps I am due to have the baby now."

"Hardly, love. There hasn't been enough time," he taunted as he lowered his voice to a whisper. "I could never forget our first time."

"You are wicked!" she said, blushing.

"And you are fickle." Jonas sighed. "Just the other night you told me I was wonderful."

Acadiana buried her brightly flushed face in her hands and discreetly turned away from the group as she remembered the nights past. Over the past months intimacy in their bed had been infrequent but full of tenderness. Jonas was gentle, almost cautious, when he took her now, and she wondered if he feared for the child, or if her misshapen figure caused him to seek her out less and less. She ridiculously tried to fan her face with the package she was holding, but the contrary gift bopped her on the nose, bounced off her belly, and fell to the floor with a thud.

"I said no such thing!" she hissed, flustered.

"No, but you were thinking it," Jonas teased.

"Non!" she denied, because she had been thinking just that. He *had* been wonderful, but reserved. Whether from the exhaustion of harvest, the fear of British invasion, or her pregnancy, there was something missing in their intimate nights together. She didn't know what, for things were much the same as they had always been except that she did not fight him now. And she knew Jonas felt it too, though he did not comment on it. He was always so careful when he approached her, unlike the early months of their marriage when the fire in him seemed to burn out of control. There were times when she almost wished for those torrid days, for him to come to her as aggressively as he once had.

It was all so confusing, she blushed again for merely thinking such thoughts. "And you still have not explained about lifting ladies' skirts and oak trees . . . and how you know about such things."

"I have a vivid imagination," he lied, using the same excuse he had used every night since suggesting the woodland tryst.

Acadiana knew very well that he was being deliberately evasive. "You are a despoiler of innocent maidens," she accused.

"There was nothing at all innocent about those—" Effectively hoisted upon his own proverbial petard, Jonas grimaced and decided there was nothing to do but retreat and regroup. "You are the only innocent maiden I've despoiled in quite a while." His voice dropped as he leaned nearer her ear. "And even with all the scratches, bites, and bruises, I loved every minute of it."

"I did not . . . You deserved . . . You are highly improper," she stammered. "Beast!"

"Ah, but you've known that for a long time."

Acadiana rolled her eyes heavenward in search of divine deliverance. *"Oui,"* she agreed, then smiled up at him with all the reluctant but full-fledged caring she felt for this beast.

It was the best Christmas Acadiana could remember since she was a child. Among other things, Jonas had given her a brilliant sapphire ring surrounded by diamonds. There were also teardrop earrings and a necklace to match. The jewelry itself did not overwhelm Acadiana, as she had never taken much stock in such things. It was the words Minette had spoken quietly that held her enthralled. She had told Acadiana that Jonas had never given any woman a diamond before, but had reserved that gift solely for the mother of his children.

Acadiana had given him an intricately carved pocket watch with a scene of a peaceful bayou and wild mallard in flight on the silver watch cover. Engraved on the inside was the inscription "Dreamfields." Jonas knew the intense meaning behind the simple word, and it touched him deeply. His eloquent look after opening the gift indicated he understood, and for a precious moment they shared a mutual dream, drawn by the bond that was strengthening day by day between them.

Close to sunset a sumptuous meal was served in the formal dining room. The Creole dishes, prepared with patience and love, were unique and some of the tastiest cuisine in the world. The feast was abundant and extravagant with over half a dozen different meat dishes including turtle soup, oyster pâté, bouillabaisse, shellfish stew, and crayfish bisque. Just for Acadiana jambalaya was added. It was more commonly associated with the people of the Delta than with Creole aristocrats. The dish gave off a savory aroma of smoked bacon, shrimp, crabs, onions, ham, tomatoes, rice, and red peppers, and had everyone's mouth watering as they waited for it to be served.

Accompanying the main dishes were various vegetables, breads, and desserts along with an assortment of flavored wine and fresh fruit with nuts. The meal was completed with several choices of coffee, each having an unusual flavor and aroma.

Jonas teased Acadiana about the enormous amount of food she consumed, but she ignored his jests and continued to enjoy herself without restraint. After the meal everyone retired to the library where a cozy fire burned. The floor-to-ceiling windows were open to let in the cool night air, and the scent of magnolias, holly, and myrtle wax mingled to give a Christmas-only fragrance to the room. The winter weather varied daily in southern Louisiana, unpredictable as a changeling from clear and warm to cold and dreary. The prevalent gulf winds over the last few days had given everyone more of a feeling of spring, but overly warm weather usually meant a cold spell would follow.

Minette took out the family Bible and read the Christmas story according to Luke, as she had done every year since her children were born. The story held new meaning for Acadiana now that she was expecting her first child. She could imagine how Mary must have felt that night as she held her baby for the first time wanting to protect Him from the harsh world outside the lonely stable. Unconsciously she cuddled closer to Jonas on the couch, feeling treasured and protected with his arm coiled about her. She dropped her head to his shoulder and didn't even notice that she sighed when the story ended.

Jonas smiled as he noted the wistful look on his wife's face. The blessed story held new meaning for him also as he contemplated the anxiety Joseph must have gone through while trying to get his laboring wife to a safe shelter.

The evening ended with a time of love and devotion. Family members gathered for a final prayer before retiring to their respective rooms where, at least for this night, they would forget about the troubles that pressed heavily upon their lives. Wrapped warmly in each other's arms, Jonas and Acadiana shared a kiss not of passion, but of hope and reverence for the babe born in the stable and for their child yet to come.

17

The rider jerked his horse to a stop in front of Courtland Manor. The beast's lathered sides heaved, foam splattered the bit cutting into his mouth from the many hard miles he had crossed to bring unwelcome news. Jonas walked briskly down the front steps, his face impassive but his insides churning as he recognized the man who must have given up Christmas with his family to ride all night. The inevitable burned in the rider's tired eyes, and Jonas knew it had happened.

"When?"

"Night before last," the messenger said unsteadily. He dragged his weary body from the mount, his legs quivering from fear and exhaustion, and he would have fallen had Jonas not dropped a supporting arm around his middle and helped him into the house. Jonas sent one servant to care for the horse and one for refreshments. Then he ushered the man into the library, where he collapsed into one of the wing-back leather chairs near the fireplace, his legs too shaky to hold him up. Jonas, unable to sit, paced the room expectantly while waiting for the man to catch his breath.

Though young, hardy, and strong, the messenger Jonas had hired to keep him informed looked as if he had aged a

decade when he took a liberal draft of wine, his eyes feverishly boring into Jonas's. "The British colonel, William
Thornton, landed at the mouth of Bayou Bienvenu two
days ago and sent a detachment up Bayou Mazant and
thence to the Villeré Canal. They followed the canal to the
Villeré Plantation and took no time occupying the area."

"And Gabriel?" Jonas asked sharply.

"Major Villeré is fine, God bless him. He escaped to warn
Jackson that the British had landed." The messenger took
another drink of wine and fought the urge to sink into the
mind-numbing oblivion of sleep he so badly needed. "General Jackson ordered an immediate mobilization of all available forces at New Orleans." The man gave a slight smile
that in no way obliterated the tension in the room. "My
contact said that Major J. B. Plauche's Bataillon d'Orléans,
stationed at Spanish Fort, dashed off for the Plâce d'Armes
and ran the entire distance. It could be true, for the army
units sure gathered quickly."

Giving in to weariness, the man dropped his head back
and heaved a deep sigh. "It was a sight to behold, Mr.
Courtland. Just as the cathedral clock was striking three,
the troops came at a quickstep through the streets of New
Orleans. Each company had its own music—'Yankee Doo-
dle,' 'La Marseillaise,' 'Le Chant du Départ.' The ladies and
children crowded the balconies as if a celebration were in
progress, while Jackson sat atop his horse with his regulars
and waited at the gate of Fort St. Charles to review the
troops as they passed."

Another tired smile flitted across the man's drawn lips
and patriotism shone in his eyes. "The first to march past
were Beale's rifles, all volunteers, mind you, from profes-
sional and business circles, ready to do their duty. It was a
sight with them in their blue hunting shirts and citizen's
hats, their long bores over their shoulders, and everyone of
them sharpshooters. Next came Hinds' dragoons at a hard
gallop. You could tell their gallantry impressed General
Jackson by the smile on his face. After that came mounted

gunmen with long hair and unshaved faces. But they were as proud as the others in their dingy woolen hunting shirts, copperas-dyed trousers, coonskin caps, and leather belts stuck with hunting knives and tomahawks."

Jonas chafed under the rambling description, ready to get to the heart of the matter, but waited patiently because the man seemed to need the diversion of patriotic talk and the chance to rest before offering an opinion as to what should be done.

"From a side street came the brave Creoles of New Orleans," the man continued, "along with Plauche's battalion, which had come up from Bayou St. John. After these were freemen of color followed by a band of Choctaw Indians. God, there must have been a hundred of them, war paint and all. Last came the Regulars. General Jackson waited until Commodore Patterson's schooner left the opposite bank of the river and moved down the current before clapping his spurs to his horse and following his army."

"And now?" Jonas urged, feeling the weight of responsibility tremble within him. He had to think of Acadiana's safety, the sugarcane harvest, and his duty to Louisiana. Shirking his responsibility in any one area would have a domino effect on them all.

"Jackson has moved his men about seven miles below New Orleans to a strip of open ground between the Mississippi River and the swamp. Do you know the place? It's near the abandoned drainage canal that acts as a boundary for the Chalmette and Rodriguez plantations." At Jonas's nod, the man continued. "The soldiers have thrown up a low breastwork on the New Orleans side of the canal. Jackson decided to attack the British while they were still weary and hit their outposts about eight o'clock that night. The battle lasted until four o'clock in the morning when Jackson withdrew to his line of breastworks. With the killed, wounded, and missing, it is estimated that the British have lost between two and three hundred men, while we have lost slightly over two hundred. Thank God we kept them from marching against the city, because it's not defended by any fortification." The man looked up, his eyes bleak. "But by no means are the British defeated. Their numbers are greater, they have not yet attacked in strength, nor have they begun to use the full complement of their artillery. They are continuing to land troops and bring up supplies and munitions. The chances for protecting New Orleans look grim, Mr. Courtland, very grim indeed."

Jonas couldn't agree more no matter how much he wanted to deny it. After advising the man to rest before moving on to the next plantation, he went in search of Acadiana. She would have to be told the grave news; he would have to leave. It tore at him, clawed through his heart and abdomen like a cancer, but he had no other recourse than to defend his country, thus protecting everything he held dear.

Acadiana scanned the message delivered by one of the Claytons' servants asking her to meet Beth at the boat landing near the border of Courtland Manor Plantation. She and Beth walked there often, sharing past secrets and future hopes, and she suspected the incident with Edward under the mistletoe had prompted Beth's need to talk.

She donned a smoky-blue cape, thankful for the warmth it provided, for the day had turned crisp.

Waving farewell to Minette as she strolled toward the bayou, she promised to bring Beth back for lunch. The magnolias were just beginning to bloom, their fragrance drifting with the breeze, filling Acadiana's senses with the most pleasant aroma. The smell brought back fond memories of her childhood, invoking a wave of nostalgia as she walked along. The remembrance was so vivid, as if she were still a child doing those things she was most fond of—shivering with cold and excitement in a decaying tree stump while playing hide-and-go-seek with Matthew, picking berries for a cobbler, sneaking out after dark to play ghosty, and discovering who was brave enough to wade into the bayou when winter was on the verge of giving way to spring. Those were good days, carefree, wrapped warmly in security. They had lacked the maturity of real adult life, had not prepared her for the dangers of world politics, the struggle of married life, or the enormous responsibilities of parenting. But they had had their place in a too-short childhood and were treasured now for their uncomplicated simplicity.

The nippy air caressed her face as she wandered farther from the mansion, whipping the cloak about her rounded figure as she left the cleared grounds and entered the woods. The chilly winds didn't course through the trees as vigorously here, and Acadiana was wont to linger in the sheltered area, picking winter flowers and basking in the peaceful solitude as she walked lazily nearer the bank of the Teche. She lost sight of the house as she strolled beside the winding bayou named for the Indian word for snake. Legend had it that a great warrior killed a gigantic serpent, and as it wound its way across the land, it died and sank into the ground, hollowing the earth, which eventually filled with water to form the bayou.

She walked out of the secluded trees into the area that had been cleared for shipping cargo to the river. This section of the plantation was peaceful and usually had a soothing effect on her, but today it was ominously still. The murky water lapped against the earthen bank in a dull rhythm, and elongated shadows stretched from the naked trees like skeletal fingers. The air was damp and grew colder as the sun slipped behind a cloud, and Acadiana shivered as the woods darkened to an eerie grayness that sapped her gay mood and left the hairs on her arms and neck tingling with foreboding. There were no birds chirping in the barren trees; even the ducks that normally swam among the cypress knees were gone. Her years near the Caddo Indians had sharpened her senses to catch anything out of the ordinary, especially in nature, and a telling chill raced up her spine, making her stiffen. The feeling was not new, but it was more real now than it had been since the Claytons' harvest ball. She stopped to scan the area for her unseen nemesis, then turned suddenly as a twig snapped behind her.

"Beth—" Air left her lungs, and a scream froze in her throat as she stared into the weak gray eyes of a madman.

A swaying wagon, crazed horses, choking billows of dust, the gleam of steel, dark red blood, the acid taste of fear. A child's cry. Adult screams. Maman! A dark, swirling mist clouded her eyes, and she loosened her hold on a reality too heinous to endure.

Otis Johnson grabbed her forearms roughly, his chipped, dirty fingernails biting into her tender flesh and flinging her back to awareness. A whimpered plea escaped Acadiana's pale lips, only to be ignored.

"Well, missy, we meet again," he snarled.

Foul, whiskey-laden breath assailed her, causing her throat to work convulsively to keep from gagging. Acadiana could not move, could hardly breathe. The nightmare was back, but this time it was real. There was no husband here to wake her from the suffocating dream and soothe her back to sleep, no mother to push her under a wagon seat. She wanted to scream, but no sound came from her parched throat. Nausea and fear momentarily robbed her of coherent thought, as if she were but an onlooker watching a hideous play from a distance. A faint numbness gripped her petrified limbs, and for a frightened second she thought she would swoon again.

Cruel fingers bit deeper into her arms, snapping her dazed mind back. She took a deep, ragged breath and summoned enough courage to speak, buying time as she tried to assess her situation.

"What do you want from me?" she said as calmly as she could even as her mind raced desperately through plans of escape. Her heart was slamming sickeningly against her ribs, but she didn't want to give this murderer the advantage of seeing her fear.

"I don't want nothin' you got now," Otis said, greedy eyes roaming her rounded figure. "The condition you in ain't liable to make it too pleasurable."

Her eyes followed his down to her stomach, and her mind cried out in agony for her unborn child. The thought of his filthy hands on her sickened Acadiana, and she knew there would be no mercy for her or the babe, just as there had been none for her beloved parents.

"Why are you here?" She quivered, fear making her voice tremble along with her body. She sucked in another calming breath, damning her physical inability to fight his grip on her upper arms. She must not panic! Above all else, she must keep her wits about her and not give in to the terror threatening to overtake her. Fiercely she fought the horror, but the encroaching fears sapped her strength, making her arms and legs feel as heavy as stones, and a part of her cried out for the protection of Jonas's arms. His handsome face swam before her, and she drew energy from the mental picture, knowing their future together would be destroyed just as her parents' had been if she did not collect herself and find a way out. She bargained for time as she repeated the question. "Why are you here?"

"Well, you see, little gal," Otis said jeeringly, "you could make life real miserable for me, recognizin' me the way you did."

She was beset with confusion for a second, then his meaning dawned perfectly, horribly, clear. Acadiana fought the urge to laugh hysterically at the irony of it all. She hadn't seen him, not until now, but she had felt him, felt his evil presence for months. Now she realized it had not been her pregnancy or her imagination; he had been watching and waiting for this chance.

She was struck by the desire to claw this monster's eyes out, to avenge her parents' death in the most savage manner, but she must do everything to protect herself and her unborn. "I don't know who you are," she lied, "or why you are here, but my husband will come after you if you harm me." Her violet eyes grew wild with a hatred she couldn't disguise and burned for revenge. "If anything happens to me, he will find you!"

"Now, missy"—Otis cackled spitefully—"I ain't so stupid as to let him think I dun you harm. Just a nice little accident to ruin his holiday season. 'Sides, he cain't prove nothin'. Ain't nobody never been able to. My word again' his. Ain't that right?" He ogled her, and Acadiana felt her skin crawl each place his eyes touched her body. "I'm sure he'll find another bitch soon enough to comfort him after the tragedy of losing his wife and brat. From the looks o' you, he probably already has him a lady friend on the side. You look like you about to pop."

Acadiana's arms were going numb beneath his relentless grip, and her legs were trembling so, she wondered how much longer they would hold her up. "Why are you doing this?" she asked with an evenness that belied the turmoil that had now settled in turbulent roils in her belly.

"Yer too much trouble. I told you that!" Otis yelled. "Your family ain't been nothin' but trouble to me fer years! Your ma and pa run me off their land ever' time I came around. I weren't hurtin' nobody, just lookin' fer somethin' what's mine." He shook her then as one might a helpless ragdoll, and increased terror seized Acadiana as she realized that whatever wrong his demented mind had attributed to her parents was now being transferred to her.

"What are you talking about?" she almost screeched in panic. "What was yours?"

"Nothin'! Nothin' you need to know about, missy. Now come on!" He jerked her roughly toward the water.

"What . . . what are you going to do?" she stammered, frantic now. She began struggling to pull free.

"Yer goin' for a permanent swim." He laughed sadistically, dragging her closer and closer to the bayou.

Acadiana dug her heels in, clenched her jaw stubbornly, and tried the same technique she had once used on Jonas.

She kicked the man hard in the shin, then bit down on his hairy arm with a vengeance.

Otis howled in pain and shock and released her, his eyes a muddy reflection of his deranged mind. Acadiana scrambled away from the water's edge, her mind racing. She must get away! Must get close enough to the house for someone to hear her scream. Almost crazed with fear, she started running headlong for the sugarcane fields. They were closer to the manse, and their tall, dense stalks would provide a protective forest in which to hide.

She tore out of the clearing, holding her stomach protectively, and screamed for all she was worth. Her movements were awkward at best, but still she raced on, sidestepping the razor-sharp palmetto clusters and darting through the trees. A biting wind stung her cheeks. It seemed to permeate her entire body as she sucked the cold air into her lungs and screamed again and again until her throat grew so raw the sounds became nothing more than a hoarse, scraping agony in her fiery throat. A root snared her foot; she stumbled, groaning in pain as her knees hit her stomach. Righting herself, she stubbornly continued to push past the trees in an effort to reach the fields. Her voice was gone now, and tears of frustration blurred her vision when she could force nothing but pitiful mewling cries that sapped her energy.

Every muscle in her body burned with the effort, but she pressed blindly on, one arm in front of her face to shield her eyes from the punishing slaps of low branches, one supporting her stomach. Just a little farther, she told herself, one foot in front of the other. Keep going . . . almost there now . . . keep going.

The forest gave way to the clearing just before the fields. She could see the break through the trees. Safety was just within reach, just out of it . . . keep running . . . victory mingled with the acid on her tongue . . . a few more steps . . . keep pushing . . . keep . . .

Acadiana drew up sharply, screamed a mute denial, then died a little inside as she doubled over in an effort to breathe. Almost retching from pain and exertion, from her foolishness and utter hopelessness, she stared in horror at the neat, barren rows. Nothing but rough stubble lay in her path. In her panicked state she hadn't remembered that the cane had already been cut.

Thrashing through the woods like a wild, enraged animal, Otis bore down on her. With a demonic gleam in his eyes, he grabbed her cloak and violently threw her to the ground. Acadiana curled her body, desperate to protect the child. She succeeded in tangling herself in the garment and clawed at the neck clasp, trying to unfasten the strangling mass of material and wrestle free. Her misshapen body prevented her from rising fast enough to break away, and she gripped the muddy earth, scraping the tender skin from her hands and knees as she tried to drag herself away from her assailant.

Otis grabbed her by the hair and yanked her roughly to her feet. Fresh tears stung her eyes as pain seeped past the numbing horror of her predicament. Acadiana fought like a wildcat, silently sobbing and screaming and clawing as he once again hauled her back through the trees, closer and closer to the dark depths of the water. She lashed out at him wildly, twisting and writhing, each movement sending sharp, biting pains through her abdomen. After jabbing at his rib cage with her elbow, she broke one arm free and raked her nails across his face as he stepped into the freezing bayou.

He slapped her arm away viciously and shoved her out in front of him. Acadiana sank down in the slimy mud that made it hard to keep her footing, and felt the panic crawl up her body as the cold water soaked first her feet, then her lower gown, then climbed past her stomach. Again and again she screamed Jonas's name, her mouth working silently to form the words while the pain knifed through her body. In continuous, soundless agony she screamed for someone to help, screamed for the nightmare to end. Cold water surrounded her head as Otis pushed her under, cutting off her ineffectual screams . . . and her air.

Her strength was waning; Acadiana reached out her hands in a last burning drive for survival, clawing at Otis's face and neck, gouging the bleeding wounds she had already inflicted there. He screeched in agony, releasing her long enough for her to rise and take a ragged gasp of air before he pushed her head under again.

The water swirled and enveloped around her, forbidding in its darkness—its cold promise of death. Her lungs burned and felt as if they would either burst or collapse. Her failing, leaden limbs weakened, then went slack as if the bayou drained her of will and life. She was so cold, so tired, her life hopelessly out of control. She could no longer fight the evil, and her heart cried out for Jonas, for a love lost before it was even realized, for the child who would never see the strong, handsome man who had fathered him, and for dreams that would never be brought to fruition. Blackness finally overtook her, and Acadiana slipped into the deepest, darkest oblivion.

Voices seemed to dip and swirl, hovering overhead then fading away. They were loud and frenzied, then soft and crooning. Acadiana tried to fight her way up from the darkness toward the light, toward the familiar, calling sounds. Someone was pulling and shouting; the soft sounds were gone. Her body convulsed, and she awoke, retching violently. Half afraid to open her eyes for fear of seeing the nightmarish water closing about her, suffocating her, she moaned and whimpered. As if from a distance, she heard her name over and over. Her eyes flicked open to see Jonas hovering over her. She was cradled in his arms, and on his face was a tortured expression as he leaned her sideways to rid her of the muddy bayou water.

Edward was there also, crouched beside Jonas, his face mirroring the deathly pallor of Acadiana's and his brother's. "Is she—"

"She's alive, Edward. Check on Otis," Jonas said, his

voice tight and hoarse with fear. "Acadiana! Acadiana, can you hear me?" he pleaded tensely, brushing her damp hair from her white face with fingers that trembled.

She moaned and rolled her head weakly from side to side, unable to force more than a rasp from her raw throat. "Hurts . . . stomach . . . *mon Dieu!*"

"My God," he echoed, his sapphire eyes dilated in shock. "Edward, leave him! I've got to get her to the house!"

Edward left Otis's inert form and rushed back to help Jonas mount his horse. They placed Acadiana in front. She was barely conscious as she clutched her belly and moaned in pain. Despite the strong arms holding her and the warmth seeping through her damp clothing from Jonas's body, she could not stop shivering. Jonas sent Edward ahead to fetch the doctor, then rode as fast as he dared.

In all his life, Jonas had never faced such terror or felt more helpless than he did as he rode back to Courtland Manor with his wife in his arms. His words of comfort and reassurance, whispered over and over in an effort to soothe Acadiana, sounded empty, meaningless as he combated the fear coiled tightly within him. He wanted to shake his fist at the heavens, to cry out his fury as she moaned in the circle of his arms—arms that felt powerless to protect her as he had promised he would.

His expression was stonelike as he carried his wife up the stairs, his soothing words coming by rote from his stricken heart. Edward had already given them family a brief accounting, and Mattie hurried to help get Acadiana out of her wet clothes and into bed, while Minette and Beth stood to the side, existing in silent torment for Cade and for Jonas, whose ravaged face and haunted eyes spoke his concern and inability to take away his wife's pain. Jonas remained by her side, grimly clutching her hand as if to absorb the tremors that racked her body.

"Beth?" Acadiana sobbed in a feverish, hazy world of horrific images. Spasms echoed through her body; her teeth chattered to the extreme that she was almost unable to speak. "You . . . weren't . . . there. I looked . . . but you weren't . . . there."

"I know, honey." Beth wept, the note Minette had found on Cade's bed clutched in her hand. "I'm so sorry, Cade. I didn't send the message. I don't know who would do such a thing!" She covered her mouth with her hands and turned away, sobbing as if she were to blame. Minette's arms went around her and pulled her away from the bedside as her eyes searched her son's.

He looked at Beth and his mother, then shook his head. If Edward hadn't told them it was Otis Johnson, the Claytons' stable hand for the past two decades, the news could wait until later after they had sorted it all out.

"He tried to drown me!" Acadiana wheezed, her eyes aglow with terror. She clutched at Jonas, begging him with those eyes to take away the fear and pain. "He'll try again."

"No, Acadiana. He'll never hurt you again," Jonas said coldly. Otis Johnson was dead. Jonas felt no remorse, could summon no sympathy for putting a hole through the evil man's heart when he found Otis trying to murder his wife. In truth, he wished he could shoot the animal again, watch him writhe in agony as Acadiana was now doing.

The only question now was why had Otis done it?

"Jonas, the baby . . ." Acadiana cried as pain washed over her. "Please."

She gripped his arm as wave after slow wave cramped her belly, making her cry out. Jonas was oblivious to his own pain as her nails cut into the palm of his hand. He thought he would go mad waiting for the doctor, listening helplessly in frustration as each of her cries tore through his heart with the sharp precision of a knife. His eyes pleaded with those around him to do something, anything to ease his wife's torment.

Mattie pushed him aside and began to run experienced hands over Acadiana's taut abdomen, covering the sides, top, then bottom. It wouldn't take an internal examination to confirm what she already knew, and her mind raced over every potion she could think of to halt an early delivery, but she knew of nothing tried and true that would work.

Mattie smiled at her "girl baby" soothingly, then patted her hand before turning away. Her eyes met Jonas's, and he could see the futile shake of her head and the single tear that slid down her plump dark cheek as she moved aside to let him nearer the bed. In that instant he was certain his heart could not sustain the blow and would splinter apart into a thousand jagged pieces. The hopelessness he was feeling must have been evident on his face, because Minette sent him a stern look that said he would have to be strong before her own expression glazed over with the fear they were all feeling.

Jonas went back to his wife's bedside and brushed the ebony curls away from her face as he bent to whisper soothing words of comfort and made promises he wasn't certain he could keep. Acadiana gripped his hand tightly and fought the pain as fiercely as she fought the fear. She could not lose this child! In the dark corners of her mind irrational voices whispered that the baby was the only thing holding her marriage together, but in the clear, untainted regions of her heart she knew the child had brought them forward. He was everything to her—as was the man who stood over her, his eyes so full of agony that she wanted to reach out and comfort him, to assure him all would be well. But pain gripped her anew, and there was nothing she could say over the grinding of her teeth as she struggled to gain control of her body.

Dr. Loreau walked into the room accompanied by a haggard Edward. At his first glance of Acadiana's wan, pain-ridden face, the doctor ordered everyone from the room.

Jonas paced doggedly back and forth downstairs, imploring God's mercy on Acadiana and the babe. Everyone had quit trying to draw him into conversation; consolation and reassurances were of no avail. Even offers of strong libation were repulsed. It was not that he meant to ignore Minette, Edward, and Beth. They were merely trying to comfort him, but Jonas could not bring himself to converse with them. He could think of nothing—not of Otis, not of Robert Clayton's possible involvement—nothing but Acadiana and the pain she was going through. It was his fault that he had almost lost her to Otis and might yet lose the child. In his greed for the land, he had coerced her into marriage and into his bed. He had conveniently brought her within the reaches of the man he now suspected had murdered her parents. Look what his lust had wrought! But it was no longer lust that made his body quicken at just the sight of her, his heart to hammer in anticipation at the slightest smile, his mind to recoil in frustration when she withdrew from him. Not lust but love. Love so strong that the thought of her lying upstairs in pain made his whole body tremble and his heart to ache as if the very life were being squeezed out of it.

Silence hung heavy and stale in the room, like a dense fog surrounding the occupants. It might only have been minutes, but it felt like hours before heavy footsteps were heard shuffling toward the library, and everyone froze, breath coming painfully slow.

Dr. Loreau walked into the tension-filled room, wiping his weary brow. "She is asleep now, Jonas. I have given her a sedative that I hope will relax her body enough to stop the contractions that were brought on by the trauma she just underwent. There is no sign of bleeding yet, but to be frank, it doesn't look good. If these contractions do not stop, there is little I can do. There's not much chance of the baby surviving if it's born this early."

"I will go to her," Jonas said soberly out of respect for everyone present. He wanted to shout at the doctor, to shake him, to force him to do more for Acadiana than he was doing.

"Wait." The doctor's look was tired but sympathetic. "The best thing you can do for your wife is to let her sleep. Sit with her if you must, but do not wake her for any reason."

With as much composure as he could master, Jonas assured the doctor he would take care and left the room. His footsteps were slow, heavy as his heart, as his feet dragged him up the stairs. His mind was tormented by stories he had heard of women dying in childbirth, of babies stillborn. What price was he to pay for desiring this woman and wanting an heir? Prayers were wrenched from his heart, but no peace followed the silent pleas. He wondered if the great omnipotent God even heard, then chastised himself for the irreverent thought. He found himself making bargains—patience, celibacy, his life for hers—but did not dare to blaspheme his Maker again.

Jonas approached Acadiana slowly, relieved to see that she slept, her dark lashes resting like thick fans on her pale cheeks. She was too frail to be burdened with his child, he thought as his eyes drank in her slender shoulders and her delicate hands where they rested on an abdomen too large for her tiny frame. But she was strong, in temperament and body, and he knew it was his own guilt that made her appear weak to him now. She stirred restlessly, moaning as she thrashed momentarily, and a jolt of sheer, debilitating panic shot through Jonas before she settled back beneath the layers of drug-induced sleep. He had not realized he was holding his breath until it whooshed out, and he commanded his racing heart to steady itself. Dragging a chair beside the bed, he sat down to keep vigil.

It was a long, excruciating night for everyone at Courtland Manor. Jonas never left Acadiana's side, and the hurt that pierced his heart each time she moaned was like nothing he had ever felt before. Never had he known one could feel so vulnerable, so bereft of power, and he wondered fleetingly if it wouldn't have been better to have entered into a loveless marriage where superficial pleasantries were the only requirement, where duty and respect were the sum total of a man's responsibilities toward his wife. The thought was snuffed quickly, for he would have it no other way. If he had never met Acadiana, never known the joy of her smile, the anger of her rebellion, the passion of their bodies' joining, he would have loved her still. In the dark and empty places of his heart, he would have loved what he had not known. And at some point in his meaningless life he would have realized that he had been cheated somehow.

The contractions began to subside close to midnight only to return as dawn rose over an exhausted household. Jonas never slept, but stayed by his wife's side in silent agony each time she cried out in semidelirium, stroking her fevered brow and riding out the storm determined to see her through. Though he appreciated their concern, he shook his head firmly each time a family member came to relieve him. Dr. Loreau gave Acadiana more sedation just after daybreak, and she fell once again into a tortured sleep.

The feeble winter sun approached noon, and Acadiana roused, but her eyes were vacant, seeing that which no one else could. *"Non!"* she cried out fiercely. "You cannot have this life too!" Her covenant made, she drifted back to sleep, this one restless but restorative.

The pains that had plagued her throughout the night seemed to fade with the declaration, and by midafternoon they had stopped. The household rejoiced when the doctor felt confident enough to leave, giving explicit instructions for Acadiana to remain in bed no less than two weeks, at which time he would return to issue further instructions pending her condition.

Her body ached, and her mind seemed incapable of coherent thought as Acadiana struggled to open her eyes. The room swam briefly before her vision stabilized, and the sight that greeted her caused her to sit up abruptly. Jonas, his eyes red-rimmed and bleary, his face unshaven, loomed over her.

"Lie back down," he commanded softly, and the smile of relief so evident on his face sent a swarm of butterflies humming through her stomach.

"My son?" she asked anxiously.

"Our daughter is fine," he answered, and the teasing

smile that accompanied those cherished words sent the butterflies racing to her heart. "She moves. See?" he said, placing his hand over hers on her abdomen.

Acadiana's smile was nothing short of blissful relief as she gazed into her husband's weary face. "He is strong," she sighed. "Stronger than you, I'll warrant. You look tired, *M'sieu* Husband."

He nodded and brought her hand to his lips. "The night was long, love. I've aged a century. I don't think I could take another fright such as the one you gave me last night."

"But all is well." It was more statement than question. She could vaguely remember the doctor's words that the danger was past. Her brow furrowed as she tried to recollect what had brought her to this point. The madman was dead. Had someone told her? She couldn't recall, but somehow she knew. God forgive her, she was glad. Her eyes, shadowed by hurtful images, lifted to Jonas's. Fatigue was outlined in his drawn mouth and the dark circles under his eyes. He must have stayed by her all night. The thought warmed Acadiana. It felt like . . . she had never felt the like before, but it was good. So good! "Come," she said softly while patting the bed beside her. "You look like you could use a rest."

Jonas's eyes squeezed shut and a tired smile split his handsome face as his head dropped back. "Ah, the wench finally beckons me to her bed when I can do nothing but hold her. Cruel, love, very cruel."

Acadiana blushed prettily and smiled in spite of his words. "Come," she simply said, and held out her hand.

Jonas undressed and slipped in beside her, cradling her body close, pulling her head to his shoulder where he could stroke her hair and lose himself in the joy of having her safely beside him. Too soon he would have to face the British invasion of Louisiana, confront Robert Clayton, and decide what he must do about both. But for now he would sleep in his wife's arms and pretend that the rest of the troubled world did not exist.

Jonas slept hard the rest of the day and all that night. He awoke rested, but found it impossible to feel refreshed with the weighty problems before him. He needed to talk to his mother, confront Robert Clayton, but the British would not await his leisure. He sent Cain for news but there was no word other than the British were still landing troops. He knew he could not delay telling Acadiana that he might have to leave, but he dreaded the confrontation with her as much as he dreaded facing the British. He could not bear the thought of upsetting her during this critical time, but if he must go, she would need to be prepared.

He found Minette sitting on the back gallery, ignoring the winter chill as she stared sightlessly across the grounds, her features wan and aged.

"Was Robert Clayton one of the men Armand Hamilton accused of trying to run him off his land?" Jonas asked without preamble.

"He was the primary suspect," Minette confessed dully. "Do you remember the Spaniard, Diablo?"

Jonas nodded, feeling sick inside. A man of ill repute, Diablo had been a companion of Otis Johnson and was always up to no good. "He was killed in a duel over a married woman some years back, I believe."

"Yes." Minette sighed. "Otis and Diablo were seen at separate times near the fires on Armand's place. Armand confronted Robert on several occasions, but he had no proof. Robert would become enraged and threaten to throw Armand out."

"Why would Clayton want to run Acadiana's parents out?" Jonas asked pointedly, the hatred burning through him more evident in his tight jaw than words. "Why would he have them killed!"

"No reason!" Minette said adamantly, shaking her head to decry the words. A single tear rolled down her cheek and she sobbed once, steadying herself. "No reason for actions such as those. Robert did not do it, Jonas."

"Then why, Mother?" he asked softly, steely. "Why did Armand think Clayton was behind it all?"

Minette dropped her eyes to the hands that lay like cold stones in her lap. It should not have come to this. All the pain and accusations were a lifetime ago. Elaine had sat before her then just as Jonas did now with the same questions, the same soulful hurt in her eyes. Then as now, Minette could not answer, could only speculate as to the reasons. She lifted her eyes to her son's.

"Robert Clayton loved Elaine Belizaire. He and Armand were rivals for her affection. After Armand won her hand, he believed Robert was out to ruin him for revenge."

Jonas glared at his mother, stricken, disbelieving. He had known Robert Clayton his entire life, and although he was a solemn man at times, Jonas had liked and respected him. "Could he have grown to hate them so much?" he whispered.

"No!" Minette said fiercely. "I am certain Robert would never have been able to do those things, no matter how damning the evidence looks. I have known him a long time, Jonas. He is not the type of person who is capable of such a thing." Minette pressed a linen napkin to her lips and shut her eyes for a moment. Her son was well aware of the trials of the Cajun people, but she hated to speak openly of it. "Robert's parents opposed his infatuation with Elaine Belizaire. No matter how sweet and beautiful she was, they could not see past the fact that she was Acadian. They were struggling to make a place for themselves in an area populated mainly with French and Spanish nobility, and felt Elaine's heritage would be a hindrance. They arranged Robert's marriage to Beth's mother, a lovely French girl, and he accepted their decision for the good of the family. I have no doubt that he hated Armand, but he had no right to vengeance. By his own decision, Elaine was free to choose Armand without bringing shame on Robert."

"Then why?" Jonas asked, his tone clipped and mistrustful. "Why did Armand suspect him?"

"Not only were Robert's men seen at the source of the fires more than once, but years before that Robert had tried to buy that land from your grandfather. When *Grand-père* Courtland sold the land to Armand, it made Robert appear the loser again, or so Armand thought."

"What about Clayton's men? Could they have been working on their own?" Jonas asked grimly.

"One would hope that is the case, yes?" Minette said, but even her own tone lacked conviction now. "But what would they stand to gain? If they were successful in running the Hamiltons out, that still left them with nothing. Neither Otis nor Diablo could afford to buy the land. What would they gain by murder?"

"Then the evidence still points to Robert."

Minette shook her head. "I know, but I have known Robert too long to believe him capable of such despicable things. He has been a good neighbor and a good friend. It is not so! I am convinced of this no matter how it all looks."

Jonas was not in the least convinced, but he nodded out of respect for his mother, her pale features a further burden to carry as he formulated his plans. He would confront Clayton himself, and he would go armed. As he rose to leave, Minette's hand reached out to grab his.

"I do not want Beth hurt."

"No," he said, but didn't know if he could avoid it.

A visit to Robert Clayton yielded Jonas nothing. Robert had seemed alarmed but had adamantly stuck to his story of knowing nothing. Jonas had been forced to leave lest he resort to violence, and had called in the sheriff to investigate.

He waited for two days, watching Acadiana's condition for signs of decline, and balancing his concern for her with his guilt for not being in New Orleans. A messenger arrived the evening of December 29, and Jonas knew he could not delay a decision much longer.

Just the morning before, British General Sir Edward

Pakenham had ordered troops forward to pierce the American defensive line, turn the flanks, and force a retreat. Thankfully, the British had run into an American sheet of shot and shell so terrible that scarcely a ball passed over or fell short of its mark, and the attack had failed.

Though he knew the worst was yet to come, Jonas was heartened by the news. It gave him a few days to see how Acadiana would fare before deciding if she was healthy enough for him to leave her, and allowed him time to procure protection for her around the clock. His most trusted servants had been warned of the danger to his wife, and armed guards patrolled the perimeter of Courtland Manor at all times. The only bright spot in the turbulent days was the fact that Jean Baptiste had arrived to give aid to the American cause, and Jonas had convinced him to remain at Courtland Manor to protect Acadiana. Outside himself, Jonas knew there was no man who loved Acadiana more or would protect her more diligently than the man who had been like a father to her.

Acadiana complied with her forced convalescence gracefully for the first few days. But after that she coaxed, pleaded, begged, and fought for any amount of freedom outside the confining bed. The knowledge of Otis's death had brought her relief from the nightmares, and she felt revived, more alive than she had in years, her energy stifled by restrictions.

"Jonas, please! Just one little walk on the veranda," she said congenially as she fluttered her coal-dark lashes in a most alluring way.

"No!" Jonas yelled for the third time that morning. "You know what the doctor said."

"Charlatans every one!" She pouted, crossing her arms over her enormous stomach.

"Acadiana," he said, sighing, "we've been through this a thousand times. I'm growing quite tired of it."

"Me too, Jonas," she said sweetly. "May I get up?"

"Damn your stubbornness! You are an exasperating

woman!" he called, slamming the door as he stormed from the room. "Mattie! Go sit with her! I cannot endure her complaints any longer!"

"Now, Mast' Jonas," the housekeeper soothed, "she just be tired of stayin' in that bed all day. The doc gonna come by in a week or so, and when he tells her she can git up, she gonna be lots easier to live with."

"Ha!" Jonas snorted. "She has never been easy to live with. Why should she start now?"

Mattie went in to pacify Acadiana, and Jonas stomped off to help Cain. He needed the distraction that hard work would bring. He wanted to throttle his wife, and kiss her, and beat her, and make love to her. But most of all he just wanted her and the baby safe.

The mild winter days had been a great asset to harvesting. Strong backs continued to heave under the great bundles of sugarcane stalks that were gathered and transported by wagon to the mill. Everyone worked vigorously to extract the sweet juice soon to be turned into sugar and molasses for export. Jonas waited daily for his messenger to arrive and strained right along with the workers, welcoming the mind-numbing toil that temporarily brought ease from the thoughts of the British. A meaty hand dropped on his shoulder, and Jonas straightened to see Jean Baptiste grinning broadly at him.

"You got troubles, *m'sieu?*" the furrier asked.

"Damn right, I got troubles," Jonas growled good-naturedly. "About five foot three inches' worth!"

Jean let out a bellow of laughter and rocked back on his heels, all the while shaking his head. "I could have tol' you that. But nobody ask ole Jean when they go to marryin' Elaine Belizaire's wild *bébé*. Foolish man what do that, for sho!"

"For sure," Jonas echoed. He extended his hand and felt the bones squeezed beneath Jean's vigorous shake. "Have you been up to the house to see her this morning?"

"*Oui,* but she 'bout made this ole man crazy beggin' to

get out the bed." Baptiste shook his head ruefully. "I t'ink it safer to come help with the cane, and less work!"

On New Year's Day the British attacked again. It was totally unexpected because the Creole holiday had begun in a dense fog. Jackson had consented to a grand review of the army, and the bands had begun to play and the Americans to parade up and down the open field behind their earthworks when the fog lifted and a blast from twenty-four British cannon broke over the line. Confusion reigned supreme as the Americans scrambled back to their breastworks to man their guns. Even though they had only fifteen guns with a mere two-thirds of the weight of metal hurled by the British cannon, the Americans once again carried the day and stopped the British from invading New Orleans.

Despite the victory, New Orleanians were fearful during the week following the Battle of New Year's Day. A messenger arrived at Courtland Manor with the news that the British had yet to throw their full strength against Jackson, and the people were beginning to panic. Jackson and Claiborne were quarreling over the declaration of martial law, and it was charged that certain legislators wished to surrender the city without a fight, and that a few had even communicated with the British. It was also rumored that a number of French Creoles were appealing to the French consul for protection as Frenchmen instead of Americans should the British capture and sack the city. British spies and American traitors were abundant, giving complete information as to American army strength and the location of troops. Everyone in New Orleans was apprehensive and many had left the city.

Jonas could wait no longer. The request had gone out for reinforcements, and he knew it was time to throw his weight behind the American cause. He gathered the men who would stand with him, Creoles, Cajuns, and freemen of color from the Teche region, and prepared to leave Courtland Manor Plantation in Edward's capable hands.

Acadiana took the news better than he had expected, and although his heart was heavy with unspoken fears, he was able to take leave of her without the confrontation he had thought would arise. She had routed his biggest concern by promising to follow the doctor's orders to the letter and assured Jonas that he should have no fear for her while he was gone but to protect himself at all cost and return soon.

The brave, dry-eyed front she had put on before her husband crumbled into a wailing mass of womanhood as soon as he rode out of sight. Acadiana collapsed on their bed with more tears than she had ever shed in all her turbulent life. It was the cruelest thing imaginable, to have a husband go off to fight, to not know if he would be wounded or, God forbid, killed. It had taken every bit of strength within her to see Jonas off with an encouraging smile while her heart was being ripped to shreds within her breast.

Once Jonas had explained the full import of what was happening near New Orleans, Acadiana had known what he must do. It didn't stop the fear from gripping her, but it helped her to act brave in the face of his departure. He needed her support, not her tears. But it had taken every ounce of strength she could muster not to cling to him when he took her in his arms for a last farewell kiss. Ever had women been forced to send their men off to war, so why did it feel like she was the only one? The child moved, and Acadiana clutched her stomach protectively as she wept and prayed, and wondered if the babe would ever know his father.

By the time Jonas and the men with him reached New Orleans, there were also two thousand Kentuckians to strengthen Jackson's line of defense. In all, the Americans had about four thousand men against eight thousand or more British. Although outnumbered, the Americans were ready. Their lives, their land, their hard-won and precious way of life were threatened. To be defeated would mean being destroyed.

The morning of January 8 broke with a heavy fog, but

the sounds that had been coming all night long from the British encampment indicated that mischief was afoot. By six o'clock the British columns began to advance in solid ranks. Onward marched the 93rd Highlanders in their bright kilts and tartans, the Duchess of York's Light Dragoons, the King's Own, the 21st Royals, and the Buck Volunteers. The American batteries opened fire, yet the British came, closer and closer still at a deliberate battle march, their boldness and bravery forbidding. But with one major mistake: Their white-webbed bullet- and powder-pouch straps crossed on their chests made them perfect targets.

When the American riflemen opened fire, not in volleys, but with each man firing as he reloaded his gun, the advancing British soldiers fell by the hundreds. The riddled units dropped back, reformed, and advanced again. Battle smoke rose lazily to sting Jonas's eyes and floated in the fog-laden air. He rubbed the sweat from his brow as he took aim and tried to deafen his ears to the staccato *ping* of rifle shot, the crash of cannon, and the yells of soldiers. The martial music of the New Orleans and Plauche bands were not enough to cover the shrieks of the wounded men and hideous screams of mutilated horses.

The pattern of advance, reform, advance repeated itself until the lines wavered and gaping holes suddenly appeared. Tension mounted as the British wounded and dying fell in groups, often five or six men deep. The Americans could feel the taste of victory on their tongues as sharply as they could the salt of their own sweat and the acrid sting of powder smoke. At last human endurance was broken. The British halted, turned, and began to run from the field in frenzied chaos. General Pakenham tried to rally his men with cheers, then tried to shame them as he ordered them to recollect, but he was thrown from his saddle by a mortal bullet, fired by one of the freemen of color Jonas had brought from the Attakapas region. British General Gibbs fell not twenty yards from the earthworks, and General

John Keane was shot through the neck and dropped at the edge of the canal.

The British soldiers who had been brave enough to face Napoleon's grenadiers began to panic and fled the field of carnage and death in disorderly fashion, running to the rear and firing in all directions. Finally the British bugles silenced; its colors trampled in the rich Louisiana earth, and its guns were unable to reply. The proud British were vanquished.

With victory in hand, the Americans broke into cheers. Jackson congratulated his men and ordered some of his troops to collect the wounded. Jonas dragged his weary but elated body onto his horse and went in search of Cain and the others who had come with him. He also tried to find Matthew Hamilton, but his search proved fruitless. At least his brother-in-law was not among the dead or wounded, as far as Jonas could determine. An armistice was declared the next day to bury the dead, and the following day Jonas was on his way home.

18

"The next four weeks are crucial for the safety of your baby, Mrs. Courtland," Dr. Loreau warned, realizing he could no longer restrain his patient. "Six more weeks would be best, but if you can carry the child for at least four, we can be assured of delivering an infant strong enough to survive."

"But I can't stay in this bed four more weeks!" she wailed in despair. She emphasized the fact by rushing back to the window, a spot she had occupied all day since receiving word that the British had been defeated. Feverishly her eyes scanned the carriage lane for some sight of Jonas. He would be home soon! She knew it, willed it to be so within the innermost regions of her heart.

"You don't have to stay in bed, Mrs. Courtland. Just please, *please* exercise caution in your movements!" the doctor said. "Why aren't you like my other patients who insist on being coddled and pampered throughout their confinement?"

"I'm sorry," Acadiana said absently, then turned back with a smile. But Dr. Loreau didn't think she was repentant at all. With the too-bright eyes and whimsical smile, he suspected she made her tall, strong husband weak in the knees. Acadiana knew this man held her freedom in his hands, and strove to be more convincing. "The baby is my foremost concern. I will be ever so careful, *oui?* I merely want to be able to get up and move about normally."

"You are doing that now without my say-so, Mrs. Courtland." He chuckled in spite of himself at her hopeful face. "But my instructions must be followed precisely, or back to bed!"

"Oui!" she said, utterly rhapsodical now that her confinement was finally at an end.

Her euphoria was short-lived, however. At Dr. Loreau's long list of restrictions, she sank into a depressed gloom, but conceded anything would be worth delivering a healthy infant when the time came. She was given permission to move freely about the house in the mornings but was ordered to return to her bed in the early afternoon for a two-hour nap.

Jonas arrived at the entrance of Courtland Manor just as Dr. Loreau was exiting. At the sight of the family surgeon, his heart gave a sickening lurch, but the doctor's hearty welcome eased his mind. After exchanging pleasantries, reassurance of Acadiana's health and her limitations, and a long and drawn-out recounting of the Battle of New Orleans, Jonas finally stopped the conversation and looked straight at the doctor. The raw question in Jonas's eyes was strictly man-to-man; no words were necessary.

Dr. Loreau shook his head and sent Jonas an apologetic smile. "Your wife is too far gone in a fragile pregnancy for you to entertain such thoughts, Jonas. Bide your time a bit longer. It will all be over before you know it."

Jonas jerked his horse around without a word and rode straight to the house. He barely had time to dismount before he was attacked from the back by a pair of slender arms. His face split into a huge grin as he carefully turned and enfolded Acadiana. "You are out of bed," he said with a firmness that sounded ridiculous when coupled with the glow in his eyes.

"Oui, the doctor—"

"Says you are to be abed this time of day. I saw him at the edge of the plantation."

Acadiana scrunched her nose up, but all the light in the world was shining in her eyes at the moment. Jonas could not resist the temptation to lower his head and take her lips in a kiss that ended up being so long and hot and utterly passion-ridden that when they broke apart they were both breathing heavily.

Acadiana's eyes were wide and dazed, her cheeks stained a most becoming shade of pink. *"M'sieu* Husband." She sighed weakly. "Welcome home." They were the last private words she would utter for a while, because at that moment the entire population of Courtland Manor Plantation converged around them.

The household had long since learned to turn deaf ears to Acadiana's pleading that she did not need to rest after so much inactivity. Jean visited when he could make time, but that was usually in the evenings. Beth chose the afternoon to pay her calls, making the time much more bearable for Acadiana. They hadn't brought up the subject of Otis. Beth was too afraid of the effect the memory would have on her friend. On the other hand, Acadiana was too concerned about the implications of Otis being Robert's hired man. She knew Jonas was keeping secrets from her, she had seen the armed men prowling the grounds, but in atypical fashion she did not speak of it. It was a time for healing, not hurting, and she trusted Jonas to protect her.

Robert Clayton had been genuinely upset over what had happened to Acadiana Courtland. Granted, he had been unsettled by her appearance the night of the harvest ball. He didn't like the way the haunts of the past revealed themselves in the form of Armand's daughter. The girl looked so much like her mother that it had unnerved him just to be in the same room with her. He had loved Elaine with such a destroying fierceness that he had grown to hate Armand, and in some ways he had hated Elaine for not being his. He had assumed Armand must feel the same about him when the man had come with accusations about his hired man. All the ancient feuding with the Hamiltons had seemed so long ago, until Acadiana had shown up at the ball. Her presence had brought back hurtful memories of a love denied then lost, and when Jonas had shown up making accusations about Otis Johnson, it was like the past revisited. He had been blind then, Clayton admitted, but he saw things clearly now. And he did not like what he was seeing and hearing.

He was through ignoring the rumors tying Otis to the death of Armand and Elaine Hamilton. There was no longer any doubt in his mind that Otis and probably Diablo had been responsible for the nightmarish crime.

Why hadn't he listened so many years ago? At the time he thought Armand was exaggerating Otis's snooping around. He had attributed it to jealous anger. However, he was sure now that Otis had been to blame. Robert felt responsible and would not rest until the answers were found.

Jonas caught sight of the riders thundering toward the mill. He walked out briskly, his heart pounding heavy in his chest, until he realized they didn't come from the direction of the main house. Robert Clayton, already surrounded by Jonas's armed men, jumped from his horse in a rage, dragging a frightened black man to the ground, then shoving him toward Jonas.

"Tell him, Ezra! Tell him everything, or I'll have your hide stripped and hung up for the buzzards! When they get through with you, I'll dump what's left of your worthless carcass in the swamp for the alligators!" Robert shoved the slave again.

"What's going on here?" Jonas asked, confused and somewhat angry as he pulled the slave upright.

"Tell him, Ezra!" Robert ordered again. "Tell Mr. Courtland what you know about Otis and what he was up to all those years!"

"Well, suh . . . ah . . . Otis . . . ah." Ezra shuffled nervously, sweat popping out on his brow as he kicked at the dust with a bare brown toe. "He think there be some buried treasure over there on that land what yo' wife has . . . Otis say it buried in the fields. He wuz tryin' to git that gold all this time. He tried way back when the Hamiltons wuz livin' there, but Mistuh Armand kept runnin' Otis off. So he tries to make them leave . . . but Mistuh Armand, he ain't goin' nowhere fer good, jest says he be back sooner or later . . . so Otis kills him."

Ezra tried to clear his parched throat, but it was too tight for him to do more than swallow. His heart was slamming so hard against his ribs, he feared it would pop out. If his heart didn't kill him, this white man surely would when he heard the rest of the story. He had felt so guilty over what Otis had tried to do to Mr. Courtland's wife that he was certain this was the Lord's way of punishing him. Robert Clayton gave him another shove, and Ezra decided that if his life was going to end he'd just as soon get it over with quickly.

"Otis think that gal dead too, till she show up back here an' sees him." Ezra lifted his frightened eyes for the first time to face the fury in Jonas's. Every inch of his short, square body shuddered at the murderous look in the man's eyes, and he knew the moment of reckoning was upon him. His mouth worked silently for several seconds before the words burst from him. "Oh, Gawd, Mistuh Courtland! Otis say he got to git rid o' her too. He jest plain crazy, suh! I told him I ain't got nothin' to do with no killin'. I swear, suh, I ain't had nothin' to do with that! All I dun wuz help him dig up that ground after Diablo died! They ain't no gold, Mistuh Courtland! That man wuz jest crazy. They ain't no gold! Otis tore all that ground up lookin' for it."

Jonas looked at the frightened man in horror. All the senseless killing—just a crazy old man hunting Acadiana's dreamfields for something that didn't even exist.

"Ezra," Jonas said bitterly, sick to the depths of his soul. "Why did Otis even think there was gold there?"

Ezra stepped back, terrified of the wrath emanating from the man towering over him. Robert shoved him forward and commanded him to speak.

"He say the pirates wuz shippin' stuff in at night down the bayou. He say they wuz hidin' it there. Otis's pa used ta pick it up an take it somewheres afore the Hamiltons moved in. When his pa dies, Otis say he gon start pickin' stuff up, but it jest stop comin'. Otis say the last haul wuz neber found. He look for it all this time."

"This is insane!" Jonas shouted, his teeth grinding in frustration for what Acadiana had been through. "Do you know how crazy this sounds, Ezra?"

"I—I knows, suh," Ezra stuttered, afraid of what this bellowing giant would do to him. "Otis . . . he be crazy, suh. He had a demon in his head sho as the world."

Jonas ran his fingers through his hair, then clenched his fists. It took a supreme effort to keep his mind clear and his hands off Ezra's neck. "Why didn't we see any signs of Otis's digging?"

"He only do it in the spring an' summer when the grass grow back fast. He always shovel the dirt back over real neat, an' the weeds cover it in no time."

Jonas's eyes narrowed, and his voice was now dangerously calm and calculating when he spoke. "Who else was involved, Ezra?"

The black man's weathered face showed his fear and horror. The whites of his eyes bulged; his full lips trembled. "No one, I swear! Ain't nobody else dun nothin' but Diablo afore he gots dead. All I dun wuz help Otis look for that stuff what weren't even there. I ain't dun no killin', Mistuh Courtland, you gots to believe me!"

He fell to his knees in the dirt, groveling, pleading for mercy. Jonas turned away in disgust, trying to summon some pity where there was none. The man had known Otis was planning to murder Acadiana, and Jonas didn't think he could forgive that. He turned to face Robert. "Get him out of here before I kill him with my bare hands!"

Robert hauled Ezra back to the horse and ordered him to get back to the fields. He then turned reluctantly to face Jonas, feeling so much to blame for everything that had happened.

"Jonas, I am so sorry . . . I don't know what to say. I had no way of knowing." Robert's face was a stony reflection of agony as he faced the younger man.

"Robert, please," Jonas said, shaking his head. "There is nothing you could have done."

"Don't patronize me!" Robert spat out bitterly. "I could have listened to Armand. He knew something was going on, but I wouldn't believe him. Elaine Belizaire was one of the strongest, most beautiful women I have ever known. I couldn't forget . . . I couldn't get over her." Robert's words faltered, and he looked around him as if searching for the right words to say. "I was weak—too weak to fight my parents." He gave a short, self-deprecating bark of laughter. "She didn't deserve me after all. I let my pride take hold and wouldn't listen to Armand. I was glad when they left, *glad* so I wouldn't have to see Elaine's lovely face, see the glow of love she had for another man! God"—his voice broke—"what have I done?"

"Robert, stop!" Jonas ordered. He was feeling his own brand of guilt for suspecting Clayton when his mother had tried to convince him otherwise. "You could not have known it would end up this way."

"I might have, if I had listened to Armand. If I had buried my pride and jealousy, I might have seen it coming. I've told myself a thousand times that what happened wasn't my fault, but then I see Armand's angry face accusing Otis and I know I'm as much to blame for their deaths as Otis was."

Robert stared off into the distance, empty yet hurting, unable to atone for the sins of his past, for the jealousy that had blinded him to the truth.

Jonas felt pity for the man who was not to be blamed but harbored all the guilt. In suspecting Robert, Jonas too had been wrong. Although the results had not been the same, he was as much at fault for misconstruing Robert's motives as Robert had been for misconstruing Armand's. A reconciliation was in order, and Jonas offered his hand in truce.

"It's over, Robert. We have to put it behind us and go on."

Robert hesitated, then took Jonas's hand reluctantly. He looked as if he might say something, but ended up just nodding his head. Silently he mounted his horse and rode off.

Jonas turned and went back into the mill to find Edward. He wasn't certain of Robert's mood and felt someone would have to explain things to Beth before she saw her father. He wanted no more bad blood between the two families, especially since he suspected a growing affection between Edward and Beth. There should be no doubts that could mar their relationship in the future.

Edward left immediately after talking to Jonas. This was one visit he did not relish making, having grown so fond of Beth. If Clayton should still feel remorse or guilt, he personally wanted Beth to know that none of the Courtlands blamed her father. Although he had always respected and cared for the young woman, there were new feelings emerging deep within him, and he would not see her hurt.

He rode back to Courtland Manor to change clothes before the confrontation and found Beth sitting with Acadiana in the bedroom. Even in his preoccupation, he noted the animated look on Beth's face as she chatted with his sister-in-law and the nice way the pink of her gown complemented her glowing cheeks. After perfunctorily greeting Acadiana, he turned to the one he had been seeking.

"Beth, may I talk to you, please?" he asked.

"Edward." She blushed at the rather pained but polite look on his face, and her heart seemed to hasten its beating. "Of course. What is it?"

Acadiana smiled at Beth's flushed cheeks. She knew her friend had strong feelings for Edward and wondered when he was going to realize it. From the serious look on his face, perhaps he already had.

"I need to speak to you privately, please," Edward said. "No offense, Acadiana."

"None taken, Edward," she reassured him. "Beth, will you come back when you are through?"

"Certainly," Beth said, very confused now. Privately? Her heart tripled its rate as she rose and followed him out the door.

Later in the garden, Beth clung to Edward's chest and wept silently, her face buried in his shirt. She cried for her father's regrets and the pain he must be suffering, and she cried in relief that the Courtlands had exonerated him of all blame. Though she had never thought her father involved in what Otis had done to Acadiana, she wasn't naive enough to believe that the Courtlands had not suspected him to some degree. She had never been brave enough to ask what they were thinking for fear of their answer. So she had hidden her grief in the hope that all would turn out well. It was a relief to know now that she had not been wrong in her loyalty to her father and that the Courtlands felt no animosity toward him.

"But why?" she cried, lifting shimmering eyes. "Why does he still feel so responsible if no one blames him?"

"No one but himself, Beth," Edward comforted. "Your father feels he must accuse someone, and the men who caused this disastrous affair are dead. He has turned the blame inward."

"I must go to him, make him see—"

"Give him time, Beth," Edward advised her. "He needs to work this out for himself. In time he will realize the truth. He is a strong, wise man; it won't take him long."

Edward stared into Beth's tearful eyes. Sad eyes, the color of dew-kissed clover. He ached to wipe away the hurt, to see the gaiety that was such a natural part of this woman.

Before he realized it, he was kissing her. Not the carefree kiss he had stolen under the mistletoe, but a slow, devouring kiss that consumed them both. He told himself that he was comforting her, offering support, but as Beth ran her fingers lightly along his jaw, Edward could not deceive himself. It was more than brotherly feelings stirring inside of him, more than friendship that was causing his blood to run hot and fast to all parts of his body. Much, much more.

Beth shivered, more from the heat of his kiss than the cold, frosty air. She had always admired Jonas, even fancied herself in love with him when she was very young, but as the years passed she had become somewhat intimidated by his arrogance and his dark moods, and her affection had gravitated toward Edward. Though she had been drawn to the gentler younger brother, she had despaired that he would ever return the feelings she was certain must be so obvious because they were such an integral part of her now. As his mouth devoured hers, she felt herself dissolve against him, weak from the heat, from the love that she had tried to hide so long out of fear of rejection. She shivered again from the force of emotions running rampant through her.

Slowly, reluctantly Edward drew away to gaze down into her eyes. "Cold?" he murmured.

"I . . . ah . . . I don't know," she said breathlessly.

"We better go back inside." He had never hated winter as much as he did right now.

"I guess we should," she said, but it wasn't what she was feeling. She wanted to stay right there and have him kiss her again, to take her away from the depressing thoughts of her father to the bliss beyond. "Edward?"

"Don't say anything, Beth," he warned huskily. In another minute he would have had her down on the cold ground, trying to seduce her. Lord, he'd gone mad!

"Why don't you want me to say anything?" she asked, mildly offended as she looked up from bashful contemplation of his coat buttons.

"Patience is not my best virtue, Beth," he replied, trying

to make light of his overactive senses. "Another kiss like that and I will carry you off to some secluded spot for something we'll regret."

"Why would you regret it?" she asked innocently. The tempo of her heart was running amuck with common sense. She didn't want this moment to end, but wanted to feel herself buried against his chest again, to have his lips on hers until she was mindless from the heat of him.

Edward stared at her, eyes wide. They were treading dangerous ground here. He was aware of what he could do with her trusting innocence, and her openness was a cruel force against his better intentions. "What I have in mind is certainly not proper," he warned in a tone harsher than intended.

"Oh, well, I guess we should certainly be proper." She sighed, feeling deflated as she hooked her arm through his and they starting walking back toward the house. "But what if I don't want to be 'proper'?" came the softly spoken question. She did not dare look at him, but stared studiously ahead of her.

Edward's head snapped up; he stopped in midstride and stared at her with narrowed eyes. "A tumble in the hayloft, Beth? I wouldn't have thought that was your style."

"I don't have a *style!*" she said, insulted by the crude insinuation. She didn't have any experience at all because she had been stupidly saving herself for him! Embarrassment stained her cheeks, and she turned her head away in mortification at her boldness.

Edward cupped her chin and turned her back to face him. "Good," he said softly, then smiled. "What did you have in mind?"

"Nothing," she returned, still piqued. "You are concerned about patience, you tell me."

But no words were necessary as Edward lowered his head once again to capture her lips.

19

$\approx$ $\approx$

Acadiana grew stronger and broader as the weeks flew by. She soon lost any hint of the gracefulness she once possessed, and although clumsy and swollen she reveled in her impending motherhood. The news Ezra had imparted to her husband had been a shocking blow, but she had accepted it with the courage necessary to go on, to look to the future as an antidote for the painful past. The child moved within her often now, and when crushing memories threatened her peace she would think of the babe—this miracle of creation that would be her legacy, the tribute to her parents' dream, and the lifeline to her future with Jonas. The four-week stress-free period prescribed by Dr. Loreau was almost over. In just two or so weeks she would be holding her baby in her arms, singing and cooing to him—or "her," Jonas would say.

It would be a boy. She was certain! A fine, strapping lad the very image of his handsome father. These thoughts engrossed Acadiana as she slowly descended the staircase and waddled toward the dining room for lunch. Jonas rose to seat her, staring at her cumbersome movements.

"Madame, you seem to be slowing down considerably of late."

"But just look how I have retained my girlish figure," she said pertly, then smiled up at him with eyes full of unspoken love. The ordeal with Otis had impressed upon them both how fragile their existence was. Perhaps it was Jonas's gentleness, or his endearing attitude, or merely the nesting instinct within her, but whatever the reason, Acadiana had been more settled these past few weeks. She hadn't been as quick to anger or rebellion, and Jonas's protective hovering had been a soothing balm that helped to heal the nightmare of the past.

She squirmed uncomfortably throughout lunch. She did not seem to fit properly in the chair. She tried leaning forward, for what it was worth, with the huge obstruction barring her way. She tried sliding down in the chair almost in a reclining position. She tried turning this way and that until she finally resumed an upright seat and stared ruefully at the food that was a considerable distance from her mouth.

"Is something wrong, love?" Jonas asked as she shifted positions again.

"*Non.*" She sighed. "I can't reach my food, but I'm not very hungry anyway. My back hurts terribly, and I need a walk!"

Against his better judgment, Jonas gathered her cape and accompanied her out to the garden. They strolled arm in arm across the lawn as a cold breeze tugged at her cloak, whipping tiny tendrils of ebony hair about her face. Acadiana stopped every few minutes to catch her breath and a faint shadow creased her brow.

"It's cold," Jonas said, eyeing her with concern as she stopped once more. "Let's go back."

"*Non!*" she said firmly, startling him. "I need to walk . . . I . . . oooh." She moaned as another pain coursed through her.

"What's wrong?" Jonas asked, frightened by the look on her face and the force with which she gripped his arm.

"Nothing." She smiled as the tightness subsided. "Just a

. . . funny feeling, it comes and goes . . . for a day or so now." Just not quite that hard!

"I think we had best get back."

"Don't be ridiculous." She quickly strolled as far away from him as she dared without causing him alarm. The look she sent him was adamant yet pleading. "If I let you take me back, you'll put me in the bed or commit me to that infernal rocking chair! I am too restless, Jonas. I need to move around. Just a little while . . . oooh . . . longer."

Acadiana clenched her teeth as another pain gripped her. Jonas caught her arm, ready to carry her back to the house, when she pulled away roughly.

"Non, Jonas, *non!"* she said firmly, giving him a hard stare. "I won't go back unless you promise you will let me stay on my feet! A squaw would never lie down this soon. They believe it makes one's labor longer and harder. I will stay up until I am ready to deliver, or I won't go back! Do you want your son born out here in the garden?"

"Daughter!" he corrected before the full import of her words struck him. "Labor . . . ? Labor!" All coherent thought evaporated from his head, then seemed to come flooding back with a rush. "You can stay up and dance a jig for all I care," he said evenly as he walked toward her. "But if you are going to deliver my child today, you will be near the bedroom!" He promptly snatched her up in his arms and headed for the house.

"Non!" she shouted stubbornly, but gripped his neck all the same lest she tumble out of his arms. "It is too soon to . . . oooh . . . send for the doctor. First babies . . . take a long . . . time. Put me down!"

Jonas held her tighter, shaking his head and seething at her defiance. It wasn't as if he could use force to bring her to heel in her condition. The damn obstinate wench would whelp right on the lawn for spite if he wasn't careful. He mounted the steps to the first-floor gallery, ushered her carefully into the hallway, then placed her on her feet with a censorious stare. Acadiana gritted her teeth against the next contraction and stared back at her husband.

"Jonas," she said with a tight-lipped smile. "I think I've neglected to tell you something."

He arched an eyebrow warily, not sure whether he ought to bundle her off to bed or turn her over his knees, present condition or not. "I don't think now is the time for confessions or declarations, my dear."

"It's not that," she snapped.

"Well, what!"

"I do not now, nor have I ever, liked pain."

"Oh, hell!" he growled, and his face lost all color. "Are you in pain?"

"Most definitely!"

"Mother!"

Mattie and Minette both came running as his distressed voice boomed through the house. Acadiana brushed them all away and paced up and down the wide entrance hall, refusing to listen to their pleas for her to explain her agitated state.

"Jonas, what is going on here?" Minette asked with concern as she took in Acadiana's pale, drawn face.

"She is having a baby. Indian style!" Jonas said, pacing step for step behind Acadiana. He looked as if he would like nothing better than to throttle his stubborn wife. "She seems to think it is best to deliver my daughter headfirst onto the floor! I suppose Indians are opposed to comfort!"

"Son! . . . our son . . . oooh, Jonas." Acadiana winced as the pain grew to engulf her entire lower abdomen, back, and thighs. "Say we'll have a son. I want him to have blue eyes and—"

"All right, Acadiana! We'll have a son. *Now* will you go to bed?"

"Non, I won't go to bed." The pain eased and she stopped pacing to slump against the wall. Her voice was weak, her words disoriented when she spoke. "Maybe we *will* have a daughter. Oh, Jonas, you won't be disappointed if it's a girl,

will you?" With dazed interest, she took in his harassed expression.

"Acadiana, please! Can we discuss this in the bedroom? I will love it no matter what it is! A daughter will be fine!"

"Son! It is going to be a . . . oooh . . . son . . . Jonaaaas." She groaned, gripping the wall for support. "I'm . . . I can't do this. I'm not really an Indian, you know." Her legs started to tremble, and she slowly began sliding down the wall as she called out weakly, "Jonas, *help.*"

With a snarled oath, Jonas caught her up in one quick motion and took the stairs two at a time. Minette and Mattie exchanged worried glances, then rushed to follow behind them.

Jonas sat Acadiana on the bed and began to unfasten her dress. She brushed his hands away in modesty. He growled back at her in protest. Mattie quickly stepped in and sent Jonas out with instructions to find Cain to get the doctor.

Mattie helped Acadiana change, made a cursory examination, then saw her situated in the bed. She was just pulling the covers up when Jonas returned in a rush.

"I can't find Cain," he said breathlessly. "He's not at the mill." His mouth went dry as he looked anxiously at his wife's pain-contorted face. "God, are you all right, Acadiana? I'll have to go for the doctor myself."

"There ain't no need, Mast' Jonas," Mattie said calmly. "They ain't gonna be enough time for the doc to git here. Git on down to the quarters and fetch Naomi. Tells her I needs her straightaway."

"What are you saying?" Jonas asked in sheer panic.

"Git, boy! That's what I'm sayin'! Go to fetchin' Naomi!"

Jonas knew better than to argue with Mattie when she used that tone of voice. He left immediately, praying he could find Naomi in time.

"Miz 'Nette, you go on and git me plenty of fresh linens, some hot water, scissors, an' string. You know the stuff." She looked at Minette's worried expression and laughed softly. "Git on now. This ain't the first baby gonna be birthed in this house."

Acadiana tossed restlessly in the grip of another contraction. She clutched at the covers until her knuckles were white and beads of perspiration began to form on her brow. Despite her protests earlier, it was good to be lying in the master bed that she shared with her husband. The familiarity of the room and the rightness that their first child should be born here comforted her as another spasm of pain gripped her.

"Mattie, how long is this going to take?" she asked frantically.

"Settle down, honey pie, you gonna need your strength for later. Just go with the pains. Don't fight 'em."

Acadiana calmed down listening to Mattie's soothing voice. She tried to relax as each contraction ripped through her body, consuming her, but it was getting harder and harder not to cry out with the overwhelming cramps.

Naomi, Jonas, and Minette reached Acadiana's room at the same time, and all three tried to rush through the doorway. Mattie pulled Naomi in, grabbed the linens from Minette, and ordered Jonas out.

"Don't you leave me, Jonas Courtland!" Acadiana cried out. She wanted him to stay by her, to give her the strength to get through the hours ahead, but her mind was darkened by the pain as were her words. "You did this to me! How dare you leave at a time like this, you coward . . . you . . . you . . . oooh!" She was the coward, lost without him, needing him to be able to hold up under the excruciating agony.

Jonas's face paled with the force of his wife's words. He stood as if frozen, staring at the strain on Acadiana's face.

"I'll call you when it's time," Mattie said, pushing Jonas and Minette out the door. "I'll send Naomi down when we got some news."

"Well!" Minette started before Mattie slammed the door firmly in her face. She turned her attention to her thoroughly demoralized and panic-stricken son. "Women say things they do not mean at a time like this," she said soothingly as she coaxed him down the stairs. "You should have heard the things I said to poor Jon when each of you was born."

"Mattie, I've changed my mind." Acadiana moaned weakly. "Tell Jonas that he can have a daughter later. I can't do this right now!"

"It's jest a little late to be talkin' like that, honey chile," Mattie chuckled.

"I mean it. I just need to rest for a little while. I'll have a baby later," Acadiana pleaded. "Oooh!" It began again. Her abdomen hardened and cramps racked her body, forcing her to cry out. *"Mon Dieu,* I'll never forgive him for this! I just know I won't! Do you hear me, Jonas Courtland?"

He did. Sweat broke out on his brow; his mouth went dry, and Minette had to forcefully pull him down the rest of the way before he buckled.

"That's right, honey," Mattie soothed, "raise a ruckus. You jest fuss all you wants, if it makes you feel better."

"It doesn't make me feel better," Acadiana argued, her face awash with fear as her body demanded things she was not yet ready to handle.

"Then jest try to relax, sweet baby," Mattie crooned. She ran a damp cloth over Acadiana's feverish face and told her about the time Cain was born in the heat of the summer, about how lucky she was to be delivering in the winter. The words helped distract Acadiana for a while until the intensity of the pains became unbearable. She gripped the sheets and bit her bottom lip until she drew blood to keep from screaming, feeling as if her body were being torn apart.

Jonas paced unwaveringly back and forth across the carpet while Minette sat demurely wringing her hands in the dimly lit library. Edward walked into the room, taking in the oddly silent scene.

"Why are you sitting in the dark?" he asked in surprise.

"You look like you've just lost your best . . . where's Acadiana? What has happened?"

"Nothing yet," Jonas said. "We're still waiting."

"For what? Uh-oh! She's having the baby, isn't she?" Edward was amazed at their calmness, unaware that his brother and mother had simply fallen into a worried stupor.

"Edward!" Minette said, startled as if noticing him for the first time. "Cade is having the baby. Mattie is with her."

Edward fell in line, pacing step for step behind Jonas in the unbearable silence. They looked like a somber marching brigade as they made several passes around the room.

Minette, with all her years of unwavering strength, could not find the words to comfort her son. Cade was her daughter, the child of her heart if not her body, and she could only pray silently for the safety of the baby and his mother. She watched her eldest son's tortured face as he strode by, knew his heart and his mind as well as her own. If there had ever been any doubt about his devotion to Cade, it would have been shattered now. He was in misery, unable to allow the excitement of the birth of his firstborn to infringe on his concern for his wife. Minette could sympathize, but let him work through the pain on his own, knowing her words would be meaningless. And as the seconds stretched into minutes, and the minutes into hours, she knew that perhaps the heartfelt agony was God's way of strengthening the bond between couples.

Their procession was halted by a piercing wail from above. Jonas bolted from the library, followed by Edward and Minette. Two more screams followed, freezing them halfway up the stairs. Minette took Jonas's hand for reassurance and drew him up.

Just as they reached the top Naomi stuck her head out with a grin broad enough to crack her face. "It be a girl! You can come see in a minute." She shut the door before anyone could say a word.

His breathing was still labored, but the tension left Jonas's haggard face to be replaced by a faint, absurd smile.

Relief washed through him, leaving his head light and dizzy. He knew by Naomi's smile that Acadiana was well, and he could hear the child, his daughter, wailing in the background. He knew a joy more complete than any he had ever experienced. His eyes stung with the force of emotion and he closed them a second to offer a silent prayer of thanksgiving. He barely had a moment to accept Minette and Edward's congratulations before Mattie stuck her head out the door.

"It be a boy, Mast' Jonas! He tiny, but he strong!" she said, slamming the door shut once again.

Jonas looked around him, shaken, his relief abruptly vanishing. "What's the matter with them? Can't they tell the difference?"

Minette composed herself and refused to face the horrors of a malformed child. As long as Acadiana and baby survived . . .

"Massa Jonas, you can come in now," Naomi said with a giggle.

Jonas rushed through the door, then stopped and resumed walking at a slower pace, almost afraid to approach his wife. Acadiana was pale, as pale as death, he thought as he moved to her bedside. "How are you, love?" he whispered. He had faced danger countless times, in the wilderness, on the battlefield, yet he felt distinctly queasy as he caught sight of Mattie and Naomi discreetly removing the bloody linens. He had confronted worse fear over the last few hours than he had faced in a lifetime, and for the briefest second he thought that if he had to withhold himself from Acadiana he would do just that not to have to go through this again.

"Tired"—she sighed, smiling—"and very happy. Jonas, that was the hardest thing I've ever done, and it hurt like . . . well, it hurt." She reached out weakly and intertwined her fingers with his. "I'm glad it's over."

"Me too." He smiled wanly back at her. "I'm sorry you had to go through it, but you've made me very happy." His voice was constricted. He brought her hand to his lips in a gesture more eloquent than words.

"That's a relief," she said in a faint but spunky tone.

Jonas laughed and reached for her other hand, kissing each finger lovingly, then dropped his head to rest on her breast. "You are well?" he asked, wondering what she was feeling there where her heart beat so slowly against his cheek, wondering if she would forgive him for putting her through this.

Acadiana stroked his sable hair tenderly, feeling her love for him swell up within her until she thought it would burst the boundaries of her mortal body, and wondered if his gentle care of her, his obvious concern, meant that her feelings were reciprocated though the words had never been spoken. *"Oui,* I am well, and I am sorry for the things I yelled at you when Mattie made you leave the room. Will you forgive me, *M'sieu* Husband, if I promise to be a biddable wife in the future?"

Jonas sighed in relief and felt the joy rumble within him until it came out in a soft laugh. He lifted his head, grinning at Acadiana's delicate features. "My love, what would I do with a biddable wife?"

"Become a biddable husband?" She flashed him a smile so bright it melted Jonas clear down to his toes. And when his laughter came it was rich and deep and surrounded her so securely that she basked in the comfort of it.

"I'm confused," Jonas said evenly. "Who won?"

"We both did," Acadiana said, pointing at Mattie and Naomi each holding a bundle.

"Twins?" he asked in mingled shock and relief. It took him a moment to recover, but when he did his face split into a grin. "I should have known, love. You never do anything halfway."

"You helped," she said wearily, "a little."

Mattie and Naomi walked over to Jonas, carefully holding their precious bundles. Jonas's eyes widened as he viewed the red, wrinkled infants. They didn't look at all like the babies he remembered seeing. "Are they all right?" he asked, unsure. "They look sort of . . . odd."

"They'll fill out," scolded Mattie. "They jest come a little early, but they be strong for twins. You best git your ma now afore she break the door down."

Jonas hurried to admit Minette and Edward and proudly displayed his new son and daughter, relieved that his mother didn't find anything unusual in their appearance. Edward's expression, however, was dubious.

"Have you named them yet?" Minette asked Acadiana as she bent to kiss her forehead.

"Not yet, *Grand'mère,* we were too busy fussing over whether it was a boy or girl."

Everyone took a turn holding the infants, then Jonas took them to Acadiana. He brushed back her wet hair and bent to kiss her warmly. She smiled up at him with so much love and pride in her accomplishment, it made his heart ache.

"Thank you," he said, kissing her again. "You did a fine job of starting our family. How did we come by twins? I don't know of any on my side of the family."

Acadiana awkwardly tried to brush away a tear while holding her babies. It had been years since she had remembered her mother making mention of such a thing. "My brother Matt was a twin. The other baby did not survive the birth. I wish he could have been here, Jonas. He would have been so proud—" Her voice broke from weariness and old memories.

Jonas took a deep breath and looked at his wife with pity. Damn you, Hunter, his heart cried out. Damn your black soul for hurting her this way. Damn you to hell for marring the beauty of this moment. He wanted to tell Acadiana about her brother but dared not. He couldn't even be sure the man was still alive.

Acadiana lifted her shimmering eyes to his. "I'm sorry. I did not mean to bring up the past. Please, I just want to rest now and hold my . . . our children." She winced and tried to shift to a more comfortable position. Coal-black lashes fluttered down to shield the pain and exhaustion in her eyes.

Jonas tucked the covers in around her, then gazed at each of his children. His eyes wandered back to his wife, and he stroked her pale cheek.

"I love you," he whispered.

Acadiana never heard his last words. She was already in a deep, exhausted slumber—her babies securely by her side.

At the tender age of two weeks, Armand Cade and Catherine Elaine were baptized. Despite his earlier reservations, Jonas was quite sure that no two children in existence were as beautiful as his; Acadiana quite agreed. As with most couples newly awakened to the role, they were proud parents, basking in the wonder of creation, diligent yet fretful in their caretaking, determined to give their all in nurturing the tiny beings whom God had entrusted to them. There was a unity of purpose for Jonas and Acadiana, strong, forged in unspoken love, and they were aglow with the deepening bond between them.

The February air was warm considering the time of year as a happy group left the church. Edward and Beth had been chosen as the twins' godparents and took the honor to heart, showering them with gifts both humorous and cherishing. There were specially engraved silver cups and spoons, intricately carved wooden soldiers, and porcelain dolls gowned in the finest linen and lace. Everyone returned to Courtland Manor for refreshments in celebration of the occasion.

"Whom do they look like?" Jonas asked as he held the two sleeping babes before handing them over to Mattie and Minette.

"They certainly don't look like my family," said Acadiana. "What little hair they have is too light."

"It will probably darken," Jonas said. "Then again, one of my ancestors was a big, blond English—"

Minette rapped her son sharply with her fan, looking

every inch the offended grand dame. "Such talk, when our own *Louisiane* has just been attacked by the British! Why, we must be thankful that New Orleans still stands! It is not necessary to draw attention to the fact that there is a taint in the blood!"

Jonas sent his mother a stern look yet spoke as if to soothe her. "General Jackson has managed to keep us safe. We can be thankful to the Kaintucks and Tennesseans, Lafitte's army of pirates, Cajuns, Creoles, Indians, and freemen of color. It was a grand effort on everyone's part, no matter what their background. But make no mistake, the British were beaten. They've returned to their own soil because their soldiers were no match for our terrain. It's being said they were defeated as much by our swamps and mosquitoes as they were our men."

"Nonsense!" Minette scoffed. "It was the proud French heritage in most of our fighters that carried the day."

Jonas realized that in no way would *he* carry the day, and reverted to his previous conversation as he studied his children. "At least they have my eyes."

A round of gentle laughter rippled through the ladies, breaking the tension. "Most babies are born with blue eyes," teased Acadiana, "but perhaps theirs won't change."

"Either way," replied Jonas, undaunted by their amusement, "they are the most handsome children."

Their conversation was interrupted by the majordomo, who admitted a coachman delivering ornately wrapped gifts for the twins.

"You two!" Acadiana laughed at Edward and Beth. "If you do not stop lavishing these babies with gifts, they will become unbearably spoiled. *Mais oui,* that is the luxury of a *parrain* and *marraine,* is it not? They spoil the children, then *Maman* is left to tolerate them."

Puzzled, Edward looked to Beth for confirmation. At a shake of her head, he turned back to Acadiana. "Sorry, we didn't send them this time."

"Jonas, *Grand'mère?*" Acadiana addressed them dubiously. "Which one of you . . . ?" The air was suddenly charged with unexplainable tension, as if this scene had been played before but the outcome unknown. A whisper of something forceful yet intangible flowed among the occupants, but none felt it more keenly than Acadiana.

"I sent them," a deep, lazy voice droned from the doorway. Everyone turned, speechless, to see a tall, dark man with cold amethyst eyes leaning against the door frame.

Acadiana sat as if frozen and stared at the familiar face from her past. His features were older, more mature, in some ways the same, yet . . . not. The eyes were guarded, the grin arrogant. She blinked rapidly to clear the specter from her vision, the ghost seeming too real, looking too real and solid for an apparition. When her eyes focused he was still there, bold as ever, and staring back at her.

"Matt? Matthew?" she asked weakly. Confusion reigned within her heart and mind. She felt disoriented. Slowly, one crystal drop at a time, tears began rolling down her pale cheeks. Her bottom lip trembled.

"Cade," he whispered hoarsely, feeling as if the whole world had just come crashing into his gut. Slowly Matthew pushed off the doorframe and walked into the room. He gave Jonas a barely perceptible nod, then let his gaze wander back to his sister. He should have allowed Jonas to tell her. Hurt and confusion was evident in her dazed eyes, in the trembling fingers pressed to her lips. His own eyes saw what his mind had not been able to credit. She was no longer a child, but a woman fully grown with a radiance of grace and beauty and the innate strength that had been their mother's. He steeled his heart against the crushing blow, but no power on earth could stop the destructive force of regret, of love betrayed by his own hand.

Flesh and blood had spoken to Acadiana. No phantom, no astral spirit from her past. No hellish dream that shattered her nights and lingered restively to mar her days. He was real and alive and standing before her bold as brass. As if a fierce wind had suddenly blown through the room, the reverie was shattered. Acadiana's face, fused with red showed her fury.

"Matthew Huntington Hamilton," she accused with all the virulence of one wronged. "How dare you! How dare you come back here alive after all this time!"

"Cade," Matthew drawled, a cynical twist to his lips at the sudden transition from dazed innocence to angry animosity. "I can explain."

So much for warm homecomings, he realized, and backed up quickly as she lunged to her feet like an avenging angel and approached him.

"Why aren't you dead? *Mon Dieu,* do you know how long I have grieved for you!" she shouted, her words cutting like a saber. "For years I have mourned the loss of my brother! Years!"

"I can explain," he warned, rounding a sideboard laden with china. He glanced at the expensive pieces, then stepped behind the sofa to put distance between them.

With commendable effort, Jonas restrained the impulse to laugh. Ah, if Jean Lafitte could see his cold-hearted lieutenant now! He also fought the urge to place himself between brother and sister and call for peace. They would have to work through the anger and hurt if there was ever to be a reconciliation for the future.

"Explain? *Mais non!* There is nothing you can say that will wash away the loneliness and hurt that has devoured me for eleven years." Acadiana's voice broke, and she struggled to regain her composure. "How could you have been so cruel? How could you have let me go on thinking that you were dead, Matthew?" The tears began again, angry and hurtful tears that she would have given anything to be able to stop. "I was a child alone, thinking I had lost everyone and everything dear to me!" She swung at him with one puny fist, but Matthew had put too much distance between them.

Hunter fought her words, the pain that could bring him to his knees, but Matthew, the brother, shared her anguish

His remorse at not informing her years ago that he was alive was compounded by guilt that even so, he could not have taken care of her, not then in the early days. It was only later that he could have given her support, but by then so much time had passed. Still, he had betrayed her and, in so doing, had betrayed himself.

Acadiana stopped suddenly when Catie began to cry. She cast her brother a condemning look, as if he were solely responsible for waking the child, then rushed to soothe her infant daughter.

Matthew breathed a sigh of relief at the interruption and turned a guilty look on his amused brother-in-law. "Jonas," he said wryly, "so good to see you again."

"Matthew." Jonas chuckled, shaking his head. "You do make an entrance."

"You knew?" Acadiana gasped, her eyes glaring at her husband in stunned and hurt disbelief. "Jonas, how could you?" Her anger was now directed toward her husband, the man she had grown to trust above all others. "How could you know and not tell me?"

"He asked me not to say anything," Jonas said simply, his sapphire eyes sincere and apologetic. It had not been pleasant, withholding the truth from her, but he had given his word. "Please understand, Acadiana, that I could not break my oath to your brother no matter how badly I wanted to." His eyes implored her to forgive what he could not change. "After the Battle of New Orleans, I wasn't even sure he was still alive. But I would have told you sooner or later, if Matthew had not come forward. I would have told you one day when I felt the time was right."

"I do not need to be coddled!" she argued.

"But I would protect you." Jonas sighed.

Acadiana sat down in a haze of mixed emotions, her eyes dry now but full of pain and betrayal. "I'll speak with you later," she said, then turned her full attention on her brother. The knowledge that Matthew was alive began to overwhelm her anger, though she held on to it with a mea-

ger, self-righteous shred of stubbornness. But it was to
difficult to remain cold and aloof toward the brother wh
had been so dear to her, who was now miraculously aliv
and well and close enough to touch.

"Matthew, you were supposed to have drowned," sh
said, her voice flat, not revealing her innermost joy at find
ing him alive. Her eyes, however, were fixed to his belove
face—a face she sensed had seen too much over the pas
eleven years to ever recapture the *joie de vivre* that had bee
a part of the boy she remembered.

"Did you see a body?" he asked, unruffled. He caught th
glimmer beneath the cool surface of her violet eyes, eyes s
like his own they spoke a wealth of feeling she was desper
ately trying to conceal.

"Non, but several people disappeared during that time
Clyde Deveraux's wife never found his body either. It wa
presumed he had drowned also."

"Deveraux was first mate on the ship I boarded."

"Ship?"

Matthew sent a sidelong glance at the occupants in th
room and sensed there would be no secrets here. His gaz
then sought out his brother-in-law, but Jonas merely shoo
his head with a This-is-between-the-two-of-you look.

"Listen, Cade," Matthew said as he walked over and sa
down beside her. "At first I thought you had been kille
with *Maman* and Papa. After I found out that you wer
living with Jean, I was too deeply involved to show myself.

"Involved in what?" she asked, confused. But in man
ways the answer no longer mattered. She had Jonas, he
children, and now Matthew. What more could she ask fron
a world that had been so troubled and was now so full? He
heart was fairly bursting with joy, and all she wanted to d
now was hug Matthew close and make certain he never lef
her again. His reasons for staying away from her hurt like
physical blow, but the healing was in seeing him again. Sh
took his hand and put it to her cheek, reassuring hersel

that he was truly alive, not some apparition from the past come back to haunt her.

"My chosen profession is rather unconventional," Matthew ventured in careful tones.

Acadiana eyed him suspiciously but squeezed his hand. "I have always been rather 'unconventional' myself." Someone chortled in the room, and it sounded suspiciously like her husband, but when Acadiana looked at him, his expression was as innocent as his sleeping son's.

"So I've heard," Matthew said ruefully. "But not nearly as foolish as myself, I'll wager."

"Some would beg to differ with you." Acadiana smiled for the first time but quickly sent Jonas a look that dared him to agree with her. "So, who is to blame here? My silent husband or disappearing brother?"

"Your privateering brother will have to accept the full measure of your wrath," Jonas said when it seemed apparent that Matthew could not find the words. "I was keeping my mouth shut only to protect my unborn children."

"Privateering?" Acadiana's eyes grew round, then narrowed as the word struck a raw wound within her. "A corsair? A pirate? You despicable creature! You went off with those men, *oui*? The ones we used to watch sneak up the bayou at night."

"Guilty," Matthew said coldly. They had spent many hours hiding in the grass, watching the boats row up the bayou when they were supposed to be sleeping. She more than anyone should have understood his fascination. He felt his own brand of betrayal as he stared into her stormy, unforgiving eyes.

"Why?" she grated out.

Matthew shrugged. If she did not now understand, she never would. How could he explain the excitement of commanding a sleek vessel on the high seas, the briny wind on his face, or the pure sensation of the hunt and chase? How did he explain to one who had treasured the land almost before she could walk the lure of saltwater and sun, the freedom and beauty of miles and miles of unbroken ocean?

"A life in league with the great Jean Lafitte intrigued me," he said with little or no regret, and the coldness in his eyes matched the utterance. "I used to watch them travel up the bayou. It seemed a very exciting life, full of danger and intrigue. Not like the life that was going on at home—tending the fields just to have them burned week after week."

"Those smuggled goods were the reason our parents were killed," she said, her tone bitter and accusing.

"No, Acadiana!" Jonas interrupted firmly. "I know you're upset, and rightly so, but smuggled cargo has come in and out of Louisiana at many points. Everyone turns a blind eye to the tariff-free imports, and most reap the benefits in one way or another. Otis Johnson is to blame for what happened to your parents, no one else."

"I'm not blaming anyone!" Acadiana cried defensively. "It was just all so needless!"

"Killing always is," Jonas said softly.

Jonas proceeded to fill Matthew in on everything they had discovered after Acadiana's attack. Matthew listened quietly, numbing his emotions to the pain of so many years that threatened to wash back over him.

"You see, Matthew, your leaving was not the cause of your parents' death," Jonas continued. "Johnson would have gotten to them one way or another. You should be thankful that you and Acadiana were spared. Had you stayed, that insane man probably would have killed all of you."

"I don't understand," Acadiana said, drained of all emotion except the aching emptiness that always followed thoughts of her parents. "Why did *Maman* tell me you had drowned?"

"Your mama was proud, Cade," Minette replied. It was the first time anyone outside of the threesome had spoken since Matthew had entered the room. All eyes turned in her direction. "She did not believe anyone, especially a young boy, could survive an encounter with the infamous band of pirates. Her pride would not let her dwell on the fact that she had lost one of her children to that type of life. Hence, she wrote Matthew off as dead, truly believing that she was justified in her assumption."

Acadiana gasped. "She knew?"

"She knew he did not drown, but she did not think he could survive long in the world to which he had run."

"Little did she know," Matthew said coolly, "that they will take anyone who is willing to work and is sympathetic to their cause."

Acadiana struggled to keep righteous indignation as a shield against the love she felt for her brother. But to see him again, to be able to talk and laugh with him as she had as a child . . . Her defenses went tumbling down around her, leaving her heart sore but open for renewal. She handed Catie to Mattie and waited for her brother to make the first move.

Matthew hesitated, then grabbed her up in his arms in a bone-crushing hug. "Ah, Cade, I'm sorry I hurt you!" was all he could manage past the constriction in his throat.

Acadiana returned his embrace with a fierceness that startled him. "Why did you come back now?" she whispered against his shoulder, tears clogging her throat.

"Once your husband discovered my whereabouts, he convinced me that it was prudent I show myself as soon as possible," he answered dryly.

"He threatened you."

"Exactly."

"He's good at that," she said in a watery giggle. "I'm just glad you are safe, Matthew, and back with me again."

"For a while," he murmured noncommittally. He knew he would not stay long, but didn't want to spoil the visit by telling Acadiana just yet.

20

Winter struggled to give way to spring. Crisp mornings tempered by warm afternoons caused a restless excitement among the occupants of Courtland Manor. As the dormant plants burst forth in resplendent colors of every hue imaginable, the very air seemed to come alive and flourish along with the foliage. Acadiana also thrived, recovering in both body and spirit. Dividing her time between Matthew and the twins, she felt almost complete. Only the uncertainty of her relationship with Jonas could intrude on her otherwise peaceful days. He had not said that he loved her, but he was patient and giving, treating her with respect and care.

There were times when Acadiana felt his love as a viable force, alive, encompassing her, surrounding her so protectively that the doubts would be chased to the farthest corner of her mind, and she wondered if the words themselves were that important after all. Still, the insecurity lingered there, crouched in readiness to rear its ugly head to abuse the trust she had put in him. It was during those times that she distanced herself from her husband and erected those age-old barriers to shield herself from devastating hurt. She had no experience with the deep, abiding love of a man and a woman that seemed to flow between them on those days when she would let herself feel, let herself experience that which she was afraid she was only imagining because she wanted it so badly.

Jonas enjoyed the healthy glow on Acadiana's cheeks but noticed it did not seem to envelop her entirely. He found himself watching her covertly and mentally ticking off the days and weeks as she still made her way about cautiously and carefully in even the simplest of tasks. It was getting harder to do nothing more than rest beside her at night, and he dare not even kiss her for fear that his passions would spiral away from him. So he waited, perhaps not patiently, but with rigid determination for the days to meld into weeks, the weeks into months.

He shifted uncomfortably in his chair as he gazed at his wife while she prepared to take the babies up to bed. It was a nightly ritual—a round of kisses from everyone for each tiny infant. He had to pull his eyes away from her gaping bodice each time she bent over to let Minette, Matthew, and Edward kiss Catie's rosy cheek. After what seemed an eternity, he allowed his eyes to return to Acadiana. Was it his overheated imagination that her breasts appeared fuller? Or had he simply reached the limits of his control and was beginning to experience delirium? He had been exercising patience that would have qualified him for sainthood, and found this aspect of marriage totally unrewarding. He was certain the fieldhands and mill workers would be as relieved as he when the waiting was over. His quick temper kept the weak-hearted scurrying and the older workers chuckling insubordinately as they recalled how it was for them each time their own wives gave birth.

Jonas rose unhurriedly from the soft leather chair in the library to follow Acadiana upstairs. The children were two months old now; surely enough time had passed. Tonight would mark the end of his waiting or would see him sleeping in another room. A man could endure only so much; he had reached his limit. Acadiana looked healthy enough, a little thinner than before, but he was certain her weight would pick up if she would agree to let him bring in a new mammy. She always looked so tired by nightfall that he had not had the heart to approach her yet. But it wasn't his heart that was ruling him this night as he ascended the stairs.

He stepped quietly into their bedroom, then hung back at the scene before him. Acadiana sat by the glow of the candlelight nursing Cade. The tranquil picture tugged at Jonas's heart and sent fiery demands to other parts of his body. His son's tiny hand rested on the curve of Acadiana's breast while his little mouth tugged lazily at her nipple. Never had Jonas witnessed anything more stirring, the gentle nurturing a powerful aphrodisiac for his strained desire.

He walked over and planted a soft kiss on Acadiana's forehead. She blushed and tried to drape a blanket over her exposed breast, but Jonas pulled it away and dropped a light kiss on the soft fluff atop his son's head. He then rose farther up to nuzzle the soft mound of Acadiana's breast.

"I am jealous of my own son," he murmured against her fragrant skin. "I used to have these all to myself."

"M'sieu, you are terrible," she whispered, her amethyst eyes provocatively mysterious in the candlelight.

She raised the sleeping infant to her shoulder and patted his back as she walked to the adjoining nursery. She placed Cade in his cradle, then bent to place a kiss on Catie's fist. Jonas watched her, his eyes hot and intense as she walked back into their room fastening her night rail.

"Don't," he commanded softly, pushing her hands away. "My children have seen more of you lately than I have."

His fingers reached out to brush the exposed flesh, and sapphire eyes locked with violet ones to send an undeniable message of yearning. Acadiana smiled shyly and placed her arms around Jonas's neck. Her fingers intertwined the sable curls at his nape as she pulled his face closer down to hers.

"I thought you would never come to me," she whispered. She had not meant to say the words aloud, though she had thought them night after night as her husband lay stiffly beside her. She felt her cheeks grow hot, and her black lashes fluttered down to shield her eyes from further perusal.

"Don't be cruel, Acadiana," Jonas moaned hoarsely. He locked his arms around her slim waist and pulled her soft body close to feel his turgid response as if in warning. "I'm being considerate of your delicate condition, but I'm not made of steel."

He felt like hardened steel against her, Acadiana thought, but she would never be so bold as to say so. "My condition is not so delicate," she said softly instead.

His eyes glittered with frustration. "Why didn't you tell me?"

"I couldn't!" She blushed from head to toe, appalled at the thought of being so brazen. "I assumed you would come to me when you wanted me again." She had begun to fear that he had everything from her that he wanted. He had the land, heirs, her respect, and her willingness to do her duty as plantation mistress. All those things he had said were important in a marriage. But his eyes. Those burning sapphire eyes spoke clearly that he would have more. The knowledge thrilled her, and frightened her, and warmed her in a way that no one but he could.

"I never stopped wanting you." Jonas groaned. He ran his fingers through her hair, losing them in the silky midnight curls as he tilted her face up to his. "After the accident, the doctor said I shouldn't, then the twins were born . . . I've just been waiting for you to tell me when you were well enough. The doctor said it would take time."

"I told you doctors were quacks," she said sassily.

"What about now?"

"I still think they are," she answered with an impudent sparkle in her eyes that brought back memories of the puckish girl in the tree and the Indian maiden, but never the wife. Not the prim lady-wife she had become.

"No"—Jonas chuckled—"I mean how are you feeling

now?" He certainly knew how he was feeling. Hot, and hard, and exhilarated that she wasn't stiffening up or re- pulsing him or any number of things that he had imagined could happen when he finally approached her. There was almost a welcome in the arms around his neck and a light in her eyes that spoke the same message.

"Mais oui, I feel terrible." Acadiana pouted. She laid her head on his chest and heaved a long, exaggerated sigh. "I have a husband who married me just for my land, and now that I have given him a son to carry on the family name, I guess he has no further need of me." She spoke the words lightly to cover the insecurity gnawing at her heart. She knew he wanted her; it had been that way from the begin- ning. But now she wanted him, needed to feel him pressed to her, needed to hear him call her name in passion. Needed desperately to feel loved by him. And it frightened her to need anything so badly.

"Shall I prove how very wrong you are, love?" Jonas asked, cocking one eyebrow so coolly suggestive it made her knees weak.

"I suppose you shall have to, if I am to believe it," she replied.

Slowly, Jonas commanded his racing heart as he slipped his arm beneath her knees, *do not spoil in haste what she is freely offering.* He carried her to their bed and placed her securely in the middle, then eased beside her and began slipping free the buttons of her nightdress. His fingers were agile for one in such a rush to experience what he had not for months. Again he ordered himself to tread cautiously.

"Jonas, wait . . . the candle," Acadiana said shyly. It had been so long, and this had never been easy for her. The birth of the twins had creased her flesh with tiny marks. Her figure was still flaccid in places, and she felt intimi- dated as always by the thought of lying naked before him. But it was more than that, a newness in this joining that made her almost feel as if it were her first time. She wanted

to please him but did not know how, and insecurity welled
up within her.

"Acadiana." He moaned, unwilling to relinquish the
sight of her. "I would see all of you."

"Jonas, please."

"No," he murmured against her ear, then traced the slenderness of her throat with his lips. "Not this time."

Acadiana shifted until she lay almost atop him, her
nightdress gaping open to reveal the glory of her full
breasts. Jonas's eyes flared, hot and searching over every
inch of her. She shifted over him more fully, stretched and
leaned . . . then promptly blew out the candles.

"Witch!" He chuckled, then tumbled her beneath him.
"You little sneak, I've a mind to light them again."

Acadiana lifted her head and pressed her lips to his to
banish the thought as her arms clung to his shoulders. Jonas nuzzled her lips then her cheek, working his way back
to her ear. He murmured things that brought a blush to her
cheeks even in the darkened room as he slipped the nightdress over her head and sent it floating to the floor beside
the bed, then removed his own clothing. Returning to her
side, he told her what she did to him as he brought their
bodies close, and what he would like to do to her as he
stroked her satiny flesh. Told her in a voice grown rough
with passion what she made him feel as the scent that was
only hers surrounded him, and he hoped she would do the
same. But she lay silent beside him, unable to put the feelings into words because she wasn't sure how to say them,
and it would have embarrassed her to do so anyway.

Jonas gave no sign that he was disappointed, though he
was. He continued to whisper his need, encouraging her
with eloquent words that flattered the woman in her. Then
he moved between her thighs to express that need in the
way he had fantasized over the long, celibate months.

The birth had not been overly difficult, but Acadiana still
felt tender and bruised. She could not help the shudder that
passed over her when Jonas prodded her sensitive flesh. He

pulled back quickly, startled, his arms rigid beside her as he fought to control the commands of his body.

"I hurt you," he rasped harshly, not wanting to cause her pain, but not knowing how not to. Damn Dr. Loreau for not warning him that this might be difficult.

"Non!" Acadiana lied fiercely, his concern flowing through her so warmly that she would have done anything to please this man who put her welfare above his own. Instinctively her slender fingers reached out to grip his hips to urge him back, but he was an immovable force of restrained muscle and sinew above her.

"I would not hurt you," he said, his voice gruff.

"You will not." She pulled him to her, digging her nails into his buttocks, but she could not budge him. Her hands moved up to cup his face, and she whispered the one thing that sent him beyond the limits of even his steel-edged control. "I want you inside me."

His heart plummeted to his gut, and he entered her swiftly, increasing the agony for Acadiana. She gritted her teeth and pushed against him, thoroughly convinced now this was not a good idea. He captured her hands and pinned them by her head as his body pinned her to the mattress.

"It's over," he rasped, his breathing quick and shallow like his heartbeat. "It's over."

Acadiana whimpered and struggled, but he held her fast and began soothing her with words and kisses, at first light and nonthreatening, then heated and exacting, meant to replace the hurt with overriding passion.

She let the manly fragrance of him envelop her, the sound of his harsh breath ignite her, and she clung to him, needing the feel of his skin beneath her fingers, his weight atop her and within her. Her body quickly adapted, and seemed to absorb his heat and his desire until it was her own.

Jonas rocked slowly, steadily against her, longing to ravish her, to unleash the pent-up strength within him and have her follow him beyond the boundaries of simple duty to the shattering heights of love-born passion where she had not yet gone.

She would have followed him anywhere had she but known how. But the old doubts and insecurities that were so much a part of their past lovemaking rose between them, an invisible barrier, along with the fear of losing control of herself when her mind, heart, and soul were awash with the passion created by him. Though none of it was done in defiance or rebellion, it existed nonetheless in subconscious ignorance of what her body needed and wanted, and worked to confuse her. Acadiana didn't know how to respond to such strong and conflicting emotions. So she lay quiet beneath him as had been her way, accepting without returning, taking without giving, and, in so doing, denied herself that which she unknowingly wanted most.

"Don't!" Jonas groaned in a voice much harsher than intended. He pulled her into a fierce embrace, steeling his body against the release he so badly wanted.

"What?" Acadiana whispered, her breath catching in her throat. He was not pleased. She could tell by the tone of his voice, and it hurt her so deeply, made her feel so inadequate that she wanted to cry.

"Withdraw," Jonas said. "Don't pull away." His voice held a frustration that she did not understand but was feeling. "It is as if you hide yourself away from me."

Acadiana could not deny it, so she said nothing, just let her gaze drop from the handsome face that held a tortured look in the pale glow of moonlight. "I don't know what you want!" she said defensively, but recognized his dissatisfaction because she felt it herself. "I don't know what to do."

"Acadiana." He sighed, hating himself for the rash words as he dropped his head to her neck. Regret curled within him, and he squeezed his eyes shut as he pulled her closer, fitted his body more deeply inside her. He hadn't meant to vent his frustration aloud. He sensed she had no answer for him, and he cursed himself for a fool. Never, *never* would he want her to withdraw further. They would reach this milestone with time, with understanding, but not with brash words spoken in the heat of passion. "Just don't pull away from me," he said, then pressed his lips to her before she could argue that she had not. He ran his hand lightly along her arm, kissed her idly, as if he had all the time in the world and his body was not torturing him with a need greater than his restraint.

He nipped her nose playfully as he toyed with the long strands of hair so dark they blended with the night where they flowed over her shoulders, then buried himself in her more fully. Acadiana gasped and arched, her eyes fluttering closed.

"Yes," he whispered darkly, thrusting with the force of his desire. "Come with me."

His words beckoned to the empty, longing places within her as his body quickened the tempo of plunge, retreat, and plunge again, just as it quickened the pace of her heart. Distress coiled tightly within her, overwhelming, snaring her breath until it was snatched away and she was left panting for air. Her body rose to meet his thrust for thrust, gasp for gasp, the strength of it all a frightening and frenzied thing to her troubled spirit. She dug her nails into his shoulders and cried out from the power of the emotional assault, which hurled Jonas completely, regretfully, over the edge. With one last, violent thrust he spilled himself into her.

Physically, if not emotionally, spent, he waited for his breathing to slow, his body to cool, and held Acadiana too tightly for her to turn away in confusion as he knew she would. For he had touched a part of her she had not wanted to reveal, brought her one step closer, one inch nearer to a place she feared to go, and he would not let her hide herself away now when she had come so close.

"You blew out the candles," he accused when he could speak calmly.

She giggled softly, trembly. Her body still thrummed from the force of their joining, clamored with unrest, and

she didn't think she'd ever get enough air in her lungs again
to stop her head from swimming.

"You weren't nearly as shy when dressed as an Indian,"
he continued. The little nibbles he grazed beneath her earlobe caused ripples of renewed delight to trickle through
her. "You had very little clothing on then in broad daylight."

"That was another time," she said, "another person."

"I would have that person here in my bed," he said. "Is
she still in there?" he asked, and placed his hand above her
breast.

Her heart leapt an extra beat beneath her husband's agile
fingers, and her breath skittered away again. "She will always be a part of me," Acadiana whispered, "but she was a
wild creature and not suitable for the role of mother and
plantation mistress."

"She is suitable anywhere that I am," Jonas coaxed, but
he didn't press the issue. If he caused her to believe that she
was lacking in some way, she would turn the blame inward,
or rebel, and he would never be able to draw her out. Although it caused him much frustration, Jonas convinced
himself there would be plenty of time later for him to find
the untamed abandon he sought in their lovemaking. If he
had that much patience.

Work on Acadiana's dream house had been begun in late
winter with the clearing of several arpents of land on the
Hamilton property, and the labor progressed steadily
throughout spring and summer. Matthew assured her that
he had given up his right to the land eleven years earlier.
The old homestead didn't hold the same appeal for him.
The pirates' participation in defeating the British had
earned them a pardon. Many, like Matthew, were going to
accept the offer of amnesty to pursue a secure and lawful
future, or so he told his sister. That future awaited him in
New Orleans.

The new crop of sugarcane had been planted, and Jonas

juggled his hours among the fields, the mill, excursions into town, and time spent with Acadiana. His duties were endless, the amount of work enormous, but he took every opportunity he could spare with his wife. He still found her elusive, yet there was a difference in their lovemaking. What was not wrought during the fires of passion was at least gentled by her acceptance of him. Sworn to bide his time, he accepted the tenderness and affection she freely gave as a stepping-stone to the greater pleasures that would come with time, with the growing awareness of her own body's needs that experience would bring. He only hoped that the small amount of pleasure he gave her now would not be enough for the vibrant woman inside her, hoped that one day she would realize that and reach for more.

As August passed into September, Matthew informed Acadiana that he was leaving. He knew it would be an emotional ordeal for her, but he was restless. The wanderlust that had plagued him as a child, the need for more adventure than the life of a planter, still pulled at him. It was time to go.

Acadiana bid him a tearful farewell—tears of joy at finding him and tears of unhappiness at losing him once again to a life she little understood. Matthew tried to convince her that he would return as often as possible to spoil his niece and nephew, but Acadiana remained fearful that she would never see him again. It had all been a lovely dream and she would awake to find him forever lost to her. Through it all Jonas was there, strong, supportive, never allowing her to stay too long in her grief. At times his comfort was solely out of his deepening love for her, at others it was purely selfish. A disquieted state of mind was the last obstacle he needed in his quest for a richer union between them.

In an effort to conquer depression, Acadiana threw herself into the plans for the new house. Everything must be just right, just as she had imagined it over the long, lonely years. Every board of cypress was cut from timber on the plantation. The bricks were molded on site for the main house, but only wood was used for the servants' quarters because many of the Negros believed that the bricks held evil spirits.

The house, innovative for its time, was of Louisiana Colonial design with Greek Revival overtones. There were wide galleries, spacious rooms, and steep roofs. Massive columns ran from floor to roof and wide hallways were employed, but the comfort of large windows and wide doors was retained from the common West Indian–style houses along with less imposing designs for the ballroom, music room, and library. Acadiana wanted the family rooms and work areas to be less confining and more comfortable. She didn't want the house to be so impressive that it projected a standoffish appearance, sharply contrasting with the warm, inviting atmosphere of her former cottage.

Although Jonas approved Acadiana's good taste in the selection of materials and design, he ordered her continually to slow down. She looked tired and drawn at the end of each day and continued to refuse too much help with the twins. By the end of the summer, she was reed thin and shadows were everpresent beneath her eyes. Matthew's departure seemed to spur Acadiana's devotion to the land and the house into a near obsession, as if she feared it would all slip in the night, and caused Jonas to worry and watch over her protectively while trying not to stifle her enthusiasm.

They stood side by side surveying the work done thus far on the house. It was a monstrous skeleton with walls, roof, and windows, but none of the interior had been completed as yet. "When will your shipping agent be here?" she asked, fanning her face. Drops of sweat formed in the hollow between her breasts and on her face to trickle down her temples. She brushed them away with the wisps of hair that defied the simple chignon she was wearing.

"Tomorrow or the next day," Jonas said, smiling. His wife looked more like a farm girl or servant in her simple gown and apron. "I wish we had a barn already built," he stated with a rakish twist of his lips.

"Why?" she asked.

"You look like the perfect wench to tumble in a haystack."

"You wouldn't!" She giggled.

"Shall I prove it?" he asked wickedly.

"There's no barn!" Acadiana squealed as he grabbed her around the waist and lifted her high above the ground. "Jonas, put me down! The builders . . ."

"You are no fun, madame," he replied as he put her safely at arm's length. "Why do you want to see the shipping agent? Has he more to offer than I do?"

"Mais oui," she said with a sassy toss of her head. "He is delivering the things I ordered for the formal dining room. Italian marble for the floor—it will be so much cooler in the summer, and we can put carpets over it in the winter—blue French china, and amber-colored Bohemian crystal."

"And will we eat anything American in there?"

"Mais non, just French Creole cuisine."

Jonas lifted one eyebrow in a gesture that had become very dear to Acadiana. "Are we to have a bedroom in this grand house of yours?"

"Mon Dieu, Jonas. Where else would we sleep?" she asked indignantly.

"It's not sleep that I'm thinking of," he growled.

"Oh," she said as her eyes widened. "Do you ever think of anything else?"

"Not often, love," he said seriously. "But right now I'm thinking that you need a rest. You look so tired." Jonas frowned as he ran a finger over the sweaty locks of hair that framed her face and took in her bedraggled appearance.

Acadiana might have been offended but knew it was true. She must look as disheveled as she felt. "It's just this heat," she excused. "It has been like this all summer. Is it ever going to rain?"

Jonas looked at the clear azure sky and rubbed the moisture from the back of his neck. "It doesn't look like it. This is the worst drought I've seen. Most of the cane is already burned. Cain has his people hauling water from the bayou for the food crops, but I'm afraid the sugar is lost this year."

Acadiana was stunned. How could she have been so pre-occupied that she had not realized what was going on around her? She touched his arm in sympathy, perceiving the grimness in his blue eyes. *"Oui,* I knew it was bad," she whispered, "but I just kept hoping for rain. How will this hurt us financially?"

"It won't help," he said evasively. Jonas knew she expected an honest answer, but he wanted to shield her from the harsh truth. "Most of our revenue was spent on the new mill, but we can stand the loss this year with our other interests. We'll just have to be practical . . . and careful."

Acadiana shielded her eyes and squinted up at the relentless sun as if she could dilute the searing rays by force of will. "Why have you let me continue to order so much for the house? I can do without the extravagance! Heaven knows—"

"No!" He cut her short. "The money has already been set aside. Nothing will stop the building of your house."

Tears gathered like violet pools in Acadiana's eyes as she looked up to face her husband. "My house? *Le bon Dieu,* I thought it was *our* house!"

Jonas cursed his wayward tongue, and his face softened at her heated admission. "It is," he said, cupping her chin in his large, tender hands, "but I could live anywhere as long as you were there with me."

Acadiana pushed his hands away. Mutiny flashed in her eyes as she stomped an impertinent foot. "Need I remind you," she said haughtily, "that I can live anywhere too! Probably better than you can!"

"No need to remind me, love. I remember quite well the vision of you in those Indian clothes."

"Jonas!" she began, but it was little use. She found it impossible to stay angry with him while looking into his smiling face. Instead, she took his hand and led him down the path to the gazebo. "Do you remember the first time we came here?" she asked, pulling him down to sit beside her.

"How could I forget?" he asked with a roguish look. "Do you want a repeat? We never did finish because of that damned squ—"

"Non!" she said, playfully slapping his thigh as she remembered their first trip to the gazebo and the animal that had interrupted the tryst Jonas had planned. How she had been relieved when the little creature had scampered by! Her smile was soft and sweet and a little awed when she recalled those early, turbulent days, her husband's thoughtfulness in having the structure from her painting built when he must have known she despised him for forcing her into marriage. "Now just listen to me a minute, *oui?* The first time we came here, my dreams were realized. Whether I wanted to admit it to myself or not, it was true." Her eyes were aglow with the love she had never fully expressed or even let herself feel. The awareness struck her full force, and her voice was husky when she spoke. "I don't need an extravagant house to be home again. I have you and the twins. That is all I will ever need."

Jonas wrapped her in his arms as her words streaked through him like a bolt of lightning, all brilliance and light and energy, and there wasn't anything on heaven or earth that could stop him from helping her fulfill her dreams. Even as her words warmed him, he knew they were part lie. She was a part of him now, flesh and blood, bone and marrow, life, and he knew the dream was a part of her, a part of them. "No, the house will be built as planned. We may have to sell more timber, and we'll mill whatever cane survives, but the house stays."

His words did not achieve the soothing effect he had hoped for. Acadiana was troubled as much by the alarming news as by Jonas's attempt to gloss over it. "What about your shipping business? Will it also suffer?"

"I turned that over to Edward when I married you." Jonas chuckled. "You were all I could handle." At her reproving look he continued more seriously. "That was Father's legacy to Edward, mine was the land."

"Beth won't be glad to hear that, if it takes Edward away too much."

"Oh, I don't think she'll be lonesome for long." Jonas smiled. He knew Acadiana would welcome the forthcoming news and hoped it would deter her concern for the crops. "Edward is in the process of selling it. He wants to settle down."

Acadiana brightened immediately. "With Beth, *oui?*"

"Perhaps," Jonas teased.

"Mais oui, I knew it. This is wonderful!"

"Whoa!" Jonas caught her in the middle of a pirouette. "He hasn't asked her yet."

Acadiana stopped her spin to look at her husband. "But he is going to, *oui?*"

"He said he would have to . . . or he would go insane, or he would dishonor her." Acadiana's shocked expression sent laughter rumbling through his chest.

"You Courtland men are all alike," she said, blushing.

"Quite true, love," Jonas admitted, thinking of the lengths he had gone to to make this woman his wife, the lengths he would have gone to if it had been necessary, dishonorable all of them, to have her. "Anyway, he will propose when the sale is completed and he's assured of being here permanently."

His attempt to cheer her did not last long once they began riding back to Courtland Manor. They traveled in a somber mood, a mood heightened by the sight of ruined sugar crops and Acadiana's guilt that she had been so wrapped up in her own plans that she had failed to notice what was so plainly before her. She cringed as she surveyed the parched fields along the way, for it looked as if no amount of rain could revive the withered, broken ground.

She glanced surreptitiously at Jonas, her heart aching at the bleakness on his harsh features, and once more she regretted her selfish expenses on Bayou Oaks. Why hadn't she noticed the absence of the afternoon showers that were a part of southern Louisiana? The cloudburst was a daily ritual, ending as quickly as it began, pouring forth its life-giving moisture to invigorate and restore the land. But there were no clouds now to break the endless and potentially destructive hazy sky.

Despite the overwhelming heat, Acadiana shivered. There was something potent and foreboding in the stillness of the air, in the whitish glare of heat waves that radiated like mist from the ground. She turned to Jonas to see if he too felt the strangely charged atmosphere, but he was already dismounting, his eyes on Edward, who was waiting for them at the stables.

There was a concerned look on her brother-in-law's face as he walked toward them. "Jonas," he said, his mouth grim. "Your shipping agent was here. There is a storm brewing at sea and headed inland. It looks bad."

"We should be so lucky," Acadiana said in a tired voice. "Is there a chance we'll get any rain in time?"

"We don't want the rain this brings," warned Edward. "It looks like a hurricane."

"How soon?" Jonas questioned, his eyes glinting as he helped Acadiana down from her horse.

"It should hit New Orleans by tonight," Edward said. "We have to make preparations immediately."

Nodding gravely, Jonas took Acadiana's arm and led her toward the house. "Go pack enough clothes for you and the twins," he said, "for at least a week."

"Where are we going?" she asked, taken back.

"I am sending you to your Uncle Grayson's, or as far north as you can get. Mother and Mattie will go with you to help with the children."

Alarm widened her eyes and she clasped his hand firmly. "I'm not going anywhere without you!" she stated emphatically. "If there is going to be trouble, I need to be here."

Jonas clenched his fists to keep from shaking some sense

into her. "Don't fight me on this, Acadiana! Think of the children!"

"What's the matter with you?" she asked, shaken by the ferocity in his voice. "Can't we withstand a little storm?"

"Not just a storm, Acadiana. A hurricane! There is no way of knowing how much damage it could do if it hits this far inland! You will be safer in Providence."

"I don't want to leave you," she said firmly. "I can help."

Jonas didn't like the mulish glint in her eyes. He recognized the determined look too well and knew she would not leave without ample cause for concern.

"Have you ever been in a hurricane?" he asked, flashing furious dark blue eyes at her.

"Non, but I can help if I am here!" she retaliated.

"You'll be in the way!" he shouted angrily, but his anger was not directed toward her. It was the fear of losing her that had his stomach twisted in knots. "A friend of ours lost his family in the last hurricane. The bodies of his two small children washed up, but they never even found the mother!" He gripped her forearms and pulled her to him. "I cannot lose you! Can't you understand that?"

Acadiana stared at the harsh planes of his face, the grim set of his mouth. But when she reached his eyes she saw nothing but fear and concern. "Then come with us. I'll be afraid for you," she said weakly. "Jonas, please . . ."

"I'll be fine," he said gruffly. "Go get your things packed." He sounded defeated, though he had won the argument. There was no satisfaction in having to send his family away. "I have to stay here, Acadiana." He cupped her chin, running his thumbs gently over her flushed cheeks. "You know I wouldn't do this unless it was absolutely necessary."

"Oui." She smiled with trembling lips. Silent tears misted her eyes, and she turned her face to kiss his palms. Were they always to face separation in their lives? Was it part of their destiny that just when they were growing so close they be torn apart? *Non!* God was not so cruel! He would not

destroy what He had brought together. Her heart felt empty already as it had the first time Jonas had gone to New Orleans to find a manager for Bayou Oaks, as it had when he had returned to fight the British. She felt the tears threaten, but was determined not to let them fall. She would be strong for her husband. Shimmering amethyst eyes fastened on to his face, pain and hunger in their burning depths, and she reached out to stroke her fingertips over his strong jaw.

Jonas's heart felt unbearably heavy as he covered her hand with his. "Things are going to be different between us when you get back," he said so seriously that Acadiana's eyes widened in confusion. "No more barriers, Acadiana."

"I don't understa—"

"I think you do." His tone was infinitely revealing as was the promise in his dark blue eyes.

"Oh." She mouthed the word though no sound came forth. The blush on her cheeks let him know she understood.

She nodded, not wanting to distress him further, but the thought of leaving him, of being separated from him again, tore through her with cruel agony. "Are you sure—"

"Acadiana!" Jonas stormed, at the end of his tether. He didn't have time to convince her of the seriousness of their situation, needed her for once to obey him without question, needed for her to go quickly before he changed his mind.

"*Mon Dieu!* I'm going!" She spun around and marched off toward the house, using what Jonas was certain was very foul language. It was, however, a mixture of Caddo, French, and English, and he wasn't exactly sure just whom she was cursing.

Acadiana hated incurring his wrath. It was the elements she railed against as she made her way angrily to the house. It was so unfair, so vastly unfair, that they should be separated again when her love for him was so new and fledgling within her, when she had not had the courage to express it yet.

"Unfair!" she cried out as she ran up the steps to Court-land Manor and almost collided with Minette, who was hurrying down the main hall. *"Grand'mère,"* she said anxiously.

"Oh, Cade," Minette said, worry evident in every classic line on her face. "We must prepare quickly."

"He means to send us away," Acadiana cried with everything her burdened heart was feeling.

"Hurricanes are so unpredictable," Minette said at the look of despair on her daughter-in-law's face. "If we had left sooner, our chances of getting away in fair weather might have been better. But now. . . ." She glanced out the window, seeing from experience that which Acadiana could not, tasting the swell and thickening in the gloaming, feeling the slow drop in air pressure. "Now it is probably too late."

"Too late?" Acadiana gasped.

"Too late today," she said. The stress on Minette's face softened to ease her daughter-in-law's distress. "If it doesn't strike tonight we still must leave in the morning. It is foolish to stay when there is no danger farther north. There is nothing of importance we can do here other than locking the shutters and getting food ready. Naomi and the others will be moved to the big house to cook for the men as they battle the elements."

Non, they would be safe, Acadiana knew. The northern parts of the state wouldn't get more than the torrential rains that were common enough in Louisiana. She and the children would be safe, but what of her husband? Her heart wept bitter tears at the thought, but she knew there was no way to convince him to leave with them.

It took less than an hour for Acadiana to pack. Mattie gathered food for the journey and Minette went about securing the huge shutters over the windows. The shutters! Acadiana dropped her packing and rushed to the wardrobe. She pulled out the old leather bundle and spilled its contents onto the bed. Selecting the frayed stable boy's outfit, she donned it in haste, knowing what she could do to help before Jonas sent them away, away from everything and everyone she had grown to love. Brushing at the tears collecting on her lower lashes, she slipped quickly from the house and made her way to the stables. After mounting Shawnee, she kicked him into a hard run for Bayou Oaks. Already clouds were gathering far in the distance, black and angry, a portent of things to come.

Minette stood in stony silence, clutching Catie to her breast as Jonas walked into the house. "Where is Edward?"

It was the first time Jonas had seen his mother's composure shaken except for the time his father died. He wanted to soothe her but knew his words would be useless. "He went to warn the Claytons, Mother." He stroked the top of Catie's head, his fingers lingering in her soft curls. "I wish you didn't have to wait for morning."

"The Claytons are not back from New Orleans yet," Minette said tersely, though her concern wasn't just for the Claytons. She and Jon Courtland had lost nearly everything they owned once in a hurricane. They were just getting starting then, and the results had been devastating. They were blessed to come out of it alive, but they had come out with nothing left but each other.

"Where is Acadiana?" Jonas asked, taking his daughter in his arms and wondering how long it would be before he held her again, refusing to wonder if he ever would.

"She is preparing for the journey—" Minette began.

Their conversation was interrupted as Edward came into the house, holding his fear in check. "I told Robert's servants to begin preparation. He and Beth are still not back. I pray they don't get caught halfway home by the storm. Come on, Jonas. We'll start on the sandbags."

Edward watched Jonas hand Catie back to their mother. He knew his brother was hurting, knew there was nothing he could say to ease the pain, knew there was nothing any of them could do to stop the approaching danger.

21

Acadiana pressed Shawnee on in the suffocating heat and humidity. It seemed to take forever to reach Bayou Oaks, but when she did she set out immediately to latch the heavy shutters. For hours she worked on the lower level, securing windows, gathering the workmen's tools, trying to find the safest place for all the things that had been brought so far to furnish the house. With every shutter she closed, with every bucket of plaster she dragged, with every crate of tile and board of lumber she lugged, she continued to stare nervously at the ominous gray clouds rolling in. She would have to work more quickly if she wished to stay ahead of the storm, but she was already bone-tired, weary from anxiety, her energy sapped from worrying about Jonas and the others at the manor. By sheer will she forced herself to concentrate on what needed doing.

The oppressive heat hung over her like a shroud, making the simple act of breathing a chore. She dragged her exhausted body to the stairs, forcing her mind to stay on the job at hand instead of the one thought she refused to acknowledge, for it brought her too much pain. A hurricane was destructive. It took lives and land without regard, sometimes leveling whole towns.

Mosquitoes and horseflies swarmed around her, as if in a frenzy, and she swatted at them with blistered hands, then mounted the stairs. There were no rails yet, just raw wooden steps, and she was careful to stay in the middle. Ignoring the cramping in her arms and shoulders, the pounding in her head, she went to work on the upstairs shutters. It was the dull throb in her heart that continued to call to mind her reason for being here.

The first drops of rain on the upper-floor gallery were almost refreshing. Acadiana threw back her head and allowed her face to catch the drizzle. The droplets splattered her skin, cooling yet abrasive as they mingled with her own perspiration to trickle down her neck. But a darkening upon the land warned her that this was more than a summer storm. She watched in horror as the black clouds rolled in like ocean waves, billowing black sea demons, the wind accompanying them a blast of fierce, dangerous heat.

She grabbed the window latches quickly and fought the wind as she tried to shove them closed. Like a drawn curtain, night fell quickly as the clouds continued moving in, stealing the last rays of sunset. The mist rising from the steamy ground crawled across the land with vaporous fingers then quickly dissipated when the downpour began. Inky blackness seeped around her, cutting her vision in half, and she forgot about securing the house. Above all now she needed to mount Shawnee and get back to Courtland Manor.

Struggling against the stinging layers of wind-driven rain, she crawled back inside the window, then dashed down the stairs and out of the house. She called for Shawnee, but the whistle was torn from her mouth and swallowed up in the alternate roar and whine of the wind. She called again and again, but each time her words were whipped away in the growing fury. She stumbled once when a gust of air took her feet out from under her, and she crouched low and fought her way back to the house, almost collapsing once inside.

She was drenched to the skin as she warred with the heavy oak doors, finally pushing them closed with her back. A flash of jagged lightning rent the dark, and she stared dully at her blistered, bleeding hands. It hadn't taken her long to become as pampered as her cousin Katherine. It was foolish of her not to have worn gloves, but her mind had not been on such mundane things. Too worn out to give it further thought, she laid her head back against the solid door, utterly exhausted, too exhausted to realize the danger she was in.

She must have slept, for she awoke slumped against the door to a rumbling sound that drew nearer and nearer. She rubbed the sleep from her gritty eyes and stood up slowly, wondering why Jonas was not beside her in this strange bed, until, her heart heavy, she remembered where she was. A sob rose in her throat at the loneliness that assailed her, but was quickly changed to a gasp at the roaring sounds that invaded the room. Torrents of rain slashed against the window, causing her to climb the stairs to the last shutter left unlatched. Every muscle and bone in her body ached as she stretched then had to recoil. She felt as if she had been slammed repeatedly against the building like the downpour outside. But the sound that woke her wasn't only rain, she realized, wasn't just moisture beating relentlessly against the panes.

Acadiana crept closer to the window, squinting her eyes in the darkness. There was a tree limb whipping at the panes. *Non,* branches, leaves, and debris flying everywhere, swirling and circling in midair, then crashing violently against the walls and window. The pressure in her ears and lungs grew painful, and she clutched her hands over the sides of her head as if she could stop it as a branch slammed against the window.

Startled, Acadiana jerked her head up then backed away slowly, keeping her eyes on the fragile panes of glass, mesmerized by the furious onslaught outside. Hurricane? Tornado? She didn't know but knew she must take cover immediately. She crouched back toward a corner, away from the window, but there was nothing with which to cover herself. She shouted in furious impotence against the roar outside, as if by naked determination she could stop the tempest. But her anger was spliced by screaming wind as the window burst, flinging glass and sticks throughout the room. A sharp object struck her over the eye, causing her to stumble back against the wall.

One tiny, lonesome tear rolled down her cheek, lost in the midst of the slashing rain, before she crumpled to the floor.

Jonas lay sprawled out in the drawing room, exhausted and distraught, his jaw throbbing where Edward had just decked him. Cain held him down by one arm while one of Cain's brawny sons held him down by the other. His eyes blazed fury and hatred at the three of them, before he directed his glacial stare to his mother. She stood over him in frigid silence, her back ramrod straight, her heart shattering into a million pieces.

They had all worked the rest of the day and into the night to secure the plantation. The windows had been boarded up and sandbags filled and hauled to the bayou to prevent flooding. They knew all the while they toiled that if the hurricane was bad enough, their efforts would be in vain.

Jonas had returned to the house, exhausted and worried about Acadiana and the children, knowing he would not be able to send them to safety now. He had returned just as the hurricane had unloaded its first full thrust to find her gone. Gone!

No one knew where, no one had seen her leave. They had all been so busy they hadn't taken notice and had assumed she was in her room. He had just struggled through the door, shucking his drenched jacket, when Naomi had come running down the stairs, a bawling Cade on her hip.

Her eyes bugging in fright, Naomi just stared at Jonas a moment, then whispered, "He needs to be fed."

Jonas had stared back at her, he remembered, frustrated by her seeming stupidity as the storm began rattling the windows. "Find Acadiana," he began, before his heart plunged to his gut.

Naomi was shaking her head, tears streaming down her brown cheeks. "We cain't find her. Oh, Gawd! We cain't find her nowheres!"

Jonas had torn through the house, his son's cries haunting him even when he could no longer hear them, for Naomi had stuck a biscuit in the child's mouth. He called his wife's name over and over, threatening her in his panic and fear, pleading with her even when he realized she was not there.

It was when he tried to go back out into the raging storm that Minette had set the men on him. "I cannot lose both of you," she had said simply, so braced that one more word, one more step, one more breath would have shattered her like fragile crystal.

Jonas had snarled at her, at all of them, and headed again for the door. Edward, no less unreasonable in his fear, but with more presence of mind, had tackled Jonas to the floor. Acadiana had found shelter or she had not. His brother's charging out into the night would make no difference, except that they might lose both of them. Like an enraged bull Jonas had thrown him off, and Minette had nodded to Cain. The huge black man grabbed Jonas long enough for Edward to gain his footing and plant a solid right to his brother's jaw. The blow had only staggered Jonas, but it was enough for Cain, his son, and Edward to wrestle him to the door and hold him there.

Liam Connelly squeezed Maeve's shoulder as she hushed her children for the thousandth time. He had seen the signs early and had rushed his family over to Courtland Manor, knowing they would be welcome, knowing the larger house

on higher ground would be more secure. Maeve shushe
them again, keeping the children under strict rein out o
respect for the Courtlands. She didn't realize the ceaseles
chatter and childish giggles were the only thing keepin
Jonas sane at this moment. He had regained what was lef
of his senses only to feel the heavy crush of his powerless
ness.

He stared silently at the empty fireplace, refusing the im
ages of his wife's mangled body washed up on the swellin
banks of the bayou, or battered against uprooted trees. Rai
slashed against the house in a frenzied assault. Couple
with the wind, it made a deafening roar, but it was nothin
compared to the roaring in his head, the agony in his heart
Edward kept the vigil along with him, ignoring the continu
ous offers of strong chicory coffee. Neither spoke of th
fears that were eating away at them.

They struggled through the day in strained silence, eac
lost in his own concerns. Cain came and went quietl
throughout the house, checking windows and doors t
make certain they stayed barred against the forces of evi
outside.

Edward paced the library, thinking of Acadiana, hi
brow creased in pained dismay as he also thought of Bet
and wondered if she was safe. He heard a child cry, sav
Jonas wince, and wondered how much longer his brothe
could remain calm before his composure faltered again.

Jonas groaned, the sound deep and aching in his throat
He dropped his head back to stare at the portrait of hi
father and felt what Jon must have felt when coming to thi
territory with his parents from the countryside of Alsace
Lorraine, France.

Jonas Edward Courtland's family had been his para
mount reason for living. He had developed this area int
one of the finest and most productive plantations anywhere
but not without the setbacks and hardships common to th
untamed country. There had been violent dangers from hos
tile Indians and beasts of prey. There were crop failure

me and time again due to droughts and hurricanes that
wiped out previous accomplishments. Always the prideful
gentleman planter, Jon would survive again and again with
even more determination and rebound.

Only once had his resolve weakened and threatened to
crumble to an almost irreparable state. The dreaded *mar-
ingouin* had invaded, causing the most devastating setback
thus far for civilization in Louisiana. The mosquito-borne
epidemic of yellow fever had claimed the life of his two
young daughters and an infant son. Of his beloved children,
only his namesakes, Jonas and Edward, had survived. Still
Jon had endured, and as his son stared at his portrait, he
knew that he would endure also, for his own children's
sake, building a family rich in tradition and devotion to
their way of life.

But he didn't know how he would do it without Acadi-
na.

A deceptive calm settled over the land by noon the next
day. The men rushed out to check the damage close at hand
while the peaceful eye of the hurricane passed over, bringing a false security for a time. Jonas trudged through the
muddy, stagnant fields with disgust and resignation, feeling
his insides churn to nausea. The bayou was rising to a dangerously high level. With the fields already standing in water, there was little chance of preventing the flooding that
would finish off the previously parched crops. He only
hoped that the normally peaceful bayou would stop with
the fields and not steal in and wreck the homes and people
who revered this life and land. He didn't stop to think how
long it would take to recoup his losses.

Because none of it mattered, nothing at all mattered except his purpose at hand. He had to get to Bayou Oaks
before the eye of the hurricane passed over and the storm
struck again.

* * *

Acadiana awoke to a horrible pounding in her head and complete silence. Her fingers went to her temple, where she felt an egg-size bump and crusty flakes of dried blood. She lay in a heap on the unfinished floor, her body hurting in places she hadn't known existed. She struggled to sit up but nausea and dizziness sent her reeling back down. She tried again more slowly and managed to slump against the wall for support. Her spinning head finally stabilized and she eased slowly, carefully to her feet. Using the wall for balance, she made her way to the window and stared out at a quiet, cloudless sky . . . and utter devastation.

Water, muddy and filled with debris, was everywhere. Trees jerked from their roots converged into twisted, tangled piles like beaver dams. The bloated carcass of a drowned cow floated like a lazy old man gone fat from excessive living. She held back a sob that threatened to split her pounding skull and slowly began to stalk the wreckage of her new home, the dream that would have been completed over the next few months. She left the room and eased down the stairs only to find that she could go no more than halfway. The muddy water was here too, as vile as a sneak thief, covering the cypress floors, the lower portion of the unfinished walls.

The stench of rotting fish rose to tumble her stomach, and she gagged, but there was nothing in her stomach to heave up. She made her way back to the upper floor. She was trapped; her logical mind knew this, but didn't seem capable of accepting it. She had to find a way out, had to find out what had happened to Jonas and the others, had to know if they were all right. Her knees trembled and gave way beneath her, and she slid down the wall. The waiting and wondering began, gnawing at her heart and mind until her eyes leaked helpless tears. What would she do? She rolled her head to the side to stare sightlessly out the window, not seeing the water covering everything, everywhere.

Her breasts were unbearably full and aching, as painful as the bump on her head, and she pressed her hands to them to stop the throbbing, feeling the wasted trickle of milk seep through her blouse. She had never agreed to hire a wet nurse, had scoffed at the idea. Who could take better care of her babies than she? Where was the wisdom in that decision now? Were they fed, safe? Did they cry for a foolish *maman* whose recklessness had separated them? Or had their cries been stilled by demon winds and water?

Her heart imploded, brutally caved in upon itself, and she sobbed, choking on her own tears because they seemed wont to lodge in a throat and chest too tight to release them. She had only to stare out the window to know the flood damage was extensive, but her eyes could see nothing, register nothing over the crushing pain. Had Courtland Manor survived? The heart that she thought could bear no more was wrenched with an agonizing twist at the thought that she might never see her children or husband again. She wanted to scream as she thought of their last farewell. Jonas had stood there so firm and solid, steadfast in his decision to send them away. But he had not been able to disguise his pain when she had turned angrily from him to stomp back to the manor. She had wanted to rush back into his arms, but it would only have prolonged the agony. Once Jonas made up his mind, he was not likely to change it, a trait she found most infuriating!

He had told her once that they were made for each other. She had not believed him then, but now . . . *le bon Dieu,* she believed it with all that was left of her aching heart! He was her heart, her life. As surely as the blood that flowed through her veins, he was her life-giving substance, and she would never be whole without him.

Jonas had given up his birthright to Courtland Manor to follow her dream of Bayou Oaks. It was no small sacrifice, but he had never let on that it was anything other than exactly what he wanted to do. And she had never really thanked him, told him how much it meant to her, told him how much *he* meant to her. In truth was only just beginning to realize the full extent of what she felt. *Mon Dieu,* I love him, she cried silently. *I love him and he doesn't even know!*

With a groan, she eased her head back against the wall, dispirited, hurting, then buried her face in her shaking hands. She vowed that if she ever saw Jonas again, he would know her love in full measure.

"God," she prayed, as if to seal the pledge, "it doesn't matter that he hasn't said he loves me, because I know he does, just as I love him. And I don't know what he will think of me, but I can no longer hold back the passion I feel for him! I have tried to be the good wife, the proper lady, but life is too short not to experience the fullness of all it has to offer. He has hinted that he wants more from me, but I don't know what he is seeking. Please, help me, give me the chance to tell him . . . to show him!"

"He always answers prayers asked in earnest" came a deep, familiar drawl from the doorway.

Acadiana jerked her head up with a start, her heart hammering against her ribs until she thought it would break free. "Jonas?" she whispered, then shrieked. "Jonas!" She scrambled to her feet and threw herself into his open arms. "You're all right! *Merci,* God! You're all right!"

"All in one piece, as you can see, as are the others," he said huskily, running his thumbs beneath her eyes to wipe away her tears before he crushed her to him as relief exploded in every cell of his body. "Just as you are, thank God!" He tipped her face back, assuring himself that his brave, beautiful wife was alive. "You are hurt," he said, grazing his fingers tenderly over the purple swell above her eye.

"I am fine," she whispered, unable to take her eyes from his face. He tightened his arms around her slim body and held her as she held him, in deep and silent joy.

"You are certain about the others?" she asked fearfully, and reached up to touch his face, his dear, familiar face. He nodded but before he could answer her tearful questions, she let out a reedy cry and pressed her face against his chest, inhaled the rugged scent of wet earth and beloved man, listened wondrously to the steady beat of his heart. *"Mon Dieu!* I am glad you are here!" She held him a moment more then tilted her head back. "How did you get here?"

"In a pirogue of Jean's," he said. "Ah, love, we were so worried!"

Jonas ran his fingers through the silk of her hair, stroked the satin of her cheeks as he lifted her face up to his. His mouth came crashing down to plunder the richness of her moist, willing mouth, his arms gathered her into a bruising embrace as if he would fuse the two of them, and dare the world ever to try to separate them again. Eventually the kiss gentled, their breathing slowed, and Acadiana's head lolled back on his arm so she could stare into his deep blue eyes. *"M'sieu* Husband, welcome." She sighed.

"Wife." Jonas smiled. "You were talking to yourself when I came in."

"Praying," she corrected, then blushed when she realized he must have heard her impassioned plea. "How much did you hear?"

"Enough," he said with a grin. "There was something about the fullness of life . . . and passion?"

"I meant it," Acadiana said, embarrassment further setting her cheeks ablaze. She lowered her eyes to stare at his shirtfront, but stayed within the security of his embrace. "I do not want you to think my thoughts are not proper, Jonas, but I can no longer hold my feelings back. Life is too short—"

"Proper? My God, Acadiana! Don't you know how long I've waited to hear you say that?" He cupped her chin tenderly in his long fingers.

"My thoughts." She hesitated. "Aunt Elizabeth would declare them wanton, and she would be right," she said boldly as if in warning.

"Thank God," he said fiercely, consumed in the amethyst eyes that held him spellbound. "I told you once before, love, our very first night at Courtland Manor, that those puritan ideas have no place in this relationship. Could you not believe me then? There is nothing, Acadiana, *nothing* improper in our sharing our love to the fullest, in any way we see fit."

"I did not want to believe you then," she whispered. "I was so confused."

"And now?" Jonas asked, searching her eyes as if he could see right down into her heart.

There were no words to express the feelings within her, so Acadiana did not even try to put voice to the overwhelming emotions that spiraled throughout her. She stood on tiptoe to show him what mere words could not convey, and kissed him with a passion so full of fire and promise that it left him breathless. Jonas pulled her to his chest fiercely, ready to prove how fulfilling their union could be now that she was ready to accept him, but this was neither the time nor the place, among the wreckage of her broken dreams, with only mud and debris for a bed, with soiled clothes in place of fine linens upon which to place her beneath him. And with the remainder of the storm yet to come.

"I need to get you home before the eye of the hurricane passes over," he said, the simple words taking more willpower than any he had ever uttered.

The babies were sated, their little bellies full, their eyelids drooping. Jonas put them in their cribs and returned to his wife, who seemed content just to stare out the window, as if she could not truly believe the storm was over and must prove it to herself. She had soaked in a hot bath, been served a sumptuous meal in bed, and felt like pampered royalty from all the loving attention. Her sore body begged for rest, but she fought sleep as she looked out over the land. Courtland Manor sat on higher ground, its magnificence untouched by the wind and water that had destroyed Bayou Oaks.

The last glimmer of sunset cast a warm glow over the

land, stretching golden fingers out across the forest and fields. Everything had begun to seep in past her relief, like stagnant water through the cracks of a wall—the horror, the destruction, the devastation. She tried to hold it back, to keep it at bay just a little longer, please just a little longer! She didn't look at Jonas but began to talk in a jumbled, disoriented chatter, firing words with the rapid, humanless *ping* of rifle fire—hiding the true fears oozing through the shelters she had erected to keep them in their place.

"Uncle Grayson said in a letter that his crops look good this year. Not like last year. Last year there was too much rain . . . *non*, that was the year before. There was so much rain that year, the cotton just rotted in the fields before we could get it out. We all picked cotton that year, even Katherine, although she didn't do a very good job of it. Aunt Elizabeth was so humiliated by us working out there like common fieldhands. But I told her not to worry, we were still house servants at heart. She didn't think it was very funny, though. She said it would rightly ruin our reputations, not to mention our skin. She dragged us back to the house and made us sit around for days with cucumber lotion all over our faces."

Tenderness in his eyes, Jonas put his hands on her shoulders then, and Acadiana's voice faded to nothingness. "Why are you rambling on so?" he asked, turning her to face him. "Why don't you ask me what's really on your mind?"

"I don't want to know," she said, eyes downcast. "I have you and the children back safe with me, and that's all I care about."

"Ah, love, you're a terrible liar." He smiled, enfolding her in his arms. She squirmed to free herself, but he held her firmly within an embrace that was as powerful as it was gentle. "No, Acadiana. You're not going to pull away from me—not now . . . not ever again."

"All right then!" she said, raising her eyes defiantly to meet his, inwardly bracing herself for the worst. "What

about Bayou Oaks? It's ruined! All the land . . . the house
. . . the crops. And what about the Connellys now . . .
What will they do? And what about Beth? How will we find
out—"

"Whoa," he calmed her, pulling her close, stroking her
hair as it fell in long, silky waves against the gossamer
nightdress she had put on awaiting his return. "Beth is fine.
Edward is with her now. The house will be fine in time; so
will the Connellys. Nothing will change."

Acadiana smiled softly, glad about Beth, glad they would
not have to turn the Connellys out, but the smile did not
quite reach her troubled eyes. "But it's ruined."

"Flooded, not ruined," Jonas said woodenly. He didn't
want to hurt her. God, the last thing he wanted to do was
cause her more pain! She had been hurt so much, and he
would have given anything to avoid telling her the truth.

"And the crops?" Acadiana continued as if she had not
heard him. But her teeth tugged at her bottom lip and her
eyes misted over as she fought for control.

Jonas remained silent.

"The crops!" she almost screamed.

"Flooded also, but, Acadiana, the drought had already
ruined most of the cane this year."

"What about the mill?"

"It sustained quite a bit of damage, but it can be repaired
before next year's harvest. We can wait another year for the
steam conversion if we have to."

Acadiana's chest rose and fell with a deep, heartfelt sigh.
"Everything destroyed," she whispered. The tears began to
fall, slowly at first, then gaining in intensity like the storm
that had swept in to see the demise of yet another hope for
her future. Acadiana struggled to turn away. She didn't
want Jonas to see how much it crushed her to have her
dreams stolen as they had been so many times before. She
felt faithless, petty, unworthy. She should be happy just to
be back with Jonas and children safe and secure. And she
was. But it did hurt. Oh, God, it did! How could life be so

full and rich one moment, then cruel and savage the next? Her chest ached with the agony of his words, her heart felt as if the life were being squeezed out of it. She wanted to escape, to sleep for an eternity until the world righted itself again.

Jonas turned her back to face him. "Flooded, Acadiana, not destroyed. Water and mud everywhere, but it still stands. You know that."

"Oui," she said, teary-eyed yet hopeful. "Water and mud, just water and mud. That is wonderful, *oui?"*

"Not too wonderful," Jonas warned. "It will take us forever to get it cleaned up."

"Forever is a long time, Jonas," she said in a small, strained voice. "Are you saying we won't be able to resume building the house?"

"No, we'll be able to . . . later. I'm so sorry, Acadiana. There is just so much damage. There is no way we'll be able to rebuild for a few years. The crops, the mill, even the cottage was flooded. We'll have to spend what money we have to repair all that and replant. Our savings will have to be used to get us through until the next harvest. Edward has offered the money from the sale of Courtland Enterprises, but I won't take it unless I have to. I'm so very sorry!"

"Don't!" Acadiana pleaded, torn by the agony on his face that mirrored the hurt in her soul. "It's all right, truly! I can wait, Jonas. As long as I have you and the twins, I can wait forever if necessary."

"It won't be forever, love. It may just feel like it."

From the day he had listened to Acadiana explain the painting in Grayson Hamilton's library, Jonas had wanted to build her that dream. There had been too much tragedy already in her life, yet she had stood there so proud, so strong and determined. Jonas knew then that he could never have taken the land away from her. Her attachment to those arpents along the bayou was as deep as his for Courtland Manor. When he really dwelt on it, he supposed she had captured him the first time he had seen her tramping through the Hamilton house in muddy clothes, mindless of the guest that awaited her. Jonas could not have foreseen what would happen when the hurricane hit, but he felt responsible. He wanted to give her everything. Now he couldn't even finish the house that meant so much to her.

Acadiana saw the traces of despair still on her husband's face. She knew the feeling too well and wanted to comfort him, to wipe away the pain. "We have forever to build our dream, Jonas," she said, and knew it was true even deep within the hurting part of her, she knew. She would spend a lifetime loving him no matter where they were, no matter what the darker side of life threw their way. Dreams could not be shattered by mortal man or fiercest demon or even the raging tempest of a hurricane. Only the dreamer could do that, and she would never give up her plans for Bayou Oaks. If it took a lifetime to see those dreams fulfilled, Jonas would be by her side and she could endure it.

Acadiana pulled his face down to meet hers and kissed him hungrily, pressing her body close to his as if fusing their strength to stand as one. With a muffled groan, Jonas clasped her tightly and pressed her slender hips to his more muscular ones, letting her feel his urgent desire. Waves of hot pleasure welled from deep inside and enveloped them. The emptiness that had long been a part of Acadiana clamored and ached to be filled. Jonas ran his other hand up her spine, losing it in the tangled mass of hair. Tearing his mouth from hers, he buried it in her scented locks and swung her up in his arms. He strode to the bed, whispering words of apology and regret for Bayou Oaks. Acadiana reached up and placed her fingertips to his lips.

"Non," she said, her eyes ordering him to listen and understand. "We will not speak of it again this night."

A smile relaxed his stern features. "As you wish," he said, then dropped her down playfully. Acadiana squealed and tried to pull him down after her, but, with a smile of indulgence, he pushed her hands away and began unfastening her gown.

Acadiana clutched instinctively at the open bodice, her heart fluttering against her breast in mingled portions of anticipation and modesty. "Jonas, the candle."

"Not this time, love," he demanded, his voice low and husky as he slipped the cloudlike material over her head, leaving his wife stretched out in all her glory. She darted a quick glance at the bedside candle, and Jonas laughed quietly, seductively. "Don't you dare. No barriers, remember? No darkness to hide our love." His breath was a warm, moist whisper against her ear. "I want to see you, Acadiana."

Our love. The words washed through Acadiana with the force of a tidal wave, cleansing, healing, carrying with it the sludge of old resentments and insecurities, and leaving only the promise of renewal in its wake.

Jonas stepped back to gaze at the beauty before him and began unbuttoning his shirt. His eyes were glowing coals of blue fire as they traveled over the unbound hair framing her delicate face like a waterfall of rich black silk. His eyes darkened as they made a hot, searing path down the slender column of her neck to her creamy shoulders, over her rose-tipped breasts, down her rib cage to her tiny waist. Acadiana fought the urge to cover herself as his gaze continued a scorching trail down her legs, then rose once again to her face. His thorough perusal was a caress, white hot and demanding, yet gentle and adoring. She shivered from the impact of it, her eyes luminous pools of misty violet as they pleaded with him to find her nakedness acceptable, to understand her shyness, but most of all not to stop the worshipful adulation that she felt when he looked at her.

She sat up shyly and reached out a tentative hand. Her fingers trembling at first, she gathered courage and boldly pushed his hands from his shirt to finish the job he had started. She had to touch him, had to feel that steel, masculine strength beneath her fingertips, to look at him as he had her. Driven by a need stronger than any she had felt before, or perhaps had ever let herself feel, she pushed the shirt off his broad, muscled shoulders, then ran her hands over his bare chest. Her eyes fluttered closed and her head fell back as she simply let herself feel all that was Jonas, his sleek skin, the mat of hair on his chest that tickled her fingers, the constriction of his belly when her hands drifted lower.

She heard his low groan and brought her head back up to gaze in his eyes as slowly, ever so slowly, her fingers went to his lean hips and began removing the trousers that held his desire captive. Her heavy-lidded eyes roamed boldly where her fingers played, marveling at his magnificence, yet almost intimidated by the force of his arousal. Jonas felt his knees weaken, and his breath hissed between his clenched teeth when she leaned forward and pressed brazen kisses over his taut abdomen, rolling her cheeks back and forth as if she'd bury herself there. The caress of her soft mouth on his burning flesh tore a growl of need from his lips, and his hands stretched to bury themselves in her hair.

Acadiana slipped the pants down and raked her nails lightly over his thighs down to his knees, then back up again. Jonas's breath caught in his throat, then was released on a low moan. Once again her eyes sought his, devouring him with the artfulness of a courtesan, yet questioning him with the innocence of a maiden.

"Ah, love," he breathed with a raggedness that spoke of his iron restraint. "Yes, touch me."

But when she did it was like setting a match to dry timber. The flames erupted into a blinding blaze of desire that drove his need beyond the edge of control. Unable to take more of this unexpected pleasure, Jonas grabbed her hands quickly, pressing the fingers to his lips, laving each one lovingly until his breathing slowed. He finished stripping quickly and crawled into bed beside her.

For a moment she lay very still, her breath a mere whisper of air through her parted lips, her heart and soul spellbound by the first real sight she had allowed herself of his full naked splendor. Though she was hardly a virgin bride, she felt timidity creep through her, and was suddenly apprehensive by the obvious virility she would meet this night without the protection of her sanctuary. Her throat grew tight and she would have fled to the safety of her innermost self save for the strong arms that reached out to gather her close, and the words of love and need from her husband that sent her nervousness and inhibitions on a swift flight to freedom. Acadiana opened herself—mind, heart, and soul—to his protective keeping.

Jonas rolled her beneath him, smothering her face in passionate kisses, drowning in the want of her. His hands played languidly over her body, petting, stroking, teasing her until ripples of delight ebbed and flowed with each touch. Her eyes burned into his as his fingers crept lightly over her rib cage, as his hand slid higher to cup her swollen breast. Her soft gasp turned into a moan, and her body began to squirm as he tantalized each hard, aching nipple. His mouth followed the path his fingers made, nipping until Acadiana's entire body tingled with expectation, her stomach tightening in a peculiar pressure that was both painful and pleasurable.

Acadiana had never been fully relaxed with his seduction, had never fully allowed him the liberties he would take, but this night she let herself go, released her self-inflicted bonds. Jonas commanded it with soft words and actions that she could not resist. She could not hold herself from him, and finally, inevitably, she realized she didn't want to. Oh, what foolish time had been wasted by her reserve! She returned his kiss with delight, running the tip of her tongue over his lips, then slipping it inside his mouth to taste the sweetest nectar on earth. The mating ritual began with the dip and swirl of tongues that danced, then retreated, then found each other again until the breaths that mingled in moist play became hot, ragged gasps. Acadiana soared with the freedom of giving herself to him, floated on the wings of ecstasy. As she moaned and writhed beneath him in cadence to the thrust and withdrawal of his tongue, Jonas slid his hands down her body and fondled every hollow and curve, delighting himself in the exploration that she had never completely allowed.

Acadiana tried to pull him closer, to join their bodies together as she reached and searched for the ultimate fulfillment that as yet had eluded her, to give back the pleasure he was giving her.

"Wait," Jonas whispered, stilling her frantic movements. "Give it time, love." As it was he could barely control the fevered need to sheathe himself in her. He was dangerously on the edge, sent there by his wife's ardent willingness.

He continued to seduce her, teaching her body how to relax and enjoy all he had to offer. Acadiana accepted his expert tutelage and even returned it with the full power of a woman in love until Jonas feared he would ravish her, until the anticipation within Acadiana's own body built to such a tortuous level that she thought she would go insane with wanting. Jonas stilled his rampaging passion. Once back in control, he gave no quarter to the writhing mass of womanhood beneath him, but blazed a trail of molten heat as his lips moved from her shoulders, past throbbing breasts to her small stomach, then dared to wander to the silken skin of her thighs. He anticipated her withdrawal and gripped her hips firmly, securely, when she would have stopped his most intimate exploration.

"Let me," he implored, "I want to touch all of you, taste all of you." He did not wait for her acceptance, but pressed his mouth to the apex of her desire, and Acadiana almost jolted from the bed as hot tremors shook her. Jonas continued with a maddening rhythm that shattered Acadiana's control and sent her mind and body reeling to collide into a mass of clawing, grasping frenzy. The spiraling would not stop, and a helpless, rapturous cry burst from her throat as she pleaded with him to end the sweet, unbearable torment.

Jonas struggled with the desire to bring her to fruition now and the need to be buried deep within her during her first climax. He let his lips drift to her thigh. Her desperate moans coupled with her nails digging into his shoulders to keep him from moving away were almost his undoing.

"There is more," he said, his voice rich and dark with the passion he was trying to control. "I swear it."

His lips worked their way slowly back up her stomach, stopping to pay homage to her aching breasts as he cupped her hips and nestled between her thighs, his breathing heavy and laborous as he tried to pace himself, to make certain that she experienced all.

"Wrap your legs around my back," he coaxed gruffly, sliding his hands over her buttocks then down under her thighs, lifting them up to meet him.

A cry of rapture escaped Acadiana as he entered her with exquisite slowness, savoring every moment of contact. Her hips rose to greet him, undulating in a rhythmic pattern that came as naturally and as urgently as the pulsations of ecstasy that swept over her, engulfing her completely, building and climbing to an almost unbearable height. Never had her body felt so imprisoned yet so free as his weight surrounded her and she could feel him deep and throbbing inside her, felt him thrusting time and again until she cried out with the intense pleasure.

Jonas watched her face, watched for the things that gave her the most pleasure as he moved within her, and fought the driving need in him that threatened to explode with every thrust. He shifted his hips, and she growled low in her throat as her head dropped back and her slender neck arched.

"Like this?" he whispered, and swiveled again.

"Ah, *oui!*" she cried out, her shoulders lifting from the bed.

Her body thrust against him wildly, but her mind and heart took flight to soar high above worldly pleasures to that place where only passion born of love can touch the soul. In giving she received, in losing control she gained it a hundredfold. Her release began slowly, shudderingly, folding her around Jonas in its velvet grip, and he increased the tempo, consumed in her, capturing her for all time as they soared toward the pinnacle of intense emotion. When rational thinking was no longer possible, when her body closed around his in convulsing waves of pleasure, he thrust faster, penetrated deeper, until they both felt themselves spiraled through space into the sun where it burst in a shower of flames that devoured their entire beings.

It was so fierce, that joining, it left them breathless and sobbing. And the tears that mingled with the sweat of their bodies belonged to both. They found the supreme measure of love that night in each other's arms, not the essence of it, nor the reasons for it, but the complete gratification and reward that accompanied love's full commitment. And neither would ever be the same.

"Say . . . you love me."

"I love you."

"Say you will love me forever."

"I will love you forever."

"Say you will never even look at Merrill LeBeau again."

"I'm hungry."

Acadiana jabbed Jonas's chest playfully, her laughter soft and rich in the glow of early dawn, then her fingers stole down his stomach to fondle him. Again. Jonas grabbed her wrists and rolled her beneath him, smiling, sated, happier than he had ever been. Acadiana squirmed beneath him, her arms pinned to the bed beside her face. Her smile was delirious, her heart overflowing, but her eyes took on an impish gleam.

"M'sieu Husband, would you take advantage of me? Ravish a helpless maiden? Have your wicked way with me?"

"Damn right," he growled, "if you don't kill me first."

"You'll die a happy man, *oui?"* She giggled.

"An exhausted one." He sighed, giving no quarter until she punched him square in the belly. "Ouch! What did I do to deserve that?"

"You did not tell me how it would be, what it would feel like when . . ."

"When what?" he asked innocently while grinning wickedly in the darkness.

"You know what! You should have told me."

"I tried, but you never listened, never opened yourself up enough to let me teach you. You were a very stubborn woman."

"I am a good student now, *oui?*"

Jonas laughed and dropped his lips to hers. "No, you are bad, very, *very* bad." And proceeded to love her affectionately, unlike the previous joining, which had been wild, almost savage, and the time before that, which had been sweet and tender. And unlike the time before that—the first time in many ways—which had been a culmination of their love.

22

Feeble sunlight filtered through the trees, illuminating the wreckage wrought by the hurricane. Acadiana choked back a sob as she was once again face-to-face with the destruction. She and Jonas had worked most of the day at Bayou Oaks, cleaning mud and debris from the unfinished house. She looked down at her stained dress. It was ruined—like the house and the land. Unlike her legacy, the dress could be easily discarded and replaced almost overnight. But it would take years to reclaim the land and finish the house. A lone tear slid down her cheek before her lashes dropped to catch the others.

"Acadiana, you're tired," Jonas said, taking in her forlorn, disheveled appearance. "Let's go home."

"This *is* home, or it was supposed to be!" she cried, fighting the urge to sink to her knees on the soggy ground. She wanted to beat at the mud with her fists as if a tantrum would rectify the situation. But she did nothing more than stare at the sodden earth as tears clogged her throat and she fought to hold them back.

"Don't," Jonas pleaded, watching her resolve crumble. She had been withdrawn since they had ridden over to see what was savageable after the water receded, but he suspected her silent composure wouldn't last much longer. "It *will* be our home. Given time it will be just like you planned it."

"I know," she said, raising a tearful, grime-streaked face to him. "I'm sorry, Jonas. You're right, I am tired, so very, very tired." Physically tired, but mentally and spiritually as well. Tired of having her dreams ripped apart, tired of fighting the forces of evil that seemed to wait in readiness just to dash her hopes. But she would win, she thought as she stiffened her spine and took in the destruction around her. Nothing—not a crazed man like Otis Johnson or the elements, or any unseen foe—could stop her dreams and hopes for the future. A future with the love of a man and her children by her side. She *was* tired! Tired of losing everything dear to her. Her eyes lifted to the man who stood beside her, and she gathered strength from the love and compassion she saw there. She would not walk alone in her quest and vowed that if it took her a lifetime, she would be the conqueror not the defeated!

"Let's go back," Jonas urged, taking her arm. He noted the light of determination that shone once again in her eyes, but said nothing. It was so much an innate part of the courageous woman he had married that he had almost expected it. "We can go back by the bayou. Edward and Cain have been cleaning out the gazebo most of the afternoon."

"They shouldn't have done that," Acadiana said with a soft half smile. "They should be at the mill."

"They were worried about you," Jonas said. "They wanted to do what they could to help."

"I'm glad it still stands. Just seeing it will make me feel better." Her eyes twinkled suddenly and a suggestive smile flitted across her lips. "Perhaps our squirrel friend is there."

"He is no friend of mine," Jonas scoffed.

Acadiana giggled and threw a hand to her brow in mockery. *"Mais non, M'sieu* Husband! You are no lover of animals!"

"Quite correct, madame," he said, leading her down the boggy path. "Only a lover of women."

"Anyone in particular?" she asked indifferently.

"Only one." He chuckled, picking her up and slinging her carelessly over his shoulder.

Jonas trudged through the muddy, rutted path with Acadiana beating his broad back with tiny fists. "Put me down, imbecile! Do you want them to see us like this?"

"It matters not to me," he quipped, ignoring her attempts to wiggle free by giving her a lecherous little pat every few feet.

They had just rounded the magnolia tree near the gazebo when they saw Cain. He lumbered through the mud as fast as his awkward feet could carry him and slid to a stop before them, gawking at the sight of his mistress slung over the master's shoulder.

"You got to come see this! Hurry up! You ain't gon' believe it!" He grabbed Jonas's arm and dragged him toward Edward, who was kneeling down by a crate with a puzzled expression on his face. Edward scrutinized Acadiana's position but wisely refrained from saying anything after taking in her flushed face.

"Jonas, get over here!" Edward urged. "You aren't going to believe this!"

"So I've heard," Jonas said, depositing Acadiana beside the old wooden box. "What is it?"

"Gold," Edward whispered in awe. "Gold doubloons! Lots of them! Crates and crates of them! I've never seen the like! They must have washed up from the bayou during the hurricane."

"Mon Dieu," Acadiana breathed. Her eyes grew wide as she realized the significance of Edward's words. "Otis was right. There *was* another shipment."

Jonas stood stupefied, staring in awe at the crates surrounding them. Half stuck in the mire and sludge, they looked like growing things rising from the earth.

"Pirate's gold!" Acadiana gasped. "It wasn't buried in the fields. It was sunk in the bayou!"

"My dear wife," Jonas said calmly, "I do believe you are rich."

"I—I am?" Acadiana stammered, her heart slamming against her ribs as she looked around her at the clumps of muddy crates that looked more like piles of refuse. Edward rubbed one of the coins until it shown with the brilliance of sunshine, then held it up for her inspection. *"Le bon Dieu!"* she gasped. "I am!" Her lips trembled on a small sob just before she squealed in pure joy and threw her arms around Jonas, pulling him in a circle as she danced with the happiness flooding her. How right it felt that her parents' death was vindicated in some small way, that Otis had not gotten his greedy hands on the gold, and that the hurricane that had almost destroyed Bayou Oaks should give something back in return. "Oh, oh, my," she said impishly, her breathing fast and exhilarated. "I suppose a person of my wealth and demeanor should certainly conduct herself in a more dignified manner, *oui?"*

"Quite right, your Highness." Jonas grinned. He bowed gallantly before her, then swept her up into his arms and tossed her into the air.

"Put me down, you beast!" she pealed. She clutched his neck as she landed in his arms, her smile mischievous, her cheeks aglow as her eyes met his. "You do not throw the queen in the air or she will have you flogged! They do flog wayward serfs, *oui?"* She giggled.

"Serfs? You forget yourself, madame. I shall be king of the castle. And I shall exile you to a faraway tower if you do not behave," Jonas said in mock indignation.

"Mais oui, most definitely king of the castle." She smiled. Acadiana's heart fluttered erratically, stalled, then began to beat wildly in her chest as she digested his words. Her mouth went dry, and her voice was nothing more than a breathy whisper full of hope and anticipation when she

spoke. "The castle? Jonas, does this mean we can finish the house?"

Jonas let her slide slowly to the ground, his hands locked around her waist as he stared into the eyes that had held him captive since the first time he had seen her. "From the look of it, madame, you can finish Bayou Oaks and several more just like it," he said.

"I just need one," she said softly, tears sparkling in her eyes like rare amethyst jewels as she cupped his beloved face in her hands. "I was right all those years, wasn't I, Jonas? All those years of wishing, hoping, longing . . . I was right. These truly are my dreamfields."

"You were right, love," Jonas said tenderly, "and we'll build those dreams together."

Epilogue

~~ ~~

Bayou Oaks—1820

A peal of childish laughter rang out from the back gallery of Bayou Oaks, accompanied by the tap of running little feet as five-year-old Cade and Catie pushed and shoved to be the first to reach the steps. Three-year-old Jon Matthias was dumped ignominiously on his plump backside as the twins rushed by and he set up a yowl, while two-year-old Elizabeth doggedly toddled behind him. Acadiana, with the newest member of the Courtland clan bundled in her arms, bent to soothe Jon, then called a warning to the twins.

"We gots to see Uncle Edward," Cade called back, heeding his mother's warning about as effectively as his father always did.

"Hurry, *Maman,*" Catie called. "Aunt Beth has the new baby."

Acadiana helped Jon to his feet, then took Elizabeth's hand to walk her safely down the steps. With the petite features of her *grand'mère* but the stubbornness of her parents, Elizabeth jerked her hand back with an adamant "I do it myself!" And promptly flipped herself around bottom side up and scooted down the steps on hands and knees.

Acadiana lifted her eyes to the land that had flourished and bloomed as had her family. At times, when the evening chorus of katydids and bullfrogs tuned up for their nightly symphony and the day's work had been put to rest, the children abed, she would slip from the house just to gaze upon all that was theirs. It was a land of plenty, the Courtland empire prosperous, but those things meant little more to her than a legacy she would leave her children. It was the value of hard work, dedication, and respect for the land that she was instilling in them, the real heritage she hoped they would take to adulthood.

Her dreams had turned into reality, and no longer was she afraid of what the future might hold. For the past five years she had embraced each new day with reverence and awe as her life unfurled to the rigors of prosperous plantation mistress and the love of a wonderful man. The house had been completed in the spring after the hurricane, and everyone had rejoiced in the strength and abundance of the new sugar crops. The flooded land had brought forth the most beautiful cane ever, and the introduction of the new steam-powered mill was changing the course of harvesting forever.

Strong hands dropped to her shoulders, and Acadiana turned to smile up at her husband. "You must do something about your children," she scolded mildly.

Jonas glanced at the rambunctious foursome surrounding his brother and sister-in-law with their own two small children and waved to Edward in greeting. His gaze then went back to his wife and the tiny bundle in her arms. "I'll take them in hand," he said, and reached out for the baby, LeClaire. She was the image of her beautiful mother, her tiny features fine and fair, but her hair was the color of golden fire and her eyes a sparkling crystalline blue. It was said that she had inherited those traits from the ancestor for which she was named, and to this daughter—this last child of Acadiana's body—would go the locket.

Acadiana turned the newborn over to her husband and felt only a dull twinge now of the pain that had accompanied this difficult birth. They would have no more children. The news had been heart-wrenching at first, but she was now able to console herself with the fact that five offspring were more than enough to carry on the legacy of Bayou Oaks.

Life was full and peaceful for the Courtlands, abundantly rich, but its wealth not measured in monetary terms, for love—unconditional and freely given—was the only thing of any worth, as Acadiana had learned so well.

Jean Baptiste called a boisterous hello. She smiled to see Minette on his arm, looking very much the matriarch next to the rough trapper. Minette whispered something to Jean, and Acadiana was pleased to see him blush like a schoolboy as he returned her secret with one of his own. Minette rapped him with her fan, but her smile was purely feminine, ageless, as they drew closer to the house.

"This was your idea," Jonas said, a dubious lift of his brow as the Connellys' wagon, full to overflowing, rolled to a stop behind the others. "Your Uncle Grayson and Aunt Elizabeth should be here by late afternoon with Charles and Katherine and their brood. LeClaire is not yet a full month old. Are you certain you can take the noise and chaos?"

"*Oui,*" Acadiana breathed. "This and more." She would never tire of being surrounded by the love of family and friends. "If Matthew shows up, we will have everyone."

Jonas wasn't proof against such sentiments as the horde of chattering people neared the steps, but he nodded and dropped a kiss to his wife's forehead. He would do anything to keep the glow of love and happiness on her face that had been there the last five years. She was still stubborn and hard-headed and defiant, but she was no longer troubled or afraid. The memory of her parents' brutal murder finally put to rest, she no longer grieved for what she didn't have but gloried in what she did. "Yes," he agreed, "if Matthew shows up, we'll have everyone."

But they both knew, with or without Matthew, with or without wealth and plenty, they had each other and their dreams. It was all they would ever need.